"Life and a time on part of the Nova Scotia coast that Bruce knows like the step of his own feet. You don't just read this book. You live it."

Thomas H. Raddall

"He has brought a poet's insight and a native's love to the delineation of his own province."

Montreal Star

"The best novel we have had on rustic life in Canada. The people and circumstances are revealed so fully that the reader commences to feel he is living among them and ultimately cannot wait to find out what happens next."

Globe and Mail

Charles Bruce was born in Port Shoreham, Nova Scotia, in 1906, and nostalgia for the fishing communities of his native province colour both his poetry and his prose. Educated at Mount Allison University, he became a journalist after graduation. In 1945 he was appointed head of the Canadian Press Bureau in Toronto. Bruce's books of verse include *Tomorrow's Tide* (1932), and *The Mulgrave Road* (1957), which won the Governor General's Award. He has written two novels: *The Channel Shore* (1954), and *The Township of Time* (1959).

Charles Bruce

The Channel Shore

New Canadian Library N178

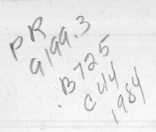

Canadian Cataloguing in Publication Data

Bruce, Charles, 1906 – 1971.
  The Channel Shore

(New Canadian library ; N178)
ISBN 0-7710-9329-2

I. Title. II. Series: New Canadian library ; no. 178.

PS8503.R91C4 1984   C813'.52   C84-003636-1
PR9199.3.B787C4 1984

Manufactured in Canada by Webcom Limited

McClelland and Stewart
The Canadian Publishers
481 University Avenue
Toronto, Ontario
M5G 2E9

You will not find the Channel Shore, so named or in exact geography, on any map or chart. But there is a province of Nova Scotia. Two provinces, perhaps. A land of hills and fields and woods and moving water. And the image of that land, sensuous with the sound of seas and voices, in those who live or have lived there: a country of the mind, the remembering blood. If it is necessary to locate the Shore, consider these twin lands: and take the edge of any county, on the coast of either one.

CONTENTS

PEOPLE OF THE SHORE

STEWART and JOSIE GORDON
ANSE, their son
ANNA, their daughter

RICHARD and EVA McKEE
HAZEL, their daughter
JOE, their son

JAMES and JANE MARSHALL
GRANT, their nephew
FRED and WILL, their sons

RENIE (FRASER) MARSHALL
MARGARET, daughter of RENIE and GRANT
ALAN . . .

CURRIES, GRAHAMS, NEILLS, FREEMANS, WILMOTS, KATENS,
LAIRDS, KINSMANS, STILESES, CLANCYS, LISLES . . .

1919 - 1945

BILL GRAHAM was standing on a garden chair, on the grass behind Buckingham Palace, when the Channel Shore came back to him.

He had walked up the Mall from Canadian Military Headquarters in Cockspur Street, presented his pass, and drifted through the building to join the sixteen hundred men of many nationalities who were gathered there on the palace lawn.

For something to do, really.

It was late May, nineteen hundred and forty-five. A bright day, soft with spring; and the war in Europe over. Across London, young men who were lucky enough to be in England talked at the bars of crowded clubs, sat in cinemas, walked with girls at Kew and Richmond, engaged themselves in the many amenities of friendship and entertainment and sexual pursuit which had made the city familiar, a second home to them, through the time of war.

But Bill was thirty-nine years old, on the doorstep of middle age. He had spent the last four years as a conducting officer, in Public Relations. His work had not been without its excitements and dangers; it was, he supposed, about as good as anyone could expect who had come down to nineteen-forty with no military experience and until that time no interest in it. But it was not as good as having faced the sea-wall at Dieppe or crossed the Moro. It was not as good as having stood hip-deep in water among the polders of the Scheldt.

Something of this, combined with a private apprehension that was not new to him, denied to Bill the relaxed sense of achievement he imagined others were feeling. It was not a sense of failure or inadequacy; more a feeling that adequacy was not enough, a lack of personal enthusiasm and the lift of youth.

And so, out of a kind of impatient boredom, he had volunteered to write a colour piece, for a war correspondent with other things to do, on the royal garden party for Commonwealth prisoners of war.

1

He already had the stuff in his notebook and in his mind. A sprinkling of names and home towns from the various Canadian provinces to lend regional interest, representative names from India, South Africa, Australia, New Zealand, to give the picture breadth. And the feel of the scene: riflemen snared behind erupting beaches; seamen taken from sliding rafts on sullen water; bomber crews who had dropped through the reddened dark under billowing silk. All here now in the King's back yard, with a faintly artificial sprightliness in their lean bodies and sun-lamp tan imposed on the *Stalag* pallor.

He stepped back out of the crowd and climbed a wobbly chair to get a better look at the King and Queen and the princesses, walking down the inner edges of that great colourful horseshoe of men. The King and Margaret Rose had reached the group from *Milag und Marlag Nord*, Merchant Navy boys and survivors of destroyers and motor-launches. It was then Bill saw the face that brought the Channel Shore back to him and began the odd awakening which was to end, eventually, his private frustration and sharpen again the colour of his life.

The face was thin, dark, no longer young, but stamped with qualities that are never youthful and that do not change with age: flaring eyebrows, sharp downward lines from nose to mouth corners, thin, faintly twisted lips; self-possession, a private arrogance, a slight continuing contempt.

And fascination, a kind of bitter charm.

It was this that Bill remembered, the fascination, even before his mind called up the name. Back of this first flash of memory was the pressure of vanished time, of life observed and forgotten and about to live again. But that first scene was brief and single. Kilfyle's Hole, and himself and his cousin Dan and young Stan Currie and Joe McKee, loitering on a Sunday afternoon. And someone coming, through parted alders: a face and a voice.

The names began to come to him then. Anse Gordon. Grant Marshall. Anna Gordon. Hazel McKee.

He stepped down off the chair, skirted a group of Essex Scottish, and edged into the knot of seamen.

He said, "Hello, Anse."

Anse Gordon turned toward him without hurry or surprise. The eyes ranged over him shrewdly, lingered for an instant with the faintest flicker of amusement on the uniform and the shoulder pips, came back to his face, and held. The mouth corners twitched in a grin touched with mockery.

"Well, for God's sake," Anse said, casually. "A Graham. Dan, is it? No—it must be little Bill."

Afterward, as they walked together through the fringe of Belgravia toward a pub called the Antelope, Bill had the sensation of moving at the same moment in separate areas of space and time. He found almost unbelievable the clearness with which it was coming back to him. And equally incredible the fact that it was years since it had come to mind at all, except in wisps of memory vague and brief, seen dimly through the closer past and the present and disregarded.

Across the years of study and work and love, of small successes and slow failures, of brief delights and long irritations, he saw the Shore again. Saw it as he had first seen it that summer of nineteen hundred and nineteen, when Andrew Graham had sent him there to stay with relatives. With Uncle Frank and Aunt Stell and Dan and Edith. To see the country he had sprung from.

The railway station at the little port of Copeland, the county town. And then the drive west in the mail-team: Steep Brook, falling down its wooded hill, and the shoal water marching in, white on green and tan, under the bluffs at Millersville. The cavernous rock-sided gulch at Forester's Pond. Blue-flags in the swamps by Mars Lake. Again the curling water, slow and dignified and deadly, on the reefs at Katen's Rocks. The little cape, with the inlet tucked into its side, that gave a name to Currie Head.

Currie Head. Home . . . But the road went on. A church on the hill at Leeds, where it turned inland for a little, and the branch road there, slanting off to Riverside. A blacksmith's shop (now perhaps a garage) and two general stores at Findlay's Bridge. And across the Channel from first to last the blue lift of the Islands, fencing the shore from the sea that runs east to France, south to the Caribbean and southeast to the hump of Brazil.

That was the shape of it, the shape of road, fields, woods and water. But more than this, the Shore was people. It was flesh and blood in buggies on the road, swinging scythes in side-hill fields, tramping summer woods, braced to the jolt of oars on rolling water, that gave it colour . . . movement . . . life. It was flesh and blood, moved by its rooted hungers, by hate, fear, love and the branch and bloom of them—by caution, daring, malice, sacrifice, that formed the story with which Anse Gordon's name was forever linked.

Bill pulled himself back to the present, this present Anse Gordon. It startled him to think that Anse must be close to fifty now. Time had touched him with indifferent fingers. Worry, concern

3

for anything but Anse Gordon, and today and the immediate tomorrow, had never come close.

In the public bar of the Antelope he turned toward him.

Anse said, "Beer'll do," and Bill remembered that drinking had not been one of the things they held against him. He ordered cider for himself and carried the glasses to a bench by the wall.

He considered wryly that Anse had not lost his taciturnity. Neither of them had yet mentioned the Channel Shore. A question waited on his tongue. He left it there, looking forward to the answer with excitement, while his mind reached back for the start of the story: and found himself and Dan on the shore road, in the dark of a Saturday night.

The night was soft, dark with cloud, and cooling off in the way it has even in the hot months along that northern coast. Himself and Dan, dropping back on the way home from Katen's, falling back to see who walked behind them.

Dan saying, low-toned: "Anse Gordon and Hazel McKee. Mrs. McKee won't like *that*."

And, in answer to Bill's question: "Oh, *you* know. Because. Anse is what they call wild . . ." A touch of admiration in Dan's voice. "And the Gordons are Catholics."

Another night, then, weeks later, when the story of Anse and Hazel was known and already fading, and the story of Grant Marshall and Anna Gordon just beginning, and before the tales were joined. Again himself and Dan. The long walk down the road ahead of the straggling crowd, homeward bound on a Sunday night from the Methodist church at Leeds. The sound of talk and laughter, and buggy-wheels away between the hills. Two boys, reluctant to leave the night and the road, walking on past the house, past Uncle Frank's house toward the next small square of yellow lamplight.

You picked it up again there, with darkness blurring the figures by Gordons' gate. The sound of voices known and liked. Sensed movement. A girl speaking.

"All right; good night, Grant." Laughter then, low and pleased. "Take care of yourself."

A man's voice: "Good night . . . Good night, Anna."

That was the way it was. It was all like that, the parts of the story you could take in your hand and say, *I saw this . . . I heard this*. Small words and private gestures, the look on a face,

4

a voice saying, *I'm going away too, Bill.* A voice saying, *Well, she's dead, that's all.* A voice saying, *No, Uncle James, I'm staying here.* A voice saying, finally, *It's like this, Bill—we're going home to-morrow* . . .

The shape of the land, the colour of moving water. The words, the gestures and the feel of people.

Bill turned to Anse, indifferently tasting beer on the bench beside him. An almost childish excitement quickened his heart as he asked his question:

"Well, Anse—and what's going on at The Head?"

PART ONE

Summer - *Fall* 1919

HAZEL

ANSE

GRANT

ANNA

1

EXCEPT in households headed by stern men like James Marshall, the women are usually the critics of family behaviour along the Channel Shore.

Eva McKee sat by the north windows of her kitchen with hands folded in her lap. Her face was placid and her glance concerned, apparently, with nothing but the slope of the field, the flowers in her garden, a buggy passing on the road. But her thoughts were inward. Now and then she turned to watch her daughter, busy with the dishes left from Sunday dinner. She rose, finally, reached down an apron from the clothes-pole, tied it around the grey satin she had worn to Sunday School, and crossed the kitchen. In the downstairs bedroom Richard was lying down. His door was closed. There was a chance now to speak and she had made up her mind to do so.

She took a wet plate from her daughter's hand and dried it with the dishcloth. She said casually, "Who *was* that outside the house last night, Hazel?"

The girl's hands were still for an instant, then resumed their work with the dishmop. She too was casual. "Last night?"; and then with a little rush of impatience, of irritation at the indirect approach, "Oh, you know who it was, Mother."

Eva lifted a plate from the dishpan and slowly dried it, as if by making speech incidental to action and movement she could reduce the conflict and still speak her mind.

"It's not sensible, you know, Hazel. It's nothing that can do you any good."

The girl turned abruptly and faced her. Hazel had in her a directness that made it almost impossible to dissemble. Eva returned the direct look and for a moment their glances held: the tall girl, her cheek-bones flushed, the lips of the wide mouth parted in impatience; the woman, dumpy with middle age, her face a mask of resolution and patience and authority.

8

The silence was brief, no more than a hesitation. Hazel broke it. "Oh, Mother" —irritation touched with resignation edged her voice— "you sound as if we were thinking of—oh, getting married or something. I like Anse, that's all. You never said anything—"

In the instant of silence Eva had felt a disturbing sense of strangeness, an illusion that the girl she faced was a stranger. This was lost at once in the unquestioned consciousness of parenthood.

She interrupted. "I know. Maybe I should've. I'm saying it now. You go to a supper with a man back from overseas; well— that's all right. A person c'ld hardly—But it don't mean you can act like you belong together." She paused. "You're getting yourself talked about."

Hazel laughed, her voice a light sarcastic parody of understanding. "Oh, I see— It's what Hat Wilmot said—"

Eva was silent for a moment, fighting down exasperation, annoyed by the girl's quickness and the edge of truth in what she said. She had watched with a kind of nagging worry the way in which Hazel and Anse Gordon were drawn together. She had felt a sharp irritation, for instance, hearing their laughter and muffled talk at the back door last night. But it was not until this morning that the nagging had hardened into the need to speak.

Hat Wilmot had meant to be funny, calling out to them after Sunday School: "Well, Eva . . . Hazel, I'd 'a thought *you'd* 'a gone to *Mass.*" But there had been an edge of malice behind the fun. And what Hat Wilmot said others would hear and say.

Eva sighed. She was tired of sparring. Her voice hardened.

"It's *not* what Hat Wilmot said. And I'm telling you now, I won't see you wasting time with somebody that's not worth . . . Who'd be no good even if . . ."

She halted to find words and went on more quietly. "Lord knows nobody's got any right, any business, finding fault with religion. *Any*body's religion, as long as they don't . . . It's not that. There's more to it than that. I wouldn't have that one hanging round if he was John Wesley's grandson. Oh . . . I'm not worrying about you—not really worrying. You've got too much sense to . . . But other people don't know that, and . . . He's no good. He's wild. You know it as well as I do."

Hazel shook her head. "Mother—it's just fun. If you know I'm not serious—why d'you bother about it?"

Eva's voice rose. "Because it's wasting time. As I said. Because it don't look right. Because I don't know what Anse Gordon— Nothing good, if—"

9

In the bedroom off the kitchen Richard grunted in his sleep. Hazel shook her head again with a warning "sh-h-".

The antagonism went out of her manner. She glanced at the clock and turned to smile at Eva. She said lightly, "Don't worry, Mumma. I won't—". She finished the sentence wordlessly, in a ripple of low-toned laughter, almost confidential, and put a hand against Eva's shoulder. She pushed playfully. "Get out of here. Get away from the sink. Go over to Marshalls' and take it easy."

Eva's face slowly softened. She turned away, twitching off her apron. Hazel had sense. In spite of her impatience with the normal ways of living, she would see what was right . . . A vague faint uneasiness troubled Eva for a moment, a recognition of the unusual in her daughter's sudden friendliness and implied surrender. Usually Hazel never gave in. She would argue briefly and then go silent, brooding. Eva brushed this thought away. The girl was too straightforward for deceit.

She smoothed her satin dress and her greying hair, stepped out on the back porch and turned east to take the pasture path to Marshalls'.

Hazel washed and wiped the remaining dishes, working quickly, singing to herself in a soft undertone:

> There's a long—long—night of waiting—
> Until my dreams all come true—
> Till the day—when I'll—be going down . . .

She would have liked to be a singer. She could have put her whole self into a thing like that. But it wasn't practical. Music had no place on the Shore except in church concerts—if you could call *that* music . . .

No. You stayed on the Channel Shore to work and marry. Or you got away from it to go into household service—but that was beneath a McKee. Or to do stenography or teach school. Not to sing.

Hazel had no chance of getting off the Channel Shore by any normal procedure. She had neither the inclination, nor the ability to concentrate on what did not interest her, to qualify as a teacher or a stenographer. So for years she had expressed her impatience with her surroundings in an outspokenness, a spasmodic irritation, an abruptness designed to impress on others an independence she had never been able to prove to herself.

Unless, in this wild secret summer, she had proved it.

10

Her mind met and faced with a sense of wonder and exhilaration the thing that for this last month had been woven through all her thought. Wonder that it should have happened at all, exhilaration which was partly the re-experience in memory of bodily sensation and partly a sense of triumphant daring. And now, far back, a faint insistent uneasiness, and the puzzlement that grew from it.

Her voice dropped to a half-whisper, as if she had simply forgotten to continue her low-toned singing while her mind ran on. She hung the dishmop on its hook behind the sink, finished wiping the dishes with the sodden cloth, and stood for a moment motionless, looking down.

In this moment there was nothing as clear as thought. She was conscious without seeing them of the range and stove-pipe, the clothes-pole over the range, the floor-boards worn down round polished spruce knots, the hooked mats on the floor, the blue-and-white-checked oilcloth on the table; the front hallway and the stair-posts, and the dim plush of the parlour through the open door beyond. The slow ticking of the clock on the shelf behind the range broke into this mindless reverie. She shook her head as if to clear it of the small inexorable sound, and moved abruptly. She crossed the kitchen, reached for an empty baking-powder tin on the shelf by the clock, and turned toward the door of the downstairs bedroom.

Richard McKee, in sock feet and the faded blue serge trousers of his Sunday suit, stirred and turned his head on the pillow, unconcerned with anything but the rare luxury of rest. Now that the women's voices had partly roused him, he was holding to the bare edge of wakefulness to enjoy this drowsing peace.

Hazel leaned inward around the door. "Father, Mumma's gone over to Marshalls'. When she gets back, if I'm not here, I've gone up to Lowries'. See if there's any strawberries."

"All right," Richard said. "Sunday, though." It was merely a caution, a suggestion that Hazel was old enough to know for herself that Eva wouldn't like berry-picking on a Sunday afternoon.

The kitchen door closed, fathoms up in the world of waking, and left him alone.

Hazel left the house, walked across the flat grass of the front yard, and up the slope of the field to the road; crossed the road, and took the cart-track uphill through the thin browntop of the upper field.

At the top of the hill the land levelled out. From there a person could look east and west along the northern fields and pastures of almost all the places at Currie Head, separated by line fences and the untidy hedges of young wild-apple trees the years had grown there. You could look west to the cross-roads, where the school-house road branched north from the shore to the school and the church, and beyond the cross-roads to the farms stretching away to the neighbouring district of Leeds. You could look east across the fields and woods of Currie Head to the district of Katen's Rocks. Or let your sight drift out over the down-sloping lower fields and clusters of pitch-roofed farm buildings to the stretch of sea they called the Channel. And beyond it to the Islands; west to the Upper Islands opposite Morgan's Harbour, or east along those island coasts, merged by distance, to the mist of the Lion's Mane, thirty miles away to the southeast where Channel met Atlantic.

Hazel turned only once, at the top of the hill. She stood there for a moment, her brown cotton dress blown lightly about her by the southwest wind, looking back. Her glance drifted eastward across James Marshall's place with its white house and red-stained barn, across Alec Neill's ill-kept buildings, and Hugh Currie's, half-hidden in clustered apple trees. Across Grant's Place, the stretch of woods that belonged to James Marshall's nephew, and Frank Graham's. Beyond Grahams', the Gordon place, its house, north of the road, also hidden by an ancient orchard, the last house eastward in Currie Head; more than a mile from where she stood. Her glance came back to the home fields directly below her. She scanned them briefly for a sign of young Joe, for assurance that her brother, normally a welcome companion, was not following her today.

The fields were empty of life. She turned north again and climbed the worm fence separating this upper hayfield from the back wood-lot, and began to go down the reverse slope of the first fold in the land.

This was the frontier of an old prosperity. By the opening years of the nineteenth century all the land along the water from Copeland to Findlay's Bridge had been taken up. Later, having served its first purpose by freeing its settlers from the bonds of Europe, the Shore was to become a breeding-place for migrants, men and women who were born there, raised there, and who left the Shore in youth for the States and the West.

But during one golden period, the forty or fifty middle years of the century, it had prospered by the standards of the time in

12

its own right. For a while it had exported products other than its flesh and blood, prospered on the basic economics of salt fish, enhanced at times by lesser pursuits—by vessel-building and coastal trade, cattle and sheep and squared hardwood timber. It was a harsh prosperity, based on circumstances that were not to last; but while they lasted the Shore overflowed, up its small and crooked water-courses, over the fold in the land, into the standing woods. Younger sons and new settlers chopped out and burned and planted new fields, a mile, two miles and more, from salt water.

A few side roads like the school-house road remained, leading back through places stubbornly kept in cultivation. But most of the back fields had returned to woods. Two and three generations later you could still find them: a stone pile among the spruce, a rock-walled hollow, an apple tree still putting forth a small hard fruit among spruce and fir and second-growth birch. Areas of almost unbroken woods, unmarked except for the grey scar of a corner-blaze on an ancient beech; still known by the names of men who had planted life and left a crop of winter firewood. Lowries . . . Kilfyles . . . McNaughtons . . .

Places to search for small fruit grown wild, to explore for no reason at all, to name for a meeting-place.

As Hazel walked down the crooked hauling-road her ears caught the slight rushing murmur of the Black Brook, riffling across a stretch of stony bottom in its course eastward to Graham's Lake. Just west of that riffle a log bridge crossed the brook and beyond it a path rose through the woods to the pasture field that was known as Lowries, all that remained of a farm. Not even a streak of rot was left, zigzagging through the growth to remind you of a fence. But in the little open break, retreating in on itself with each year's growth of young spruce, wild strawberries grew.

As she climbed the slope beyond the brook she was touched again by the breath of her uneasiness, her faintly growing puzzlement.

When a girl crossed from innocence to experience the fact was supposed to have a mysterious importance, almost like birth and death. This was implied in every attitude of the women and girls she knew: the care for reputation, the fuss over weddings, the tight-lipped shock at transgression. And there was the outgrowth of that, the story-book thing about love, shared tenderness, lasting as life. . .

Hazel had never believed this. She had never believed in the attitudes. She had never believed the step out of innocence had

13

any mysterious importance. It was simply the end of curiosity; and, in her own mind, a kind of rebellion . . .

She had seen nothing on the Channel Shore, nothing in Richard and Eva, nothing in James and Jane Marshall and all the rest of them, to show that anything but the habit of living together had grown up in the soil of intimacy. No . . . Whether you found it once or a thousand times, in marriage and a home or a hollow in the woods, experience was a physical fact; important for what you found in it in the moment of its passing. Or, if you stepped aside to find it, for the secret satisfaction, the private rebellion.

Yet, just now, just in these last few days, there was this uneasiness; despite the exhilaration, this sense of something missed, and the puzzlement of why it should be so.

It touched her mind with a light curious insistence. She shook it away as she reached the clearing, the stream's hurry growing fainter in her ears.

Now again the wonder, memory and anticipation, yesterday and tomorrow, merged in the flowing now. Curiously, at the edge of sharper memories, one from the long past. Once for no reason except to try something new and daring, she had walked through the woods to a hidden inlet of Graham's Lake, had stripped and waded shuddering into cold spring water until it closed around her shoulders. Later she had sometimes repeated the experience, approaching each repetition with the remembered shock of that first submergence quickening in her flesh.

What she felt in her marrow now, a thousand times intensified, was the dark excitement, the chill of the lake, its cold insistent meaningless message along the nerves of the lower body, the breast, the mind.

There was no one in the clearing. She crossed it to the cradle-hills along its northern edge and crouched to search for berries while she waited.

Anse turned slowly in the door-yard, scuffed out a cigarette and glanced around him, half noticing with a mild contempt the hen-house, the wood-pile, the manure-cart tipped with its shafts high against the barn wall. There were times when he lived on the juice of his own feelings. At such times he could look with amused tolerance, almost with liking, at the commonness of life and things at Currie Head. At other times his mind ranged with a hard scorn on the whole of it.

Today his mind was light, controlled and expectant. After the novelty of return from overseas had worn off he had begun to feel the impatience and restlessness, the old contempt for the Shore and everything on it. He had let his instinct rove restlessly for the outlet that would restore the inner feeling, the evidence to himself of the power he was.

It was this that had turned him to Hazel McKee, sensing some spark of life or daring or discontent that livened to meet him. In a sense he had found the outlet. Discovery was complete. It remained only to confirm possession, prove mastery, establish a continuing relationship that could give him a lasting sense of triumph. Until he should tire and go on to something else.

He stepped out abruptly and headed north through the fields. At the edge of the woods he took the hauling-road that led back to Graham's Lake.

On either side of the track lay small clearings where four years ago, in the last winter before his enlistment, he and Stewart had cut box-logs. Fallen tops and old brush made a scattered tangle and through these skeleton branches young raspberry canes were pushing up. For a moment, as he remembered, Anse's mood darkened. Four cents for a seven-foot stick, five inches across the small end. Work, from cold sunrise to raw dark, and after. Night and morning the barn to tend. Work, and nothing else, except for hanging around at Katen's and once in a while a dance at Forester's Pond.

It was all part of the Shore picture, the dullness of it. Hugh Currie . . . Frank Graham . . . Stewart Gordon . . . the lot of them. He grunted in bitter amusement, thinking of Stewart and the boat.

Three years before, while Anse was in the army, his father had built a twenty-four-foot two-master for the mackerel fishing—when everyone knew the Channel run of mackerel was done for good. Through some cycle of habit of which the secret was lost in tidal time, the fish had ceased to follow the Channel in their great migrations. At a time when even the last die-hards had come to see this, Stewart built his boat.

For two springs Frank Graham had continued to sail with him and fish an empty sea. But now even Frank was through. The two-master lay in a disused sheep-shed attached to the barn. Once this spring, as they put the horse away after hauling top-dressing to the fields, Anse had nodded sideways through the stable door: "What you keepin' her for? A souvenir?" Stewart had merely looked baffled and reproachful.

Stewart and all the rest of them . . . The boat was a final foolishness. Foolish, because they couldn't see beyond the Shore.

15

They lacked the sense to see that what had been done by their fathers could be done again.

Anse grunted in his mind. This whole shore once had looked toward the sea. They had trawled for cod and haddock and in the spring the two-masters had gone far beyond the Channel. Men had sailed east from here to the Cape Breton coast, to shack on the beaches and fish the waters off Petit de Grat and L'Ardoise and Port Hood.

But when the mackerel failed in the Channel the backbone had gone out of them.

Down-shore where the land was hard to work they still stuck to the trawling. But from Currie Head west they had turned inward to hay and oats and sheep, cattle and butter and eggs, strawberries and vegetables. Only the single month of herring to remind them of another time. A time when there was pride in owning your own boat, a time when the back places where men stuck to the land were known contemptuously as Bogtown, a time before the beam trawlers, when there was money in in-shore cod. A time before the mackerel went away.

All this moved through Anse's mind like shadow. The Shore had gone soft. No one thought of the possibilities . . . No one saw that what was foolishness in Stewart, for instance—foolishness as long as you looked only at the Channel and the Shore—could be carried beyond that into something new and strange. New in this generation.

Put a gas engine into a boat like that and you could still do it. Sail again to the Cape Breton coast, or through to the Atlantic side of the Islands. Shack on the beach there. Go where the fish were.

The odd thing. The unexpected. It was something to think about, a break in the dullness of the close future, as this thing of Hazel McKee was a break in the flowing present.

His mood was light again. Presently he came out on the shore of Graham's Lake and began to walk west up the beach of small uneven stones until he reached the shallows where the Black Brook enters the lake. He picked his way across, the shallow water splashing the work-boots he was wearing with his brown serge Sunday suit. He tramped a short distance north then through ferns and alders to the old back road.

Here the going was easy. This had been designed as a wagon-road to serve the back places, paralleling the shore road and meeting the school-house road a mile or so north of the cross-roads. Now it was nothing but a track for woodsleds in winter, but it was clear of brush and its swampy spots were bridged with corduroy. The road followed the brook and he could hear the faint sound of it off to the left behind the spruce as he walked west, and occasionally see a loop of it in its shallow valley where softwood gave way to open stands of young birch, or an old clearing remained. As he crossed the back of Frank Graham's land and then the northern edge of the strip known as Grant's Place, his controlled excitement began to grow.

Suddenly, from the direction of the brook, voices. Just ahead the road widened and sloped down along a little intervale where the stream was wide and slow. Boys. Four boys squatted there on the narrow ledge of bank between the road and the water—Frank Graham's Dan and his cousin, the kid from Toronto. Stan Currie. Joe McKee.

Anse halted, irritated. He could leave the road and circle through the woods, but one of them might look up at any time. Absently through his annoyance he heard young Dan's voice.

". . . Kilfyle's . . ."

And Bill's question, "Kilfyle's? Why?"

Dan was indifferent, staring down into the pool.

Stan Currie said, "Fellow called Tim Kilfyle farmed back here. Eighty, ninety years ago. More, maybe. The land's no good. Swamp and rock."

Anse felt a flicker of contempt. Stan Currie. The only son old Hugh had produced. A quiet one who took care to stay out of mischief. Hugh Currie had gone away to Boston as a young man, failed in the grocery business, and come back a widower with a baby son to raise and educate and send away again. When Anse thought of the Curries he was touched with an inner contempt for admission of failure, for regular school attendance, for gentle ways.

He considered. Too noticeable to hurry past. He parted the alders and walked to the edge of Kilfyle's Hole.

Dan Graham grinned. "Anse! Where *you* cruisin' to?"

He squatted by the Hole, running his glance from boy to boy, and laughed. "Nowhere much. Takin' a short cut to church, maybe . . . Where's your hooks-and-lines?"

He said this with a teasing drawl, knowing that for the Grahams, the Curries, the McKees, for all the Methodists of Currie Head, fishing on Sunday was forbidden.

Dan Graham recognized this with an apologetic grunt. "No trout in the Black Brook anyway."

Anse sprawled into a more comfortable position, his back against a dried and barkless stump. "Don't fool yourself. There's trout

17

all right. Watch the holes when the water's middlin' high." Irritation at the break in his journey was passing into something else—a kind of private satisfaction in the deference these boys had for Anse Gordon, the wild one. In their minds when they thought of him would be their knowledge of his doings before the war. The time he had left home, telling no one of his going—or where he had spent the two weeks of his absence. The time he and Lon Katen had made a midnight bonfire of James Marshall's backhouse. The time he had chopped Fred Marshall down with his fists, on the road one Sunday night, when Fred jumped him for a word said about Lola Falt.

The legend was there in their minds. It amused him, even, to sense Stan Currie's subdued dislike, a dislike edged with embarrassment and the fear of malice. Stan was carrying on his conversation with Bill Graham about the woods, in a low-toned aside to Dan's talk of trout and mushrats and rabbit-snaring.

Stan was saying, "We own it now. We're directly back of our place, here. The next one west's McNaughtons', back of the Neills'. McNaughton was a blacksmith. There's another old place behind the Marshalls', belonged to a man they called The Frenchman. Next to that's Lowries'; the woods there belongs to Mr. McKee. Part of it's still cleared off. Joe's father used it for a horse pasture up to a few years ago . . . Didn't he, Joe?"

It amused Anse to glance at Joe McKee and to know that these boys suspected nothing of what brought him to the woods today. There was almost a touch of regret in that. Whatever satisfaction you felt, the final satisfaction was in the thing known . . . He put that thought away, feeling the mounting of his present excitement. On the whole he was pleased now at this momentary delay. It was better not to be too eager, too soon at the place.

He got up lazily and brushed spruce needles from his clothes. "Well, stay out'v trouble."

He lifted a hand and turned back to the road. Behind him was silence, then low-voiced talk. He could make out Dan Graham's words, spoken in answer to an indistinguishable something from Stan Currie. "Aw, you been listenin' to the women," was what Dan said. Anse grinned.

He caught himself hurrying as he crossed McNaughtons', and cut his pace to a saunter. He crossed The Frenchman's slowly. Less than a stone's-throw short of Lowries', when he could see the open of the clearing through scattered spruce and birch, he halted. No sign of Hazel. He lit a cigarette.

18

Her mother, perhaps. A chore she couldn't escape. Or Sunday visitors from up the Shore. He had recognized the possibility of such snags when he had talked to her last night in the dark . . . "I was through Lowries' today. Lot of strawberries there. You better go picking tomorrow."

One thing he hadn't thought of seriously was the possibility that she would stay away of her own will. They couldn't do that when you made the arrangement in words that shaped a statement, not a question. When you had the hardness to back it up. Anse had the hardness. He wasn't worrying about any hesitancy in Hazel McKee.

The whole thing, though, had taken him by surprise.

A little more than a month ago he had asked Hazel to accompany him to a church supper at Findlay's Bridge. It was not the sort of thing he would ordinarily have gone to, and Hazel McKee was certainly not the kind of girl he would ordinarily have asked to go with him anywhere. It was this impulse to the unusual, sprouting in a mind already beginning to feel the nagging of the humdrum and the habitual, that had caused him to ask. As it turned out, he had enjoyed the attention paid him as the first Shore boy back from war, and the glances exchanged by the up-shore women, seeing him there in the Methodist Hall at The Bridge with Eva McKee's daughter. He had enjoyed hanging around the church at Leeds the following Sunday night and walking home with her. He had enjoyed the wild imagining that crept into his mind then. He had enjoyed the craftiness with which he had dropped behind the others, spaced out on the road in the dark, and the audacity with which he had drawn her up the school-house road and into Clem Wilmot's hayfield above the school-house.

But it had taken him by surprise. Particularly her response. For he had found an eagerness that matched his own, that lacked his calculated control. An eagerness that did not wait to be drawn into a protesting shivering surrender. And no tears afterward. No pleading for assurances. And yet . . . without experience. An awkwardness, a momentary tension, had made him sure of that.

No tears. Only, in their wild hazardous meetings since, the beginning of something else. Anse frowned, thinking about this. Softness annoyed him. He couldn't respond to it. Flattering, perhaps. But vaguely dangerous. And out of character with the forthright way in which she had met his calculated urgency; tenderness was a thing that developed in the frightened or the weak, and Hazel was neither.

19

Anse glanced at his watch. If she hadn't come in half an hour he would go back along the hauling-road. If he felt like it he would walk up to Leeds church again in the evening, about the time service was getting out. When she made excuses, he could say he had come to Lowries' and waited till dark, or he could say he hadn't come at all.

Then he saw her. She had moved out from behind a clump of low bushes and was crouched on the slope, moving her hands in tall grass where the long-stemmed berries grew. She rose suddenly and scanned the woods openly. Anse grinned. He himself could be furtive in a manner that seemed direct. It was almost impossible for Hazel to be furtive at all. He rubbed out his cigarette carefully against a tree trunk and walked out of the shadow of the spruce.

Hazel watched him approach, feeling the tingling in her flesh, the fascination.

He said, "Hello. Finding any?"

She said with faint mockery, "Where's your dish? Anybody hangs around here has got to help."

Anse laughed. "I don't work Sundays. That's my day for the girls."

"From what I hear, then, every day's Sunday."

He laughed again.

But boy-and-girl sparring didn't come natural to her. She said abruptly, "Glad you got here, anyway. Drives me crazy, sitting around the house."

"Me too." He made it sound sincere. "Give me the can." He tucked it between the roots of a sun-dried stump, humorously contemptuous. "Quite a size, that. Take all of ten minutes to fill it, once we get to it. Let's look around . . . I snared rabbits here, one winter when I was a kid. D'you ever see where the old house was?"

She nodded. "Years ago, I guess. I've not been any farther in than the berry patch for a long while, though."

"Come on, then. It's back here a-ways." He took her hand.

They walked slowly toward the fringe of trees at the northern edge of the clearing. There he slipped an arm round her, drew her gently round and kissed her briefly but long enough to feel the beginning of her body's answer. He dropped his arm indifferently, as if the caress had been a wink or a careless word.

"Come on," he said. "Up here."

Something that once had been a path slanted up through spruce and fir and birch to the level place, itself partly overgrown, where the house had stood. The cellar walls had fallen in and been covered by encroaching earth and the yearly fall of leaves until nothing remained but a hollow, a grass-grown cradle in the woods. Anse slid to the edge of it, leaning on an elbow with Hazel beside him.

The cold excitement and the eagerness were here, but not the tension. And even now in this renewal of revelation, while her flesh responded to a kind of remorseless insistence, there was something that remained aloof.

This was the underlying thing in her consciousness, that even while her senses dulled and quickened in waves, in a slow mounting frenzy, a person now remained aloof and alone in her mind. And the person was Hazel McKee.

Anse lay on his back in leaves and grass, eyes closed. Hazel examined his face with curiosity. The long dark hair had fallen back from his forehead. The features had lost some of their arrogance in the peace of accomplishment. Even in fulfilment her blood stirred at the pull of his physical attraction.

And yet . . .

In what she felt, despite the answer of the flesh, there was nothing now of tenderness. She did not know why this was so. Was it memory? Memory of the controlled irritation with which he had met the softness and the yearning that had surprised even herself, the last time they had lain in grass together? Or was it simply the lack of that, now, in herself? An answering hardness?

Whatever it was, there was no impulse now to move the lips gently along the plume of the eyebrow, or trace with a finger the dark curve of the lips.

The puzzled uneasiness troubled her again.

Why should it matter?

She sat brooding, arms around her knees, chin down. After a little Anse stirred, sighed and sat up grinning.

"Well . . . I s'pose we got to pick strawberries."

Hazel said nothing, and he turned to her slowly, taking in the silence, the brooding, the withdrawn expression on her face.

He said, lightly, "What now?"

After a little further silence she spoke. Not as if she were answering his question but as if she had come to a conclusion in her mind. "It's no good, you know, Anse . . . We might as well admit it. You don't give a damn."

21

Soft protest, perhaps, or angry denial, were what she had expected. She got neither from Anse. His face hardened. She had taken him, again, by surprise. But this was as good a time as any to make things plain.

He laughed. "What is it you want, Hazel? A ring or something?"

She turned to look at him, curiously, studying his face, and shook her head. "No. Anybody can buy a ring. And get a dispensation, I s'pose. If that's what you call it. No, I'm not looking for a ring . . ."

He said sharply, "Well, what *do* you want, in the name of Christ?"

Her anger flared at the callous shape of the question.

"Nothing . . . I won't tell you. I won't bother . . . It's not worth it. Because—if you want to know—I don't give a damn about *you*."

"Oh!"

Anse put understanding into the word, and irony. He rose and put on his coat and slapped away clinging needles and tags of moss.

"You don't, uh? Well, Hazel, you're a pretty fair hand at make-believe." He said matter-of-factly, "Come on, now, we've got to get busy."

He reached down and pulled her upright and pushed her playfully toward the clearing.

They picked berries without talking much, making casual conversation now and then about the unusual size of the berries, other places one or the other had picked in other years. Conventional talk that ignored the thing between them. Anse whistled softly through his teeth. They could hear distant voices, boys getting close to the clearing. When the can was full he walked with her as far as the juncture of the old back road with McKees' hauling-road and kissed her briefly over the heaped can at parting.

He said pleasantly, "Next Sunday if it's fine—oh, I'll be seein' you before that. Won't be up to church, tonight, but . . . Anyway, next Sunday we'll take a walk on the east side of the Head. Nobody goes to the beach on Sunday. You know where Rob's House is, don't you?"

Hazel looked away. "Yes, I know." She had tried to say, "I won't be there." But honesty and indecision had intervened.

22

2

Off the beach at Currie Head small sounds stirred and drifted in morning dusk: the Channel's slow and even breathing, the soft thump of rowlocks, the slight hollow sound of an oar hauled inboard, the whispered echo of a voice.

There in the shadowed calm before sunrise men leaned across the gunnels of flats, grasped the tail-buoys of herring nets; peered downward, while they hauled on dripping head-ropes, to glimpse the shifting flash of silver; and hauled out of tidal darkness the black wet mesh, studded with twitching fish.

This was secret from the Shore, a ritual of the Channel and the calm dusk before the morning wind.

Later, in early daylight, the Shore would see them rowing in, their flats low in the water, and the first faint flaws of wind beginning.

There on the beach they would clean the fish while gulls skirled and dived around them. By the time the herring were salted in the huts, the summer-long southwest wind would be making up and the Channel flashing under the climbing sun.

By then the Shore itself would be alive. Inland from the Head and the low ridge of beach the sunlight blew on hayfields patched with oats and the narrow strips of root crops, dull green on brown. Potatoes in drilled rows along the brows of hills were coming into blossom. On the branches of ancient apple trees where a seething foam of petals had bloomed and faded and vanished on the June wind, the tiny knobs of small hard fruit were forming, lost in a sea of leaves.

In this time now between planting and haying, from almost anywhere at Currie Head a man could see here and there a horse-drawn cultivator moving along side-hill turnip rows, smell the land and the smoky rumour of distant brush fires, hear the echo of an axe, a shout from house to barn, and the small far-off snarl and whine, down the road at Katen's Rocks, of Rod Sinclair's mill.

A mile and a half up the school-house road, far back where the fields finally gave way to woods, old Ed Kelley lazed in his kitchen, waiting for his latest batch of home brew to mature. Down past the church toward the shore road, Sam Freeman puttered at the job of replacing sleepers under his barn. Next door, just above the school-house, Clem Wilmot was patching a worm fence between his front hayfield and his horse pasture. On the main road itself, now that school was over, children hoed and sprayed potatoes, weeded gardens, and loafed. Or picked cultivated strawberries for James Marshall at two cents a box. From Marshall's fields, from anywhere here at Currie Head, they could look out over the Channel and see, far off, Anse Gordon's dory crawling along its line of trawl in the range of the Rocks; and closer in, if the hour was early, the herring flats, rowed by Richard McKee and Hugh Currie and Frank Graham or their sons; or by Stewart Gordon, alone. Closest of all, the star-shaped design of Alec Neill's salmon net, anchored by its leader to the shore.

Day by day this desultory activity went on, in blowing sunlight or under clouds heavy with unshed rain. And in the evening men and women sat in kitchens, lighted lamps for a brief while between late dusk and dark, and went finally to bed. Boys and girls and younger men and women called at McKees' for the mail, drifted down the road to Katen's store for cigarettes and strawberry pop and laughter and pursuit, and went home together in the dark.

There was about all this a sameness, a pattern repeated with small differences through the seasons, month after month and year after year. Snow, sun, cloud and frost. Planting, haying, digging, woods work, and for the few at Currie Head who still bothered with the Channel, the brief season of fish.

School, church, the mail, Katen's. Now and then a picnic on the Head in summer, and in winter a box social at the school . . .

This was the sameness that for years had eaten at the core of Hazel's mind.

Now, she hardly thought of it.

There were times in the week after the meeting at Lowries' when she wished she had said it, clearly and finally—*I won't be there*. When you made a statement it was something you could stick to. And yet . . .

She had put it off. She had put the time of decision away.

The week was gone, now, a blur of puzzled thought, of memory and anticipation, of inner argument and counter-argument. Now the time was here.

Richard and young Joe had gone to the pasture bars to milk. Eva came through the back porch to the kitchen, stopping to sniff in distaste at the tub of soiled clothes in the corner of the porch, ready for tomorrow's wash.

She said, "Fish! You can't wash out the dirty smell of it. What your father sees . . . What anyone sees . . ."

She went on, repeating the old complaint. There was nothing now in fish, except perhaps for salmon. If they'd stay home, away from the beach. If they'd fix fences and roofs, tend to the farms . . .

Hazel made a wordless sound of acknowledgement, one woman's recognition to another of a situation neither one could help. She felt a sense of shame about this. Last year, six weeks ago, she would have said, "Oh, it's only one month a year. And it's Father's business, not ours. Let's just put up with it." But now she was going out of her way to be agreeable.

This realization sharpened further the acrid humour of her mind. You went out and established your independence, a secret dark independence, and found yourself sacrificing the little independences you had taken a kind of pride in. Covering up. Saying "m-m-m-m-" to opinions you didn't agree with. She felt a flush of exasperation. Just this morning she had hidden in the shop the snapshots of herself and Anse at Katen's Creek, snaps they had borrowed Ede Graham's camera to take . . .

Covering up. Because perhaps you had some idea of paying for deceit with pleasantness. Or because, when you didn't openly disagree, there was less chance of anger, less chance of temper lost, less chance of a probing watchfulness.

And then after all, in spite of the secret independence and the physical release that went with it, and beyond the small shame of subterfuge and the shadowy fear, you faced this sense of something still unsettled and unsatisfied. And what to do about it.

She said, "Mother, I think I'll run down and see Ede Graham for a while."

Eva said indifferently, "All right. If you want to. It's kind of a long walk, though."

Inwardly Eva was pleased. Hazel was getting—manageable. The slight shiver of doubt that had crossed her mind a week ago touched her again. That was the kind of thing you might think was . . . But Hazel hadn't the art to be deceitful. Anyway, there was nothing now to hide. She hadn't gone down to Katen's in the evening for a week or more. The Anse Gordon thing—a kind of whim. She was all right. The girl was all right.

25

Once out of the door-yard, Hazel began to walk quickly. Walking solved no problems, but it helped to quiet the mind. Alone with Eva she could never escape uneasiness. Alone with herself she could at least face it, face the lack of purpose, the dissatisfaction, the new and puzzling discontent that displaced the old.

With a kind of calm desperation her mind ran over the possibilities and the alternatives.

What is it you want? A ring or something?

Marriage hadn't even crossed her mind in the course of their first wild meetings. But during this past week she had considered it, as she had considered everything which might in some way help to the decision she had to make.

She considered marriage, not as a likelihood or even as a possibility, but as a theory, an idea, a starting-place for the range of her speculation.

Did she want to marry Anse?

No. Not Anse or anyone. Not even if that were what Anse wanted. Marriage with Anse . . . she didn't care about "turning". People got used to it. That part of it wouldn't bother Anse, either. He'd just as soon be a Protestant unless he thought someone was trying to turn him into one. But marriage with Anse . . . It might get a person off the Channel Shore, in the end. But she couldn't see herself tied for life to Anse Gordon.

What, then?

Well, there was the future Vangie Murphy had found, years ago, after Dolph Findlay got her in trouble. A broken-down house, a couple of kids with different surnames, a wild kind of calculated abandon when someone got drunk and came to call. And hand-outs of second-hand clothes from the Grahams, the Wilmots, the Marshalls, the McKees.

The McKees. Hazel laughed out loud at the crazy picture she had been painting in her mind. Hazel McKee . . . No.

For a moment she had thrilled with fear, and it was new to her. Fear, outright fear, was something she had never felt about those wild and secret hours. Somehow when it was you, and the other one was there, down the road, a person you could touch and see . . . Anyway, for every one who was caught, ten went their way unscathed. No; that kind of fear hadn't come into it. Even now, it merely touched her flesh and vanished.

The thing would go on for a while, then, and—peter out.

That was all you could expect. That was all she had ever expected. Anse had been, what?—the opportunity to prove something to herself. A thought shocked her a little. It might have been anyone, in Wilmot's field that night. Anyone with the boldness to match her mood.

She had no right to expect from Anse a thing which she herself had not been seeking. Something that even now she could not put into words, could think of only as a lack, an emptiness. Something toward which her tentative tenderness had been exploratory, a groping beyond the moment.

She thought: we're alike. Anse and I are alike.

The difference was in the questioning, the groping toward something missed. Something that Anse Gordon had never looked for and would never need, and that she perhaps had lost the chance to find.

Reason told her to forget it, to accept the things she had looked for and found and forget this puzzled wonder about a thing she could not name. Her trouble was that she could not forget.

She walked on, past Marshalls', Neills' and Curries'. Between Curries' and Grahams' lay the stretch of woods known as Grant's Place, the woods, never cleared, which old James Marshall had bought for his nephew. Before his enlistment Grant Marshall had done a little chopping there; he had swamped a hauling-road into the middle of the stretch that lay south of the shore road.

Hazel told herself that when she reached the spot where the hauling-road turned off she would have to make a choice. There she would have to end her indecision—go on to Grahams', or turn down through Grant's Place toward the beach and the Head and Anse.

Supper was over and cleared away. Anna Gordon sat on the back steps, smiling to herself. Gordons' back door, like others at The Head, was really a side door, opening eastward. She let her glance run down the southern slopes of the lower fields toward the edge of woods where the land rose before it fell away to the beach and the Channel.

Behind her in the kitchen Josie sat placidly, the outdoor light falling on the work-shirt on which she was replacing buttons. In this first week of July the days were still long with light, but indoors a grey dusk was gathering.

Anna looked back over her shoulder, through the open door, and said idly, "You'll hurt your eyes, Mama." She said the words merely for something to say, to make an idly affectionate contact. There were times when you wanted to share light-heartedness, and now the special moments of inner excitement were becoming more

27

frequent. You went along as usual, only happier, and then this happiness would be alive and tingling.

Josie shook her head. "Plenty of light yet." She glanced at Anna a little curiously.

Anna made a small laughing sound. She supposed something of what she felt showed in her face. Certainly when the moments came she must seem to Josie a little absent-minded. Stewart wouldn't notice, anyway. But Josie had said nothing. Nor had Anse.

Anse. When she turned to speak to her mother she could see him, across the hall in the parlour, sprawled on the lounge. It amused him, she supposed, to lie there alone in the curtained room that was never used except for company. But she had long ago given up bothering about what Anse thought or did, except as it affected Stewart and Josie. Let him do as he pleased. For a moment it worried her a little, but she put it away. Nothing ever worried Anna long.

She had a little ridiculous thought. If she were to sing out: *Grant's coming home! Grant's coming home!*

What would Josie say?

What would *anyone* say?

The thought tickled her; she giggled as she met Josie's glance.

Actually it was ridiculous. She had no idea just when Grant would get back. But the return from overseas was well along. First, in early May, the Artillery, and Anse. Then a little later Dave Stiles and Jim Katen, with the Twenty-fifth. Then three weeks ago, the Highlanders—the Eighty-fifth—Will Marshall, and Jack Laird from up past the cross-roads, and a dozen more. Grant would be among the last because he had reached Army age late and never got past England. But he would come. Before the end of summer he would come.

Across the hall Anse got up and stretched and threw a cigarette butt at the Franklin stove. She turned to watch him as he walked to the open front door and through it, not turning to look at Josie. For a little he was lost to sight. She heard Stewart speak to him on the front porch and felt a twinge of irritation; he hadn't bothered to answer. Then he crossed the road, tall and indifferent, and went lounging down across the fields toward the beach. He vanished from her mind.

After a little she got up and strolled across the kitchen and out through the narrow hall to the front porch. The low insistent grumbling of the Channel, never entirely still, was pleasant to her ears, too familiar to be noticed. A faint smell of barns and fields and gardens hung in the warm, almost windless, air. A mile away, beyond Grahams', beyond Hugh Currie's and the Neills', she could see James Marshall's windows winking in the sun-down light. She laughed again and glanced down at her father.

Stewart Gordon sat on the small porch in a rocker, his head bent in frowning concentration. Anna touched it playfully with her left hand, running her fingers through the thinning silver hair.

Stewart looked up over his glasses in faintly embarrassed response. The outward signs of affection were not in common fashion along the Channel Shore.

He voiced a mild complaint.

"This Marx. Trouble is, you have to learn a whole new language. Listen to this: 'The two phases, each inverse to the other, that make up the metamorphosis of a commodity constitute a circular movement, a circuit: commodity-form, stripping off of this commodity-form, and return to the commodity-form.' Now I've got to go back and figure out commodity-form again."

Anna laughed. As she went down the path to the gate and turned up the road she was still laughing to herself. Josie must know that she and Grant had a liking for each other. Probably they all knew. But if they knew that on this Sunday evening she was walking up the road just to sit on a stone and look at Grant's Place, they'd think she was crazy.

Her mind went back in amused wonder, remembering the little things. The closeness they had shared in spite of the long intervals between their meetings. In spite of the differences . . . In spite of the fact that one family was Methodist and strait-laced and dry-footed, the other Catholic and born to oilskins.

What was it they had had, when you looked at it? Brief meetings at Katen's store. Chance walks together, if both happened to call at McKees' for the mail at the same time. Perhaps a row on the inlet on The Holiday. Occasional meetings at Frank Graham's, sometimes, when Grant came over after chopping in The Place.

They had never put into words the current of light-heartedness that ran in them when they were together. Anna was not sure she had even thought about it until he had gone away. But the memory of it, and the thought of having it again, were real and clear in these moments when the dream of his home-coming rose in her heart like tide.

She glanced toward Grahams' house. Young Dan and Bill were perched on the veranda railing. She waved a hand and went on.

A line of gnarled old cherry trees fronted Grahams' and straggled to an end at the line fence where Grant's Place began. There, along the road, maples grew on a stony plateau, but south to the

29

Channel the place was thick with softwood, touched here and there by the lighter green of hardwood clumps. From the road you couldn't tell where the clearing was in which Grant used to work. North of the road the slope went back to the skyline in unbroken spruce.

Midway along the stretch of main road that passed through these woods, Grant's hauling-road turned off. Opposite the turn-off a silver birch stood, and at its foot a flat smooth boulder nested in a bank fringed with ferns. One evening just before Grant had sailed, he and Anna had sat on this rock in silence, content in being there and in being together.

Anna crossed the road-side gutter. Seeing the rock, touching it, was like meeting a friend. She sat down and let her mind go out to Grant.

Hazel walked slowly, her eyes on the packed dust and gravel of the road. Now that she was nearing the place she could feel the excitement, the quickening of her heart, in the knowledge that now she must choose. Here and now she must give in to the logic of her mind and her body's urging or finally reject them for the sake of a feeling, a feeling blurred by strange mists of pride.

She glanced up and saw Anna Gordon and halted.

She felt at once an angry annoyance that for the time being her power of choice was gone. She could not turn down along the hauling-road with Anna watching, if that was what her choice was to be. And a forced decision to do otherwise would settle nothing.

She thought quickly of turning back. But Anna had seen her. She would have to go on now. Realizing this, a slight sense of relief touched her, mingling with frustrated anger.

Anna sat on the smooth rock, leaning back against the trunk of the birch, one raised knee clasped in her hands. She watched Hazel coming and smiled slowly and quizzically.

She said lazily, "Hello, Hazel," and added indifferently, "You headed for Ede's?"

Hazel said, "Yes." She stepped across the gutter a little hesitantly and let herself down on the verge of grass. She did not quite know why she was doing this. The thing to do was halt for a minute, exchange a word, and go on. Go on to Grahams'. Make the choice there. Wait for Anna to go home, and then decide. To stay the evening with Edith Graham or find an excuse to get away, to the beach and Anse.

30

But she found now that she had a curiosity about Anna Gordon, an interest stronger, momentarily, than her impatience. This sister of Anse . . . The moment was suspended. She was pulled away from private preoccupation, and the sense of this was pleasant.

She said, making conversation, "Well, I s'pose Grant'll be home soon."

Perhaps it was an association in thought, the fact they were sitting there looking into the woods that belonged to Grant Marshall, or a memory of the boy-and-girl attachment between Grant and Anna.

Anna was looking at her gravely, a little wonderingly. She said, "Yes. He will. But not for a month or more, he expects."

Hazel said, "Expects? Oh, you hear from him, do you?"

This was a little startling. Still, a lot of girls wrote to boys overseas as a kind of community duty, and the boys replied. There could hardly be more to it than that. Considering Grant, silent and shy and almost as unsociable as his Uncle James. And Anna Gordon, lively and full of careless mischief. And the difference in religion.

Anna said, "Oh, yes." She laughed a little, almost to herself. "They're kind of funny letters . . ."

Suddenly Hazel realized that Anna wanted to talk about Grant Marshall, and she felt the oddity of this. Letters. Love letters, maybe, between Grant Marshall and Anna Gordon . . . Passing through her own house, date-stamped by Eva McKee, or by herself; and she hadn't noticed . . .

She said, "Funny?"

Anna was hesitant. "Well, there's nothing in them anyone couldn't see, but . . . Oh, things over there're always reminding him of home."

She had in fact received four letters from Grant in the year or more he had been overseas and it was not until she had got the second that she had caught on to what he was up to. Casually, as if searching for something to say, he had made it a point to mention days and places and people that recalled to her the times they had been together. A lane in Sussex was like the stretch of road between McKees' and Grahams'. A beach on the coast near Bournemouth reminded him of The Holiday. The Regimental Sergeant Major had a moustache like Adam Falt's.

Her mind forgot Hazel McKee, remembering these little things.

Hazel saw the withdrawal and self-possession and above all the serene confidence in Anna's face. She looked away. Grant Marshall and Anna Gordon. Whatever there was between them was more than anyone imagined, then. More than . . . more than . . .

She looked again at Anna with a feeling close to intimacy and realized the strangeness of what was happening in herself, the sprouting of sympathy with others, the recognition—in the strange soil of her own problem and her private indecision.

Anna Gordon. She had never really considered Anna as a person. Anna was just a girl younger than herself, at an age when a couple of years could make the difference between intimacy and mere acquaintance.

She looked at Anna now. At the rounded face and honey-coloured hair, the girlish body that was somehow mature and entirely womanly for all its youth.

Hazel felt a flush of envy, almost of anger. But it was not envy of the physical.

She said meditatively, "You're fond of him."

Anna was silent for a little. Hazel's tone had taken her by surprise. On the Channel Shore any reference to a boy-and-girl relationship was likely to be cloaked in banter. She didn't quite know what to make of Hazel McKee. Now and then lately she had thought of Hazel, knowing there was something between this girl and Anse and idly curious about it. But she had not thought of her as the sort of person who would say "You're fond of him" in that curious voice of discovery and understanding.

She said, "Yes. Yes, I guess I am." They sat for a short time without speaking and finally Anna rose and brushed her skirt.

She was about to suggest they walk down to Grahams' together. She had an impulse toward closeness, the wish to talk about Grant. But there was something in Hazel's manner. Hazel was thinking of something else. It was as if she had withdrawn, gone away. Anna said, "Well . . . I think I'll go on up to Curries'. See you later." She turned and was gone up the road.

Hazel watched her until she was hidden by a curve in the road and then sat on for a while alone. Once she glanced down the hauling-road toward the beach. She could not have said that the look on Anna's face or the tone of her voice as she spoke of Grant Marshall had proved to her that there *was* a gentleness that could grow between people; that there *was* a tenderness, linked with bodily attraction or simply there, existing, with which and in which the physical and all other relationships grew together. It was not as clear-cut as that.

But something glimpsed in this half-hour with Anna had created in herself a mood that was like sadness, as though discontent had been transformed into a sorrowful certainty; a mood in which there was a quiet almost impersonal envy, but nothing now of indecision. She got up, crossed the gutter to the dust and gravel of the road, and turned east toward Grahams'.

Later, she sat with Edith Graham on the back steps of the house, idly talking in the dusk. Somewhere behind the barn there was laughter. Dan and Bill, their voices mingling with the cowbell sounds of late evening. In the early darkness she saw Anse, an indistinct figure, lounging up across the slope of Gordons' lower field, going home from the Head.

3

FELIX KATEN's store stood on the south side of the road a half-mile east of Gordons'. Behind the store and just east of it the Katens had built a new house on a steepish knoll, a square mansard-roofed structure that looked more like a town place than a farm-house. Its back door faced south across pasture and spruce bush to the Channel and out to the low thrust of rock a mile off-shore which had been named for Felix's great-grandfather and which in turn gave a name to this district of the mainland.

Not everyone at Currie Head had seen the inside of Katens' house. This was the beginning of down-shore, different country from The Head and Leeds and Riverside. Here at The Rocks began the stretch of shore on which men still gave most of their time to fish—trawling for cod and haddock, netting salmon, and setting their herring-baited pots for lobsters. And it was Catholic country. From The Rocks to Forester's Pond the Protestant families could be counted on one hand—Sinclairs at The Rocks, Browns at Mars Lake, Foresters at The Pond—just as, up the road, Catholics were few and far between.

Down-shore there was dancing and card-playing and a church with a cross on a steeple at Forester's Pond. Up-shore there were box socials and strawberry festivals and small white box-like churches at Currie Head and Leeds.

These differences were matters of inheritance, something a man couldn't help and which couldn't be held against him. But apart from this there was the character of Felix Katen and his sons. As a young man Felix had worked as a street-car conductor in Boston. It was generally believed that he had palmed enough fares, eluded the spotters long enough, to come home and build his house and store.

There was something worse than that. The Canada Temperance Act was in force in Copeland County; Felix Katen had been tried three times, though never convicted, on charges of selling rum. That was all in the past, but it was still believed that if you searched Katens' Woods down by the Channel you would find a cache—and risk a smashed face or a broken arm at the hands of Lon or Jim or even young Wilbur.

In Lon particularly the bad blood was dark and obvious. Vangie Murphy had sworn to Lon as the father of her second child, the little girl Etta. Her word was worthless and she could prove nothing; but you couldn't mistake the Katen look. Lon had refused to help support the child and Felix wouldn't even let Vangie or her children inside the store.

In the view of Currie Head the Katens were "not even good Catholics". So, except for Anse Gordon, hardly anyone from The Head climbed the knoll to Felix Katen's house.

The store was another thing, a public place. The Shore bought most of its necessities at Copeland or Findlay's Bridge. Felix Katen had no wish to be a harassed general merchant with half the county owing him money. He did a steady trade in tobacco, candy and pop and his store was there if you ran out of kerosene oil or molasses, sugar or tea. He even kept a small amount of bagged flour and feed in a shed at the back. He made money.

The store was a low pitch-roofed building, long way to the road, with a single front door between small-paned windows. Its shingled outside walls were labelled with tobacco advertisements of stamped and coloured tin. The door in warm weather stood always open and in the evening the white light from a big gasoline lamp overflowed on the verge of grass outside.

Inside, a long oak counter, hatched in the middle, stood out from the back wall. Behind this Felix lounged in vest and shirt-sleeves, a small man, almost hunched, with wispy grey hair curling on his head and shrewd eyes behind steel-rimmed glasses. He said little.

At the west end in front of the counter the sugar barrels and molasses cask stood, and at the opposite end the oil barrel. Three or four years ago Felix had bought a gramophone; it sat on the counter by the hatchway, a square walnut box with flaring horn attached, and wax cylinders which gave out a variety of metallic sound.

A round-bellied stove stood in the middle of the long room. Round this in winter customers and casual visitors pulled stools and boxes. But in warm weather the gathering-place was outside on the grass. When new varnished pews were installed in the Methodist church at Currie Head, Felix had bought the discarded benches. Five of these were arranged in front of the store for convenience. Sometimes the church trustees, James Marshall and Sam Freeman, regretted this. There was something disturbing about seeing in front of Katens' place these benches on which generations had sat to sing and pray and listen. But it was too late now. Secretly James Marshall had made Felix an offer for them. The offer was refused.

Inside, summer and winter, the place smelt of kerosene, molasses, tobacco, lead-foil and tea.

This was where the young people of Currie Head and Katen's Rocks, and now and then their elders, gathered at random in the evening. Katen's store was a place of casual companionship, rough hilarity and political argument.

It was a place, too, from which boys and girls, on those evenings when something seemed to draw them to Katen's in numbers, walked home together in the dark, paired off or in little groups of a single sex. Almost as they did from church, but with more hilarity. Katens' was in fact a little piece of Town, set down by a patch of woods on the Channel Shore.

Anse went down the road to Katen's on Tuesday evening.

During the week between the afternoon at Lowries' and his futile wait on the Head he had dropped in at the store only once. It was just as well to leave a few chances missed and let her wonder a little. He did not know whether or not she had come down the road during that time, and there was no one he felt like asking, and he didn't greatly care.

The wait on the Head changed that. Monday night he stayed at home endlessly smoking in the parlour, his long body drawn up on the lounge, living again that hour when he had sat on the grass-grown rock pile of Rob's House, watching through the trees.

By Tuesday night some of the anger had burned out. There were reasonable explanations. Any one of many things might have kept her from coming. It was best after all to be careful; there was plenty of time. He told himself this, but a doubtful uneasiness lay at the back of his mind, and a kind of anger—that anyone should give Anse Gordon cause to doubt.

He put on the brown serge suit and left the house. There was no land breeze; the day's heat lingered. He walked slowly, his mind on Hazel. He would treat her casually and make no effort to draw her apart from the others until he was ready. He would walk home with her then, listen without comment to her explanation, and take in the end what chance and darkness offered.

Thinking this, he came to the rutted lane that led in to the Murphy place south of the road. The hayfield there had grown up in spruce and fir until you couldn't see the house. Whole panels of roadside fence had rotted and fallen away.

He saw now that Vangie herself was standing there, leaning on the bars that served as a gate across the lane.

He stopped and grinned at her. "Well, Vangie—waiting for somebody?"

She said indifferently, "Well, Anse."

On impulse he turned up the stony lane and leaned back against the bars across the fence from Vangie, hooking his elbows on the top rail. It pleased him to think that if anyone passed they would see him there talking to Vangie Murphy.

There was nothing wrong with it. Vangie lived on the Channel Shore road. A person's name might be entered on the books in Hell, but as long as she was a neighbour, dealing with the same earth and weather and people as anybody else, she must be, in some sense, acknowledged. But they'd talk about it all right, and it pleased Anse to think of the conjecture. It would be nice if Hazel should see him there.

He said casually, "Nice night," and turned his head to listen. Somewhere up the road, the sound of buggy wheels.

The rig rounded the turn below Gordons', the horse walking now, and he saw that it was Sam Freeman. The thought of this added to his mild and casual pleasure. Sam Freeman was one of those solid likeable people who are dogged always by small things, the slightly ridiculous. He was hard-working, intelligent, upright and respected. But he spoke with a slight lisp, exaggerated in anger—and he was quick to anger; and he had fathered five daughters. No one would say anything deliberately to hurt Sam Freeman's feelings. But even gentle and unmalicious people like Frank Graham and Hugh Currie laughed a little, privately, and referred to his family sometimes as Tham Freeman'th girlth.

Two of the girls were beside him on the buggy seat.

Sam nodded. Anse could see him flush as he chirked to the horse, and could sense his discomfort in the presence of his daughters, at finding Anse Gordon and Vangie Murphy together. This Anse enjoyed. He glanced round at Vangie and laughed.

She was following the buggy with her eyes. She said, "After something at old Katen's, I suppose."

Anse grinned at the tone, a tone almost of outraged righteousness.

He said indifferently, "I guess so," and then, on a note of confidential daring, "Was it really Lon, Vangie?"

She turned to look at him. "You shut your mouth, Anse."

He was surprised to see that she had reddened. Vangie Murphy blushing.

He said, "I know. But a man can be curious, can't he? Can't help it. The youngster looks like the Katens." He changed tone and said evenly, "I didn't mean to hurt your feelings, Vangie. . . . I been mixed up in a war, and it changes the way you look at things. I'm not making fun of you. I wouldn't do that."

After a little silence she said, "Well—maybe *you* wouldn't, Anse. But—"

He said, "I know—"

In the small silence that followed, he knew what she was feeling, resentment softening to accept a basis of conversation that was strange to her. In his matter-of-factness there had been neither the cold reserve with which she was habitually treated, nor the rough obscenity to which her position sometimes made her subject, and to which he supposed she responded as a matter of course.

He turned on Vangie a smile of understanding, feeling in his bones a wonder that in years of growing up next door to her he had never noticed the fact that if you disregarded the charity clothes, the baggy sweater, the sagging skirt, the chopped-off men's rubber boots, you might consider Vangie Murphy a good-looking woman. She was older, of course, must be over forty, and he had not been much more than a kid when the war took him away. And there had always been the feeling that she was not as other people were.

Now he felt the stirring of excitement and power, knowing that simply by a careful friendliness he could get freely the favour that Vangie Murphy, when she was up against it, was said to sell for cash.

He smiled again, and thought with a bluntness he was careful to keep out of his speech: *hooked; she's hooked like a fish.*

He considered calmly whether to press this experiment now, and decided against it. No good being in a hurry, and tonight there were more important things to think about.

Hazel. Hazel McKee. The oddness of their relationship ran in the mind, the strangeness of the fact that it should have happened at all. It was really something, to possess a Currie Head girl, one of the holy ones, under the noses of the righteous people who shook their heads over Anse Gordon. To do what you wanted . . .

But the thought of Vangie tickled him. He took his elbows off the bars. "Well—I guess I'll go on down and see what's going on. See you again, Vangie."

Dan and Bill Graham were sprawled on the grass in front of Katen's, drinking strawberry pop. The two Freeman girls sat prim and silent in the dusk, away from the pool of light falling through the door, silently waiting. Anse ran his eyes over the boys, faintly grinning, and went on through the open door.

Lon Katen in dusty overalls sat tipped against the wall at the oil barrel end of the store, a wad of tobacco making a knobbed wen in one stubbled cheek, a straw between his teeth. Dave Stiles from down the road occupied the end of a grocery box beside him, elbows on knees. Sam Freeman, gathering together his tied-up bags of sugar and rolled oats on the counter while Felix figured on brown paper with a stub of pencil, was the only customer.

Anse had been looking forward to Katen's. He wanted to hear meaningless talk and laughter while his mind stood aside on its private hill. He wanted to sense the deference—uneasy and mixed with dislike but still deference—of the Currie Head youth who came there. He wanted to see Hazel. But now—the place might as well be empty.

An ugliness found its way into speech. He walked down the store toward Lon and Dave Stiles, and as he passed Sam Freeman he spoke.

"Well, Tham. Howth thingth in Bogtown?"

He didn't halt, but he could see the sudden reddening of Sam Freeman's face, the impulse to violent speech, and the smothering of the impulse.

Dave Stiles glanced up, his face loose with surprise. Felix Katen frowned. Even Lon stopped chewing the straw and shifted his wad of tobacco from port to starboard cheek.

Anse squatted on a backless chair, got out a cigarette and let the moment lie, taking a small satisfaction in the little cruelty. They never knew what to expect from Anse Gordon and that was the way he wanted it. Liking was a soft thing. The other thing was better, the hard dislike painted into a reddened face by simple words, sudden and sly and unexpected. Anse grunted. He had been pretty easy-going since coming home. Perhaps they thought he had tamed down, these holy people at Currie Head. He laughed aloud, a brief ugly laughter.

Sam Freeman gathered up his parcels and went out, and the girls got up from their bench and followed him in silence to the buggy. Outside there was casual talk. Anse could hear Dan Graham chattering and then the sound of a girl's voice, laughing. He t   stening, but it was only Edith Graham and Anna; they came into the store with Lol Kinsman. Lol bought cigarettes and

Anna came down the store to set the gramophone going. The metallic music boomed from the horn, accompanied by an unctuous wheezing voice relating an encounter between a negro preacher and a grizzly bear. Anna stood there, tapping a toe, and then with a laugh and a look at Anse and Lon and Dave Stiles, turned and followed Edith and Lol out of the store.

Grunting a curse, Anse got up and turned off the machine. He went back to his chair scowling. It was almost fully dark now. Outside, the Graham boys went off up the road. After a little he saw Anna, with Lol and Edith, vanish from the circle of light outside and turn toward home.

They sat in silence, Dave Stiles saying and doing nothing, Lon tilted against the wall, occasionally devoting himself to his cud. Finally Lon stirred, expelled the tobacco into a sawdust box, and said:

"Guess she ain't comin' tonight, Anse."

Anse controlled the impulse to cut Lon down with his tongue. That would be the natural thing to do. Or he could treat it lightly, laugh it off. But either thing would be a kind of admission. And Lon didn't worry him; he had always been able to handle Lon.

He said evenly, "Well now, I guess maybe she ain't."

There was neither anger nor lightness in his voice, merely interest and a touch of disappointment. Let them try to figure it out.

He rose after a minute or two, bought cigarettes and strolled out of the store. For a moment he had an impulse to call Felix aside and wheedle a drink out of him. But liquor had never greatly appealed to him.

He walked off up the road, humming to himself. At Vangie Murphy's lane he halted. No light shone from Vangie's windows. He laughed and turned in and climbed the bars.

Anse stayed away from Katen's for the rest of that week.

He spent the days running trawl and hand-lining, splitting fish and turning them on the flakes he had set up behind Stewart's hut on the beach. Stewart worked alone at the herring. As he rowed out to his trawl beyond the herring grounds Anse would see his father there in the morning dusk, bending over the dark coils of dripping mesh. Sometimes they walked to and from the beach together, Anse silent and Stewart talking endlessly about small details of the herring run, endlessly regretting the days before the mackerel had vanished, when a man could make some money out of fish.

Sometimes after his cod were split Anse would lend a hand at cleaning herring. At other times as the mood took him he would squat on the warm stone of the beach or fall asleep on the bunk in the hut while Stewart cleaned and salted alone.

Now and then his mind returned to the half-formed ambition he had considered for the fall . . . an engine in the boat, mackerel-gear, the beaches beyond the Islands . . . But the taste of the idea had been washed out, staled in the tides of his dull continuing anger.

He spent the remaining evenings of the week in the hut on the beach. On Friday and Saturday nights he slept there. But on Sunday he returned to the house for supper and set out to walk the three miles to the Methodist church at Leeds.

On the Findlay's Bridge circuit service was held in alternate weeks at the two mission churches, in the morning at Currie Head on one Sunday, in the evening at Leeds the next. The fortnightly evening service at Leeds was the one from which the courting couples of Leeds and Riverside and Currie Head walked home in pairs.

As a Catholic Anse would stay away from the service itself. He had gone into the church on a couple of occasions for no reason but the talk it would cause, but the novelty had gone out of that. He would wait, along with the four or five up-shore youths who didn't care what their elders thought and so remained outside the church till service was over. Then he would see.

The road was empty as he walked past Grahams', Curries', Neills', Marshalls', McKees'. Past the cross-roads and the Laird and Kinsman places beyond it, and up the long slope to the church, the first building in the district of Leeds.

Service had already begun. Through open windows the music of the cabinet organ and the voices of the congregation singing one of the opening hymns were a blended sound, husky and low and sweet, not quite melodious.

Anse, turning in to cross the wooden platform across the gutter, half listened as the blended voices brought the slow tune to an end . . .

> My gracious master and my God,
> Assist me to proclaim,
> To spread through all the earth abroad
> The honour of Thy name . . .

41

A brief silence followed the long-drawn-out *Amen,* and the minister's voice began, keyed to the conventional plaintive pitch of supplication in the long prayer.

Anse walked round the building. Sprawled there on the grass under the windowless back wall were the usual loungers who came to church for nothing more than something to do. He grinned at them, let himself down to the grass, and lit a cigarette.

There was little talk. The members of this group were quiet enough, knowing that any interruption of service would not be tolerated. Anse glanced at the buggies tied up to the churchyard fence. James Marshall's double-seated buggy was there, and Frank Graham's brown mare, but not Richard McKee's rig.

Perhaps this was another place to which she had not come . . .

No. You couldn't figure it that way. She usually walked up with one of the other girls. If Lol Kinsman were there to walk home with Edith Graham, he could pair up with Lol and overtake the two of them as they walked down the hill.

It annoyed Anse to find himself concerned with these details, planning a thing, doubtfully, that was as simple as rolling off a log.

Behind the whitewashed wall of the church the routine of the service went on, faintly muffled. Collection . . . sermon . . . benediction . . . doxology . . .

Now there was the creaking stir of the service over, voices at the front door as routine devotion lapsed into social intercourse. Anse and the others with him came round to the front to watch and wait.

He saw among the forty or fifty people coming out of the church that Will Marshall was still wearing on Sundays the dark blue-and-black tartan of the 85th Nova Scotia Highlanders. He was coming out flanked by old James and Mrs. Marshall, and shaking hands with the minister. Anse spared a moment to indulge his contempt for the bearded figure of stern piety who was Will's father, and the whole idea of people like the Marshalls. What Anna could see in the young one, Grant . . . The incidental thought vanished. Hazel was there, with Mrs. Graham and Ede, but apparently Lol Kinsman was not. Mrs. Graham had stopped on the steps to speak to Mrs. Jack Graham, one of the Graham cousins from down the side road to Riverside. She said to Ede, "Bring the horse round, will you, Edith?" and turned back to Mrs. Jack.

Edith said, "All right, I will," and hooked a hand in Hazel's elbow. They walked past Anse, toward the fence where the horses were hitched, without a sidelong glance.

42

What Anse felt, perhaps in imagination only, was the boring of curious and contemplative eyes. The eyes of young men and women and boys and girls, waiting for him to follow Edith and Hazel, to take Hazel McKee by the arm, pull her away from Edith Graham, and turn her with casual arrogance toward the road.

He couldn't do it.

He could not take the chance . . .

Cold with anger, he watched with outward indifference as Edith and Hazel brought the buggy round and Stella Graham climbed in beside them. A little later, when the crowd had cleared away, straggling off on foot and behind horses to Currie Head and Leeds and Riverside, he went down the hill in the dusk with the aimless young men who came to church for something to do.

Lee Wilmot was the last of these; after Lee turned up the school-house road, Anse was alone and glad of it.

The feeling he had was something outside his remembered experience. He had lacked the confidence, the gall . . . He had lacked the guts to take the chance of a public turn-down. The sense of this fused with an anger at the circumstances and people responsible that flushed through his mind in sickening waves.

He glanced at the lights in Richard McKee's house down the slope of the field from the road. A figure moved across a downstairs window, but he barely noticed this. He was not thinking directly of Hazel. For the time being his mind was concerned with an inclusive anger against it all, the Shore and its people.

Lights still burned in the houses; Marshalls', Neills', Curries', Grahams'. Frank Graham's front windows were open and he heard laughter from the front room in the dark, and Anna's voice, talking to Edith. Grahams' buggy, its shaft-tips on the ground, stood by the barn where someone had unhitched and left it after the women came home from church.

Anse went into his father's house by the back door. The kitchen was dark. Across the hall Stewart lay on the lounge in the parlour. He had been reading, but the book lay face down across his chest and faint snores escaped him. Josie had turned down the lamp. She looked up from her rocker as Anse went upstairs. He did not return the look, but groped his way straight to his room and changed into old clothes.

A little later he came down and went out and stood for a little in the door-yard. Dark scud crossed the sky slowly, moving east, momentarily letting moonlight through. The Channel's endless sighing was heavier than usual, a deliberate grumble, and although it was mid-July, the air had a chilling cold. Anse was conscious of these things, but he did not think about them, or watch or listen.

For a moment, standing there, he had an impulse to turn east to Vangie Murphy's. He put the thought aside with a hard impatience. The need in him was more than physical, a bitterness beyond the reach of Vangie's promiscuous favour.

He crossed the road and went down the path to the beach, lit the lantern in the hut, and reached down from the beam where he had hidden it a bottle of Demerara rum he had bought in Copeland weeks ago and never broached. He prised the cork out with a knife blade, set the bottle on the floor, and reached for the water-jug and cup. He sat on the bunk then, letting the rum slide back over the roughness of his tongue, feeling the hot bite of it as he swallowed. As usual with him, the black rum left no mellowness; it merely heightened the rankling in his mind.

Outside, the Channel's grumbling was broken down by nearness into separate sounds, the rising phrase of the swell's edge reaching up the slant of gravel, the low roughened sliding of moving pebbles as the swell withdrew.

Once Anse rose and went to the door. Everything now was overcast. He could see only the faint recurring spark of Princeport Light a dozen miles away. He returned to squat on the bunk, communing with the rum . . .

To want and not to get. That was one thing, and a thing you could deal with. You could plan and see a plan fail and there was still the ambition, the chance of achievement in the end.

To win, to make the grade, to take; and to treat possession lightly. That was another.

But to take and fail to hold . . .

To see the fact of belonging to Anse Gordon held worthless and disavowed . . .

There was no answer to this failure, none that he could see, on the Channel Shore. Some gesture that went beyond anything possible to him here was needed now to restore the sense of well being and of private power. Toward daylight, he thought he saw what it was.

He did not row the dory off to pick and bait his trawl. Instead he curled up on the bunk and slept.

At some time in his sleep he sensed Stewart in the hut, and heard his tentative voice, "Anse!", and grunted "All right; I'm sleepin' in." It was early evening when he finally got up for good and stretched the sleep out of him. He went home then to eat and wash and shave.

When it was dark again he put on the brown serge and walked down the road.

4

In NINE years of driving the Channel Shore mail Adam Falt had seldom travelled farther west than Findlay's Bridge or farther east than Copeland. Those were the limits of his route, twenty-four miles down on Monday, Wednesday and Friday and twenty-four miles back on Tuesday, Thursday and Saturday.

As a young man Adam had left the Shore and worked on the ice-teams in Boston and later sailed out of Gloucester. He was one of those matter-of-fact men to whom the various parts of the world are places in which to make a living. His father had driven the Shore mail for years and when the old man died Adam had simply come home to carry on the route.

Since then he had not thought much of going anywhere and the idea of boredom had never occurred to him. His wife and boys and girls ran the place in Leeds where he had been born and where he had brought them back to live; Adam spent most of his time behind his horses, on the road. The variety of people who lived along it was wide enough to satisfy his interest and every one of them he knew by name.

Most days there was nothing new. The same men and boys, harrowing and seeding in the spring, making hay in late July and August, digging potatoes in October, ploughing in October and November, working in the woods when the snow fell. The same women, seen against a background of blowing sheets on distant clothes-lines, or swinging hand-rakes in a sweeping motion behind the hay-rack.

The same weather, cold and windy in March, bright with sun under tall clouds or overcast with brooding rain, from June to fall; frosty or wet or white with snow in winter.

In all these usual things there was something to interest a man.

But now and then there would be a change in the pattern of the usual and for this he had a special eye.

Adam's first thought when he caught sight of Anse Gordon on the station platform at Copeland was hardly a thought at all;

merely a quickening of interest at seeing someone from up the Shore at an unexpected place. Then he frowned, puzzled, wondering how Anse had got there. Must have gone up to Morgan's Harbour last night or early this morning and taken the steamer down the Channel, Adam thought.

He rested for a minute from his work of pulling mail-bags from the postal car of the up train.

He called, "Hey! Anse!"

Anse ran his glance up and down the platform. A grudging grin creased the annoyance in his face.

He said, "Oh, hello, Adam."

"Where you bound for, Anse?"

"Nowhere much, Adam."

"Nowhere much, eh?" Curiosity persisted. Adam said, joking, "Not leaving us, are you, Anse?"

Anse laughed. He said, "Just a trip, Adam."

"Just a trip, eh?"

Anse didn't reply. He walked off down the platform. Adam took the last Channel Shore bag from the mail-clerk; the coach jerked, its wheels slowly turning and slowly gathering speed. As the passenger coaches swung past, he eyed their windows. Behind dusty glass, Anse ignored him as the train pulled out.

Adam stowed the bags from the up train under the tarp on the back of his waggon and went into the station restaurant to eat and wait for the down express from Halifax. He checked in his mind the list of errands he had to do. Pick up a pair of barn-door hinges for Will Francis at Steep Brook, a keg of shingle nails for Rod Sinclair at Katen's Rocks; for Bert Miller's wife at Millersville, three bars of Surprise Soap.

His mind stopped there for a pleasant minute. He and Bert Miller had bunked together in the eyes of the same Gloucester banker, twenty years before. Passengers on the mail waggon sometimes noticed that Adam stayed longer than necessary when he took in the Millersville bags, and came out sucking his moustache. Bert Miller was a comfort to him on raw days when the wind blew off the Channel.

But today, all through his lunch and the down train's brief halt and his preparations for departure, the figure of Anse Gordon kept getting mixed up with the errands and the people. Adam talked to himself a little on the road between post offices, and he was muttering as he swung the horses down the single street of Copeland for the slow drive up-shore.

". . . just a day or so, I s'pose." He lapsed into silence, and then pulled from a pocket the copy of the *Herald* the mail-clerk on the Halifax train had tossed him. Tuesday, July 16. He scanned the headlines:

Politics . . . *New Dominion Cabinet Soon to be Announced . . . Sir Robert Borden Tells What Canada's Industrial Needs are* . . . Adam skipped it; he voted Conservative by inheritance and didn't have to read about it. *Aerodrome Needed Here . . . Handley-Page Bomber to be Repaired where She Lies at Parrsboro* . . . His mind drifted, encompassing for a moment the world beyond the Shore, this passing summer . . . flying . . . Hawker and Grieve . . . Alcock and Brown . . . the R-34 . . . That fellow who hung head down; what was his name? . . . Locklear . . . peace . . . and old men talking in a hall outside of Paris . . . And Germans, sinking their own boats at a place called Scapa Flow . . .

Dull paper today, though. During two summers on the Boston ice-teams Adam had developed a mild interest in baseball. He turned to the sport page. Ty Cobb looked out at him, brandishing a bat . . . tough customer, Cobb . . . *drops to fifth position in batting race* . . . The Red Sox had lost at Chicago, 9-3 (*Williams and Schalk; Jones and Schang*); and the Cubs had trimmed the Braves . . .

He put the paper away and sat hunched and wordless while the horses made their own gait up the long grade through Steep Brook. When he spoke again it was to say a word or two without conscious meaning, a reflection of the play of his thought. Not thinking, really, but the absent-minded observation of a pattern, woven of memory and experience traced in the fabric of his brain by years of human contact on the Channel Shore road. He said without emphasis, "poor old Stew . . ."

Stewart Gordon carried a load of wood into the house from the pile in the yard and dumped it in the wood-box and glanced hesitantly at Josie. He said irrelevantly, to himself or the world at large, "I guess I'll mow tomorrow, anyway."

Josie filled the kettle from the pail in the porch and said nothing. No answer was called for. Stewart was a poor farmer; he hated horses and machinery, had no touch for either. He still mowed the place by hand. She had persuaded him to get an early start, even though the herring run was still on. To get a little done, anyway, in hours that would have been spent idling on the beach, so that they would still be making hay when it was time to mow the oats. But a man can't make hay alone and there was no sign of Anse.

Her mind dwelt on Stewart. He had been brought up to study for the priesthood, but in the end it had been necessary for him to quit school and look after his ageing parents whose small prosperity had faded away.

Sometimes Josie wondered what it would have been like, the relationship of priest and parishioner instead of husband and wife. But always she realized that the qualities that made Stewart an indifferent farmer, the indecision, the gentleness, would have unsuited him also for the hard life of the glebe. Father Gordon. No. He was too soft. Too soft. But his presence had something comforting in it.

Josie always checked herself at this kind of thinking when she caught it flowing through her mind. Checked herself with a little half-formed apology to the vague saints. Such thinking was almost blasphemous, she supposed. And irritation with herself would fuse into exasperation with Stewart, for the sheep that roamed the pasture unshorn into June, the wood-pile used up by mid-summer, the two-master built for deep-water fishing when deep-water fishing was a thing of the past. Or the endless reading. She was sure that a lot of the stuff Stewart read would be condemned to the stove by Father Morrison if he knew about it.

And Anse. There had been a time when she nursed the faith that the dark first child of their marriage might go on where Stewart had left off. The priesthood. She was glad her thought had remained unspoken, except to Anse himself. Anse hadn't even finished grade nine. There was something in Anse you couldn't reach. Josie was not a demonstrative woman, but something in her had broken, three years ago. Anse. . . . They had known he was free on embarkation leave. She could still see Stewart in his cane-bottomed chair at supper-time, starting up at the sound of wheels, hurrying out to watch Adam Falt approach from Copeland. But Adam's waggon had not stopped at the Gordons' gate with the dark grinning passenger they watched for.

And yet, when he had come home this last May, first to return to Currie Head from the German War, the pain of that earlier time had been almost forgotten for a little while. Something unreachable, but a quality in him that kept you reaching.

Josie sighed. It was better perhaps not to worry; to leave your troubles with Holy Church and the saints and the Mother of God. You could do that, but the ache remained, a silt in the mind. And the little nagging worries, the things you could hardly bother a saint with.

For a moment her mind escaped, back to childhood. The Reilly place at Mars Lake—others owned it now—and her father and mother, who were saints of God and pictures on a parlour wall. . . . Herself and Mamie. They'd been the youngest. Crazy, the way scraps of memory came to you. She was thinking suddenly of how proud they'd been, she and Mame, of the brothers who had gone away. Sylvester who was a fireman in Boston, and Martin, skipper of a vessel out of Gloucester at twenty-three.

But even in the memory of childhood there was no real escape. There was that morning in early fall, when she and Mame had gone barefooted across frosty pastures, and come home to learn that Vesty was dead. Smothered in smoke in a warehouse fire. The scene was clear as life: she and Mame warming their feet where the cows had lain, and coming home, and their mother's face . . . It was later that consumption had taken Mart; they had known for months *that* was coming. Curious. It was hard to think of Mame, married long ago in Halifax, as that little girl . . .

Anna came in behind her father, carrying a small pitcher filled with the year's last strawberries and pressed the door to with her back and shoulders. Josie was almost startled, caught again by a feeling that had come to her at unexpected moments lately—a feeling that she had never quite realized Anna's beauty as a person apart from her character as a daughter. This was not quite the girl who washed dishes and made the beds with whimsical complaint that she'd rather be hoeing potatoes. This was a friendly lovely stranger wearing a smile that was all open happiness, and in the fact that the happiness was all hers, all Anna's, the smile in spite of its openness was therefore private and secret too.

There was something in the way Anna used to look at the Marshall boy and speak to him that in memory sent a vague fear coursing through Josie. Grant Marshall. He was all right. A good boy, but—the fear pulsed and shivered—a Protestant . . . Well, James Marshall would never . . . But things had a way of happening on the Channel Shore sometimes, a way contrary to all the rules of living. And after the first startled talk, a way of being accepted and absorbed into the pattern of the place. Even sin and remorse, heresy and regret and failure, were dark colours in the pattern.

Anna glanced from Josie to Stewart and said, almost with a touch of impatience, "Don't be so down-in-the-mouth. He'll turn up tonight or tomorrow. 'Tisn't as if he hadn't done it before."

Josie sighed. Anna had a kind of cheerful common sense that was close to tactlessness but somehow left no sting.

She said, "I guess that's right." Actually, she believed this. Even when he had stayed away, that time before the war, he had come back . . .

Possibilities occurred to her. One of the Mars Lake boys back from Newfoundland or Lunenburg with a gallon of rum in his clothes bag. Or a trip to Forester's Pond, where, they said, the Johnson girls . . .

Well, that was the kind of thing a man came back from, wasn't it? Without harm, really. But she didn't like to remember the anger she had sensed in Anse in this past week, a grown-up version of the sulking violence that had gripped him as a boy when his will was crossed.

Stewart crossed the kitchen and stood irresolutely on the back porch. Anse . . . he thought impatiently of Anse, with irritation and annoyance and a querulous immediate concern, but without much tenderness. He went round the corner of the house then to sit on the front porch and watch the steamer crawling west, far away, up the Islands' shore.

He was still there, musing, when Adam Falt's horses slowed for the turn east of the house. He saw with surprise that Adam was pulling up at the gate, and went down the path to see what he wanted.

Adam said, "Hello, Stewart. I picked up a *Herald* in Copeland. Not much in it, I guess. But it might help to pass the evening."

Stewart reached up mechanically and took the paper. "Well, thanks, Adam, I . . ."

The mail-driver went on, casually, "Saw Anse at the station today, Stew. Taking a trip, is he?"

Stewart looked up, twisting the paper in his hands. "Anse? Did you? Station . . .?" He was silent for a little, then mumbled something meaningless, confused words—"Sydney . . . mines . . . steel works . . ."

Adam nodded. "Never been down that way myself. Well . . . So long for now, Stewart. See you later."

He spoke to the horses, turning it over in his mind. Anse Gordon. Where had he heard Anse's name—in connection with some girl? Hazel. Rich McKee's girl. His mind mused on Richard, and the stiffish woman who was Richard's wife. A Laidlaw. Eva Laidlaw from Morgan's Harbour. Adam had been in the States at the time of the marriage, but he remembered hearing about it, and wondering how Rich McKee had come to hook up with a girl from Town. His mind came back to Anse and Hazel, vaguely.

He thought he had better tell Richard McKee about this, anyway, when he stopped to change bags. Richard had a kind of a way with him, for all his quietness. He would know how to handle the telling of it to others, tell it in the proper way, so they'd know how to act to Stewart and Josie . . .

Richard broke this news in his own home at the supper table. He spoke diffidently, hardly looking up from his plate.

"Adam says Anse Gordon's . . . well, skipped out again."

Richard was habitually silent as if suspicious of words. It was not shyness so much as impatience with needless talk. People spent their lives chattering, telling each other things that anyone with sense must know already. They debased the coinage.

Anse's desertion was a piece of news that had to be told, but he told it without drama and with a flat reluctance.

Eva had gone to the stove for the teapot. She paused in the act of filling her cup and set the pot down.

"Skipped? . . . Skipped out?" Her voice was incredulous. "What? Why?"

Richard shook his head. "I don't know." He added drily, "I guess he didn't say."

Eva said, "But—" She glanced down the table at Hazel and across at young Joe. Hazel's face was serene, but Joe was grinning. The fact that youngsters of Joe's age, most of them, had an admiration for Anse Gordon exasperated Eva. She said sharply, "It's nothing to laugh at," and then, "Some kind of trouble, I expect."

She questioned Richard. "But—skipped? How did Adam know? How does he know it's not just—"

Richard said, "Well, he was talking to him at Copeland. Stewart said something about the steel works. But it was the Halifax train Anse left on."

There was nothing more to be got out of him. Eva resigned herself to thinking that after supper she would have to go over to Stella Graham's. The Grahams would know, likely. She glanced covertly again at Hazel, but the girl's face showed only normal interest. That *was* over, then. But if it was something shameful that had driven Anse away—the possibilities crossed Eva's mind: something shady, like theft; or a girl in trouble down the Shore— if it was something shameful then some of the shame would linger round Hazel, who had gone around with . . . some of the shame would linger round the McKees.

You couldn't touch dirt without getting smeared. It was something to be thankful for that Anse was gone, if he stayed away. But the relief in that was balanced by the irritation that, for a while at least, when people thought of it they would think of Hazel too.

After the dishes had been cleared away Hazel and Joe went down to the pasture bars behind the barn to milk. Richard usually shared this chore with Joe but tonight Hazel took the pail from his hand. She was aware of his dislike for milking, for many of the small things a man had to do around a farm at fixed times; and now she felt a little sense of pleasure in giving him this small relief. This in its fleeting way was evidence again of the new thing that seemed to be sprouting in her, the thing she had felt consciously little more than a week ago as she sat by the road with Anna Gordon, looking into Grant's Place.

She did not really consider this. It was only after taking the pail from Richard's hand that she thought of it at all. Her motive had been to get away from the kitchen, away from Eva's speculating tongue with the edge of accusation in it and the hint of triumph and of prophecy come true. Away where she could let this news lie in her mind and consider what it meant to her.

The two cows, Bess and Spot, ruminated under the ancient apple tree on the pasture side of the bars.

Joe said, probing, "What d'you think of it, Haze?" He up-ended a box and squatted to strip the milk from Spot.

She said absently, "Think? About what?"

Joe said, "You know. Anse."

She shook her head. "Oh, I don't know. What's anybody s'posed to think? It sounds kind of crazy."

There was only the sound of the milk, hissing and splashing in the pails, the thin whining of insects, the swish of Bess's tail, the small dragging sound of a hoof shifted on sod, the sound of rhythmic chewing, of a far-off motor somewhere up the road. Joe was silent, and Hazel wondered how much he knew or guessed. How much anyone knew or guessed. From the Rocks to Leeds now, the talk would start.

She didn't much care about that. What mattered to her, about Anse, were her private feelings. These now were a blend of relief and emptiness. Relief that temptation was gone. Temptation. She hated the churchy sound of that word. It was not temptation in itself, the yielding to something called "sin", that she had feared. It was the thought of weakness, of being beaten, the possibility that her body could still betray the pride of her feelings. Never a night in these last weeks but her flesh had urged her out to the road, to the smell of the fields, the laughter and talk at Katen's and the chance of an hour alone with Anse.

That was gone and there was relief in its absence. Relief—and emptiness. And now again at the edge of consciousness, fear. Now she had time for fear.

Joe had finished with Spot. He turned away up the path to the house, the full pail in his hand. Hazel rubbed the coarse roughened silk of Bess's flank and stood for a moment looking down the pasture to the beach. Under all the small sounds of summer, rose and fell the old deliberate murmur of surf on stone, the voice of the shore. She turned and followed Joe.

Later after Eva had gone down the road to Grahams' and Joe had disappeared in the other direction, to spread the news to Lairds' and Kinsmans' she supposed, Hazel spoke to Richard.

He sat as usual in the corner beyond the range near the bedroom door, where the lamp's light scarcely fell. Hazel found herself thinking that between her and her father there had never been, as far as she could remember, a harsh word. When she was a little girl, before Joe was born and while he was still a baby, Richard had sometimes taken her to the beach. Never out to the nets, but sometimes hand-lining or picking net-rocks or just to play around the fish huts in the sun. In a sense he had treated her like a little boy.

All long ago. After Joe came it had ceased, or almost. Probably to Eva's relief or at her orders. The beach was no place for a girl. And she . . . she had almost forgotten. The memories came to her now with a peculiar newness, so long had they lain unregarded behind the growing up, the immediate discontents.

What had there been between them, since then? She couldn't remember ever having talked seriously to Richard about anything. When a question had to be settled—oh, something like the buying of a dress or whether you stayed in school another year after grade nine—Eva had settled it. If it were necessary to talk to Richard about it, Eva did the talking. The only relationship between herself and Richard had been a surface thing, off-hand and casual.

And yet, she told herself now, there was some kind of alliance, some kind of closeness.

As she came up the path with the milk she had thought the small ridiculous thing she wanted to ask of Richard would be hard to find words for. Now it was natural and easy.

She said, "Father," and waited until he lifted his head to look

54

at her. "Father . . . when d'you—when're you going to start the hay?"

Richard said after a small pause, "When the herring're over, I s'pose . . . Marshalls've not even started yet," and then indifferently, "Why?"

Hazel stirred and shifted on her chair. "Oh"—she laughed a little —"I'd kind of like to work at it."

Richard let another small pause fall. Then he laughed. "First time I ever heard of anybody *wantin'* to make hay."

Hazel shook her head, joining in his low indulgent laughter.

It was hard to explain, this restless wish to be active, in the open, away from the house, in sun and wind. She groped for words but Richard spoke before she found them.

"Be all right, if your mother . . ."

No need to explain that. Years ago hay-making had been a month-long job at which everybody worked, men and boys with hand-scythes and pitchforks, women with forks shaking out the heavy green swaths, turning the spread hay to the sun, raking-after behind the loaded racks. Now horse-drawn mowing machines and rakers were getting common. A farm could be made in a fortnight or less and it was becoming unusual to see a woman in the field.

Richard still liked to take things slowly. He had taught Joe to mow with a hand-scythe and if he had had his way would probably have made the place by hand still. But Eva had argued him into exchanging work with the Marshalls, and the Marshalls used machines. For years now after James Marshall made his own place he had brought his horses and machines to McKees'.

Hazel said, "You tell her you need me."

Richard looked at his hands and half-nodded. He said, "Well, we'll see . . ."

After a little while he got up and went outdoors to look at the sky and came in to go to bed. At two o'clock he must get up and rouse Joe and heat the tea and beans. They would go down to the beach then and row the flat out to the nets on the calm of the darkened channel.

5

ALONG the Channel Shore from Copeland to Findlay's Bridge timothy and browntop moved in the wind on the low breasts of fields, divided by fences and brook-water and fingers of dark woods reaching toward the sea.

Between the low beach and the upland forest the places lay, a patchwork of green and green on the county's edge, tilted toward the salt south-west wind in the afternoon and dark at night under a land-breeze light as breath.

Down-shore they were not thinking of haying yet. On the banks off Millersville and Forester's Pond, cod and haddock nosed the baited hooks of trawls in seven fathoms. Closer in, the painted buoys of herring nets lolled on the moving swell. At high tide off Steep Brook the markers of lobster pots stood up and swayed like scattered bean-poles rooted in the sea.

Ashore, at widely separated intervals, small clusters of men in yellow oilskins streaked with blood stood in the land-wash at gutting tables, splitting fish, stripping the guts from cod and haddock and sending the cleaned fish on to the wash-barrels, the brine and the drying flakes on the hump of the beach.

But up-shore at Currie Head, except for the few who were still concerned with herring, haying had begun.

On James Marshall's place James himself sat the double-mower, pulled by his two work-horses, while the shuttling blades laid down a widening ribbon of mown hay on shaven ground. Gradually the chosen square of grey-green timothy narrowed inward from its edges until only a scalp-lock remained. Then James would raise the cutter-bar, back the clicking machine, and make his final sweep before going on to assault another square or oblong of his wide upper field.

In the moments when the bar was up and his own blades silent, he could hear across these northern pastures the small swift cricket-chirring of other machines: Clem Wilmot's and Sam Freeman's off to the northwest, up the school-house road, and Kinsman's and Laird's between the cross-roads and the hill at Leeds.

On the level top of this first fold of land above the shore road, one seemed measurably closer to the white cloud-banks around the horizon, and the arching blue of sky, than when one worked below. From this ridge the land sloped away in both directions, south to the Channel and north to flat woods of the abandoned places along the old back road. Beyond that again one could see the far shallow slopes of a second northward rising, the wilderness of tangled barrens and forest stretching away to the gulf.

James did not indulge in undue fancies about clouds and distance, but there were times as he worked in the fields when he felt a kind of exalted pride. Now and then he grew faintly uneasy about this, but the uneasiness vanished when he reminded himself that it was a righteous pride, tempered with thankfulness to a power other than himself. Hard work and careful figuring and virtue. The Lord helps those who help themselves—if they serve Him. There was a justice in this which James understood. It was only fair.

Resting a moment, he let his mind run again to the northwest, beyond the cricket-sound of Wilmot's and Freeman's machines. When haying was done here on the front place, they would move the machines and horses back to the old farm he had bought there, from some people named Scott who had gone away. Again he felt that little sense of power. A home farm here in full cultivation, another back there from which he took the extra hay he needed for his sheep and cattle, and down the road a piece of woods that stretched from the Channel north.

He glanced eastward, thinking of that wooded land he had bought from Frank Graham's father, and of his purpose in buying it, but almost at once his mind was caught by other things.

Along the eastern line fence between this field in which he worked and the northern stretches of the Neill place, Fred, with a hand-scythe, was mowing out the patches of hay along the fence where a machine could not be brought to bear. James frowned. Alec Neill . . . They had the usual arrangement about line fences. Each built half the fence between the Channel and the road and between the road and their back lines. James, years ago, had put up wire. It annoyed him now to see his clean lines of six-strand wire joined to the staked zig-zag of Alec Neill's worm fence.

Across the field to the west, between his land and Richard McKee's, Richard at least had serviceable post-and-rail. In that direction Will was working behind Polo, the road-horse, turning with a tedder the hay James had mowed that morning.

An odd mixture of thought and recollection drifted in James's mind. Foolish to keep so fast and fine-drawn a horse as Polo . . . But Polo between the shafts of the rubber-tired two-seater gave one a feeling of—position, perhaps. He thought of the turn-out driven by Bert Stevens, the Morgan's Harbour merchant: two horses and a rig with a green fringe round the top.

Will—it was good to have Will back from the war unharmed. But Will would go away to business college. Fred was the one who would work this land when James was gone. Fred would be the Marshall on the shore then. Fred, and, of course, on the place down the road, Grant . . .

Grant . . . A wave of something indefinable flowed through James as he dropped the cutter-bar and spoke to the horses. Grant . . . It was right here, here in this upper field that Harvey, laughing, had announced his decision, years ago.

Harvey. The thing James thought of was an overcast day in May with a raw wind blowing and Harvey heaving at the side of the stone-drag. Dumping in a fence corner—it was worm fence then— the load they had picked from a ploughed and harrowed strip in this upper field. Harvey laughing. "By God, Jamie boy, when it warms up I'm getting out of here. I'm bound for Boston."

Across the cluttering activities of nearly thirty years, James still could feel the mixture of his own sensations. Inner disturbance at the blasphemy; secret warmth in the fact that Harvey always called him Jamie; recognition that Harvey meant it, meant this light-hearted threat to leave the Channel Shore.

Grant . . .

James returned to the present and glanced down the slope of land and westward along the shore road. In Richard McKee's lower field two small figures moved, slowly, one slightly ahead of the other, along a selvage of standing hay. Each to the left of him was leaving a narrow humped wake. Richard McKee and young Joe, swinging scythes in the slow mower's march. And behind them, shaking out the green wavelike swaths, a girl.

James shook his head and raised a hand to his beard in irritation. He had always felt the oddity in Richard McKee. But to make his hay by hand, when in a week or so James Marshall would be ready to turn his mower to the job . . . It was worthy of people like those who lived down-shore, neglecting the land for the endless gamble of the Channel. Worthy of someone like Stewart Gordon. He turned to his team in controlled exasperation.

Richard swept his scythe through standing hay where the swaths ended at the edge of a strip of oats, tidied away the last tufts of timothy with a short thrust of wrists and blade, and straightened, flexing his shoulders. He brought the scythe up then until the snath stood upright, rested his left elbow on the heel where the blade was bolted on, and reached into a back pocket for his whetstone.

The stone rang thinly on tempered metal, crinch-crinch, crinch-crinch, crinch-crinch, while the numberless concerns of life ran idly in Richard's mind.

He was not particularly a worrier. It was just that the mind was never empty. You tramped along, hunched behind the moving scythe, and the distant sound of James Marshall's mower and the ache in your own shoulders reminded you again that this was needless labour. Reminded you of Eva's tight-lipped unpleasantness about it. Carried you along from that into the old knowledge, submerged far below the outward things of living, below church, town, sleep, work, and the talk you had with neighbours. The old knowledge of aloneness and the conflict between a mind concerned with paint on the house, shingle-stain on the barn, walnut in the parlour, and Sunday serge and satin; and a mind concerned with the feel of wood, and what your hands could do with it, the smell of net-tan, the look of the Channel, the drift of seasons, the sound of certain voices . . .

Richard never dwelt on this if he could help it. He did not blame anyone. Long ago he had achieved a sort of open-mindedness, a private stolidity close to fatalism. But there were times when he could not stop the condition that underlay his life from breaking surface and coming up to be dealt with in conscious thought.

It had reached the surface more than once in these last few days, borne up on the tide of Eva's annoyance and the uneasiness that seemed to have touched both her and Hazel. That somehow had even touched himself. Everyone but Joe . . .

Richard grinned slightly and tossed the whetstone to his son. Joe had finished his swath and stood now sweating at the edge of the oats, wiping his scythe-blade with a twist of hay. He was a big boy for fourteen, Joe. Fourteen? Nearly fifteen, now, and ready to quit school. The thing about Joe was that he didn't mind anything. He liked work. Joe would go away, in the end. There was nothing at Currie Head to hold him. But in the meantime he was learning to mend nets, splice rope, shave staves and caulk a row-boat. Just as he had learned to handle a mowing machine at Marshalls', and a double-bitted axe. And he didn't mind getting up in the morning to go to the nets.

Richard's mind drifted as he walked back to begin another swath . . . Himself and Hugh Currie and Alec Neill and Frank Graham and Frank's brother Andy, who had gone away . . . Gathering net-stones and ballast-rocks for the whale-boats. The boats in which their fathers sailed, far down to the Cape Breton coast in early spring, after mackerel. Even though the fishing had almost vanished, diminished in these last summers to nothing but the four or five weeks of herring, something about the beach remained . . .

Richard's living was taken from his land and the timber of his wood-lots. But the part of his life that was made up of pride and affection and boyishness, the thing in him that regarded as unimportant so many matters that meant so much to Eva, was coiled like a net's head-rope round the weeks of early summer that somehow stretched themselves across the drifting seasons . . .

In winter after a day in the woods he would bring in from the shop the brown bun of a tied-up herring net, loop its coils to a nail in the window-sill, and mend. When he chopped box-logs for Sinclair's mill, his eyes would be alert for a straight spruce that might make up into a pair of oars, or a white pine to watch and hoard until it was big enough to be sawed and planed into planking for a lap-seam flat.

In spring he would steal a sunny day or two from harrowing and seeding to caulk and paint the boat, with Joe learning how. This craftsmanship would never be of any use to Joe, as Eva complained, any more than it had been to Richard. The thing was like an instinct.

Soft darkness at three o'clock, before the morning wind. The tail-buoy inboard, and then the anchor, and then the glimmer, far down, sliding, vanishing, sagging to the surface: the net alive with twitching fish. Ashore, the gutting-knife flashing under the sun, while gulls screamed and the sou'west wind came up to set the Channel marching. The bite of coarse salt on chapped hands. And sixty dollars perhaps, from Bob Fraser's fish company at Princeport, at the season's end.

All this drifted at the back of Richard's mind. To him there was nothing illogical or impractical about it. He really didn't think about it much. Salt slop on thwarts. The mean job of fish-cleaning. The back-breaking labour of lugging hand-barrows over the hump of the beach. Long half-silent conversations with Frank and Alec and Hugh, or Stewart Gordon . . . the core of a life that for eleven months a year was concerned with chopping wood, cleaning stables, ploughing, getting in the hay . . .

He halted in the middle of the swath and glanced down at the Channel. They might as well haul, soon. Already he had beached four of his eight nets. Couldn't fish and make hay at the same time. It was too tough. They would haul another fleet in a day or two, and leave the last for a while . . . He thought of this with regret. The last days of July, when all that was left of fishing was to pick the dirt out of drying nets and stow them in the loft—it always left an emptiness.

He began to mow and his mind turned again to Eva. This was the thing in him, the unreason of the beach, reflected in everything he did, that exasperated her. He sensed this, felt it with something in him less precise than thought. As he halted at the swath's end he glanced up over the fields toward the toy-size plodding of James Marshall's horses. James came of people who were all clerk and farmer, who didn't know a gunnel from a thole-pin. Respect, yes. You had to respect James Marshall. Liking was another thing. He had a sudden thought that Eva should have married somebody like James. Wryly, he grinned and was momentarily light of heart.

The grin was still on his face, playing lightly there, as he loafed, leaning on the scythe, and watched Hazel approach, shaking out the swath behind Joe. And again, the scattered wisps of memory: mackerel-fishing, years ago, with Alec Neill. The row in from the anchorage where the two-masters were; the beach, and a small girl, straightening, dropping handfuls of coloured stones as she ran bare-footed on wet sand to be on hand when the flat crunched in to a landing . . . Richard felt an ache in his throat. It was all past, he hadn't thought of that for years. It was, now, like something that had happened to another person, in another country. But . . . that person was himself, the running girl his daughter. He had a curious illusion, here in the hayfield, of time long past, forgotten, drawn close around him. Immeasurably far away, and yet close. Of old things new again in an intimate strangeness, touching his throat with recognition that was a kind of pain.

Hazel thrust the fork into the green wave of the swath and scattered fresh hay over mown ground. Outdoors in sun and wind with space around her it had been possible during these last few days to feel at times that nothing much had changed. She did not know why this was so, or consider it very deeply. The sweep of the Channel, the banked clouds, the side hills quilted in varying shades of dun and green, the shape of the land and the colour of flashing water . . . They were unchanged, and in them she had found a kind of comfort.

Indoors, with the earth and sky and sea shut out by walls, and life a thing of people, habit, talk, of guarded glances and idle chatter and sudden silence, there was no defence . . .

When she sat in church with Eva now the speculative eyes were on her. Behind the good-natured words of boys and girls, dropping in for the mail, she could hear the undertone of words unsaid.

Last week, just after Anse's departure, she had gone down to Katen's one evening with the Lairds. The Lairds had a new Ford, the first car at Currie Head, the first on this part of the Shore, except for Katen's truck. Edith and Lol Kinsman had gone down with them; and Dave Stiles and others were there, others from The Rocks. But not a word, in her hearing, had been said about Anse. Not a word about the one thing you'd think they'd talk about . . .

Probably, she told herself, some of this, some of this thing she felt, was imagination. But not all. Last Sunday after church a little knot of women, Hat Wilmot and Ida Freeman and Sarah Kinsman, had been talking about Anse. Nothing unusual in that. What was unusual was the silence, the sudden silence touched with embarrassment, when she and Edith Graham had edged round them, through the churchyard gate, to take the road home.

That, and Edith's obvious considerateness. Edith hadn't mentioned either the talk or the silence.

So now in the open air and in bodily exhaustion, Hazel tried to find relief from this sense of being watched and considered, and from the fear that was overtaking her.

She was not sure when this sense of fear and foreboding had become definite. At the time of Anse's disappearance, there had been nothing but the vaguest sort of doubt. It had hardly been in her conscious mind at all at the moment when, half-laughing, she had asked Richard to let her help with the hay. Gradually it had grown, was growing, in her mind and flesh.

She felt the flush of it now, amid the heat and the insect-singing and the smell of hay, and found herself imagining . . .

Easy enough to get to Morgan's Harbour. The Lairds' Ford was on the road nearly every night. She saw herself slipping away from them, away from the crowd at Carter's ice-cream parlour, slipping down the street to Dr. Brickley's house. Confiding in the old doctor. Hearing his brusque voice—*Go on home, there's nothing* . . . Or seeing the veiled eyes, hearing the voice, the other verdict . . . *Well, it looks . . . we'll have to talk to your mother* . . .

She couldn't do it. If her fears were groundless, then she'd have put herself in the position—What if you told, laid the secret bare, and for no reason?

If they were not, if the worst were true, then the telling would have to be done over again. Over again. Endlessly over again.

She washed the imagined scenes out of her mind. Even doctors couldn't be sure. Not this soon.

It came to her now that after all there wasn't much real relief in the sky and the land and the Channel. In these things there was only temporary escape from people. And from yourself. That, and the chance to achieve a tiredness of flesh and bone that brought the troubled ease of sleep.

6

HAZEL woke one morning and knew she could not bear, alone, the burden of her fear.

She had fallen asleep earlier than usual and wakened several times throughout the night. Her first thought on rousing finally was that she had slept late; she could hear Eva moving about the kitchen below. She lay in bed a minute, watching squares of sunlight on the yellow spread. For the last few days she had felt sick in the morning. She knew now that when she threw back the spread and drew herself upright the sickness would begin. She got out of bed, and it was there.

She dressed quickly, conscious only of the sickness, which would pass, and the long fluttering apprehension. Eager to get downstairs and force herself to eat something, and escape to the fields where there was work with which she could try to deaden the waiting and the fear.

Then, between slow strokes of a hairbrush, the waiting was over. The fear was final and realized, and something she must share. There was in this a sense of something like surrender and the beginning of a strange relief.

She stood for a little with the brush in her hand, looking into the mirror. The face that looked back at her was calm. The brown eyes showed little of the tumult in her mind. But the wide mouth was pinched and the cheeks colourless. She thought her mother was right. She didn't look too well.

Eva was busy with breakfast when Hazel came through the door from the hallway. The damp warm porridge-smell hung in the kitchen like faint mist. Eva said, "Morning. You're a little late. A good thing. Why you have to—"

She broke off, shook her head, and glanced directly at Hazel as the girl took her place at the table.

For an instant she stood there with a plate of porridge in her hand, her eyes on Hazel's face. A vague alarm and something close to sympathy edged her voice. "Hazel, you're—you look—you're white as a sheet . . . Sick? Are you sick?"

64

Hazel stumbled to her feet, grasping the edge of the table. She said, "No. No. Oh, Mumma, hush." She walked quickly from the kitchen, out through the porch to the yard.

Behind the barn, out of sight, she stopped to retch. For a moment there all the torment of her mind and body were blended in a gasping helplessness. She straightened and went on slowly, weak and unsteady. A kind of hard calm was taking possession of her mind.

As she crossed into the lower pasture she glanced back, once, and saw Eva standing in the porch door, and felt a sense of sorrow. She waved her hand in a gesture of attempted reassurance and went on. Eva would not shout or follow. Hazel almost wished she would. Wished she would break down and forget appearances and come rushing after her, even though it were in anger . . .

Richard had his own road to the inlet shore, but the scow he and Joe used to cross the inlet would be on the other side . . . The long walk round, then. She climbed the fence and crossed Marshalls' lower field to Alec Neill's land. A little farther on she saw Christine Currie, far up the slope of Curries' field, moving between house and hen-house. Christine stopped to look, across the quarter-mile of field and pasture.

Across Grant's Place she could hear the rushing of Graham's Brook. Farther east the faint rattle of Sinclair's mill, just starting the day's work, came into the blend of morning sounds, of bird-song and crow-caw and the sighing of the Channel on its thirty miles of shore. She turned down Currie's road and walked through Rob's yard, on across the neck and up the inlet's southern shore to the beach.

There was no wind here, but somewhere far to the southeast, unseen beyond the Lion's Mane, the Atlantic heaved and swayed, and the Channel stirred lazily with the muted echo of that heaving. Its glassy movement was slight and regular and slow, hardly perceptible except on tide-packed gravel where the shallow edge of sea ran in and up and forever slipped away.

East of the Head the Grahams were rowing their flat in to the beach with Frank in the stern and one of the boys at the oars. Farther out Hugh Currie and Stan were still at the nets, hand-lining after having picked their fish. Hazel could hear a word spoken, a far unbodied indistinguishable ghost of a sound. She looked up the beach toward Richard's hut. He and Joe had landed and were cleaning herring in the land-wash under a cloud of screaming gulls. Even as she looked she saw Richard glance up and realized from his sudden momentary stillness that he had seen her. He turned to say something to Joe and turned back slowly and began to climb the beach toward the hut.

As she faced Richard by the door of the weathered building she felt a moment of reaction. For a little she saw only a man, middle-aged and slightly stooped, with a stubble of yellowish whisker on his face, in ragged shirtsleeves and oilskins stained with blood.

Nothing . . . There was nothing here to end aloneness . . . For this instant her mind swam in the depths of a blind sea, lost and without hope, and there was nothing she could say.

Then Richard spoke to her, and fear vanished in the sound of his voice.

He said evenly, with a casual quietness, "Come into the hut, now, girl, and tell me what it is."

7

THE green and ochre and gold of August smouldered along the Channel Shore. Even down-shore, now, haying was in full swing. At some of the Currie Head places, James Marshall's among them, it was over. At others the fields lay half cleared and half standing, or heaped with bundles ready for the rack. In mown fields the green oats waved in separate patches, like islands surrounded by flat stubble. Along the side hills early sown with oats for ripening, the faintest haze of yellow began to tinge the greyish green. In roadside gutters the darker yellow of ragwort was dull with time and dust.

Except for the floats of Alec Neill's salmon net, nothing broke the smoothness of Channel water off The Head. The last herring nets had been hauled, cleaned and dried and stowed in the lofts of huts.

In early evening of the second Sunday in the month the three Marshall boys were lazing in the last mellow sunlight at the back of the house. Will sat on the porch steps in shirtsleeves and sock feet, polishing his shoes. Fred tipped his chair against the house wall and grinned up at Grant, squatting on the step between kitchen and porch.

Fred, the eldest, had been forced to stay at home while first Will and then Grant went into the army. But there was no resentment in Fred about anything, Grant thought. Fred was the sunny one. He could get a laugh out of anything, even the precise and serious way in which Will shined his shoes. It was Fred who had fried the ham and eggs for supper and washed the dishes afterward. Suddenly Grant felt a little rush of feeling, dumb and indescribable, for these cousins, for this family which treated him like a brother and a son. Fred, the barrel-chested farmer, who worked like a horse and laughed and never worried. Will, the silent shrewd one, who would make a place for himself soon in some city or other, far from The Head. Aunt Jane, Uncle James. He thought of the three half-grown ash trees set out on the flat grass in front of the house. Set out there, years ago, by Uncle James, in some unusual moment of whimsy, to represent the three boys. Momentarily this family feeling blurred for Grant the other thing, the slow excitement growing in his mind.

Fred said, "Ain't you puttin' on your uniform for church, boy?" and Grant felt a little inward laughter. Uncle James had tried to bring them all up to be painstaking in their speech, but it hadn't had much effect on Fred. The friendly bantering voice went on, "We fin'ly got the plaid peddycoat off Will; but they'll expect brass buttons up at Leeds, your first Sunday home."

Grant shook his head. "Nope. I took her off for the last time." He had worn his khaki serge to Sunday School in the morning, had sat through Bible Class because Uncle James expected that. He said, off-hand, "I don't think I'll be going up with you tonight, anyway, Fred."

Fred said, "What? Why? . . ." and was silent. Will began to put on his shoes. A slight constraint gathered round the three of them, a kind of doubtfulness.

Fred said, "They'll be to church there, on the way home."

Grant said, not in answer to this observation but as if he had not heard it, "I think I'll take a night off."

He knew what was in their minds. Uncle James and Aunt Jane had driven to Findlay's Bridge after dinner to visit cousins. On the way back they would go to church at Leeds, and Uncle James would expect to see them there—his two sons and most of all his nephew on his first Sunday home.

Fred laughed, breaking the small odd silence. "Y'heard that, 'd'ya, Will? He's got somethin' on his mind. Well, good luck to him."

It was hearty and clumsy but it ended the brief constraint. Will knotted a shoelace and said contemplatively, "Maybe he's going down the road," and Grant laughed.

A little later he watched from the northern windows of the kitchen as Fred and Will walked off up the lane to the road and turned west. Shortly afterward Dan Graham and Bill, Harry Neill and Stan Currie sauntered past and halted at Richard McKee's gate. Joe was going up the slope to the road to join them.

Grant wondered whether Richard and Eva would be driving up, and felt a pang for Richard and Joe and Hazel. Regret lay at the back of his mind, faintly troubling, faintly clouding what he felt at being home.

He had heard the story yesterday in Adam Falt's mail waggon, somewhere between Steep Brook and Millersville. Adam had been silent for a little when Grant asked him, merely making conversation, what was new at The Head. Then he had told the story.

Grant shook his head, remembering Adam's words: "No, not together. He just vanished. Hazel—she's gone to Toronto. With relations, so Eva says. Dress-making. Nobody knows exactly . . ."

He was thinking of this, and of the talk that would be going on, and the disquiet he had felt at Adam's words, when Frank Graham's rig went by. The mare was travelling at a walk, and Mrs. Graham and Edith were in the buggy. Grant felt a small amusement; they hadn't been able to argue Mr. Graham into going.

He had seen Mrs. Graham and Edith and the boys at Sunday School, but not Frank, yet. It was a little strange to him, the inner glow he felt at seeing again each familiar face. Through the time away when he thought of home three things had made everything else seem dull and formless: the place here, and the family—and related to that, the strip of woods between Hugh Currie's place and Grahams'; and the girl. Now he was finding in these first days at home that everything wakened a warmth, a response. It was all a pattern, growing clear again, and even the background threads of it were pleasant . . .

He took the jacket of his blue serge from a hook in the hall and slipped into it and felt the tightness across the shoulders; must have grown a bit, he thought, in his year and a half away. "Filled out", was what Stella Graham had called it when she shook hands with him at Sunday School this morning. Well, he could stand that. He had always been conscious of being just a little smaller than average, and slender. He glanced at himself in the hall mirror. His shoulders were heavier, all right, but his face had lost its chubbiness. It was lean and tanned under the crisp, short, brown hair. He looked into candid blue eyes and had a small wish that he didn't appear so serious; even when he felt finest, his feelings didn't show, and even Anna sometimes teased him about it.

He went out through the front door, and halted, and considered crossing the lower pastures, then rejected this in favour of the road. The strip of packed dirt curved away in front of him, past Alec Neill's and Curries', a friendly brown ribbon roughened in the centre by the impact of innumerable hooves, with strips along the inside of its low shoulders pressed smooth and hard by the passage of iron-tired wheels.

No sign of life at Alec Neill's. Perhaps Mrs. Neill had persuaded Alec to go to church. Grant thought of turning in to find out; the wry laughter that ran like an under-current in men like Hugh Currie and Frank Graham was almost a tide-race in Alec. He felt good, thinking about it.

The other impulse was stronger. He went on, past Curries', to the stretch of woods beyond. Opposite the big birch he stopped, musing a little. It would not have surprised him to find Anna sitting there, but he felt no disappointment in the fact that she was not. Things didn't often turn out by chance the way you wanted them. Sometimes they did, and up to now he had been satisfied with that. But now he was thinking that maybe things could be given a little help, a little arranging.

He turned down the hauling-road. Fifty or sixty yards from the main road he came to the clearing. Here, two years ago, he had made a start; had begun to turn spruce and fir and yellow birch into box-logs and fire-wood. But concerned mainly with laying the land open to the sky. He found the level stump of a spruce they had sawed down, one evening when Fred had come along to lend a hand, and sat on it now, feeling a grave elation.

This fall and winter he would chop, and next spring burn a new field and plant potatoes in the ash-covered cradle-hills. Probably if you wanted to farm it would be more sensible to go to Boston and haul ice or do carpenter-work until you had saved the price of a place. There were places you could get, on the back roads, now that the younger people were drifting away. But Grant didn't want to go to Boston, or anywhere. He wanted to work land that was new, to bring it into stumps first and then pull the stumps, and grow the first hay and oats himself, as the settlers had done a hundred and fifty years ago. He was twenty years old. Not quite twenty-one. There was plenty of time . . .

He didn't linger long in the woods of the Place. Time now stretched endlessly ahead, the days in which he could work here, clearing ground, burning stumps, fencing off a pasture and field. Years away, he could see a house on a concrete basement, with running water; a big high-shouldered barn . . . He didn't have to stay in these woods to think of it. This was a picture that slipped into his mind whenever he thought of this wood-lot, and it stayed with him as he turned east out of the clearing and picked his way through the woods in the deepening dusk toward Frank Graham's line fence.

Before his enlistment he had worked in the clearing in the evenings, ignoring the banter he had had to take for doing winter work in summer, for working at all when you didn't have to. Before going home at dark he had sometimes crossed to Grahams' to sit

70

on the back steps with Frank or young Dan. Sometimes Stewart Gordon would come up the road, for Frank's companionship. Or Anna, to talk to Edith . . . The houses were barely an eighth of a mile apart, the Grahams' south of the road and the Gordons' north of it. Between these families the differences seemed to be ignored; there was no feeling when you saw Frank Graham and Stewart Gordon together that they were different because one was Catholic and the other Methodist.

Grant's mind ran for a moment on the differences there were, even in a place as small as Currie Head. Not only in religion and politics. In his own time in school they had called the youngsters from up the school-house road Bogtowners. And they in turn had called the kids from farms fronting on the Channel, the Fishguts . . . He grinned in the dusk. The Marshalls lived out front but he couldn't remember that anyone had ever called Uncle James a Fishgut.

It was nearly dark as he picked his way between the trunks of spruce, on green moss prinked out here and there with the salmon-pink of pigeon-berries. He climbed Frank's rail fence, dropped into the pasture and went on across its hollow and up the slope of the mown hayfield to Grahams' back door.

No one was about, but he could hear voices. He went round the house and found Frank and Stewart Gordon on the veranda, and pipe smoke faintly acrid in air laden with the smell of hay.

Frank got out of a wicker chair and came to the steps and put out a hand.

"Grant! They told me you was home. Come up and siddown." The hand pulled him up the steps.

Grant laughed, a little shyly. "Hi, Mr. Graham. How are you, Mr. Gordon?"

Stewart Gordon peered over his glasses with his slight habitual air of bewilderment. Anything unusual seemed to puzzle Stewart until he got used to it. He was silent for minutes while Grant and Frank exchanged casual talk. Then, his mind recovering from the surprise which had jolted him out of preoccupation, he settled back in his chair with a gentle pleased interest.

He said, "Grant. Well. Didn't know you were back . . ."

"Yesterday, Mr. Gordon. We landed at Halifax Friday and I came up yesterday with the mail."

Again the rush of regret ran thinly in his mind. As he talked idly with Frank and Stewart Gordon, he found himself quick with a painful sympathy for Stewart. And Mrs. Gordon. She must

71

be . . . But he didn't really know her. It was Stewart who wakened the laughter and love in Anna's voice.

Anna. The vague disquiet whispered in his mind. He had never thought of her really in relation to anyone but himself, and as Stewart's daughter. But—she was Anse Gordon's sister. She too would be touched and troubled by anything Anse did. He had felt this vaguely from the moment he had heard the story, but now the sense of it was clear and sharp. Troubled and hurt and talked about. He felt a cold hard anger. At Anse Gordon, at circumstance, at the malice of talking tongues.

He hardly heard Frank Graham say, "Here's Anna . . ."

She came through the gate slowly and up the short path toward the veranda, a careless girl in a white middy-blouse and dark skirt, friendly and casual. Grant got down to meet her, his flesh tingling.

They did not touch hands. Anna said, "Hello, Grant. You're back . . . I caught sight of you . . . How are you, anyway?"

He said, "Fine, Anna. I'm fine." And then in his own shy tone, the conventional words he would have said to Edith Graham or Lottie Kinsman or any other of the girls his own age he had known for years, "You're looking good."

She laughed, light and careless, and spoke to Frank and Stewart: "He's got to come over to say how-d'you-do to Ma . . . Come on, Grant."

There was nothing to say. It was all said in the fact of being together. But as they walked down the short stretch of road the fingers of her right hand slipped into his. She left them there until they turned in at the gate.

Josie was lighting the lamp in the parlour. She turned toward them, the burnt match in her hand, the yellow light gradually flaring out to make a luminous pool round her as the flame rose on the wick. For a moment Grant felt a diffidence that was close to fear. In this dark-eyed woman with the lined placid face he could feel no warmth of welcome. Only a tolerance, a doubting reserve.

They said the conventional words. Josie remained standing; and before constraint could settle, Anna said: "Let's not sit around, Grant. It's too nice outside." She tucked a hand under his elbow and turned again toward the door. He let himself be led, feeling the capability of Anna. Over his shoulder he said, "Good night, Mrs. Gordon," and heard her expressionless "Good night."

But once they were outside, alone together, he felt all sense of trouble vanish. Again Anna's fingers found his own.

She said, "Let's go down to the bridge."

"All right."

They began to talk now a little. About meaningless things. The things that had been going on along the Shore while he was away, and his time in England. Again Grant felt the curious wonder he had always known, since the moment of first sensing it, in the presence of Anna Gordon. His shyness vanished whenever he was with her. For all the urgent sense of her as a girl, a woman, there was between them none of the sparring, the mock pursuit and the feigned retreat of courtship.

Suddenly out of a moment's silence she said, "I s'pose you heard about Anse. And all that . . ."

He said "Yes . . ." and let it lie.

She said, "Well, then, you know as much as we do," and added on a little note of irony, "maybe more."

She was getting it over with. Washing away the sense of things unsaid. He pressed her fingers lightly and said nothing.

Vangie Murphy's place. Katen's . . .

A mile east of Gordons' a railed wooden bridge crossed Katen's Creek. The road there was screened by hardwood growing in the creek valley. An ancient beech and a giant maple overhung the bridge itself, darkening even in daylight the sliding water.

Night had fallen. The bridge was a pocket of darkness under the trees, but a moon approaching the full rode the sky, and stars half-hidden by faintly stirring leaves. Below, the creek slipped almost soundless down-valley toward Sinclair's mill and eventually the Channel; from somewhere in that southern distance they could hear the whispered rumour of swell on gravel, and far up-stream the slight ceaseless hurry of brook-water over stone.

Grant stood leaning back with an elbow on the railing. Anna came into the circle of the elbow, looking down across arm and railing toward the almost invisible water, a hand on his upper arm. There was no urgency or embarrassment or expectation in the contact. Simply a kind of recognition, wordless and unemphasized.

Grant laughed, and felt the question in her slight stirring.

He said, "Oh, nothing. I was just remembering the first . . . When I started feeling . . ."

Anna let the pause last a moment. "That's not nothing."

"No." His tone matched hers for lightness. "Oh, it was the Holiday, one time. The way you looked."

73

He let it go at that. He could think of it and of all the moments they had ever spent together; could call them up to be lived again when he was by himself. But to talk of them to Anna . . . No, there was something childish about that, and something that seemed to him vaguely like the disturbance of another's privacy. Not his, but hers.

How could you explain it, anyway? The moment when he had first felt knowingly the beginning of this private excitement was one without importance, a scrap of time, an incident that must have passed unnoticed by any but himself, that must have left no impression even on the memory of Anna.

Three years ago. That was where it always started in his mind. The Holiday. The summer Saturday when the people of Currie Head and Katen's Rocks and Leeds got together on the beach for an afternoon of sunlight and rowing and eating in the open. Nominally it was a children's picnic, but it brought to the beach all ages.

He had arrived at the beach late. Most of the youngsters were rowing on the inlet under the Head's western slant. Their mothers were already setting out plates on plank tables, their fathers squatting on warm beach rocks, talking of the days when mackerel had swarmed in the Channel, when fishing had been a way of living instead of something to fill the pause between seeding and haying time.

Some of the older boys and girls of what Frank Graham called "sparkin' age" were standing around the two tall spruce between which an ox-yoke had been slung as a swing. Grant saw that Tarsh Findlay, Vangie Murphy's twelve-year-old, had been left behind there by the children of his own age. This was unusual, because they had been taught to treat him with consideration. But there was a perverse streak in Tarsh. He would stay out of things sometimes unless urged directly to come in. Grant wondered for a moment whether there was some unobtrusive thing he could do, and could think of nothing.

The swing slowed. Elsie Laird and Lee Wilmot slipped to the ground laughing. Anna turned to pull herself into the seat and Lol Kinsman dropped the rope on which he had been pulling to jump up beside her. Bantering argument began then. Grant had picked up one of the ropes, but Lee Wilmot and Fred Marshall each insisted the other should take the one on the off side.

Anna said, "You fellas—what gentlemen!" and then, "Hey! Tarsh! . . . Get busy. Give us a hand."

Lee Wilmot said, "Yeah. That's it. Come on, Tarsh. Get to work."

It was simple instinct. Anna's eye had caught the boy's aloneness. As the swing gradually gathered way, the chains creaking, she glanced down at Grant and winked.

Nothing that Anna would ever remember. But Grant had felt the wink in his backbone. In that moment Anna had become for him something more than a figure of flesh and blood. Something more than a girl who stirred you, the way girls did, when you thought about them. There was nothing in this quiet elation to be ashamed of. Bodily disturbance, certainly. But this seemed part of something that was long and slow and inevitable, not a thing to be brushed out of the mind. He had grinned across under the soaring swing at the dark face, intent with effort, of Tarsh Findlay, Vangie Murphy's bastard . . .

But he had said now as much as he wanted to say. *The Holiday, one time. The way you looked* . . . How could you put it into words, anyway, this quality of hers, this feeling for people? This thing he felt himself, sometimes, deep down, but could not really show?

Dimly perhaps Anna understood. She did not need words. She moved close and turned to him, and he took her in his arms. Her body lay pliantly against him, without reserve, answering the pressure of his own. Her mouth was soft and suddenly troubled with a breathless hunger.

After the first long kiss they stood for a while relaxed and without tension, lightly touching, his mouth moving along her eyebrows, searching the channel in her parted hair.

Anna said casually, "What makes it this way for us, Grant?"

"Oh . . . me and you."

Far down the road there was a faint humming; light touched the high branches of the hardwoods and flickered and held. Anna said, "Car coming." She sighed, "I s'pose . . . ."

"Yes," Grant said. "Best getting back."

The car passed in a swish of gravel, vanished along the road westward. Grant and Anna walked up the road alone.

At the gate she turned to come into the circle of his arms again. Then as if answering some unspoken doubt, she said: "It'll be all right, you know."

"I know."

"All right. Good night, Grant. Take care of yourself."

"Good night . . . Good night, Anna."

He walked up the road alone now, thinking of Anna. This was something he could do. He could go back and relive the time he had spent with her, bringing his mind up through each of the moments as one does with the lines of a familiar poem. But for him there was a special meaning, a sense of anticipation, because it was unfinished. For him the poem was unfinished. The phrases still unknown, the living lines, must continue as long as time remained in which they could meet and talk and touch . . .

This absorption was not exclusive. In the dark ahead of him near Grahams' he could hear voices. Boys. Dan and Bill, the kid from Toronto . . . The Place, next, and Hugh Currie's lights. The whole incidental living detail of Currie Head and the Channel Shore was a shadowy background to his thought of her.

But now, there was a difference. They had lived on moments, remembered moments and the dream of time to come. But now, a difference. They had learned something tonight, he and Anna.

He walked up the slope of the road past Alec Neill's. The lights of home, of Uncle James's house, were bright behind the ash trees.

Home. He turned down toward the house, toward familiar things and people. A ridiculous thought came to him. If he were to be placed blindfold in any kitchen at Currie Head he could tell in whose house he was by the smell, the blend of wood and paint and year on year of cooking. The central scent that clung to Aunt Jane's kitchen was that of molasses cookies. It bothered him briefly that he couldn't recall the smell of Josie Gordon's.

He walked down the lane toward the lights, not thinking; feeling his long affection for his family and the Shore, and love, and a vague misgiving.

8

JAMES wakened to the sound of softwood thumping gently against cast iron. For a moment he lay relaxed, conscious at once of a sense of pleasure and of something else, an irksome nagging that merged with pleasure and dulled the edge of it.

That was Grant, out there in the kitchen. He could tell from the quietness, the sensed movement. Grant, who had come back and picked up where he'd left off . . . Mr. Marshall sat up in bed. Grant. His mind was warmed by memory. Grant, the cheerful early riser, and a thousand kitchen fires; in bland daylight or the cold dark of winter mornings before sunrise. The moment of wordless companionship before the rest were up.

Grant. He frowned and moved his head as if to shake away the complex irritation that troubled him: a person loved and a small unworthiness; the need to speak, to make it clear; a kind of anger at his own reluctance . . .

He swung night-shirted legs to the floor. On the Channel Shore most men slept in drawers and undershirt, as do men who work in the open anywhere. But not Mr. Marshall. He brought a kind of dignity to the hard business of farming dubious soil. Flannelette nightshirts, a tended beard, grammatical speech, a big downstairs bedroom in which, his wife having passed the age for conceiving children, he slept alone.

He dressed methodically, pulling on drawers, undershirt, grass-stained grey trousers and socks; working his feet into ankle-high work-boots, criss-crossing leather laces round brass hooks above the eyelets. This done, he walked through the kitchen and back porch without a word to Grant, and down the path, wet with dew, to the outhouse behind the workshop; returned to the porch and splashed water on face and neck, dried himself on the roller towel and returned to the bedroom to don a shirt. Until the private routine of backhouse and basin was completed, Mr. Marshall never spoke to anyone.

He opened the bedroom door and came into the kitchen again and said, "Good morning."

"Morning, sir."

Grant closed the damper a half-inch, judicially, and listened to the small cheerful rush of sound in the fire-box, the sound of flame getting out of the kindling, into the bigger wood, and drawing.

His uncle stood with dignified nonchalance by the kitchen table, his eyes apparently concerned with the things he could see through the north windows. The three ash trees that fronted the house, the sweep of his upper field beyond the road, or just the thin morning light. Grant sensed uneasily that in a moment he would speak.

Mr. Marshall turned and said evenly, "You were not at church last night."

"No, sir, I . . ."

Grant hesitated. Fred's feet were on the stairs. Aunt Jane's footsteps lightly crossed the floor above.

"Never mind."

Fred pushed open the door between hall and kitchen and came in, whistling.

Mr. Marshall turned again to the windows. He spoke over his shoulder, "Fred, you and Will can go on cleaning up at Scott's. I'll go to work on the barn today, I think. With Grant."

Fred said "Yes, sir"—casual acknowledgement from one who knew that work on the Marshall place was laid out ahead, and had no particular interest in the fact that his father, uncharacteristically, was outlining it again.

Grant merely noted that his uncle was giving notice that he would return to the interrupted conversation when they were alone together, later in the morning.

Jane Marshall crossed the kitchen, removed a stove lid with the lifter and poked at burning wood. This was habit. The fire was blazing steadily, the kettle beginning to give off the faint tuneless note of water in the grip of heat; but it was necessary for this small competent woman to assert her own concern with all the phases of life in her house. A pail of water on the sink must be moved a quarter-inch, a pair of boots by the wood-box must be shifted to the corner by the coat-closet.

If James Marshall had ever noted this in his wife it was long ago. He was no more conscious of it now than he was of the fact that Jane accompanied everything she did, floor-sweeping, cooking, bed-making, with a casual commentary, a sentence addressed to one or all or no one, a hymn-tune half-muttered and half-hummed.

She was singing now in a not uncheerful undertone, "When mothers of Salem, their children brought to Jesus . . ." She slipped plates from the dish-cupboard to the red-and-white oilcloth of the kitchen table. "The stern disciples . . . Fred, that shirt's a sight, you've got to . . . the stern disciples . . . and bade them depart . . . But Jesus . . ."

No one listened. Fred and Will and Grant, straggling out to milk, were conscious of Jane's fussiness merely as something that blended with a thousand other things to make a person, a small compact woman with drawn-back hair, still unaccountably black.

As for James, he would have dismissed with puzzled contempt any suggestion that Jane's mannerisms were traceable to himself—were the slight persistent reaction of a personality that must develop some kind of self-assertion when faced for a lifetime with the immovable, the impervious.

His present difficulty was that he was *not* impervious. Without thinking of it directly he had come to recognize again a crack in the granite of hard sense and righteousness.

This had nothing to do with Jane, moving from stove to table now, halting to glance out of the porch window at the speck on the Channel that was Alec Neill's boat. It was something else, this other thing that had bothered him at times for more than sixteen years. Something that went back to a Boston-and-Maine day coach, clicking through the dark, and a four-year-old boy asleep on green plush.

Duty was another word for life to James, a straight road, uphill, between the fences of labour and religion. It worried him to find his eyes drawn by the grassy by-ways of affection.

His meditation was interrupted by the sound of the young men's voices, their boots on the steps, the drone of the separator.

There was little talk over the oatmeal porridge and fried eggs. Only Jane's commentary, unlistened to. Grant's mind turned back in rueful amusement to the wisps of thought it had played with last night, the smell of kitchens. What was it, now, that Gordons' kitchen smelt of? He would mention it to Anna; it was the kind of absurdity she liked to laugh at.

The sense of difference . . . More obvious than ever now, since Anse—Grant wondered how things were between James and Richard, now that Hazel . . . Fred had asked him if he knew the story, but no one else in the house had mentioned Hazel or Anse.

He thought about this as he and James went to the workshop for carpenter's aprons, loaded the pockets with shingle nails, and climbed to the scaffold across the north gable of the barn.

Other considerations vanished then in the crawling excitement that had always assailed him at the knowledge that his uncle was about to speak to him alone. It went up his spine in waves. A blend of obscure emotion: gratitude, fear, pride and the fear of pride, respect; something like love, perhaps. He knew only that it was a feeling he couldn't help. Couldn't help, any more than Uncle James could help withholding speech instead of saying what he had to say before the family, as he would have done if it concerned Fred or Will.

He began carefully to lay shingles, thinking absently that there was a good deal to do around the place. A shed to build, a machinery shed. Uncle James had said there was too much stuff cluttering up the threshing-floor in winter-time. Already sand and gravel for the concrete lay in heaps near the east wall of the barn. Building. The kind of work he liked . . .

James waited until they had got into the staccato rhythm of the work, adjusting edge against edge, driving nail after nail. They had laid a full course across the barn before he spoke.

"You were not at church last evening."

Grant said, "No, sir. I intended to go up, and then, well—sort of, I didn't feel like it."

That was all he could say. James wouldn't know about the meeting with Anna, and that was something Grant felt he must keep back. Partly through the secretiveness of personal possession, partly through a caution he had not quite defined.

He had an impulse to laugh and blurt it out: "I'm sorry, Uncle James. But I had a girl to see. *You* know. Anna Gordon."

That was impossible. It was the sort of thing Fred could do, or even Will. Because James's sons, when they broke the rules, could take what was coming simply as the other side of a bargain. Could take the cold rebuke without hurt, like punishment from a school teacher, whose approval or wrath meant equally nothing. But, just as James could not call Grant down in the presence of others, could seldom be blunt and forthright even when they were alone together, so Grant could not speak frankly to this man who was less than a father, and more. Reluctance to hurt and to be hurt; something like affection, perhaps . . . tempered in the frost of pride.

James laid another shingle. Grant wondered whether he would speak of this again, this small thing that irked him. Perhaps he had had his say.

Through the association of wood and nails and work, a scene from his childhood came to him. An evening when Uncle James had been coopering in the shop. Young Will, nine or ten years old then, had overstayed chore-time, down the road at Neills'. James had cut him across the bare calves, coldly and repeatedly, with an unbent barrel-hoop. Will had howled in pain, not humiliation. But Grant remembered how he himself had trembled with shock, partly on Will's account but partly from an imagined conception of the shame that would shake him if *he* were guilty of conduct that called forth such treatment. At times since then, through carelessness or bravado, he *had* been guilty. Uncle James had always corrected him privately, verbally, indirectly. Nearly always . . . Once, in the presence of the family, he had cuffed Grant sharply for persistent noisiness. Grant remembered his own numb surprise and the sense of resentment this had left until he realized the inwardness of that blow: James Marshall's sudden impatience at his own sensitivity where Grant was concerned, the need to establish as fact before his family the fallacy that all were equal in his sight.

When James spoke now he used a pattern of indirection with which Grant was familiar, the formula that time will teach.

"You will come to learn in time that obligations are more important than whims . . . more important than inclinations."

Grant thought, irrelevantly, that James's courtly speech could be irritating at times, like an affectation.

"You have just come back to us, Grant. I don't intend to . . . If you have some proper reason for something . . . for doing something other than what is expected, I think you will always find me reasonable. But it distresses me to think you would choose a time when your aunt and I were away—to follow a course—to stay away —to follow a course you might have explained beforehand." He added, "If there *is* an explanation."

Grant thought, That I might explain now if I could, but he knows I can't . . . He knew what it was that rankled in James's mind. More, perhaps, than the simple fact of staying away from church when James wanted him there, wanted him there to be seen, was the suggestion of underhandedness. Deceit, and the hurt to pride. The fear that someone at Currie Head or The Rocks or Leeds could say Grant had picked a time to carry on some pursuit of his own while the old man was away.

James's words worried him without stirring his conscience as once they might have done. His regret was that the circumstance was there, a difference in outlook you couldn't get round.

James went on: "I am responsible for you, you know." He added clearly, "To God and others."

Grant was startled. James was inflexible in religion; he held family prayers at night and would not hire a man who swore or drank. But it wasn't often that conscious piety crept into his daily speech.

To God . . . and others. For a moment Grant felt a sad humility, remembering. Remembering what he knew more by hearsay than experience. Humility touched with envy. For Uncle James had known Harvey Marshall. Had possessed with a brother's intimacy something that was known to Grant, except for a picture on the wall, only as the shadow of a face whose living lines he could not even trace in memory. A face like the imagined features of a character in fiction, and a man's voice, low and gentle, singing, almost whispering, a childish lullaby of which neither tune nor words remained.

And somewhere, another voice: impersonal, careless, without malice or rancour, or feeling of any kind. The words were clear: "Sure. I guess that's best. He's a good brat. If there was any way . . . But take him. Take him. It's better—"

It was only a play seen, a book read. Life as life began a little later. Days or a day or perhaps only hours later, in gaslight on green plush. The backward rush of clicking drumming darkness and a face that was neither vague nor distant. Seen across the years it was somehow gentle. He glanced up now and searched it again for the kindness he could not find.

James had left the subject poised, awaiting a reply, but while he sensed this, Grant was deep in the old and private dream.

A picture of Harvey Marshall hung in the parlour, fuzzy with enlargement and tinted like the face of an embalmed corpse. He couldn't connect it with the imagined features and the lullaby that lay in memory behind the rushing darkness. But James had said, once, "You're the living image of him."

The living image. What was it Harvey Marshall had been, in the late seventies, in the eighties, in that other century? A boy who laughed at James's dour silence? A boy whose careless laughter as they nested apples or set their rabbit-snares had been light and a song to James?

Grant didn't know. He could only guess. Except for a rare reminiscent word, years ago, James had never talked about Harvey. Had let Grant's questions go unanswered, as if he hadn't heard. And long ago Grant had ceased to ask.

But as he thought about it now on the scaffold across the barn's gable he felt himself again a part of something he didn't try to explain or understand. Something old and continuing, a blend of today and the past and the future. The future. For a moment the other thing, the pervasiveness of Anna, almost vanished from his mind.

The prodding words came, then. Sharper than any he had heard in years.

The words were like a blow.

"Did you hear me? While you live with me you will fit yourself to the conduct of this family. Do you understand me, Grant?"

He felt the flush of an old resentment, sudden and unfamiliar. He said, "Yes, sir. I understand you."

"Then that's all there is to be said."

The hammers tapped their repeated rhythm, a slow step-dance along the barn wall. The sombre sense of belonging was dimmed and blurred. But no resentment could wholly drown that contact with the generations. Anger itself was proof of this. This was a feeling that came from the roots of family. Otherwise, there would have been only impatience, a kind of indifferent dislike.

He turned slowly once to look out across Alec Neill's pasture and across Hugh Currie's lower field and the wooded valley of Graham's Brook. Across his own land. Uncle James's land. The Place. Beyond Frank Graham's barn he could see the Gordons' apple trees, at the edge of the woods, and the remote grey square of the house.

What was it Anna had been thinking of?—"It'll be all right, you know."

He had said, "I know." The thing that pierced him now, for the first time really, was the fact that when you wakened from the dream . . .

Of course, you couldn't know.

9

A WEEK went by before Grant again crossed the pastures to The Place.

By Wednesday night they had finished shingling. On Thursday the Shore woke to an overcast sky; Grant and James rode the hay-rack up the school-house road, with Fred and Will, to cock up the mown hay at Scotts'. By mid-afternoon rain had begun to spit and at dark was falling steadily. Friday dawned in a drizzle that turned to a watery sunlight in the afternoon. Fred and Will took it easy while Grant and James worked in the shop, glazing window-frames for the porch, shaping felloes from a piece of dried birch and fitting them into the rim of a manure-cart wheel.

On Saturday the grass was dry before noontime and James judged the weather had settled enough to risk shaking out the cocked hay; by Monday it should be dry enough to haul to the barn.

Next day was Church Sunday at Currie Head. Grant walked up with Fred and Will. The weather was holding fine, banked clouds and sunshine and a light west wind. On Monday they bundled up the last of the hay at Scotts' and hauled it home.

Throughout this week of concern with ordinary jobs and usual chores, James did not mention the thing that had driven him to passionate speech on the scaffold across the barn gable. *Then there's nothing more to be said* . . . It was as if with that closing word all memory of the moment had vanished from his mind.

Except perhaps for an unusual softness, a kind of considerateness. Less than an hour after that stormy moment Grant had sensed his uncle observing him briefly, sidelong, watching the way he joined shingles and drove the nails. There had been something in James's face, something like a reflection of that remembered face in gaslight leaning down over green plush. In the shop, later, as Grant tapped a felloe into the rim of the wheel, James had said out of nowhere, "Your father was good at things of this kind; good with his hands . . ." The voice had been almost regretful, touched with a reminiscent affection that yet had something grudging in it.

He had gone on to talk of the fixing-up there was to do. He and Fred had let things slide a little while Will and Grant were away . . . Too much to do on the land to bother about other things, James said. But now there was time. Fences that needed seeing to, and brush to clear. A dozen things that wanted catching up with. The unfinished room upstairs to sheathe and ceil. The machinery shed, against the barn's east wall . . .

For Grant the week had been a time of drift. After the first resentment he had slipped into the groove of habit, almost unworried, putting the time of worry away. He had not seen Anna.

That was not unusual. They had never tried to arrange meetings. A time would come.

But on Monday evening, with the last of the hay from the Scott place in the barn, he felt a restlessness and a need to be active. He took his axe from the chopping-block by the shop, grinned at Fred and Will on the porch steps, and headed east across the fields.

While he walked, across Alec Neill's pasture and into Hugh Currie's, a slow excitement began to grow. Should he go on over to Grahams', toward dark? Would he find Anna there? A sense of troubled subterfuge invaded the excitement: the shadow of a barn wall, the sound of tapping hammers.

He found himself thinking of his time in England and the dreams that had lived then in his mind: the family, and his life as part of it, Aunt Jane's fussy kindliness, the warmth of winter fires, the feeling it had given him to find approval in Uncle James's eyes or voice, the blunt companionship of Fred and Will, The Place. And Anna, the laughing and the foolishness, and the deeper something you could feel but never say or even form in thought; the feeling . . .

Both real. Both realities. In memory and in looking forward the dreams had merged and blended, become one, the shape of life imagined.

It was one thing to blend the shape of dreams. Another to merge the two realities.

When you saw that, the thing you felt about that lonely time across the sea was curiously like regret, the memory of a lost happiness.

Memories of memories . . . Grant grunted in impatience at this kind of thinking. When he reached the rutted grass-tufted path that led from Hugh Currie's to the neck of land connecting the mainland with the Head, he turned up it on impulse toward the Currie house. The sound of voices came to him as he topped the rise of land. He saw that Hugh was sprawled on the door-sill, with Stan and young Bill Graham below him on the steps.

Stan called "Hi, Grant!" as he came into the door-yard. He walked over to join them, acknowledged a word from Hugh, and let himself down on the grass, his back against the porch wall.

Young Bill grinned at him, shyly, but went on with a question he was pressing on Old Hugh.

". . . but the cellar; where'd the cellar come from, Mr. Currie?"

Grant sensed Hugh turning slightly to look south across field and pasture toward the Channel where the land rose in the wooded ten-acre hump of the Head.

Hugh considered. "Rob's House?" He gave a small meditative laugh. "Uncle Rob . . . He was red-headed. Like Stan. Rob didn't care much for in-shore fishing; the farm either."

Grant had a curious feeling. Hugh was living back for a minute in a time unknown. Part of this would be direct memory of a man in leather knee-boots and oilskins, part of it the memory of words, scraps of taciturn conversation, overheard as he worked at his copy-book or listened idly in candle-light. His mind would be running back, picking up the faded colours of things all but forgotten; remembered little by little at the insistence of listening boys.

Grant's own interest was caught. This thing Bill and Stan were after—it was like his own probing in childish memory. Hugh would be thinking back to boyhood, of what he had seen and heard of older Curries, Grahams, Marshalls, McKees. People who had left the Shore as the families branched. Branched into brothers, nephews, nieces, grandsons. People whose flesh and blood were third and fourth cousins now, in Gloucester, Quincy, Haverhill, in California and on the western plains.

Harvey Marshall, too, had gone . . .

It crossed his mind that Hugh Currie would have the simple answers that were all he cared to know. *What was he like, Mr. Currie? My father? Like Uncle James? Like . . .?* But, as always when he had felt this impulse, in the presence of Frank Graham or Alec Neill or Richard McKee, he knew he could not ask. How could you ask, bluntly, of outsiders, a thing you should have learned by your own kitchen fire, in your own woods and fields?

After a short interval of silence Hugh was speaking again.

"Uncle Rob was father's brother. Sailed in trading vessels. That was before the railroad hit here, and steamers weren't common. Not on this shore. Vessels used to take cured fish down to Halifax and bring back stuff like rope and salt. Anything people needed.

Uncle Rob built one, the *Star of Egypt,* down on the neck. The place they call Rob's yard. That was before I was born. Bought a bigger one, later. But he got tired of that, too. Ambitious, I s'pose. Began going foreign. I can just remember the winter they cut timber for his house. He'd cleared a place on the Head and planned to build there. Growed up since, of course. The cellar was dug. They'd started to build. He was due to get married, the next spring, and finish it up."

Hugh was gazing out across the hump of the Head toward the Islands, squinting distantly at the little coastal steamer working slowly up the Channel out of Princeport on her course for Morgan's Harbour. His voice was impersonal, almost disinterested.

"He took a three-master out to Sierra Leone, one trip. Freetown. Crew of seven or eight, all from 'round here. That was the end of it. She was never heard tell of."

Grant, watching, realized now that all this was known to Stan. An old story. He had staged this scene so that Bill Graham should hear it in the voice of Hugh Currie, in which no boyish bragging could be suspected.

Old Hugh went silent, and then began to talk again, mild and contemplative.

"So Rob never did get married, and they never finished the house. One of the Grahams. Old Frank Graham's sister. Your great-aunt, Bill. Her father, that'd be your great-grandfather—Long George, they called him. Long George Graham. He bought that place . . ." Hugh glanced across at Grant's land. "Grant's Place, now. He bought that from a fellow that took one look and left the country. Never even took an axe to it. Long George give it to the girl for a kind of a wedding present. They planned to live on the Head and clear that piece if Rob ever got time, I guess." Hugh paused and added thoughtfully, "She was a handsome woman, Fanny Graham. Married, later. Ran away with the mate of a Yankee barque, in here for ton-timber . . . It was quite a thing, at the time."

Grant heard Bill Graham sigh as the story ended. The story of great-aunt Fanny and Rob Currie. Rob Currie, who had sailed his tern schooner down the Channel, long and long ago . . .

As he rose and picked up his axe, Bill slipped off the steps and they went together down the road toward The Place. Aunt Fanny's . . . Grant had heard Frank Graham use the term, but had scarcely thought to wonder. He had never heard the story. He hadn't known that this land Uncle James had bought was a part of history, of tradition at The Head. What had the land meant to Bill Graham's great-aunt Fanny, with Rob Currie forever gone? The Yankee mate. Was that romantic love, or escape from the piercing reminders, the familiar things? No one would ever know. But what they knew was enough.

Grant walked without hurry; his mind returned to the sense of trouble and subterfuge, and was bothered by a ridiculous irritation. At The Head men rarely talked about the past. Their long concern was with the present, today and tomorrow. But when they did look back, there was a warmth in it. They talked of ships built, farms cleared, women who ran away with Yankee mates. But Uncle James—the past to him was not the warmth of people and a place, but the cold pride of family. Only that softness, when, rarely, he spoke of Harvey. And even that had in it something else, a curious undertone of shame.

Bill took the axe from Grant's hand and hefted it and they exchanged grins. Without asking, Bill turned down the hauling-road when they came to it. Grant had a hint of what must be in the boy's mind. This was land that had been his great-aunt Fanny's, land a red-headed man had planned to clear in the times between his voyages. He felt a little of it himself. Last week this had been merely a big wood-lot which people called Grant's Place. Now it was land with history, land with life. Aunt Fanny's and Grant's Place, merged in a marriage of time. Land with a past and a future.

Bill said, "Where you going to build the house, Grant?"

Grant halted as they neared the clearing and took the axe from Bill's hand. He considered.

"I think we'll put her up close to the road, on the flat where the maples are. Leave enough of them standing to make a row along the road. Useless. But nice in summer."

The Place, like all this land, sloped toward the Channel. From where they stood bemused in the August evening they could hear the steady rush of Graham's Brook, and nearer by the small intimate treble of the branch that ran through Grant's land itself.

Grant said, "I think we'll dam the brook under the slope some time, and have a trout hole."

For the first time in his life he was talking about The Place. The sensation was strange and satisfying. Odd to be talking this way to a kid from the city, a boy you'd known less than two weeks. But perhaps that was it. You could talk safely to a youngster who would be going home in a month or so; you'd never see him again. James Marshall was not the sort of man you went to with talk of dreams, even though it was his generosity, his sense of family, that made the dream possible. Fred and Will were all right. They were fine. But they had other interests. And Anna . . . They had never really talked about the future. The present was always too golden and clear. He had always avoided the future until that moment of revelation by the bridge. It came to him now that there must have been something instinctive, deliberate, about that avoidance. For almost in the moment when he had ceased to avoid it, truth and certainty had begun to merge with the beginnings of uncertainty. He could not talk of it to Anna. He could not talk of a dream and a common future while his mind heard a precise and certain voice, the rap of iron hammers on a barn wall.

But he could talk to Bill, almost as if talking to himself, knowing that no flicker of amusement would cross that intent young face. And if—the thing he talked of—if it faded and vanished, Bill would never know.

He said, "The house there, where the maples are. We'll clear fifteen acres or so, next the road, for hay and oats. And some for pasture. The rest of it, down by the Channel and back to the Black Brook, can stay in woods. For now, anyway. There's some beech trees down there, about the middle of the pasture. We'll let them be . . . How d'you think the place'll look, when we get the grass-seed and oats into it?"

"Wonderful," Bill said.

No one had worked at The Place while Grant was away. In earlier winters he and James had cut firewood there and hauled it out over the wood road he had swamped, and up the main road, home. The place was heavily timbered in red spruce, balsam fir and occasional clumps of hardwood.

Grant glanced along the southern edge of the clearing, marking with his eye the middling-size spruce he could fall with an axe without trouble. Box-logs. He had to be thinking now about money. There was money in the bank, he didn't know how much. They had saved his pay and the next-of-kin's allowance for him. But when you were planning a house . . .

He cut his front notch, stepped round the tree and went to work. When the spruce fell, he began to trim, using short competent strokes, the axe held near its head. Bill began to pile the brush.

They were working on the second tree when Anna came down the hauling-road. Grant was startled, and a little confused. And even in this confusion, a childish thought came to him. There was no way of describing her. If you paid special attention to her nose, her mouth, the shape of her face, it broke down the wholeness. It had taken him months, when he had first been conscious of her as a person, to notice the colour of her eyes, a dark and laughing blue.

She sat down on the flat stump of a fir he and James had sawed down more than two years before, and laughed at them.

She said, "Hello, boys; and how are they usin' you?"

Grant said, "Hi, Anna," in a tone of mild questioning surprise. "Who let *you* out?"

She laughed. "Well, I don't know as I have to be let . . . It *is* kind of a nuisance, though, when you got to come scratchin' through the woods to see a person's friends."

Grant laughed and went on trimming. "Oh, Bill and me . . . we work for a living."

"Yes, I noticed that," Anna said. "Bill manages to get across the road now and then, though. There's work over at our place, too. We've got Bill trained so he can milk, now. He's pretty good. You ought to come down some time and take a hand. I think we could make a milker out of you."

Grant started to speak, to fall into the careless casual banter, and closed his mouth. He had no heart for it. He lapsed into a frowning abstraction, started to speak again, and stopped trimming to listen. Someone else was coming down the hauling-road.

He said, "Maybe you better scamper, Anna."

She shook her head. "No; I like it here."

James came into the clearing briskly. He was carrying a cross-cut saw in the crook of one arm. Grant glanced at Anna. If she was flustered she didn't show it.

James nodded politely to her.

"Good evening, Anna."

His glance and nod included Bill. He said to Grant, "Chopping is slow work. I thought I might give you a hand, for an hour or so." He turned back to Anna, "How is your father?"

"Oh, pretty well, Mr. Marshall," Anna said. "I'll tell him you were asking."

James nodded. Grant sensed that both Bill and Anna were a little afraid of Uncle James, made uneasy by the studied manner, the precise speech. In that moment Grant was suddenly impatient with all of them, Anna and Bill and Uncle James; angered by the uneasiness their presence here together caused him.

Anna glanced at Bill, stood up and brushed her skirt. "Well . . . Good night, then, Mr. Marshall. Good-bye for now, Grant . . . Bill, you coming? If there's nothing else you've got to do, it's time we milked."

James said, "While the two of us are here we might as well get at a few of the bigger ones. It might be as well to figure on some of the best stuff for lumber, don't you think, Grant?"

"Yes, I s'pose so." Grant spoke noncommittally. He could never really tell what James had in mind. Now a whole series of pictures came to him. Lumber . . . He had told himself that some time soon he should be thinking of lumber, of getting the stuff out for a house . . . planking, sill-logs, shingle-junks. In his own mind this had never gone beyond the thought that some time he would do it; he had never discussed with James the matter of beginning on his own. Was this what James was thinking of? Or was it merely conversation, or the natural inclination of a shrewd woodsman not to waste big straight stuff as firewood or box-logs?

James measured a spruce with his eye and chopped a notch. They eased the cross-cut saw through the bark behind and above the notch, and began to saw.

When the tree crashed, Grant again went to work at the trimming while James rested contemplatively on a stump. After a little he rose leisurely and measured off the butt log along the trunk and nicked the bark for the saw-stroke. When they had completed the cut, Grant began to knock off the under-branches which had held it horizontal while they sawed.

James stood nearby, leaning on the saw. After a little he said, casually, "Grant . . . Are you . . . You are interested in Anna Gordon?"

Grant felt a knot untie in his mind. He came out with it flatly. "I'm very fond of her, sir."

He was not quite sure what he hoped for. Perhaps a laugh, a kindly, "Well, good luck!" But that was beyond hoping.

James nodded. He said nothing for a moment. When Grant had finished trimming the butt James began to move toward another spruce. His voice, as he walked, seemed to carry a severe regret; what he said was a blend of intimacy and stilted rhetoric.

"It's too bad, that. Too bad that things so often make it impossible for us to follow . . . to do what we would like . . . to follow our inclinations. Impossible for you . . ." He shook his head. "For anything except perhaps friendship . . . But that is what we *know*, from experience. Difference in outlook, religion, thought—"

He was notching the tree a foot from the ground. He straightened and said, "I've seen six or seven mixed marriages in the last thirty years along the Shore, Grant. They failed. All failed. Nothing left but remorse."

He motioned Grant to bring the saw round behind the tree. As he bent down and reached for the handle, he said, "These things are—well, hard. But you must know—you must have realized that the way to ávoid involvement"—he amended the sentence—"to avoid pain . . . is to avoid the person . . . to avoid meeting her. When you can't—"

The saw bit into spruce. When the tree had fallen, James waited until Grant had begun to trim. Then he said, "You're young, Grant. You're very young. Pain—the pain will pass. There will be someone . . . There will be a woman who can share your life, your home—the home you're making."

It was a studied speech and carefully done. Merging in Grant's mind with the sense of surprise that Uncle James had known the way his heart was turning, was a kind of bafflement. There was nothing in that speech he could take hold of and prove wrong. Nothing he could meet solidly and deny.

As he trimmed the spruce, his hands going through accustomed motions that needed no thought, he was desolate and alone, his mind plagued by the puzzle of what it was—failing the laugh and the voiced "Good luck!"—the puzzle of what it was his heart had hoped for.

10

THEY began to build the machinery shed on Tuesday. A hundred sheds along the shore rested their sleepers on wooden posts or low walls of loose stone, but that was not James's way. This was to be a building based on concrete, which would continue to take the weight of carts and trucks for years after he was gone.

For two days the four of them mixed gravel, sand and cement and poured the grey slush into foundation forms. It was hard work, and welcome; for Grant there was satisfaction in it. He had never handled concrete; he got from it the same small sense of achievement, a new thing learned, that he had felt in boyhood when James first let him lay shingles, and later when he had sawed out the frame of a screen door on a mitre-box.

It was curious that this satisfaction could exist in one compartment of his mind while the rest of it was dark with worry and a growing fear.

On the Monday evening when he had walked back up the road from the clearing, wordless beside James, he would not have considered it possible that a day or two later he would be able to go on for hours, his hands and mind concerned almost wholly with concrete and wood, and find a kind of goodness in it.

But this was so. It was only in the evenings that the shadow drew in to flood the senses. Even then, he was not fully engulfed. It was as if he were aware that the darkness was there, but stood and moved at the edge of it, watching from no more than the corner of an eye.

His full glance was turned backward in the old sweet habit, thinking of Anna, the girl, and of the hours they had spent together, with others and alone.

He found that he could not go to The Place in the evenings. Something in the thought of it set the shadow rolling and brought it close; the thing men feel for towns, streets, houses, where they have known shame or the betrayal of a thing loved.

Instead he began to spend the evening time in James's lower pasture, pulling and piling with his hands the small seedling spruce that continually encroach in that country unless the land is grazed by sheep.

There, alone, leisurely busy at work that took no thought, he let his mind go back. Anna, on the beach, laughing down from the soaring swing; Anna on the veranda at Grahams', glancing at him across .Stewart's bent back; Anna, on the rock opposite The Place . . .

Through two or three of these evenings he refused to admit in thought that it was not the same. It was not until Friday night that he really faced the truth. Always before he had been able to live again in memory the moments he had spent with her. He could not do it now.

The quiet sense of something sweet and continuing, the feeling of fulfilment and eagerness that had always come to him in these small journeys back and forth in time . . . They were no longer there.

There was nothing now in dreams. What he must have was the sight and touch of her, the knowledge that she was there, the sight of the Gordon house and fields, if that was the best he could do . . .

The words echoed thinly in his mind—*to avoid involvement . . . to avoid pain . . . to avoid meeting her* . . . And even while he planned his small strategy he was bothered by a furtive dissatisfaction, a shadow of guilt, the guilt of evasion.

Well, he had to see her.

He and James had worked on the framework of the shed that day while Fred and Will stretched wire along fence posts at the bottom of the lower field. After supper Grant sat idle in the kitchen instead of going down the field toward the pasture to pull brush. Now and then he closed his hands and felt the soreness where spruce needles had pricked, between patches toughened by years of pitchfork, axe and scythe handle. He thought indifferently that the army hadn't softened him, not even his hands. He was good and tough.

Jane was moving about the room fussily. She opened the stove door with a lifter and put a stick or two on the dying fire, to keep, as she said, the edge off the chill. Fred and Will were at the barn and James in the downstairs bedroom with the door open; Grant could hear the opening and closing of a bureau drawer.

He said, "You wouldn't be wanting anything from Katen's, would you, Aunt Jane? Thought I might take a walk."

Jane said, "No-o-, I don't think so; we're not short of anything you could get at Katen's." She spoke the name with a slight cast of unconscious contempt. There was no malice in it, nor objection. She was merely expressing a casual opinion of Felix Katen and his sons and their reputation.

Despite the way he felt, Grant grinned inwardly. There was a kind of unspoken friendliness between himself and Jane.

He rose and stepped out on the back porch and glanced around for a sight of Fred and Will, and heard James come out behind him. James said, "If you're going down the road, why don't you take the light buggy? Give Polo a run. We could use a bag of cracked corn, also." James felt in his pocket for his leather draw-string bag.

Grant said, "All right," and added, "That'll be great." Thoughtfulness of this kind was unusual in Uncle James. He glanced at the bearded face soberly as the money was counted out. James was smiling bleakly but for a flying second Grant caught in his eyes the flash of softness.

The effect of the moment stayed with him as he harnessed the black gelding and drove out through the field gate to the road, even though he thought he could see what James's motives were. Kindness, after laying down the law. For three nights, as he plucked the tiny spruce in the pasture, Grant had half-expected James to join him there, had half hoped he would talk to him again, reopen the conversation in the clearing. But James had not come.

James thought it was all over, Grant supposed. Nothing more to be said . . . But, there was that kindness . . . The power of Polo's track-horse gait communicated itself to him through the shafts, the traces, the buggy's moving frame. Good form, good legs, an easy mouth. He thought: we ought to put him in the trots at Copeland. For a little his mind was almost empty of the purpose which had led him to build up, in casual conversation, the idea of a trip down the road to Katen's.

A walk to Katen's, planned to appear unplanned. He grinned to himself. Uncle James's offer of Polo had made it almost an expedition. The responsibility of a horse and rig cut down his freedom of action, but it was almost worth it to feel Polo stepping out.

Past The Place, and Grahams'. Grant held the horse in a little, abreast of Stewart Gordon's. From the corner of his eye he could see the grey house, the front stained with streaks of worn-off white-wash, and the apple trees. He resisted the impulse to bring the gelding down to a walk, to let his glance run over the place slowly, finding in the house, the barn, the yard, the warmth of things touched by a person loved.

He was passing Vangie Murphy's when he saw her. She turned at the sound of the horse's hooves just as he looked up, and waited on the shoulder of the road.

She was laughing as he pulled up beside her. "You and your rubber-tired buggies . . . A person could get run down and never know it."

Grant said, "Get in here, Anna. I'm just going down to Katen's."

She said, "So'm I."

It was still there. The laughter, the warmth, the lightness. Still there, when Anna was there. For the moment he put away the worry and uncertainty and the shadow of fear. He handed the reins to Anna and leaned back. She glanced at him with a smile that was half delighted giggle.

As usual, Bill and Dan Graham were squatted on the grass in front of the store. Through the open door Grant could see Felix squinting through his glasses at the brass bar of the counter scales. He was weighing out tea for Mrs. Clem Wilmot. Grant felt a quick annoyance. Hat Wilmot would hang around on the chance of a lift up the road.

The white light of a mantle lamp flooded the store and overflowed to the grassy margin of the road. It was early dusk and the evening was luminous, but Felix liked a lot of light.

Lon came out of the house on the knoll and halted on the veranda, hands in pockets. As Grant hitched Polo to the rack the tone of Aunt Jane's voice came back to him. The tone Mrs. Graham or Christine Currie might use—regretfully, for they were more tolerant than some you could think of—about Lon's latest spree: "Well, of course they're not even good Catholics." As he walked into the store behind Anna he wondered whether Mrs. Josie Gordon ever said of—well, of Clem Wilmot, perhaps: "Well, he's not even a good Protestant."

Religion. An odd thing. You were born with it, like politics, but it was beyond argument. Without much bearing on the way you got along with people, but as much a part of living as work and sleep.

Good Catholics and good Protestants . . . Bad Catholics and bad Protestants . . . Perhaps the difference grew from thinking of people not as people but as groups, the best tainted by the worst.

"Catholic people . . . the Gordons and the Katens . . ." Well, the Gordons weren't much like the Katens. Except of course for Anse.

This passed through his mind quickly, the sum of previous unconscious thinking; and as he saw Anna there, greeting Hat Wilmot, it related itself to her. A difference you couldn't understand but had to accept. Anna . . . he tried to apply it to her, and could find nothing, no difference of look or speech or manner, that would have told him, *She's a Catholic*. No outward thing. An inner thing, then. For it was there.

The thought drifted in his mind as young Bill and Dan came into the store and up to the counter to turn in their empty pop bottles.

Hat Wilmot turned from Anna to Grant and spoke to the world generally: "Well, look who we've got here."

Grant hoped he could keep the dislike out of his face. Hat Wilmot. Hat was a woman in her early thirties, and so considered herself at home among either the girls or the middle-aged women. Four or five months from now she would be presenting Clem with a child, and this fact was embarrassingly obvious. Hat carried herself with a kind of pleased ostentation while her tongue travelled the Channel Shore.

Her voice now was all pleased surprise; but in her eyes, the pursed set of her lips, a little special implication sparkled and sang. She saw us get here, all right, Grant thought. The fact of Anna Gordon and Grant Marshall buggy-riding together was worth speculation and comment. Something of the pleasure she would take in this, tomorrow or next day, was obvious in her greeting.

"Handsome couple, aren't we, Hat?" Anna said. Under her hand as she leaned on the counter she made a face at Grant. He felt it in his blood like a tide, the warmth of her presence; the personal softening for him of the look she wore for everyone. But this private happiness was tempered by irritation at Hat Wilmot's smirk, her gossiping voice—and a slowly-realized irritation at Anna for being smart, for making fun of Hat in that way.

He said, "Good evening, Mrs. Wilmot," and turned to Felix. "Can I get a bag of cracked corn, Mr. Katen? . . . Don't bother, I'll lug it out myself."

He went to the rear of the store and got the bag of feed and swung it to a shoulder. As he carried it out to the buggy his annoyance was transferred to himself, annoyance at his irritation with Anna for being flip to Hat Wilmot. It was just that Hat— well, her tongue was dangerous. He stowed the feed in the fly.

97

The chore was done now; he could go back and hang around the store, say hello to people from The Rocks and The Head if they came in, and be with Anna for a while in their peculiar personal isolation.

He turned and found that she had sauntered out behind him to the hitching rail and stood now smoothing Polo's neck. She said, "He's a nice animal, Grant . . . Aren't you, Polo?"

"Yes, he's a good road horse. Friendly and easy to handle," and with a touch of pride, "and pretty fast."

"I'd like to go for a drive, Grant."

"Would you?" He hesitated. "I guess, a lift when I go up the road—that'll have to do for tonight, Anna. Anything more'd look, well—it'd look—kind of conspicuous." He added, "You know Hat Wilmot."

Anna said, "Hat? Sure . . . But who cares? What's *that* matter?" She turned to him, teasing, "I don't care who gets a look at us. Do you?"

Puzzlement shadowed the laughing provocation in her face. "By gosh, Grant . . . I believe you *do*."

"No. No. Don't talk that way, Anna. It's just—"

"Never mind." She rubbed Polo's nose and said regretfully, "All right. No drive. I'll take that lift home, though. Any time you say."

"All right," Grant said. "I'll just see if Mrs. Wilmot's ready. S'pose I'll have to offer her a chance up."

Anna threw her head back and whooped with laughter. She recovered and spoke quietly, with suppressed amusement.

"You've sure got yourself mixed up, haven't you? . . . With a mess of women . . . You should've brought the two-seated buggy, Grant, to handle the traffic. No. I don't feel much like bouncin' around on Hat's knee . . . Or takin' her on mine." She eyed him, head slightly tilted. "And I s'pose you wouldn't dare hold me on yours. I'll run along, Grant."

She walked off up the road, and looked back once, laughing.

Grant swore to himself. The good moments had slipped away. Everything had fallen flat and so quickly he had had no chance to do much about it. Something more than irritation plagued him as he walked back into the store. A sense of futility and failure. He wanted time to think it out.

Homeward bound in the buggy, Grant set himself deliberately to keep part of his mind free from the impact of Hat Wilmot's running comment. This was something he could do through long practice in listening half-consciously to the flowing conversation of Aunt Jane, though Jane's talk was usually free from gossip. Hat's required more care.

He was glad to have Bill and Dan Graham standing in the fly with the feed bag, their hands on the seat-back to steady themselves. With the kids there Mrs. Wilmot's attention would be divided; the chance was less that she would say something that demanded thought, something he would have to find a sensible answer for.

He sifted the chatter as it came.

"Look at that . . . Bushes from one fence to the other. You'd think she'd at least make that Tarsh keep the front clear, wouldn't you? You would now, wouldn't you?"

Grant grunted assent.

Anna . . . *But who cares? . . . What's that matter?*

She was right. Unless you were ready to acknowledge affection, acknowledge it with pride before everyone, you had no right to run to the warmth of it. If you disregarded that, if you sought the warmth anyway, in hidden moments, in a private look across a roomful of people—

You couldn't do it, if you wanted to keep your self-respect.

No. You couldn't taste the sweetness of day-dreams unless you were doing what you could to make them true. In the slow exaltation of these dreams he had forgotten the facts. Before he could dream again and believe in what he was dreaming, there were roads to clear in the mind, roots to tear up . . .

He had kept Polo to a walk, not wanting to overtake Anna. Now he flipped the reins and set the road horse into a trot. Hat Wilmot for the moment had run out of talk. Suddenly Dan Graham said, "Hey! Grant!" He realized he was jogging past Grahams' and pulled up to let the boys down.

As he put the horse into a trot past The Place, Mrs. Wilmot said, "You doing much work here these days, Grant?" She went on, a prodding invitation in her voice, "I s'pose you'll be thinking of building for yourself before long."

He laughed, "Oh, there's lots of time, I guess."

He thought: By God! The truth is I didn't want to take Anna driving because I didn't want Uncle James to hear about it.

That was the blunt fact and the sum of it, and it was something Anna's open heart would never understand. Oh, she would come close to understanding. She would see his concern about the hurt to other people. But not the fact that there *was* something hurtful, for anyone, in the affection that bound them.

He didn't blame her. The thing that gnawed him was the circumstance. The fact that it was both necessary and impossible to cross the will of Harvey Marshall's brother. To cut through pride and harsh kindness, the melancholy sense of position and family.

They were passing the home place now, going up the slope toward Richard McKee's and beyond that, the cross-roads. Hat was talking again. Looking down toward McKees', talking with an insinuating wonder about Hazel, away. She didn't mention Anse Gordon, but it was in her voice, the curiosity, the sympathy, the odd unrealized malice.

He thought: I must have known. I must have known there was this, in Uncle James, all the time . . .

And yet, it was only since the knowledge had been formed in words, hinted on the barn wall, stated flatly in The Place, that he had begun to feel the real force of it in himself, destroying the common poetry of remembered moments and the present music of moments shared.

He turned up the school-house road, past the school. Polo slowed to a walk on the uphill stretch toward Clem Wilmot's place. The buggy wheels jolted a little in the ruts.

If he could make it clear to Anna . . . But she would never really understand. And it wasn't good enough. The things they should be having now—long walks in the evenings, and on Sundays; Anna close to him at the box socials, the winter skating on Graham's Lake; and a slow looking-ahead, a confidence . . .

You could know that, you could reach that truth in your heart, but that didn't tell you what you were going to do about it.

He pulled in by Clem's gate and cramped the wheels. Mrs. Wilmot got down, clumsily, gathering her parcels to her.

He said, "Oh, don't mention it, Mrs. Wilmot," in answer to her thanks, and backed the rig round. As he trotted down the road past the school-house the answer to one vague puzzle came to him: the shape of what it was he had half-hoped for in the clearing, failing the laugh and the voiced "Good luck!"

How simple it would have been if Uncle James had left no choice but a break. If Uncle James himself had cut the bonds of pride and family. If Uncle James had come out with one blunt sentence: *Stop fooling with this girl, Grant, or I'll . . . or you'll regret it.*

11

THE hay was made and in the barns. The days were somnolent, the nights closed in with an early chill. This land now began to slip unnoticed into the long pause between the end of haying and the beginning of digging-time, between late summer and the cold of fall. This was the beginning of the mellow season, a time of sunlight and haze, splashed now and then with windy rain, the pause when men took in the oats at leisure, patched roofs, fashioned storm windows. Working slowly, halting to look down the slopes of fields, to note the wavelike growth of after-grass, the ripening of apples . . .

On Sunday afternoon, the last day of August, Anna left the house and took the road of rutted grass through Gordons' lower field toward the beach. It was nine days since she had walked home from Katen's with exasperation growing in her heart.

Conspicuous . . . What else should people be, if they felt like it? You didn't have to make it obvious. Being together sometimes, as often as you could, would do for now. But the idea of caring because people knew . . . Silly. It was simply silly. You couldn't hide . . .

That was the way she had felt about it. For a day or two her mind had played with dreams of hurting Grant. Dreams in which all hurt vanished when he learned, finally, that only one thing mattered.

There were fantasies in which she left home, drove down to Copeland with the mail, and took the train to Boston. Sometimes in this imagined drama Grant would hear of her intention and come down the road to plead with her not to go Sometimes she slipped away proudly, saying nothing beforehand. She had pictured herself in a black dress and a white apron, setting out linen and silver on polished mahogany in a house in Back Bay. And a ring at the door . . .

There was nothing impossible in the locality and circumstance of these imaginings. The kitchens and factories of Boston, the forecastles of Gloucester, were full of Nova Scotians. Couldn't toss a penny in Scollay Square, they said, without hitting one. But Anna's mind was too realistic to take the dream seriously. How could you get away, anyway? How could you leave Stewart and Josie, with Anse gone?

As the days passed the practical side of her nature had taken charge. She would see Grant and talk it out. She began to realize then that this was not as simple as it seemed. He did not come to Katen's any more. Each evening she had made it a point to drop over to Grahams', but he did not come; there was no sound of axes in The Place. To ask him why he was avoiding her became as important as the necessity of asking him about his manner, his troubled caution when they last had met. Yet that, she thought, was silly; it was all part of the same thing . . .

So, last night, she had crossed to Grahams' as soon as she had finished an early supper, and walked up the road with Edith for the mail. This was a small adventure. Since Hazel's going, by some tacit agreement the Grahams had been bringing down the Gordons' mail, when there was any.

Anna missed making these trips. In earlier summers they had given her a chance to see Grant, in McKees' kitchen while Mrs. McKee sorted the letters and papers, or on the road afterward. Now, without saying anything to Josie, she had decided to go again to McKees'. You couldn't go on forever avoiding people because of something someone else had done.

Josie . . . Anna didn't want to discuss it with Josie, to open up subjects better left as they were. She had noticed Josie watching her lately, and had felt a little thrill of fear that her mother was about to speak, to ask questions. She did not want to talk to Josie yet.

She had crossed to Grahams' before the mail-team went by, so that she could be there before Edith or the boys left to go up the road; so that she could say, without stressing it, "If you're going up, I guess I'll go along with you."

There was a certain sense of ordeal in this. She wondered whether McKees' kitchen would be crowded as it used to be on mail nights, as young people from the two roads came in. They would stay and talk after the letters were sorted, before going home or down the road to Katen's. Now with Hazel gone there would be a constraint among them. Less talk, less lingering. Except for those who would ask Eva or Richard, curiously, what they heard from Hazel, how she was getting on, away . . .

As she and Edith passed Marshalls' she glanced down over the slope of the field. She saw no one except James, going from house to shop.

No one was at McKees' but Alec Neill, and he was standing up to go as the two girls came through the back door. He said, "Well, girls," and regarded them from under shaggy eyebrows, pausing before he slouched out, with a look that was like a friendly embrace. Anna had an impulse to giggle. The look of Alec Neill was laughter; it relaxed the tightness in her throat. She took a chair beside Edith.

Alec's grin and presence made it unnecessary for Eva McKee to say anything by way of greeting. She got up from the table on which the mail lay in small heaps and handed a letter to Edith and the weekly paper to Anna. That was all. No look, no word, no gesture to suggest the thing that lay between the Gordons and the McKees.

Young Joe came in then, said, "Hi, Ede; hi, Anna," and clattered through the kitchen and upstairs. Edith glanced at Anna and together they got up to go. There was nothing in any of it to indicate anything except a casual call for the mail.

As they started up the lane to the road Edith said, "There's Grant; wait a minute." He was climbing the fence between Marshalls' pasture and the field. They lingered until he came up to them by the corner of McKees' house. Edith glanced from one to the other and said, "Well, Grant . . . You can overtake me, Anna," and went on up toward the gate.

There was no coquetry in Anna. She waited a minute for Grant to speak and said bluntly, "Grant—what is it? What's the matter?"

"It's hard to explain, Anna."

"Well, you might try, anyway. Get it off your chest. You ought to know by this time, you can—tell me anything."

He shook his head. "It's not that easy. That's what—Look, I don't know whether I could get it straight if we had all day. But I'll try. When can I— Where can we—?"

She said, "Tomorrow, about three. Come down to our fish hut. Nobody goes to the beach on Sundays; not this time of year."

So, now, she walked through rutted grass toward the beach.

Grant took the path through the pastures. In earlier years it had been usual for him to follow this route on a Sunday afternoon to spend an hour or so in the Place, alone or with one of the youngsters who might happen to join him—Dan Graham, Stan Currie, Harry Neill, Joe McKee.

But today he veered south, short of the line between Hugh Currie's and The Place, and followed Currie's road down across the neck connecting the little cape of the Head with the mainland. He went on through the black spruce swamp there to the beach.

He passed the seaward edge of The Place, walking east, crossed on stones the shallow estuary where Grahams' Brook meets the Channel, and scanned the long curve of the beach, stretching away eastward. The day was almost windless, with hardly a curl of surf on the Rocks. On the hump of the beach the small grey shape of Frank Graham's hut was half-hidden by spruce which had sprung up in the years since Frank had used it only for salting down herring. The flakes were gone. Only a capstan, rotting away with time, to remind a man of the mackerel fishery. Farther down he could see Stewart Gordon's hut, with Stewart's small herring-flat and Anse's dory bottom-up behind it.

This was strange country to Grant, even though his own land, the land James intended for him, came down to salt water. Strange not in physical fact, but in its atmosphere and in the talk of his neighbours when they used it. The Marshalls came down from English officials who had followed the first settlers to Nova Scotia when the province was still a colony. They had never worked under circumstances that demand continual adjustment to the never-quiet pulse of the moving sea, nor experienced the thing known to every fisherman or seaman, however unimaginative: the sense of flesh and bone shifting with that immeasurable movement, of kinship with all others whose lives are tensed or relaxed to meet it.

There was no sign of life. Fishing for the year was over at Currie Head. Even Alec Neill's salmon net had been hauled up two weeks ago. The curious calm of Sunday, a different climate from weekday wind and weather, lay over the shore. Grant approached the plank door of Stewart Gordon's hut with hesitation. He finally seated himself on the warm beach rocks sloping down to the falling tide.

Now that he was here his mind was quiet, like the mind of one who has forced himself to a doctor's waiting-room, certain that no medicine can cure his ill but ready at last to speak of it.

He did not hear Anna come down the path through the fringe of woods; he was not aware of her until she called.

It struck him as odd that she was laughing. She said, "You

looked funny from behind, Grant. Hunched over staring at the Channel. Like an old man."

Her easiness put him at ease. "I *feel* kind of like an old man these days."

"Well, come on in."

An ancient whale-boat rudder propped the hut door. She threw it aside. The door sagged open.

One small four-paned window had been set into the end of the hut away from the door. It was curtained with cobwebs and polka-dotted with dead bluebottles. The tied-up brown buns of old mackerel nets hung from wooden spikes in the rafters. A dozen bundled herring nets had been flung along the wall. Half-barrels full of salt herring were tiered across the building's end wall; the air was acrid with the smell of brine, cutch, tanned rope and dried fish-scales.

"Sit down and make your miserable life happy."

Anna squatted on a coiled net. She went on, "If I'd been a man I'd be a fisherman . . . out of the house and away from the stone-drag—"

In the run of her uncomplicated talk, he was possessed by the illusion that this unworried ease was the only reality; the hard facts of relationship and religion and family loyalty a shadow moving with the sun.

The fact that her presence could do this to him, could almost shut out the aching truth, perversely seemed to make it easier to say what he had to say. He wanted to speak now, quickly; as, when a small boy he had not been able to sit idly by the kitchen fire while a chore remained undone. He turned his head and his eyes caught Anna's. Her voice stopped; her own eyes sobered, waiting.

He said abruptly, "Did you ever think of what it means? I mean . . . How would you go about telling your father and mother, say—that you and I were—well, wanted to get married?"

Anna laughed, and sobered quickly. She thought about it. Finally she said, casually serious: "Oh, I don't know. It'd be a little ticklish, I guess, with Mother. Let's see—perhaps I could— I can tell Father on the quiet, and get him to talk to Father Morrison and get him to fix—a dispensation, I think they call it. Get it fixed up. Then I could ask Mother to ask Father Morrison what he thought of—well, of you and me. That's kind of a long way round. But no sense looking for trouble. You know Papa. I could marry a nigger if I liked him. He likes *you*.

Mother'll kick. Kick like the devil . . . I s'pose you wouldn't turn, would you, Grant?"

He said, "Would *you*?"

A moment slipped by.

She said, "Why—I hadn't thought about that. Things don't . . . Things don't happen that way, usually. *Do* they? It'd be . . . Even Papa wouldn't . . . Mother . . . I guess she'd try to forget I was even alive."

She turned, slowly. "You weren't . . . were you thinking . . . it would *have* to be like that?"

"No," Grant said. "No. I just asked. I didn't figure you could. Any more than I could. It's just one of the things—Oh, as far as I'm concerned, personally . . . Suppose families didn't come into it, Anna. Didn't come into it at all. How'd you feel about it?"

She turned, on the cushioned net, and said, "I'd feel the way I do now; I'd feel this way."

Her arm was around him, her face drew close to his; he could feel the pressure of a full breast against him; the eyes were dark with affection. He stiffened, turned his face slightly away and took her elbows in his hands. There was something in him, a streak of puritan denial, that would not permit a lapse into tenderness. He could not steal for a moment something he was not sure he could have openly for life.

He saw Anna withdrawing into herself, hurt and baffled. He said, "That's the way it is with me, too. Sometimes I wish I was an orphan."

She said bluntly, "Well, aren't you?"

Grant flushed. "I s'pose so, actually. But not really. That's the trouble, Anna. It'd be easier, a lot easier, if I had a mother and father living. They bring you up, and that's expected. If there's something you want to do when you're grown up, something they don't agree with, well—you can go ahead and do it, without feeling you're cheating. What they've done for you's nothing more than usual. But Uncle James . . ."

Anna interrupted. "That's what it is, then, is it? That's what's been making you keep away? Stewing by yourself . . . Your Uncle James."

He said, "He didn't have to look after me. He could have left me in the States. I could have been raised by my mother's people. He went out of his way to bring me up. To make a son of me."

"Well," Anna said, "where does that put us? Did you talk to him about it—about us?"

106

Grant said, "Yes. It's hard to . . ." He tried to find the words that would make understandable to Anna that brief conversation in The Place. The conversation itself and its continuing echo in his mind. You couldn't communicate the meaning of Uncle James without going back for generations.

He said, "He took the attitude—seemed to think—the whole thing . . . Well, that it's something not to think about at all. Out of the question."

"Is that what *you* think?"

"No. Of course it's not what I think. But I don't feel right. I'm no damned good at acting. I can't go on seeing *you*, being with you, counting on things coming out all right—unless I'm able to figure how. Do you see—a little—what I'm up against?"

She said nothing for a moment. When she spoke again the argument was not with Grant but with James Marshall.

"But—it's not good sense. What's he got against us? Against me? If two people—no one's got the right to come between . . ."

Grant shook his head. "How can I explain that? It's just the way he sees things. Feels things. Feels about it."

"Well, my Heavens," Anna said, "it's not the right way. What right has an old man got, who's never laughed in his life—or loved anything, as far as I can see . . ."

Grant could feel the protest growing in his mind; the response to common origins, a thing that may be overlaid even with anger and dislike for one of your own blood, but comes welling up to meet the threatened blow or the caustic word of others.

"Wait, Anna. He's—Uncle James is all right. He's a good man."

She laughed shortly. "A good man? You can say that when he's trying to run you? When—the way you feel . . .?"

Grant moved his head again, shaking something off. "Yes. It's not his fault."

Anna said, "I guess Lon was right."

"Lon? . . . Right about what?"

Her face was drawn with exasperation. "I didn't know what he meant. I do now. He asked me if I thought I was worth as much as ninety acres of woods."

Grant felt the anger flushing along his nerves. He could see Lon Katen, the amusement he would take from the planting of that sly seed, the crop of belief growing in the softly-spoken conjecture of the Channel Shore.

He said, "Anna, you don't believe that."

107

She flared out, "Well, what am I supposed to believe? What is it, Grant? Are you going to do what he wants? What the old man wants?"

Ridiculous words came to the surface of Grant's mind. He had an impulse to shout: Stop calling him old! He's fifty-four! He managed to achieve personal dignity. "That's the whole thing, Anna. I don't know what we—what I *can* do. All I'm trying to say is that whatever it is, somebody's bound to get hurt. Can't you see it's not easy?"

Anna said nothing. She realized that Grant's mind was full of trouble, but the trouble was not entirely real to her. In her straightforward soul there was little struggle with doubt. You did the best you could. The thing to do was find the easiest, the least bothersome way, and go ahead with it. She could understand some part of James Marshall's attitude, but not the depth of Grant's concern for it, the implications of his little private hell; the silent voices, the alternatives that nagged at him; the urge to take her on any basis, the new impulse now to prove that The Place and its possession had no bearing on himself and her. And on the other hand the restraints of a knotted loyalty.

She had no way of knowing that James Marshall's arguments had no weight with Grant, since argument is addressed to reason and Grant's only logic was that of feeling; she had no way of knowing that it was almost the same thing in him that responded to herself that was torn also by its ties with James.

The struggle was in his mind, the whole mind of flesh and nerves and blood. James Marshall's reasoning counted for nothing. His life, his pride, his iron kindness and sense of family, for more than Grant could say.

In the back of her head the question was still ringing, angry, insistent and unspoken: All right, then. Does that strip of woods mean more to you than I do? She did not believe it. She was angry at having allowed the thought to live. But it was there.

The low grumble of Katen's Rocks was a slow distant undertone to the soft lapping of swell on packed sand at the Channel's edge. Grant sat without speech or movement until the sombre rise and fall of it seemed like something inside his skull, without beginning and without end. Anna rose abruptly and walked out of the hut, into the sun.

Grant followed, and in the open searched her face. It was non-committal, impersonal, the face of a casual acquaintance.

She said, "Well, Grant, let me know what — When you work it out. What you decide."

As if, he thought, he could decide anything.

She hesitated and went on, her voice controlled and expressionless, "Whatever it is, you know, things won't be quite the same."

Grant said, "No. No, I don't suppose they will."

What depressed him most as he walked up the beach was that he had failed to say what he might have said. It could have been done. Briskly: "Look here, Anna. You and me — nothing's changed. In the end we're all that counts. I'm sorry I've been . . . I should have tried to tell you, right away, there'd be things to think about that bother me more than they do you. It's just that it may take time."

If he had said that, and taken her in his arms. He turned once, to look back. But he knew he could not have done it.

12

THE need to talk to Anna . . .

Many times in these last days Josie had felt the resolution form. Sometimes she had come so close to words that in imagination she could sense the mind's release. In those moments she could feel the spectre vanish; or at least take shape as something known and actual that could be met and dealt with.

The imagined relief faded always in a renewal of fear. She had not been able to take the cold plunge into words. She had not been able to question Anna. She had not been able to say, "What is it? What is it that bothers you?"

If she could have done that, and if she could have put into words the things that haunted her own heart, perhaps that frankness would have induced an equal frankness in Anna, would have opened Anna's trouble to sympathy and advice. But Josie had not been able to do it. She had not been able to share pain.

Why, she did not clearly know. Except that she had always been an ingrowing woman. And on the few occasions when she had followed another impulse, laid bare her heart — well, the scars were still there.

She thought of this with part of her mind as she lay in bed beside Stewart in the room behind the parlour, on the last night of August. The times years ago when she had spoken, a little, to Anse about their hopes for him. The priesthood; or if that were a thing he had no heart for, anything. An education, a training, that would get him away from the gurry-barrels and the beach, the shore and the commonness, make him a man to be proud of . . .

She could see now the composed face of the fourteen-year-old, listening. Listening, while his mind planned. In those days Anse had planned: schoolbooks hidden by the roadside while he circled through the woods to find the Katens . . . Sudden sickness on Sunday morning when it was time to take the buggy down the road to Mass. It was only later, when time had ravelled finally the ties of family authority, that he had abandoned guile in his dealings with her.

And Stewart. There was no guile in Stewart. Only the endless absent-mindedness, the something that was almost shiftless. Nothing she had ever said had altered this in Stewart. And now, since Anse had gone . . . It galled Josie to think of the Graham boys, always around; always around to help. Getting the cows or carrying in the wood. As if Stewart were sick, or something. Her heart thumped under the assault of a sudden fear. Tonight, at supper, she had reminded Stewart about the porch roof; rain a week ago had begun to drip through until she had to set out pans. Without lifting his head, Stewart had mumbled something about getting Anse at it . . . She had let it pass, refused to think about it. Now, alone in the night, she faced it. Absent-mindedness, simple and complete, or something more? A crumbling in the mind?

She stirred in bed, and sighed, and prayed for sleep. Anna. Anna was the opposite of herself. Anna could talk and laugh about anything. Anna's off-handedness had been almost an exasperation. Until lately. But no longer . . .

Josie searched her mind again for the time when Anna's silence had begun. Anse's disappearance, the root of her own grief, was not the core of Anna's trouble. Through the bitter first days after Anse's going Anna had kept her head up and her laughter alive.

It was through Anna, really, that Josie had come to realize the link between the departure of Anse and that of Hazel McKee. Her mind went back. There was Vangie Murphy, halting by the gate; Vangie saying, "Well, Mrs. Gordon, and what d'you hear from Anse?" And her own reply, "Nothing. We've not heard from Anse yet." And Vangie, her voice unaccountably bitter and vaguely sly, "They tell me Hazel McKee's gone, too. Gone away to be a dress-maker. That's what they *say* . . . "

She had asked Anna, "Hazel McKee; has she left home?"

Yes, Anna said. Mr. McKee had taken her to the train at Stoneville, the day before. And then, into a silence, "You knew Anse used to chase after her, didn't you?"

Josie hadn't known. For a moment she had felt a queer hope. If it were true . . . If they were together . . . But that wasn't possible. Not when you knew Anse. She had felt the waves of shame wash through her, the revelation of an enormous and furtive cruelty.

111

That was Josie's shame, but it was not Anna's. It was since then that the light careless voice had lost its lightness. It was only lately that the sparkle had faded to a dull abstraction. Or become a parody of itself, forced and affected. There was something more important to Anna than Anse.

For a moment, once, a shocking possibility had occurred to Josie. That friendliness in Anna for Grant Marshall . . . Was it possible there was something that wouldn't bear thinking of? As there had been—as people said there had been—between Anse and Hazel McKee? She had dismissed this almost at once. Not Anna, her instinct said. And not Grant Marshall. She realized with something like surprise that instinct told her this also: not Grant Marshall.

Her mind kept drifting back to Anse. It was like the knowledge of unbearable pain, blocked off by the mind's busyness . . . Anse. This present Anse. She had faced it fully weeks ago. She had let her mind speculate unshielded in the talk she could not hear. In the kitchens and parlours, the workshops and fields of the Channel Shore. On the wonder in the minds of men and women, the curiosity of children. The wonder, the malice and the pity.

She had faced it all then, and felt love die, and turned away. Now she did not face it directly any more. It was a thing that must be recognized and accepted; but it was not a thing to hold in the heart and examine, except when you couldn't help . . . Let the knowledge lie in the shallows at the far reaches. Let the heart turn away.

She felt the burning flush of it, dangerously near, and moved her head abruptly in the hollow of the pillow, forcing her mind again to Anna. It was Anna she was thinking of, Anna and Grant Marshall, as she fell asleep.

She woke to kitchen sounds and the indistinct sound of voices. Morning; but the light was lifeless, the reflection of a sunless overcast. Josie put out a hand, flat on the lower sheet. Stewart was up and gone. She thought about that. Her own troubled mind kept her awake till all hours, left her dull in the mornings; Stewart's wakened him early, got him out to build the fire and roam the yard before sunrise.

She could hear the voices again, but could not distinguish the words, except that she recognized the one word "Anse" in Stewart's monotone. Then Anna, answering, and a little later the closing of a door.

112

Her heart lurched again, remembering the porch roof, the little scene at supper. She threw back the patchwork quilt and sat up on the edge of the bed, a bent figure in a white cotton frill-necked night-dress, with disorderly greying hair. She dressed quickly and then deliberately took her time, washing face and hands, tucking in hairpins. She was outwardly placid when she went up the hallway and into the kitchen.

Anna sat on her heels, facing the open door of the stove. She held close to the red wood-coal a piece of bread on a long-handled fork. Her face was flushed with heat.

Josie said, "You're up early."

Anna said indifferently, "I heard Papa."

Josie crossed to the east window. Stewart was standing in the middle of the yard, watching the Channel. The sky was a sea of high grey cloud, roofing out the sun, the Channel its darker reflection, ridged here and there with white. After a long moment he turned and walked slowly toward the barn.

Josie returned to the stove, picked up the teapot's glossy earthenware and filled her cup at the table. Anna dislodged the piece of toast from her fork, closed the stove door, straightened, and ladled her mother a plateful of porridge. When Josie said, "You'd better have another cup of tea," she obediently poured it out for herself and sat down at table opposite her mother.

Josie began to eat her porridge. Deliberately she spread preserved strawberries on toast and drank the hot strong tea. While her mind was busy with the thing she wanted to say to Anna, her eyes observed the toast-crumbs round Stewart's empty plate, his cup with sodden tea-leaves in the dregs, the table-cloth with its little stains of food from last night's supper. She found her mind changing focus, concerned now with sorrow and anger and shame, now with the dirty dishes on the table, the dreariness of little things. And suddenly they were all one, all parts of the same thing. She had an impulse to shout . . .

Get out of this, Anna. For God's sake get out of it! Away from the whole of it. Dirty dishes and crumbling minds, the curiosity, the sympathy, the sneers . . . Away from Grant Marshall, away from hurt and temptation, away from the Shore. . .

She controlled that impulse. It had never been more than a thing of the imagination. Violence would not do.

She felt she could talk calmly to Anna, now. But she no longer wanted to carry on a discussion with Anna. Somewhere in the night and the morning she had lost the impulse to question, to probe, to search her daughter's inner feeling. What she wanted for Anna was—freedom.

She said indifferently, frowning, "When was it your Aunt Mame was here last, Anna? Trying to think . . . Five years ago? Or was it six?"

Anna glanced at her mother's face and saw only abstracted curiosity, a looking back.

She said, "Six. Year before the war started. Why?" She was faintly curious.

"That long? Oh,—I don't know. Been thinking about them lately, sometimes. We ought to keep in touch more, but—"

She continued, indifferently, "It's too bad we don't see more — Maybe you might visit them for a week or so, Anna. It'd be a change."

Again Anna searched her mother's face; there was nothing in it but that looking-backward, a casual quietness.

She said slowly, speculatively, "I s'pose I might."

Excitement and puzzlement began to mingle in her mind. To go away . . . to let Grant see she could do without . . . To make him feel what it was like, her absence from the Shore . . .

The fantasies began to form. She had dismissed all that. Even after their talk on the beach yesterday, she had refused to think of it as something she could do. Boston was impossible.

But a visit, that was another thing. A visit to relatives, less than a day by train away. She wouldn't have to let on it was only for a week or two. Her mind skipped. Maybe it *wouldn't* be . . . Perhaps she could find work for a while in Halifax. Doing housework. She'd be near if they wanted her, and— her mind slipped again to the edge of dream—it would be easier for Grant . . .

She looked toward Josie again, feeling something like suspicion. What was in Josie's mind? What was behind it?

Josie had risen and was clearing off the dishes, stacking them to carry to the sink. Her face was placid.

Anna remained seated, thinking. She remembered Aunt Mame McDonald as a tall woman, dark and good-looking, a year or two younger than Josie. She had never seen Uncle Howard. There were pictures of him in the parlour closet—a big heavily-moustached man. Worked in the shipyards or some place. But Jesse and Gladys . . . Glad was her own age. Jesse and Glad had been along, that summer six years ago when all of them were kids.

114

Funny they'd never visited back and forth again. She'd hardly thought of them.

There was bitterness in this reflection. For—how long was it?—she had thought of hardly anyone but Grant. Bitterness and loneliness, and despite that, the lure of something new.

She said, "I don't know . . . There's Papa."

Josie said, "Well, if we get around to it, I'll talk to your father. A visit—he won't object to that. There's only train fare. It don't amount to much."

Anna said, "No, I guess not; I guess it'd be all right." She wondered whether Josie had deliberately affected to misunderstand. It was not any objection of Stewart's she had feared. It was the ache in her own throat at the thought of him, that aimless figure, bewildered and alone.

She did not try to explain this to Josie. Her mind was ranging, on to Halifax, the McDonalds, and back again to Grant . . .

13

Anna sat with young Bill on the shop steps at Gordons'. Down by the wood-pile Stewart bent over the grindstone, holding a scythe to it while Dan Graham, squatting on one knee, turned the crank. Now and then Stewart would straighten and raise the scythe, peer closely at the curved blade's edge, brush it with his thumb, and apply it again to the turning stone. Scythe and stone and the wooden axle of the crank made a small gritty screeching sound as Dan laboured.

Anna was thinking of the friendliness of people. How friendly they could be, some of them, without making a fuss about it. Gradually in the seven weeks since Anse had gone it had got so that one or other of the Graham boys, sometimes both of them, was always around when there were things to do; the casual man-and-boy jobs that add up to half the work of one-horse farming, and which Stewart more and more forgot.

Without being obvious about it, Frank Graham was keeping an eye on Stewart. Frank and the boys had helped him finish hay-making after their own fields were made. Frank had told Stewart they would swap work; Stewart could help him later on with the oats.

Even the Katens. Lon, sent by Felix probably, had turned up to help Stewart haul Anse's abandoned line of trawl, and Stewart's herring nets. And Rod Sinclair. Rod had used his shook-boat to get Stewart's salt herring to Fraser's fish plant at Princeport.

It went beyond the circle of near neighbours. They might talk among themselves, Anna thought. How could they help it? Josie was bothered by that, hating the thought of it. But there was a considerateness along the Channel Shore.

The Shore—even while her mind turned to Halifax and a time of escape from the trouble in her heart, she could feel the familiar friendliness of it. The same thing Grant had always seemed to feel.

She said idly, "You have a good time this summer, Bill?"

"O, yes. I like it here."

"You'll be going back home soon, I s'pose."

He nodded. "Pretty soon. About the middle of the month. I heard from my father. He's letting me stay a couple of weeks more, long as I go to school here."

Anna said, "I'm going away too, Bill."

He looked up quickly. "Away? Where?"

"Oh, just up the line. To Halifax. To visit an aunt and uncle. Not for long, I don't expect. Couple of weeks, maybe. Then again—it might be longer'n you think for . . ."

She stopped, wondering why she had picked Bill to tell this to.

It had all been settled quickly, today, with Stewart hardly seeming to realize what Josie was talking about. There was no secret about it. Anna meant to tell Edith Graham tonight, and perhaps the crowd at Katen's if she went down. But here she was, talking to Bill first of all. Bill, who was close to Grant.

He said, "When 're you leaving, Anna?"

"Tomorrow," Anna said. "With the mail."

Grant had been pulling young spruce in the lower pasture as usual. With dusk coming on he glanced up the slant of the land toward the house and saw James, a small far figure standing on the porch, and wondered if his uncle would come down to join him. And if at last he could find in himself the resolution to talk again about Anna, to argue, to try to convince . . .

He saw Bill Graham then, angling slowly across the cradle-hills toward him, and felt the little sense of liking, and a sense of shame. Young Bill—he knew more than he let on for. Bill had sensed the closeness between himself and Anna, he was sure of that, and in some slight wordless way had shared it. And it was to Bill that he had talked about The Place. This odd and likeable youngster . . . He would have caught, of course, the feel of trouble.

Grant brushed his hands, stinging from the spruce needles, and sat down on a cradle-hill and was pleasant to Bill. They talked about a dozen unimportant things, about fall coming on, and the apples beginning to mellow; and Grant went on to talk a little, answering Bill's questions, about how it would be later on. November, and the mushrat season open, and ice in the wheel ruts in the mornings; the first snow, and withered hay stems thinly speckling the white smoothness of it, and sometimes a cautious deer in the orchard at daybreak, nuzzling for frozen apples.

117

There was something wistful about Bill tonight. In the end Grant said, "Well, some year you'll be back, likely; and stay longer." Then, on impulse, yet with an imposed off-handedness, "'ve you seen Anna lately?"

He wondered at once why he had asked this question and realized there was no reason except the need to hear the sound of her name, to have the sense of contact, thin as smoke, that came from talking about her.

"Sure," Bill said. It seemed to Grant almost as if the boy had been waiting for the question. There was a hint of eagerness and relief in his voice. "I was talking to her tonight." And then, obviously casual, "She's going away for a while."

"Away—?"

The word caught in his throat.

A visit, Bill explained. She'd be back in a couple of weeks. That's what she'd said, anyway.

Grant barely listened. He spoke, now and then, making conversation. But he could never afterward recall what he and Bill had talked about in this small interval of time.

Away . . . It was as if the sum of his senses had slipped, inched downward, crumbled and settled on a level of helpless pain. Absurdly, he could feel the ache of tears in his throat, a sense of utter and hopeless loss.

After a little an odd sense of duality came to him, as if he were two men, two Grant Marshalls, and this was happening to one of him while the other stood aside, observing. Watching himself and Bill, and Uncle James coming slowly down the pasture . . .

Then James was nodding to Bill and the boy was getting up off the cradle-hill to go. Uncle James was saying, "It gets cold in the evenings, now. You ought to have some kind of jacket on . . . Fred cut some apple-wood. There's a fire going in The Room . . ."

As he walked up the path behind James this feeling of being both watched and watcher vanished. He was one, again. The thought in his mind was pointless and trivial. Uncle James was beginning to show a stoop. Was, after all, getting old.

By the time they had reached the house he was chiding himself for having been invaded by that unreasonable sense of shock. She was going away. For a week, two weeks, perhaps longer. What of it? And why, as things were, should she talk to him about it?

118

He argued this with himself, reasonably. What, after all, was a fortnight's absence? It had no importance at all. You could realize that, you could tell yourself that; but it was still true that he had himself destroyed the lightness, the openness . . . Or watched it be destroyed. The wave flowed back, the helplessness and loss.

He stood in the yard for a little in the dark, under the ash trees, while James went up the front steps and opened the door and remained there, waiting, in the dimmed edge of light from the parlour lamp.

If he went down there, now . . . down the road . . . But what could he say to her?

He turned and followed James into the house.

14

IN THE fringe of red spruce between his cleared land and the Channel, Frank Graham was engaged in the beginning of a new enterprise on the Channel Shore.

Farther west in the county the pulpwood buyers had been busy for the past two years. On small hill wood-lots near the coast, in time spared from farming, men and boys with saws and axes were attacking spruce and balsam; sawing it into four-foot lengths, peeling and piling it by the sides of roads and on the banks of streams and on the beach.

A tramp freighter would be coming into Morgan's Harbour in October to load the year's cut. Frank had made a deal with the company. 'If he could put fifty cords on the beach they would pick it up. With Grant Marshall to help him and Bill and Dan peeling and piling after school, he was working long hours to fill out the contract.

The Marshalls' machinery shed was finished. James had not objected when Grant proposed to lend Frank a hand, though he had looked at him a little oddly. Wondering, Grant supposed, why he didn't go to work in The Place.

Frank's talk and easy ways made life a little more endurable. In the warm mornings and afternoons and the cool of the evenings while they chopped and sawed, Frank's voice ranged over the Shore. They were building a cottage hospital at Copeland, and a power station to make electric light . . . Down at Forester's Pond they were after the government to dredge a harbour entrance; always trying to get the government to do something, Frank said. The new school-teacher; a good-looking girl, wasn't she? . . . daughter of Bob Fraser's, over at Princeport; boarding with the Freemans; one more skirt around the house, but Tham wath uthed to them.

There was neither time nor breath for talk while they bent to the saw, but in the easier moments, while they trimmed the felled trees, or walked up to the house for the noontime meal or supper, and in the little spells of idleness that men indulge in between bursts of work, Grant found himself listening to Frank with something like enjoyment.

There was nothing in any of it to lessen the trouble in his heart, the mixture of guilt and self-justification and the smouldering bafflement, the anger at himself and circumstances. There were times in the depth of his aloneness when the sense of this flowed up in a dark and maddening tide. He would fight his way out of that and go back, retracing in his mind the things he might have done.

If he had said, on the barn wall, *I had a girl to see, Uncle James* . . . If he had said, in the clearing in The Place, *Well, I don't intend to avoid seeing her* . . . If he had driven with her openly up the road from Katen's . . . If he had turned back, that Sunday on the beach . . .

If he had been able to take the present for what it gave, and let the future look after itself . . .

If he had been able to walk down the road to Gordons', the night before she went away . . . But what could he have said to her? He could have said, *Forget it, Anna; there's nothing worth a damn but you and me* . . . He could have said that, or he could have said good-bye.

This final *if* was the one that touched most sharply the soreness in his heart.

There was nothing in Frank Graham's talk and manner that could change the fact of his own responsibility and his inability to deal with it. But there was something in it that altered a little the sense of his aloneness. People and the things they were doing . . . He began to think of himself as one of many, to think of Grant Marshall in relation to all these people on the Shore, rather than in relation only to James Marshall and Anna Gordon. One evening as they sat on the porch steps waiting for supper he heard a scrap of talk that opened a little wider the door of his inner thought.

The boys had not turned up in the woods that afternoon. Stewart Gordon was laid up with a lame back, Mrs. Graham said, so there was more to do over there than usual. They'd be along soon. While they waited, Frank returned to a subject he had mentioned once or twice before in the course of making conversation. Stewart was in a kind of an odd state. Had been ever since Anse left, but it had been getting worse, lately. Half the time he didn't seem to know what he was doing, or care much. Be a blessing when Anna got back . . .

121

Grant heard this, noting it with regret but without feeling much about it, and found himself listening absently to the kitchen sounds behind them. The boys were coming into the yard now. Stella Graham had a hot supper-fire going. She crossed the room to raise the window a little, and as Bill and Dan went up the steps into the house, Grant caught the smell of sizzling ham and part of a sentence: "—what she can do; there's nothing . . ." Stella's words were lost as she turned from the window and broke off at the boys' entrance. But the words, the tone, the breaking-off, brought something to the alert in Grant's mind. Hazel McKee. They were talking of Hazel McKee. He felt a small definite alteration in the drift of his brooding. The aloneness in the heart of everyone . . . Hazel . . . Richard . . . himself . . . Anna . . . Stewart and Josie Gordon . . . Even, perhaps, Anse . . .

This was something sharper in the heart, clearer, more penetrating, than the sympathy he had felt for Richard and Stewart in those earlier days after his return from England. Or his formal regret, hearing Frank talk of Stewart, just today. The first had been a surface sorrow, almost forgotten later in his own pain. And his concern with himself had blunted the reality of what Frank had said about Stewart today.

What he felt now was hardly sorrow at all. It was more a kind of iron understanding.

Afterward, he was not quite sure how it was that he and Frank crossed the road to Gordons'. Most evenings they had returned to the woods after supper to get in an hour's work before dark. This evening Frank wanted to see Stewart, to reassure himself. They found Stewart sitting in an armchair from the parlour, drowsily resting. There were sounds in the pantry; Josie came up the step into the kitchen with milk pails nested under an arm.

Frank said, "Let's have them buckets, Josie. We'll look after that." He turned to say, "Take it easy, now, Stewart," as they went out to go to the little fenced yard behind the barn where the boys were barring-in the two cows.

When they had finished milking, Frank stopped in the kitchen to talk to Stewart while Grant carried the milk on through to the pantry where Josie was preparing to separate. He said, "I'll do that, Mrs. Gordon," and took the crank from her hand.

Small half-thoughts drifted in his mind, accompanied by the high seething drone of the separator. This room—there was a sag in the floor. Smaller place than the one at home; earthenware crocks and pans and platters . . . Except for the milky smell and the job itself there was little to remind you of Aunt Jane's big spotless milk-room with its shiny neatness. The noise of separation made talk unnecessary, but he was conscious that Josie hadn't left the pantry. She was standing between the machine and the kitchen door, watching the separate streams fall into the pans. When they thinned to a trickle and stopped, Grant straightened and glanced at her with the ghost of a smile.

The small job had created a shared atmosphere, something in common, momentary and slight. Grant said, "What d'you hear from Anna, Mrs. Gordon? She like Halifax all right?"

A brief silence. Josie said, "We had a card when she got there. Since then we've not heard a word."

Grant's question had been unwilled, spoken because the situation called for words, for some casual remark. What could be more natural than a reference to Anna, visiting away? There was nothing in it consciously of the craving behind the question he had asked of Bill Graham among the cradle-hills. And yet as soon as he had asked it, it seemed to him that for the last half-hour he must have been working up to it. In the little silence that followed he felt as if he had done a daring thing. The normality of Josie's answer brought a feeling of relief.

Yet, *had* her answer been wholly normal? She had spoken without emphasis, but with a suggestion of irritation. *Since then we've not heard a word.* Perhaps it was an irritation that masked an inner worry.

Grant said, "Wasn't planning to stay long, was she? She'll turn up in the mail herself one of these days."

Josie made an indifferent sound, added, "Like as not," and went into the kitchen.

As he crossed the road again with Frank, Grant wondered at the thing in him that had been able to add that casual sentence. The thing that was like acting, and yet was not acting because in the moment of talking to Josie he had been one person making sincere if casual conversation with another. The thing that could come to the surface of behaviour while the mind lay captive to frustration and regret.

After that in the evenings he went over to Gordons' with Dan and Bill or Frank whenever he could do so without appearing to have an obvious purpose. Stewart's back was better; there was little that needed to be done. It was just that Frank was keeping an eye on the Gordons.

Some nights Stewart would come to Grahams', as he had done for years, to smoke on the steps with Frank while darkness fell. Grant stayed, listening, sharing the companionship. Now and then, briefly, he saw and spoke to Josie. It was as though he were possessed by an ambition, unformed in thought but there in feeling, to know all he could know, by these small contacts and associations, of this man and woman who were Anna's flesh and blood.

He had no plan. There was no change in the tangle of his loyalties. But he was no longer quite alone. There was now a kind of kinship for all others isolated in their aloneness, stricken by circumstance, caught without an answer to the riddle of living. A new sense of the future, of being one among many who must move and change with time.

15

WHEN dinner was ready Josie went out on the side porch to call Stewart. For a little while she stood there watching him, across the field, as he shuffled along a swath of ripe oats with swinging scythe.

She thought, September . . . In less than two weeks they would be into October, the season of white moonlight and clear crisp days and nights. Squirrels gathering beechnuts. Children stopping on the way home from school, to climb the fences into roadside pastures, after mullein stalks and cat-tails. For a second or two Josie tasted girlhood, the pithy flowery flavour of ripened haws.

She called "Stewart! Dinner!" and saw him halt, glance up and around and lift a hand in a half-wave. Stewart had been a little better lately, less sunk in absent thinking, except that every now and then he would look around in a lost way, and then, remembering, ask when Anna would be back. She recognized this, a little grudgingly. It had hurt her pride to see others doing for him—for them. Now pride was—well, it was all right to have the Grahams coming around. With people about, Stewart was all right. With some surprise she realized that in her thinking about this, about the boys and Frank, her mind included with them Grant Marshall.

In Grahams' lower woods she could hear the axes.

She turned toward the door and twisted again suddenly to face the fields, the Channel, the wooded slopes eastward, already beginning to colour, and was stricken suddenly by the emptiness of the house behind her. She felt again the surge of a wish that was almost violence, urgent beyond all common sense. She wished, simply, that Anna would write.

After dinner Stewart got up from the table to return to the field, but halted on the side porch. Something in his manner made Josie curious. She joined him there.

Slowly, from the east, the sky had begun to darken. A cloudless amber twilight was settling on foliage and stubble, a deepening of natural colour on the woods and the Channel. The land lay at the bottom of a still sea of dark and silent air.

Over the rim of spruce cresting the wooded southern pastures of the Murphy place and Felix Katen's, they could see the slowly advancing selvage of purple and grey, clouds massed in a single cloud. An air of wind, chilly with something colder than the breath of late September, brushed the headed oats, and crossed the field, and touched their faces.

Stewart said, "Weather." He went down the steps and crossed the field and carried his scythe to the shop, and came into the house to stand by the eastern windows, talking half to himself.

". . . . blow before night. When she blows up easterly you c'n expect it dirty . . . No wind, much, and rollers walkin' up like they come from Ireland . . ."

The first splash of rain fell, a brief squall borne on gusty wind. Through the south window Josie saw Frank Graham and Grant Marshall coming up to Grahams' from the woods.

Stewart went out to sit on the steps of the front porch, facing the Channel, watching the odd illusion of suspense that hung along the sky.

Around supper-time the rain came straight down and hard. Josie lit the lamp. It was odd to be eating off lamp-lit cloth when the windows should have been letting in the mellow light of evening.

When Dan Graham came over to help with the evening chores he was wearing a black slicker of Frank's and a round oil-hat with chin-strap wagging. Stewart put on his yellow oilskins to go to the barn.

At bedtime the rain still fell, and the wind was up now, dashing it against the windows in dollops and streaming volleys. The house creaked and strained as the wind struck and rushed round it, not blow after blow, but with a steady and growing power.

Josie went to bed early, leaving Stewart by the fireless stove.

On the shadowy borderline of sleep, while rain fell in rushing torrents, her mind was alive with waking dreams.

Anse and Anna, herself and Stewart, moving through the routine of the farm and the house. Stewart and Anse unloading firewood from the sled in the yard on a frosty morning, the

126

horse stamping balled snow from the hollow of a hoof . . . Anna laughing for no reason, at the sight of bursting bubbles in steaming porridge . . . Slush on the kitchen floor from the men's boots . . . She started into full wakefulness at the girl's voice, soundless but perfectly clear, some winter long ago: "You fellas. You're more bother than you're worth . . ."

There was no comfort in this dreaming thought. Over it all lay the fear of something lost. Josie's mind went back to the little worries of early summer—so clear and touchable when compared to this vague, empty, endless hoping that was hardly hope. So simple, because the objects of it then were near, were present flesh that you could see and touch. Except for a trace of fatalism, a contempt for futile wishing, Josie would have made a bargain with the saints: *Let it be as it was; I won't complain again . . .*

Satisfaction in Anna's escape . . . she had thought of it as that, hoping that Anna would be caught up in city life, that some way would be found . . . Satisfaction in that was gone, gone with the absence, the loss of the winsome manner and teasing voice. Gone, in Stewart's lost look, when the mood took him. Gone, particularly in these midnight hours when true sleep would not blur the shadows of the mind. She turned restlessly in bed, half-resolving to go over to Grahams' tomorrow and try to get through to Halifax by way of the open phone line to Findlay's Bridge. To reassure herself, to hear the voice . . . But half the people on the Shore would hear.

Her mind drifted back to Anse. Anse and Hazel McKee. She tried to close a door on that by a pure effort of will.

She heard Stewart moving cautiously about the room, heard him stumble over a chair, and felt the bed creak and sag as he got into it. Eventually she fell asleep and was pursued by dreams.

In the morning the rain had slackened to gusts and a blowing mist, and the wind was down. Stewart splashed his way to the barn in rubber boots. Under the higher notes of the wind, the occasional wet splatter against glass, the desultory buffeting of walls, Josie could hear the undulant curling roar, the smothered thunder of surf on Katen's Rocks.

After breakfast she went out to the side steps to look. Stewart was already beginning to think of the storm in terms of the Shore's history. He was almost boyish. "Hard a blow as any I remember. Can't hardly recall the August gale, y'know. I bet you this one hit the whole east coast. We'll hear about it . . ."

The old Balm o'Gilead in the lower field was down, its trunk sprawled across a wrecked panel of fence and its top broken off in the road. The unmown oats lay flat, as if tramped down by marching men. Graham's Brook droned full and washed into the fields.

Out of nowhere Stewart said, "We'll likely hear soon, y'know, Josie."

He stepped off the porch, hesitating what to do first.

There was no way of knowing whether he meant a letter from Anna or word of Anse. Perhaps he didn't know himself. But his voice had been firm and full of compassion. For just a moment a small flag of respect flew in Josie's mind, over the sense of threat that lived there. Respect for an ageing and sorrowful and bewildered man who could think to say a word well-meaning and meaningless. Meaningless; and yet, watching him walk stoop-shouldered down the muddy road to see what he could do about clearing away the shattered Balm o'Gilead top, her heart was not as heavy as before.

She kept an eye on the road as she washed the breakfast dishes and carried out scraps to the hens. A team splashed east through the road's mud, but the driver was a stranger to her; not Adam Falt on his way to Copeland. Not a letter, not a line, from Anna . . .

Exasperation flushed through Josie's worry. Maybe she was homesick. Well, why didn't she write, then? Grant Marshall . . . Another bargain almost formed itself in her mind. She shook her head in impatience, not at the idea of coupling a Marshall and a Gordon in the same thought, but, again, at the futility of imagining time turned back.

She watched the road for Adam Falt. Mail usually came on the up trip, Tuesday, Thursday, Saturday. But it was freakish. They were using the road from Stoneville now for the mail to Morgan's Harbour, and sometimes a letter slipped through that way and reached Currie Head on the down trip.

She thought that after Adam had gone by, she would make an excuse to walk up to McKee's and see. No. Except at a distance, when Eva McKee came to call at Grahams', she had not seen Eva since Anse had left the shore. Despite the shortness of that mile of road, there had never been any closeness between them, anyway. She knew that Eva now took some kind of bitter pride in ignoring talk, in going out to church, visiting neighbours, marketing at The Bridge. But her own pride was of another texture. She did not want to see Eva McKee.

Bill or Dan would pick up whatever there was. She glanced at the clock. Only eleven. Adam was more than two hours late this morning.

She heard his waggon then and saw it halt by her front gate, and wondered. A letter would have gone to McKees' in the bag. She hurried down the clam-shell path to the gate.

Adam had climbed down from the rig. He was holding a yellow envelope in his hand, and there was something . . .

He said a little awkwardly, "Josie, it's a telegram. They didn't want to phone it because—well—the line's down, anyway. But it's bad news, Josie. I—"

Down the road, out of the corner of her eye, Josie noted that Stewart had been able to do nothing alone about the Balm o'Gilead. Two hours and more puttering . . . Bill and Dan Graham had come across and they had finally hauled it to the roadside. They turned to look curiously at the mail-team. They were coming up the road . . .

She reached out and took the envelope and stared at it briefly, reading the address through the transparent panel: STEWART GORDON CURRIE HEAD NS PHONE FROM FINDLAYS BRIDGE.

She said, "Is it—Anse?"

Adam shook his head. "No, Josie. It's not Anse . . . It's Anna."

She was suddenly still. Then with awkward fingers she opened the envelope and read the message. As the slip fluttered from her fingers her knees began to bend. She did not feel Adam Falt's supporting arm, or hear young Bill Graham's frightened shout as he ran toward Grahams' gate: "Aunt Stell! Aunt Stell!"

16

THE coffin lay in the small unused room at the back of the house, across the hall from the downstairs bedroom. This was where Anna had slept as a child. Tomorrow they would take her body on a spring-waggon to the church at Forester's Pond for the requiem mass and committal to the earth; but tonight she lay in the room of her earliest girlhood. Candles burned in the room. The single small window was open, but their flames were steady in the still night air. When a breath of wind stirred the curtains, or the door opened to a new arrival at the front of the house, they would dip slightly and waver.

Kitchen and parlour were filled with people. They would come into the house by either door, blink around to find Stewart and Josie in the parlour and walk up to them with outstretched hand to say their word of sympathy. Mame McDonald or Stella Graham would take them down the narrow hall then and into the little room with the candles and the faint scent of barns and flowers, to see the face of Anna.

All evening they had come. Hesitant in the doorway before going on to grasp Stewart's hand and Josie's and speak their halting hurried words. There was a formality about it. Grant had heard the ritual repeated again and again: "Sorry . . . sorry for your trouble." Words spoken as if they had been learned from a manual of usage in which were printed the formal salutations for luck and love and fortune and disaster.

Perhaps that was it. Usage. Habit. Curiosity. This thought touched him, but without conviction. There was something more than that. From where he was standing, in the hall, lounging against the jamb of the parlour door, he considered all this with detachment. Frank Graham and Felix Katen sat on the parlour sofa. Stewart was between them, elbows on knees, kneading a handkerchief. Stewart, in his faded blue serge Sunday suit and a clumsily knotted tie. Josie sat across the room, with Stella Graham and one of the Clancy women from Forester's Pond, so that when newcomers arrived they had to cross the room twice, to shake the hand of both. Some were in Sunday suits, some in working clothes. Lon Katen. Rod Sinclair. Hugh and Christine Currie. Stileses and Clancys and Reilleys from down the shore . . .

That was natural enough. Close neighbours, or people of the same faith.

But what caught Grant's interest most was the presence of these others. The Freemans and Wilmots from up the school-house road. The new school-teacher, a girl from Princeport. The Lairds, Richard and Eva McKee; the bitter pride in Eva must have been very great, to bring her here . . .

During this bitter summer he had learned a good deal about the meaning of difference. It came to him now that one thing at least could blur the difference down.

Usage. Yes. But something wonderful and gentle when you saw through the awkwardness and beyond the stilted words. In the mind of each the hovering shadow, eternal and personal and known to all—the awareness that some day or night he too, she too, must lie apart in that strange stillness, beyond the warmth of work and talk and long companionship . . . And each ignored . . . tried to ignore . . . that shadow, banishing fear in a sorrow shared and immediate; and in a strange sweet private loss . . . the girl who moved in their world of dreams, their common memory . . . that shining careless girl . . . Despite the voiced *Thy will be done*, a sense of waste, a furtive human anger.

In the parlour they talked in undertones. In the kitchen the voices too were low, but concerned outwardly with usual things. The storm. Crops. The prospect of a steady pulpwood market. Dave Stiles questioned Alf Laird about the cost of running a car. Was thinking he might get one, he said. But questions and answers came perfunctorily, with a kind of inattention . . . And now and then all talk would cease and the voices fade into restless silence.

Grant heard Ida Freeman's, curiously emphatic:

". . . a lovely girl; a lovely, lovely girl."

Edith Graham made a stifled sound, almost animal; she got up abruptly from her chair by the parlour organ and hurried through the hall, outdoors, into the dark . . . Edith, the quiet, the self-possessed; and Anna had been only the girl next door, never an intimate.

Well, his own ordeal, the shaking anguish of it, was over. There remained the shadow . . . Not, for Grant, the shadow of a cosmic fear; but still, the shadow . . . endless and for him alone.

His eyes roved over the Curries, over Alec Neill, James Marshall, Frank Graham, young Bill. Odd, that a kid—but Bill had been fond of her.

They had all been fond of her. His glance was caught briefly by a pleasant face, hair the colour of dark rust. The school-teacher. Fraser. Renie Fraser. She didn't need to come, but when you came to a district to teach, you did what the people who lived there did, became for a while one of them.

Well, he was one of them already. Even if he should leave, go away, and the impulse to that had been strong a little while ago, he would think of the Shore, in rare moments when he thought of it at all—rare, since what is part of you is a thing of feeling rather than thought—he would think of it as home. But he would not go away. The surface play of his mind merged with the deeper conviction, the decision he had come to and the bargain he had made with Josie. He already knew what he would do, and there was a kind of hard peace in knowing. Peace, and excitement. It remained only to tell James. Where and how to tell James. He wondered at his own concern about this: you reached a decision that made you a new man, gave you this sense of iron freedom, and still the tendrils of mental habit . . . Some way to tell him, to get it done with. Easier, he thought, if he could feel hate.

James Marshall sat on a stiff-backed chair near Grant by the hall door. He moved the fingers of one hand in the smooth flow of his beard. He was thinking that he and Grant had been here long enough. It was the proper thing, and he had no doubt that Stewart and Josie Gordon found some kind of comfort—comfort, pride, something—in the presence of all these people, himself among them. But one didn't have to linger. He supposed that some of these people would stay all night, would hold a kind of wake . . . Jane could come down tomorrow and spend an hour if she liked. They had never been close, the Marshalls and the Gordons. The formal aspects of sympathy were enough. Out of place, to try to share the rights of closer neighbours.

Grant had been too forward, unpardonably so—hurrying down yesterday as soon as they heard the news. And again today—at daybreak, apparently. An unheard-of thing. James frowned. He had been slack with Grant lately. He hadn't questioned his wish to work with Frank Graham, though hiring out was something Marshalls didn't do. Grant. Anxious to help Frank, and

132

to pick up a little money wherever he could, James supposed, since he would want to start establishing himself on The Place some time soon. Despite the queer pang he felt at the thought of home without Grant in it, he had no quarrel with that. It would be satisfying to see Grant making a home out of that strip of woods. James had been looking forward, almost, to seeing him make a start—as soon as one could be sure he no longer harboured in his heart the threads of that dubious attachment . . .

But—working for others; it wasn't necessary, except in the ordinary way of exchanging help. And even that — there were four Marshalls. Self-sufficient. Oh, Frank Graham was all right. But James distrusted casualness, laughter, garrulity, wherever they were found. There were things about people like Frank Graham and Alec Neill and Hugh Currie, and even Richard McKee, that he would never understand.

But he had been lenient with Grant, yesterday and today. One had to make allowances. The boy had been fond of Anna Gordon. Perhaps even with a fondness that was more than the lust of the flesh. James doubted that. The carnal had a way of masking itself. But he would have to make allowances . . . even for Grant's bluntness . . .

The scene came back to him. The washed blue of the sky, with tattered clouds slowly moving, the ground spongy underfoot. It had been too wet, of course, to think of working in the woods. He and Grant had gone into the lower field to see the damage caused to potatoes and turnips by the storm's rushing runnels. That was where Bill Graham found them. Young Bill, rushing out of breath across the field to blurt the news . . .

James considered that. Even now, across the room, Josie Gordon's sister, the McDonald woman from Halifax, was repeating the story . . . A shaken head, a sympathetic sound of tongue and teeth: ". . . no tram stop at the corner. But she didn't remember . . ."

She had been coming home, they said. Setting out for the station in the blowing dusk of morning. Smashed down by a street-car . . . He could hear Mame McDonald's voice, hushed, but the hush a mere token of consideration for Josie and Stewart; the voice was clearly audible: ". . . mercy of God—she likely hardly knew—when they got to her, laying there, she never made a sound . . ."

James thought sententiously, God moves in a mysterious way. His mind came back to Grant. At last he would be free of the long temptation.

A ripple of personal feeling and ancient affection stirred in James's flesh. He could see Grant's face from where he sat, without directly searching with his eyes. Its resemblance to another . . . again he thought of that overcast day in May, years ago, and Harvey.

Other pictures drifted across that point of reference in remembered time. The woman, the wife Harve had brought home the summer of—when was it?—'ninety-seven. A city girl, full-breasted and tall, and a talker. His sense of shock, hearing the voices in Harvey's room on a Sunday morning, the woman's suddenly clear: "Well, all right, Harve. If we've *got* to. But church! . . . Kur-ist! . . . I don't like this play-acting." Now, more than twenty years later, a word flickered redly in James's mind. He brushed it away. His thought moved on, to plush and veneer in the parlour of a tenement in Boston, and Harvey dead, the crepe already gone from the door, and the same voice: "He's a good brat. If there was any . . . But take him. Take him. It's better . . ."

No. James would not admit that he was glad Anna Gordon was dead. Put it another way. He was glad temptation had been removed. The fact that death was the agent was incidental.

An iron freedom enclosed the long sadness in Grant's mind. At Bill Graham's words, panted through shortened breath in the turnip field, there had been a moment of swift and utter shock. A blow, incredibly savage. A blow that numbed the flesh . . . and yet lighted the brain, the senses, with a nightmare incandescence. In the white flash of it, there, he had felt it all—the finality and the hopelessness and the guilt.

From that inexorable moment of reality he had come back to the reality of wet clay and watery sun; Bill Graham's face, James Marshall's voice. James, saying something meaningless, well-meant and meaningless . . .

Grant had said, "Well, she's dead, that's all."

His voice had been rough with hate. But in the space of a glance he had begun to glimpse the thing that now was fully realized. He felt no resentment against James. Felt nothing about James Marshall, except that here was a man, a person, entitled to the respect and sympathy of one man for another. Respect for honesty and sympathy for blindness. Entitled to nothing more.

He had begun to build the wall, then, against the formless world of black despair and self-reproach and something else, only hinted in that moment of flashing clarity . . . The wall between that formless world and this . . .

He had gone down the road, after a little, with young Bill Graham. He hadn't entered the house at once. Stella Graham was there with Josie, and Frank was looking after Stewart.

It was curious the way old Stewart talked about Anse. All afternoon, as he moved restlessly from shop to barn and back again, fidgeting and talking. Scarcely a word about Anna. Only about Anse and Josie.

". . . come home, if he knew. Fond of his mother, whatever they . . . if he's fond of anybody. Queer, y'know. Not his fault . . . It's what you're born with. Restless . . . When we're gone . . . sell the place and go West or somewhere. Unless he's gone for good already. Don't believe it. We'll hear . . . He'll turn up . . . She feels it. I—me—I can stand anything."

Yes. Grant supposed that stoop-shouldered old man *thought* he could stand anything. But Josie knew better. And it was with Josie that he had made his deal.

Strangely, he had slept soundly last night; and wakened early, while it was still dusk, with a sense of looking ahead, looking forward to something. He had dressed and gone downstairs and stood for a moment listening to the faint breathing of the dark house. For a moment he had faced the cold range; then he had gone out into the overcast morning and walked down the road.

Fourteen or fifteen hours ago, that was. Time was queer. It seemed like years. And yet those moments were, would always be, the eternal present.

He had found Stewart standing in trousers and undershirt in the open back door, his braces round his hips. Stewart had not been at all surprised to see him; he had simply said "Grant" and stepped aside to let him enter the kitchen. Grant had a curious feeling that for Stewart yesterday was half a life-time, the people he had been with yesterday the friends of years and years.

The kitchen was steeped in gloom. He had raised the blinds a little and looked round and squatted by the cold stove to build a fire. The stove was not a modern range like Aunt Jane's but a low affair with a big fire-box and an iron neck supporting the oven. Across the damper raised letters were cast in the iron, the word WATERLOO and the name of the manufacturing company. He remembered Anna's telling him that Stewart had taught her the alphabet off the front of the kitchen stove.

Now, standing there, he could feel it come. Not the guilt. That was accepted. Accepted and possessed and walled away. What he felt now was the other . . . the hinted thing he had seen at the edge of that blaze of light . . . Seen; and turned away, as one unworthy . . .

Now the stone of his will crumbled. He stood with an unlighted match in his fingers, facing the stove, and met the dream of Anna. The eyes, the softness of lips, the sound of laughter . . . the clutch of fingers . . . the pressure of a breast.

The truth that never again . . . It went through him and all over him, a horror in the blood. He was left shaken and fumbling, his throat crying for the ease of tears. Instinct took him. The instinct to turn and find hiding, to crouch and bury his face on crossed arms and let the flesh give way.

He turned. Stewart Gordon was standing in the door, gazing out at the fields, his braces still round his hips. Slowly Grant turned to the stove and crouched and struck the match and held the tiny flame to paper.

When the kindling caught he straightened and listened to the fire. A clock ticked slowly on the mantel behind the stove-pipe, an old alarm-clock with a glassless face, yellow and fly-specked. The hands stood at twenty-two minutes past six.

The day, then . . . today, drawing to an end now in faces, men and women grouped in kitchen and parlour, moving down the little hall to the room where candles burned, and back to the front of the house, with faces fixed and solemn . . .

Mame McDonald was talking again: "Glad tried to grab her, but she stepped right out. Slippery, y'know, and dark. The street-car . . . No chance. No chance at all . . ."

Today . . . There was a convention about death. Until the funeral was over relatives did only the work that was necessary. They sat in the house in Sunday clothes, contemplatively, acknowledging in a hushed way the words of those who tried to be helpful.

Frank Graham had kept Stewart out of the house. They had puttered around the workshop. Frank had got Stewart busy mending a herring net. He had sat there facing the road and the Channel through the open door, his hands moving the net-needle in and out, fashioning the meshes. The exercise of this simple skill seemed to quiet him. Even to alter his bewilderment. As he looped the twine over the mesh-board, drew the needle through and made his knots, a kind of concentration was reflected in his face.

There had been one bad time when the truck arrived from Copeland and on it the plank shell which enclosed the coffin that held Anna. Stewart had looked up with an expression of puzzlement and fright. Then he had begun to tremble. Frank Graham simply said, "No need to go in yet, Stewart: that's all looked after." In the end the truck had driven away and Stewart had gone in with them to look on the face of the dead.

The face of the dead. Grant had forced himself to look, with Frank and Stewart. The violence that struck her down had left the face unmarked. But—nothing there. Nothing there. A face of wax, expressionless . . . Whatever that was, it was not Anna.

He glanced across at James now and saw his hand move from his beard and rest on his knee in preparation for departure. It came to him that now was the time. No waiting for the right time, no concern for persuasion or argument. The break, sudden and complete.

Josie glanced across the room, at Stewart. Some instinct of dignity was bearing up that bewildered spirit and bracing the tired body. He sat between Frank Graham and Felix Katen in a simple and accepting quiet.

Josie had travelled a long way since Adam Falt's waggon had stopped at her gate. She wished it was all over. All over, and the new phase of life begun. If you could call it life, when all you would ever feel was pain. When the nearest thing to joy you could ever know would be a moment's easing in the ache, a moment's forgetfulness of guilt . . .

She knew this was unreasonable. Anna's going had been sane and sensible, the beginning of a way of escape. But what had the heart to do with reason? The images rose in her mind, accusing and true . . . Stewart, aimless in the cold kitchen, the morning she had gone . . . Anna, in Halifax, the day before her death: *Oh, sure, Aunt Mame. It's great. I'll come again. But right now I got to get back. I got to get back . . .*

At the back of Josie's mind a curious feeling flickered and was lost. Anna: Anna was out of it, young and unsullied and safe. It was as if Josie had flown forward in time to a day when, despite her present grief for Anna and her reasonless guilt, that guilty grief was softened, mellowed, all but gone . . . And in its place, another. Here in the midst of sorrow, shame; the thing she had forced from thought; the memory and the face of Anse . . .

Her glance strayed or was drawn to Grant Marshall. A cross-current of feeling touched her. For a moment she felt re-

137

sentment at the sight of him. If it hadn't been . . . If he hadn't been part of her fear for Anna . . . But she recognized that this resentment was not genuine. It was something induced and artificial. It would be convenient to feel anger, to lighten your burden with the relief of blame. But it was something she could not feel was true.

He was blaming himself. Why, she wasn't sure. He had not mentioned Anna's name. All he had shown outwardly was concern for Stewart. It was about Stewart that he had said what he wanted to say.

She looked across at James Marshall. Well, she had done her duty. What Grant Marshall planned seemed impossible, crazy, not to be thought of. But—he was leaving home anyway, he said. In the end it was her own guilt at the thought of Stewart that had caused her to agree.

She didn't know . . . she didn't know . . . But it was out of her hands now, and she was glad of it.

James rose. He spoke with courtesy and sympathy.

"Stewart . . . Mrs. Gordon . . . If there's anything . . ."

Well, this was the moment. They wouldn't know what it meant, these people here, Grant thought. And that was just as well. They would learn in time.

James turned. "Perhaps we should go home, now, Grant."

It was a direction, not a query. For one black shameful moment Grant felt a faltering, a helpless sense that despite the spirit, the flesh must follow . . .

He answered gently.

"No, Uncle James," he said. "I'm staying here."

17

FALL comes to Nova Scotia like the late fulfilment of a boyhood love, half forgotten for half a lifetime and then at once alive and golden, new and strange.

The late-August easterlies and the line storms have blown themselves out. Slowly the slopes begin to blaze with reds and yellows, wild splashes of cold dramatic fire along the sombre hills of spruce.

The days are crisp and clear, or windless under a mild and clouded sky. The nights are those a man remembers, looking upward through the murk of cities, his instinct looking back. There are nights in the full moon of October when darkness is a kind of silver daylight, when the sea is a sheet of twinkling light, the shadows of barn and fence and apple tree black and incredible, the air vibrant and alive but still as a dreamless sleep.

This is the time when men thresh grain, pull their turnips from the ground and apples from the boughs, dig potatoes from cold clay and gather eel-grass for winter banking . . .

Grant straightened and raised the two-pronged hoe and let the handle slip backward through his fingers till the head caught on his clenched hand. Absently he rubbed earth from prongs worn smooth and blunt by years of use. He sighed for no reason except that the job was done.

Digging time. He had always liked the fall of the year and disliked the digging that went with it—back-bent labour in cold clay among blackened dead potato-tops, the picking and the cleaning and the hauling.

He dropped the hoe and rubbed his hands across the bib of overalls crusted with dried earth and turned to glance up the field. Along the edge of the patch potatoes lay piled in tubs and ruddy pink in the aftergrass, drying out before being hauled to the cellar. Grant had not thought of it before but it came to him now that for the first time in his life there had been a kind of satisfaction in digging-time. He was almost sorry it was over.

He watched as Stewart crossed the road and took down the bars and led the horse and cart across the dark fall grass to the top of the patch. Grant walked up the slope to meet him.

Stewart looped the rope reins over the hames. "Tubs first? . . ."

Grant nodded. "Some of the loose ones're still damp."

They bent together and began to heave the tubs up to the floor of the cart, and he could feel the lift of a curious satisfaction. Ten days ago Stewart would have grasped a loaded tub with his own hands, struggled to heave it to the support of a knee with the bulk of it against loins and belly, strained to raise it to the cart by his own uncertain strength.

In the last three weeks they had finished making the oats, picked apples, put down a new hewn-pole floor in the cow stable, ploughed a stretch of ground in the shadow of the woods behind the house. The thing Grant had noticed from the first was that if the plough-point caught in a boulder, Stewart would go at the rock with his hands. If a sleeper needed shifting he would strain at the heavy timber without waiting for help. He had never learned to work the easy way.

Now he was learning. Grant shoved the last tub home and slipped the tail-board into its channels and let his eyes rest on Stewart as the old man made a mouth-sound at the mare and turned the cart uphill toward the house. The old man . . . odd to think of him that way . . . but years of working alone . . . It was as if all those years of clumsy ineffectual effort had been added up and laid on Stewart's shoulders. As if in this year of Anna's death and Anse's desertion some quality of resistance had given way, and left him at fifty-five a shaken man of eighty.

And yet, in the soil of those gathered years, something new was growing. Something almost sprightly.

Grant walked behind the cart and watched Stewart's bent back and marvelled again at the older man's serenity. The flesh might be shaken, but within a circle of work and space and time that was drawn round the present, the mind was clear and calm. It was only in idleness, while he sat unoccupied in shop or kitchen, that the puzzlement appeared . . .

Well, Grant thought, that was all right. Time on his hands was something he could not face, himself.

The loaded cart jolted across the road and the cross-way into the yard. Stewart backed the mare to the cellar door behind the

140

house and they began to lug the tubs down uneven stone steps to the gloom of the cellar.

Inside, the mould of time mingled with the fresh earthy smell of potatoes they had dumped here yesterday, in the only bin, Grant thought, that looked as if it might stay dry. When they had finished setting the tubs on small platforms of brick and stone on the spongy plank floor, he straightened and looked around him and moved to the light of the doorway. He said reflectively, "I guess this'll be next—our next job."

Stewart said, "Job? . . . What?"

Grant said, "The cellar."

He noted again the walls built of boulders crow-barred from the earth nobody knew how long ago. Most of the mortar had crumbled to dust. Here and there a rock had come loose and fallen, and lay in the angle of floor and wall. He said "Look," and pressed a foot on the flooring. It sagged under him. An ooze of thin mud came up through ragged cracks.

No one for a generation had attended to the small rottings and crumblings that attack a house from the minute the last new nail is clenched. In the spring, he thought, he would floor the cellar with concrete and patch its walls. The house should be raised, by rights, its whole foundation replaced with concrete. But that was a job too spectacular to think about yet. Too provocative for Josie and too exciting perhaps for Stewart. Whatever needed doing, the important thing was to keep the climate of the household undisturbed.

He said, "The drains. We could dig out the drains. Put down a bit of pipe to keep her dry."

A horse and buggy was passing slowly down the road as they rounded the house to return to the field. Dave Stiles, going home from a marketing trip to Findlay's Bridge. He brought his rig to a stop to exchange words.

For an instant Grant felt the familiar clutch of something close to fear. There were moments still when he experienced a childlike helplessness as he faced the fact of what he had done and what he was doing. When the task of making his way alone, of meeting an assumed responsibility, seemed utterly beyond him. This was linked in a curious way with talk . . . the talk that must be going on . . . When these moments came they caused a torment in his mind.

He could not explain this. At the heart of life was a hard exalted independence, an utter confidence beyond embarrassment. Almost beyond remorse and grief. At heart and for himself he

141

feared nothing, cared nothing for what people thought and said. The sense of this was final and complete. It was almost as if the Grant Marshall of a month back had been another person, someone who had used this body in another existence, a long time ago. This was true of the heart and the spirit. The difficulty was in the habits and sensitivities of the flesh and the nerves—in these the old Grant remained . . .

These moments now were growing fewer. Early in his first week at Gordons' he had left Stewart one evening with Frank Graham and gone down the road to Katen's. For no reason except to see and be seen, to begin to face it out. He had gone there with his mind made up to the fact of slanted looks, the feel of talk behind his back. To make a start at getting used to it. There had been something of that in Lon Katen, and a suggestion of things unsaid behind the careful friendliness of Sandy Laird and Lol Kinsman. But from the moment he stepped inside the store, it had ceased to bother him while he faced it. He had gone to bed with a sense of accomplishment that was out of proportion to the incident. A beginning made . . .

So now, listening to Dave Stiles mention the clearness of the weather, the fact that they were early through with digging, he felt the fear for an instant and felt it pass. He summoned up a grin as Dave put his horse in motion, and went on down into the field with Stewart, confident again.

They sorted potatoes, filled tubs, loaded them into the cart; and he was close to happiness. At the edge of thought the shadows lurked, the fading fear of talk and people and distrust of his own competence; and the darker shadow which would never wholly fade. But in work, in talk with Stewart, he could feel the hard and forward-looking peace at the core of his existence. Numberless things, besides his single-minded resolution, came into this. The firmness of the turf beneath his feet, the strain of heaving up a loaded tub, the look of Frank Graham's house across the field. The weather, even.

He straightened and stretched the kinks out of his back and looked eastward along the shore, at the dark slopes of spruce and fir, scarved with red and yellow. He had learned long since that nothing in nature could close the wound of loss, that familiar things, familiar beauty, could be a shame and a reproach. But the shore today, the simple look of it, was part of what he felt.

They were loading the cart for the last time when he caught the faint sound of a distant tuneless whistling and looked around. Dan Graham had climbed the line fence and was crossing the field toward them, looking oddly dressed up. He hadn't changed into overalls from the knickerbockers Mrs. Graham insisted on for school.

Grant picked an apple from the grass under an ancient tree at the corner of the patch and threw it hard. Dan plucked it out of the air and bit into it and crossed the dug-up ground, chewing. There was something about Dan . . . small for his age and cocky and talkative. Grant's mind ran briefly on the Grahams. Young Bill was gone, a part of that previous existence . . . But Frank and Dan . . . There was nothing in their manner, except perhaps a pointed friendliness, to suggest that anything he had done or was doing was unusual. In a way this brought home the oddity, because it *was* unusual, and to ignore this was to emphasize the strangeness. But . . . no touch of fear, no test of poise . . . It was good to have the Grahams.

Dan stood for a little, crunching the apple, viewing the cleaned-out potato-patch judicially until he got round to what he had come to say. They were going back to the lake that night, he said, finally. Himself and his father and Hugh Currie and Stan and Alec Neill and Harry. There'd been a north wind all day, what there was of it. The trout should be biting. "Thought you fellahs might like—", Dan said. "You got any gear?"

Grant laughed, Dan's adult mannerisms rippling the surface of his mind.

Stewart said thoughtfully, "Pole in the shop loft, somewhere. Used to be, anyway. Hooks in the chest, I sh'ld think. You could rig a line with net twine . . ."

Grant laughed again. "All right. Maybe we will, Dan. See you up there, if we get around to it."

As they crossed the road behind the loaded cart he glanced back once to watch Dan climbing the fence into Grahams' field. Except for Frank and Dan, his contacts with people in these last three weeks had been deliberately sought out, a test' of fortitude, or faced in that spirit. It was strange and pleasant to look forward with no such purpose, no such bracing of the mind . . . forward to the evening . . .

The woods round Graham's lake stopped abruptly some twenty feet from the water's edge at the top of a low bank. From the foot of the bank to the water and on out until it fell away steeply into depth, the shore was a shallow rim of stones. No surf beat there: the stones were small, dark and angular, un-rubbed by the violence of water and unbleached by sun.

143

Along the western stretch of the lake's southern beach the water deepened sharply fairly close to shore. Here earlier Curries and Grahams and Gordons had pulled together narrow stone standards, on each of which a man in rubber boots could get within casting distance of trout-water. Each fall in early digging-time, and the weather fine, men and boys would come at nightfall with shaven fir poles, twine lines rigged with hooks and whittled net-cork floats . . .

Grant found the Curries and Grahams and the Neills already on the beach when he emerged from Gordons' hauling-road. He walked up the stony strip toward them. Alec was still rigging his line; the others stood half-way to their knees in water on the standards, motionless and silent, peering out at their bits of cork on dark water. Now and then one would lift his pole, let the hook swing in to a waiting hand, examine his bait and whip the line out again. An air of wind still blew from the north, setting up the smallest suspicion of a lop at the water's edge, drifting the corks gradually shoreward. Grey froth stirred in the slight land-wash, the dried foam of yesterday's wind.

Alec Neill said, low-toned, as he baited a hook, "Hello, Grant . . . You got here . . . Where's Stewart?"

Grant said, "Decided he'd stay home . . . I'm wearing his rubber boots . . ."

Alec grunted. "Well, he's not missing much. Nobody's got a bite yet."

They waded out on adjoining standards, Grant thinking idly that there would be no point in explaining to Alec that Stewart was deep in *Nicholas Nickleby*. The fact that Stewart was taking to reading again in idle moments, that he no longer followed Grant with his eyes when some small circumstance called them apart, was a thing for private satisfaction, a step forward in the task he had set himself. It was not a matter for talk.

The last of the wind died. The lake lay smooth and dark in a kind of fluent stillness, circled by darker woods ragged against a scarcely lighter sky, where slow cloud blurred out the risen moon. It was good to stand in rubber boots on piled stones in the falling dark, straining to see a floating cork on shadowed water; with other men, on other jetties of stone, and water chill round booted ankles . . .

Far out beyond the corks scarcely discernible circles began to appear. A trout leaped clear of the water and splashed back.

Frank Graham grunted. "Flies. They won't go for worms when they're jumpin'." Almost at once he whipped back his rod. There

144

was a sound of tearing leaves in the alders on the bank above the beach, the small thumping on stones and moss of a landed trout, the flash of its belly . . .

Now it was Alec Neill's rod springing back, a commotion as Alec splashed ashore, and good-natured cursing: "A damn eel! Hold still, you slippery bastard; if you swallah me hook—!"

Frank Graham said "Sh-h" and made a small sound of disapproval and then laughed. Somehow when Alec Neill swore it wasn't swearing.

Here in the chill of an October night, in this renewal of an old pursuit, Grant came close to living in the moment. Felt the cold, heard and felt the slap of water, sensed companionship. Memories of other nights like this, and the warmth of kitchens afterward, merged with this, were part of it. But regard for the past and concern for the future were very faint, low-lying at the mind's horizon.

The tiny circular ripple of his cork going down wakened him from the stillness of this endless moment within the present. Instinctively he whipped the trout out of the water and through the air, stumbled ashore to unhook and string the small threshing body on an alder-fork. As he turned to bait up and wade out again, Stan Currie's rod arched and swung . . .

The night grew dark and lightened. The rim of clouds drifted to show an edge of moon; a loon laughed. And all at once the time was over.

They stowed their rods among the stumps of trees along the bank, compared fish, began to pick their way single file up Grahams' hauling-road. There was scant opportunity for talk as they felt their way through the woods, but once they had reached cleared land at the top of the rise, it began. Talk of digging, ploughing, threshing, and of the men and boys engaged in these pursuits.

The darkness here was a silver light, deep as the sky, the Channel luminous, the stubble barred with black shadows. They made a little knot of men and boys for a few minutes by Frank Graham's gate, saying almost nothing, reluctant to go indoors.

Eventually Hugh Currie said, "Well—Alec?" He turned homeward with Stan.

Alec Neill said, "No, I'm out've chewin', Hugh. I got to go down and see if my credit's good with Felix . . . You go on home, Harry."

He fell into step beside Grant as Frank and Dan went into the house.

In an atmosphere faintly altered by absence of others, he said, "How's old Stewart anyway? Better?"

Grant said he thought so. He thought Stewart was coming along all right.

Alec said, "Sure. He's all right. He'll be all right. But they need somebody there. Him and Josie, both. It's a good thing, you stickin' around . . ."

Grant was startled. This was close to putting into words what must remain unsaid. Anyone but Alec Neill . . .

But Alec left it at that. When he spoke again it was about the work around the place. Stewart had never been much of a farmer, Alec said. No system. He asked casually, "What d'you think you'll do with that strip by the woods? You ploughed up quite a piece there. That field ain't been broke up for years."

Grant's mind halted. The ploughed strip . . . He hadn't even thought of what they would put into it. All he had been thinking about was the occupation the ploughing afforded.

He said, "Oats. Oats, I s'pose. With a grass-seed and clover mix."

They had reached Gordons' gate. He could see Stewart sitting by the lighted window, bent over the table, reading.

He said, "Good night, Alec," and went in.

There was something in this, some small thing Alec had said . . . Like a light coming on in a room far-off, revealing against the lamp the shade of hoped-for things.

He could not tell at once why this was so. The faint pleasant puzzlement lived in the back of his mind as he crossed the doorstep and put his three trout in the wash basin and carried them into the kitchen to show Stewart and Josie.

He went out to sit on the back steps then and cleaned the fish, and when this was done came into the porch and pumped cold water into the basin. After he had washed his hands he stood for a little in the open back door, letting his sight run over the moonlit fields and woods, hearing the soft grumbling murmur of the Channel. Josie, behind him, was closing the damper of the stove, preparing to follow Stewart to bed. Grant turned, shut the door and hooked it and said to her, "This kind of a night—it's nice enough, you could soak in it."

Josie turned away and closed the book Stewart had left open on the table and placed it on the window-sill. She took a small lamp from the lamp shelf over the table and lit it and blew out the larger one Stewart had been reading by. Her voice was expressionless as she said, "Good night," and turned and went down the hall toward the bedroom.

Grant stood by the table for a moment, the faint vague pleasure ebbing from his mind. Josie . . . never a light word, a friendly glance, a smile . . . He shook his head and picked up the lamp and went into the hall and carefully upstairs.

He was touched again by the thing he could almost forget at times: the tight-rope feeling; and with this a small unreasoning anger. He shook this away. There was nothing in the deal he had made with Josie that implied warmth, that said she had to like it . . .

The thought drifted from him as he undressed and got into bed. His mind calmed. As he lay at the edge of sleep the things he had to do marshalled themselves before him. Drains to dig . . . firewood to cut . . . more land to plough . . .

The faint indefinable pleasure he had felt at Alec Neill's words flowed back . . . and now he saw what it was. *What d'you think you'll do with that strip by the woods?* That wasn't the kind of question . . . That wasn't the sort of thing you asked a man, if you were doubtful. You didn't ask what he planned to plant or sow unless you took it for granted . . . Unless you knew, without thinking, he'd be here to do it . . .

Meetings on the road and contacts at Katen's had hardened his sensitivity, shown him that he fitted into the pattern of day to day, the present. This was something that went a little beyond that, a further step.

His spark of thought leaped a gap in the moving mind. Without knowing how he had got there, he found himself thinking of The Place, letting himself think of it. Feeling not shame and revulsion but interest and anticipation, anticipation and doubt; and finally, something like resolution. James. No sense putting it off. He would have to talk to James.

18

GRANT stood by the gate and watched the buggy disappear round the turn; Sunday morning, and Stewart and Josie off to Mass. He waited for a little, his hands on the gate-pickets, his mind almost empty of thought, consciously idle, concerned with surface things—clouds banked behind the Islands, wind flattening the smoke from Grahams' chimney, hardened mud ruts in the road—but knowing that in a moment it must return to a harder reality, the past and present and the future, the immediate thing he had to do.

He flexed his shoulders finally and made an impatient movement and turned toward the house. In the porch he threw off his mackinaw, pumped water into the basin and washed face and hands and neck. Upstairs, he drew the flowered curtain back from the alcove in his room, took down the blue suit, and began to change his clothes.

Church . . . This was a harder thing than any he had yet attempted. To appear among the gathered men and women of James Marshall's generation . . . But the need to see James had been growing in him since Thursday night, the night at the lake. And the way to see him, first, was casually and in public. This was, in a way, the last thing left unfaced.

He wedged a collar-button into the neckband of his shirt and affixed the collar, thinking momentarily with a twinge of affectionate regret about Aunt Jane. She had been careful to include the one white shirt he owned and two starched collars in the suitcase of clothes Fred had brought down the morning of the funeral . . .

He frowned as he worked his arms into the shirt, dissatisfied at a memory, ashamed of it; and irked at himself for feeling this way, for caring, now, about the way in which he had confirmed to James the decision voiced in Gordons' hallway . . . A brief written note, given to Dan Graham to mail at McKees'. Childish to do that, to write, formally, through the post office. He shook his head. What else could he have done? Once the word was said any deliberate attempt to explain had become impossible . . .

He uttered a wordless sound of exasperation as he hunched into the tight serge coat. You made a clean swift decision that freed you from doubt and fear, lifted you out of anger and remorse; in one clear moment you saw the answer, saw it all . . . And then, you learned that decision in itself was not enough; that whatever new plane your life was lived on, there were still people you must meet and talk to, relationships you had to make, customs you had to follow. And an inner something, almost as persistent as the hard resolution that shaped your days, that checked you, kept you questioning your acts . . . Was there, he wondered, anyone in the world who could step free, not caring . . .? He thought suddenly of Anse Gordon.

The thought of Anse startled him. For no conscious reason, then, his mind began to run tranquilly. If he could have cut clear, gone away, he thought, none of these problems would live to plague him. Only the other, the endless guilt . . . He saw now almost as a new thing that he had never thought of departure, had seen no answer anywhere but on the Channel Shore.

Well, that was that. And now there was something to be said. Life to be lived. Meetings with people in ones and twos and at Katen's had given him a sense of precarious ease. The evening at the lake and Alec Neill's words had carried him beyond that to the sense of having reached a definite objective from which the view was longer, the steps of life from season to season instead of from day to day. Well, some sort of relationship with James must be established. You couldn't live in a place . . .

He had realized this from the first. Now he could afford to think about it; almost look forward to it, to getting it done.

He went downstairs slowly and crossed the road and walked up the verge of grass toward Grahams'. He could hear Dan's voice in the barn: "Get over there!" and the clink of harness.

He went into the house in the usual way by the kitchen door and heard Mrs. Graham making her regular Sunday morning effort: "You'll be coming up with us this morning, won't you, Frank?"

And Frank's voice: "Well . . . look, now, Stell. If I go up in the buggy it'll just mean Ede'll have to walk—"

Frank was lying on the lounge in the dining-room in vest and trousers and socks. He looked up and saw Grant grinning in the doorway between dining-room and kitchen and swung his feet to the floor and sat up.

149

"Well—I s'pose I could walk, if I had to. You goin' up, Grant?"

"I was thinking about it," Grant said.

As he passed the Marshall place with Frank and Dan, Grant had an absurd apprehension. He glanced down the slope from the road and saw that the three ash trees were there, their leaves turning slightly in the wind. He had had a reasonless feeling that one of those trees might have been chopped down . . .

At the cross-roads they caught sight of Fred and Will ahead of them. Fred looked back and saw them and waited, and they walked together in a group, up past the school-house, edging over to the shoulders of the road now and then to let a buggy pass. One of these was driven by James, with Jane on the seat beside him. He lifted his whip in greeting, going by at a jog.

All the way up the hill to the church Grant was conscious of that buggy slowly climbing ahead of them, hardly faster than they walked. When they reached the church James was hitching Polo to the fence of the surrounding yard. They passed him and went through the gate and up the narrow gravel path toward the building. It was not quite time for service to begin. The women had gone inside and Grant could hear Ida Freeman coaxing lugubrious parts of tunes out of the organ, but a knot of men and boys stood around the open door. Sam Freeman, Clem Wilmot and his brother Lee, Alfred Laird . . . In a moment he would be one of that group, and so would James.

James crossed the grass outside the fence and came up the path behind them. He nodded to the Wilmots and Sam Freeman and Alf Laird, said, "Good morning, Frank," and, precisely casual, "Well, Grant."

Grant said, "Good morning, sir."

Politeness. Indifferent recognition, neither warm nor cold.

Whatever passion of sorrow or anger lay behind the even glance of James's eyes, or hardened the face masked by that careful beard, there was no open hint of it. For a moment, meeting that glance, Grant had been shaken by fear, regret, all the old sensitivities he had tried to banish from his flesh. The moment ebbed away and left him poised and quiet.

He would not have cared too deeply if James had glanced at him without words, as if he did not exist. Not too deeply. In some ways there would have been relief in that. But this was best, this outward indifference and cool recognition and surface calm. Let them look at that and make what they liked of it.

150

He knew enough not to try to talk business on a Sunday. When the service ended, in the bustle around the door as the congregation shook hands with the minister and gathered outside to linger and gossip and depart, he moved to James's side on the steps. He said, "Uncle James—some time it's convenient . . ."

James said, "Come to the house tomorrow night."

Tomorrow night.

He entered the house through the back door. Jane was alone in the kitchen, mending a dress in the lamplight at the table. The room was overly warm from a fire in the range and he caught the fresh smell of molasses cookies. Oddly, at this moment he realized that he now knew what the smell of Josie Gordon's kitchen was. A dried-soap smell, the smell of a woman's house dress.

Jane smiled at him and he noted that at a time like this when you might expect fussiness, she was quiet and self-possessed. She said on a note of chiding friendliness, "Well, Grant . . . It's about time . . . Your Uncle James is in The Room."

A cheerful fire was going in the Franklin. James lowered his paper to his knees. Grant saw that as usual he had changed from working-clothes to a suit for the evening. He said, "Sit down. Sit down, Grant," and raised the paper again and appeared to read it for a moment before he put it aside on the table by his chair.

How to begin . . . There was no point now in explanation. All that was done with. Let it go. James would want no explanation. Whatever conviction and condemnation already lay fixed in James's mind were not to be changed by words.

Grant said, "Well, sir, I was thinking about The Place." In spite of his resolution his voice was hesitant, full of doubt and deference. "I'd like to—like to make some kind of arrangement. Like to buy it, if—"

James said nothing for a minute. In this small period of silence a curious insight came to Grant. It was almost as if he were inside James's mind. And what he felt was this: that James would never be able to think directly of a certain moment in Stewart Gordon's house without a surge of hate. But hatred of what? Circumstance, perhaps. Grant could not feel hatred for himself in James. What James felt for him now, he thought, was a kind of sad revulsion.

He heard James's word, matter-of-fact and half-thoughtful, "Something could be arranged, I suppose."

151

James had been on the point of asking, "Do you plan to stay here, then? On the Shore?" He caught the question back. He could not afford the indignity of curiosity.

He thought: I could stop this boy. I could refuse the thing he wants. Refuse to see or speak to him. There would be a hard satisfaction in that. Not revenge. Revenge was beneath the dignity of one who . . . Revenge was unrighteous. Not revenge, but the application of a stern and sudden justice. He had a disturbing thought that perhaps there was an obligation on him to apply that justice. He rejected this. Mercy. There was such a thing as mercy. His mind began immediately to question this rejection, as he had questioned it in all the bitter endless wrangling that had gone on in the dark of his thought for days. If he cast out Grant completely, he would go down in the estimation of his neighbours, these people here at The Head. Not in their surface dealings with him, but in their hearts when they thought of him. Was he being swayed by this? Was he letting this determine his acts and colour his belief in what was right?

He shook it all away in a hard impatience, angry at all of it, angry at Harvey Marshall across the years, angry at himself, angry at this boy with Harvey's face, with nameless blood in Marshall veins, who sat there opposite him across the flickering fire.

He said evenly, "The place cost five hundred dollars—back in nineteen-eleven." He meditated a little. "The wood itself should be worth close to that now. If you want it at that price, I can deed it over. You can give me a note if you're pressed."

Opposite the hauling-road into The Place, Grant met Joe McKee going home from Katen's. They lingered a little, talking in the dark. He recalled that Joe had finished grade eight and dropped out of school this fall. Before they parted, Grant said: "Joe, I s'pose there's a good deal to do around home. But . . . Well, if you've got any time to spare, maybe a little later we could get together. I could use a man with an axe, now and then."

When Joe had gone on up the road, he went down the hauling-road into the clearing for the first time in many weeks. In the dark there was nothing he could see, but he could visualize the stumps, the piled logs, the brush; and the way it would look as the clearing widened. He stayed only a little while, getting the feel of it.

19

On a mild morning in late October Grant stood by the shop door, for the moment idle. The last of the roots were in, the turnips and the garden stuff. He had fashioned and hung a new outside cellar door and located and patched a persistent leak in the porch roof. The drains were working, the cellar dry. For a little there was time.

Behind him in the shop Stewart busied himself with twine and net-needle. Grant glanced at his face and his moving hands and away again, with something catching in his throat. For days, weeks, the attachment had been growing.

He thought again with a sense of thankfulness of Stewart's peculiar insulation from the effects of this bitter year.

Once, as they walked the hauling-road back to the lake, looking over the spruce and fir that still stood there, and which they would get at later for winter firewood, the old man had said, conversationally: "We cut quite a bit of stuff in here from time to time, Anse and me." The oddity was not in the words but in the tone. As if time and the companion he spoke of were half a lifetime away.

This curious illusion of time drawn out was there also in his manner toward Grant. It was as if Grant had been around the house and the woods and the fields for years. Stewart had never questioned his presence, never taken thought, for all anyone could tell, except perhaps in those early moments of shaken puzzlement, of the strange circumstance that Grant Marshall should be sleeping upstairs in the Gordon house, doing the barn work, chopping the wood.

He took an almost childlike satisfaction in everything they did together. As he watched him now, Grant was startled by a thought that seemed to sum the image of this present Stewart: for the first time in life he was enjoying the help and friendship of a younger man, living in his house. A son.

But Josie . . . Grant put that thought away. Thinking about it got you nowhere. It was something time would have to solve, and there were other things that claimed his attention now. For the dream was back. A dream austere and realistic. He was not thinking now of a house like James Marshall's and a high-shouldered barn, but of a single storey, three rooms perhaps, and for the time being no barn at all. A place for a man alone, a man who must be free within the limits of the Shore to move where the business of making a living called him. To Morgan's Harbour to work at loading the pulpwood steamers; to Forester's Pond if they started dredging there; to Rod Sinclair's mill, cleating box ends, when nothing else offered. Even beyond the Shore, perhaps, to the timber-cutting in the west end of the county, if a man could do that and still fulfil his duty here . . .

But at the moment there was no task that immediately pressed. He said meditatively, "May as well haul eel-grass this afternoon, I guess."

Stewart glanced at the sky and the Channel and nodded. "Yes. All right. It'll soon be time to bank . . ."

After noon Grant harnessed the mare to the manure cart and turned up the road. He walked beside the cart, the reins loose in his hand, glad for once to be alone. Feeling his body's strength and lightness. Glad to be on his feet instead of riding the jolting cart; but aware of the wheels jolting in the ruts, the faint smell of dried manure-dust, the brown shining of the mare's flank.

Only one thing troubled him. The thought he had put away returned, faintly nagging, and for a moment he let this occupy his mind. At dinner he had met again the cold reserve in Josie. He had made a remark about Dan Graham, laughed a little about Dan—he'd stopped complaining about being kept in school. The new teacher had them all working for her, Ede said . . .

From Josie there was no response.

Many times in the course of these last weeks he had tried to draw her into the casual circle that enclosed himself and Stewart, and at its outer edges, people like the Grahams. Comments on day-to-day incidents, facts, conditions, that were woven into the formless pattern of the Shore. Josie made the answers necessary to close the subject. She avoided open curtness, but that was all.

Again he told himself he had no reason to expect more than that. There was nothing in the agreement he had won from Josie, the day after Anna's death, to lead him to expect the warmth of friendliness. His mind went back to it . . .

He had been on the watch for a chance to speak, from the moment he had faced the clock in Josie's kitchen that bleak

154

morning and known what he had to do. But in the end the opportunity had come by accident. He had been filling up the kitchen wood-box, carrying in armloads of split softwood while Frank Graham looked after Stewart in the shop and Stella Graham and Mame McDonald and Josie made whatever arrangements they had to make in the room where Anna lay. He had turned from piling wood in the box, quietly so as not to make a disturbance, and found Josie standing in the kitchen, watching him.

She said, as if the words were drawn from her grudgingly by some instinct of courtesy, "It's been good of you—"

Earlier he would have been embarrassed but by then his resolution had given him a sense of presence, a kind of poise.

He had said, "No, it's the least—," and then, carefully, "I've been thinking about a lot of things. Thinking about Mr. Gordon. There ought to be someone . . . If you wouldn't mind—I'd like to stay here a while. Give him a hand, a few weeks perhaps. Or somewhere handy. At Grahams', if—"

She had said, after a pause, "Your people—," and gone on to try to find the words to explain the impossibility of the thing he planned.

He had shaken his head. "No. That doesn't come into it. It's time . . . Well, I'm getting—I'm on my own now, anyway. That doesn't come into it."

She had said, finally, "Well—," and made a movement of the shoulders. When he returned to the kitchen with another load of wood she was gone.

There had been nothing in that, and nothing in the wordless way in which she had directed him to an upstairs room when the night watch was over, to lead him to expect anything more than the bare tolerance he found in her now. And yet he felt a disappointment that no warmth was there. It was not merely that this was withheld from himself. There was no warmth now for anyone.

There was something in it and beyond it which he did not fully understand. The fact of grief. That was understandable. Now and then he had surprised on Josie's face a look of lost and utter desolation. That was understandable. Anna . . . The dream of Anna. But . . .

He knew something of that. He could share that. The room they had put him in was Anna's. Someone had cleared away all evidence of her one-time presence. Closets and bureau drawers were empty. There were only hooked mats and a home-made wooden bedstead to show that this room had ever been inhabited.

He knew it had been Anna's from the fact that the only other upstairs room which was finished and papered had been occupied by Anse. The gunner's uniform and other odds and ends still hung in the closet.

Once in settling away the few shirts he owned he had noticed a faint ridge under the yellowing newspaper pages with which the bottom of the drawer was covered. He turned the paper up, idly, and faced his own handwriting. An envelope, the envelope in which he had enclosed his last letter to Anna from the transit camp in England. The letter itself was gone.

The thing that he had resolutely accepted and thrust into the background of his mind had caught him by the throat then and held him stricken . . . Dead . . . No longer a face, a voice, a dream in the past and a golden urgency in the future . . .

There had been other moments like this. There still were. There still would be. It was the same thing, he supposed, that drew that look out of Josie Gordon's heart and carved it on her face. And yet . . . people who had known sorrow—they accepted it. They might feel that never again could they know joy—and yet they achieved somehow a pleasantness; they let the little companionships, the quiet jokes, come into the habits of day to day.

The moments of visible grief he could understand, but not the continuing iron calm.

He shrugged this out of his mind again as he turned the mare down Currie's road. The weather would harden soon, and he could then get to work in the woods. In Gordons' woods between the fields and the lake first, for fire-wood and fence rails. Then, The Place. Long straight butts for lumber, tops for pulpwood and box-logs.

He would mark out soon the place where he would build, and in the spring . . . Some of the stumps were too tough for a hand-puller or even a horse. Simpler and faster with dynamite. Sam Freeman knew about dynamite. He would get Sam down.

He moved up to walk beside the cart, down through Rob's yard and round the inlet shore, hardly conscious of the familiar landscape he was passing. He slapped the mare's rump with looped reins to urge her over the hump of Currie's beach. There, on the southwesterly slope of the Head, the eel-grass lay in tide-rows, thrown up by the wash of seas, grey-brown and dry on the surface of its ragged folds, green-black and heavy to the fork beneath.

For generations men along the Shore had come to this beach in the fall of the year to harvest eel-grass, pile it in door-yards, pack it into low plank-walled tunnels round the foundations of their houses as winter approached.

He had filled the box of the cart and was heaping it with the heavy dark grass when he heard a sound from one of the huts. Richard McKee had closed and padlocked his hut door and was walking slowly down the beach toward him, rubber boots crunching in the stones.

Must have been straightening away something left undone last summer, Grant thought. Fishing at Currie Head had ceased months ago. He thrust his fork into the cartload of wet eel-grass and brushed his hands and turned to speak to Richard.

Richard said, "Bankin' . . . How's Stewart?"

Grant said, "Oh, he's fine, Mr. McKee. Fine." On a faintly mischievous impulse he added, "He's knitting a hen coop."

Richard raised his head and said mildly, "He's what?"

Grant said, "Knitting a hen coop. Josie complained. The old coop was—Well, we'd no laths or poles. Wire either. Mr. Gordon made himself a mesh-board, smaller than the one he uses for the nets. We got some twine, coarse stuff, and he went to work on it."

A slow grin flickered over Richard's face. He said with a kind of wondering sigh, "Knittin' a hen coop," and then, curiously, "That your idea, Grant? . . . Or Stewart's?"

Grant grinned, "Well—"

Richard threw back his head in a short gust of laughter. It came to Grant that he had rarely heard Richard McKee laugh, had seldom shared words with him at all, for that matter.

Before his time in the army it had been usual to see quite a lot of Mr. McKee in haying time, and when he called for the mail, or at church. But not to talk to. He had always felt a warmth, an instinctive liking, but the reticence in them both had come between. And always when they had worked together at haying, there was James in the background, dignified and humourless.

It was strange to find laughter in Richard, particularly now. Grant thought: this was the pleasantness, the acceptance of small laughters, despite grief and the memory of grief, that he could not find in Josie . . .

Richard had lapsed into silence, resting an elbow along a wheel of the cart. He said, "A hen coop . . ." He seemed to wander in thought for a moment and then said, meditatively, "Harve . . ." He

157

shook his head slightly. "That kind of a thing—some way . . . it reminds me of Harve . . ."

Grant glanced at him and waited and said, "Harve . . ."

Richard came back out of his thought. "What? Oh—your father. He was a great one for . . . You never knew what to expect . . ."

Grant said carefully, "My father was—a friend of yours, was he, Mr. McKee?"

Richard glanced at him a little quizzically. He answered slowly. "Friend?" He seemed to be turning the word over in his mind, like an unfamiliar thing. "Harve used to come over to the house to bunk with me, when old Henry'd—when your Grandfather'd let him . . ."

He paused, searching in thought for some memory, some incident, that fitted the meditative mention of Harvey Marshall that had come to his lips in the presence of Harvey's son.

"We had mushrat traps out back of the lake, one fall. Mr. William Freeman—before your time; you wouldn't remember him; Sam's grandfather—old Mr. Freeman used to trap too. A mean man, kind of. He'd spring our traps with sticks if we set too close to him—that kind've thing. So Harve—" Richard stopped to examine the memory—"So we took a dozen or so salt herrin' out with us one mornin'. We sprung old Mr. William's traps and left herrin' in the jaws and got down in the bushes to watch. It was comin' on light when he got to the line . . ."

Richard shook his head, "Mister man! . . . We couldn't keep still. Harve had to laugh. Couldn't help it. Couldn't stop. Not even when he took after us, him with a shotgun . . . All Harve could do was run, and fall down, and whoop with laughin' and get up and run . . ."

He fell silent, and after a moment began again to speak.

"I remember one time . . . Do the kids still nest apples? I s'pose they do."

Grant said, "Sure, I guess so. *We* did."

Richard nodded. "They taste all right when you've left 'em wrapped in grass . . . Henry Marshall had trees, along the back slope of his upper field. They wasn't supposed to be picked, but Harve and me—we'd sneak a few, now and then." He made a small laughing sound. "James couldn't make up his mind. To tell on us or not. Never did, though . . . We had nests half a dozen places along the road to school, and through the back pasture. Half the time we'd take the long way, through the woods. S'posed to be a short cut . . .

158

"Now and then we'd get to work eatin' apples behind a slate, in school. Till Macnab caught up to us. Maybe you wouldn't know about Macnab, last man teacher they had around here. Here for years. Here when I was born. There was a clump of alder out behind the school-house. When Macnab tanned anybody he'd send him out to cut his own switches. Half a dozen or so. Macnab'd swish them up and down and make a show of it, and pick out a good limber one and lay it into you. Cross the legs, if it was early fall or spring and you was barefooted . . . He sent Harve out to cut the switches for him and me." Richard halted, remembering, and laughed. "What Harve did—there was a dead corner in that bunch've alders. Harve brought back a bundle've switches and laid 'em down on Macnab's desk. Macnab gets up and picks one and makes a swipe in the air. Breaks off in his hand, 'v course. He picks up another one and slaps the desk with it. Breaks into three or four pieces.

"Harve's standin' there, all the time, waitin'. Interested and all surprised, y'know. Sort of polite and regretful. By this time the whole school's begun to snigger . . ."

Richard meditated. "We must've got it proper, then, I s'pose. With the pointer, likely. But I don't remember. All I remember's the look of Macnab, and the look of Harve . . ."

They talked briefly of other things. Grant said he hoped it was all right, his speaking to Joe about cutting in The Place, if he ever got around to it and Richard could spare Joe.

Sure, that was all right, Richard said. Eva'd wanted the kid to stay in school, but he wasn't cut out for it. He'd be glad to have Joe chop with Grant. After a little he said almost abruptly, "Well, I mustn't keep—," and walked off to his row-boat on the inlet side of the beach.

Grant walked home behind the jolting cart with a light pulsing elation singing in his flesh. His thoughts were careless, a drifting web of simple things . . .

Alders. He laughed in his mind. There were alders still, out back of the school-house.

You couldn't nail this feeling down to any sense of logic. One laughing glimpse or two across the darkness of a generation. But this was enough.

He did not really think of it, but he could see, hear, feel, the colour and light. The talk, the laughter and the anger. The work, the sweat, and the wind cooling the sweat. Burning hayfields

159

and spring freshets, the snow and the frost. The whole moving dream of the Shore, a generation gone.

And in this at last he saw the face and heard the laughter of Harvey Marshall. Harvey, a Marshall, touched by the thing that pulsed in the Grahams, the Curries, the Neills, the McKees. The thing that was not exactly warmth, not sentiment, not . . . The thing that was alive, that was not cold doctrine or property or measured pride, but simple feeling. Life and death and achievement and failure. Laughter-wrinkles in a man's face, and the taste of tears. He was not thinking consciously of all this as it touched himself. This was not thought, but feeling . . . From this day on he would know without thinking that all he did, and all he dreamed of, were woven into that.

20

By THE third week in November Grant was at work along the fringes of the clearing in The Place, with Stewart and Joe McKee. It was early for work in the woods but he could not be fully satisfied with small tasks about the farm buildings and he did not feel ready yet to look for work in Copeland or The Bridge or The Harbour which would keep him away between Sundays from those daily tasks and from Stewart.

Through the early part of the month they had cut fire-wood as the weather permitted. The swamps back of Graham's Lake were still soft in spots, pooled with standing water from intermittent fall rains, but the rising land between the house and the lake was dry. A good deal of spruce and fir stood there. In the upper reaches of The Place, also, streaks of hardwood grew. There they had chopped birch and maple to lend staying quality to winter fires, and piled the cut wood beside old hauling-roads to be sledded out on snow.

After ten days of this Grant had switched to his clearing south of the road and enlisted Joe.

This was heavy stuff they worked in now, close-grained spruce and ancient hardwood that required back-breaking labour with the cross-cut. He was careful to include Stewart in all they did. The old man's strength was up to swamping out roads and trimming and it was necessary that he have both the occupation and the companionship of work. But on the other end of a cross-cut Grant needed someone young and wiry like Joe.

He made a simple deal with Joe. For every day they worked together in The Place they would work together later in McKee's lower woods; Richard had told Joe he could cut pulpwood there. Joe, in the surge of eagerness to rush into manhood that went with his release from school, had a mind full of schemes for making money, of which that was one.

The odd thing about it, Grant saw, was that Joe's schemes were practical. Not mere dreams, but workable plans. Joe's

161

mind was fixed on getting away from Currie Head eventually, but he did not talk much about that. What filled his talk was the immediate future. He already had a job lined up at Sinclair's mill when Rod Sinclair should be ready to saw shooks. Next spring they would tackle the pulpwood, and in the summer . . . Well, there was a salmon berth vacant off Gordons'. Frank Graham had an old net he'd probably sell reasonable. If Joe could persuade Richard to let him buy it with the mill money, and help him mend it, and there was a good run of salmon . . .

Good plans. Plans compounded of small certainties and the eternal gambles of wind, weather, markets, the run of fish . . . the chances that added up to life on the Channel Shore.

Grant listened to Joe while they chopped and sawed in The Place, and found in listening a quiet continuing enjoyment. His own life, too, was a blend now of certainties and gambles. In years past it had been all certainty. Almost all. On James Marshall's place life came down as close to the rock of certainty as James could make it. The army, too, had been like that, unless you got into combat, and that was something he had missed. He had got used to certainty.

But now the moorings were cast off. He was afloat on the same sea as Joe. Joe and all the rest of them. It seemed to him now that this was what he must have been looking forward to, this tingling sense of life half plan and half chance, in the days when he had traced his dream of the future here in The Place. But—he had been dreaming in terms of certainty or something close to it. He had not seen the contradiction.

It was on the last day of the two weeks they worked in The Place, a Saturday, that Joe mentioned Hazel. The reference was incidental. Grant could not decide whether it was merely casual, made without thought, or made out of something like Eva's pride of face, or made as a kind of confidence, a pledge of trust . . .

He was to recall the remark days and weeks later, and years later. Years later, when all that remained of Joe McKee on the Channel Shore was memory. Memory, and an envelope now and then addressed to Richard and Eva in purple pencil, postmarked from northern Alberta. He would recall Joe's voice and wonder. But it didn't matter. Motives—you couldn't always pin them down. And it didn't matter.

Joe had been talking about his own scheme for getting out pulpwood. He said, "Look, Grant; why don't you go after the trustees to let you cut the wood for the school-house? There's a few dollars in it. And next year . . . Instead've foolin' around,

162

why don't you get stumpage on a lot of places? Put in a crew and go after pulpwood big? You could make a go of it . . ."

Grant laughed. "Maybe I will. Pulpwood . . . Would you give me a hand?"

Joe said, seriously, "Sure," and added, "If I'm still around here."

Grant said, "You're really set on leaving, are you, Joe?"

Joe said, a little self-consciously, as if this were something secret and privately important, something he hesitated to talk about, "Yeah. I'm goin' all right, some time. West. Next year or the year after. That's what I want a stake for. That's all a man can do around here—raise a stake to get somewheres else."

Grant laughed to himself. "Well, maybe you're right."

"Sure I'm right," Joe said. "I'd've tried to get them to let me go west on the harvest excursion this fall—you can get clear to Saskatchewan for fifteen dollars—I'd've tried to go this fall, if it hadn't been for Hazel . . ."

He stopped, not in embarrassment, but as if what he had already said carried the explanation far enough.

Grant said, "Yes. It'd be hard for your father and mother to get along alone."

Hazel . . . he had been on the point of asking how she was, how she was getting on. But he could find no words that would not sound like curiosity, probing, prodding.

The moment lingered in his mind. Hazel. The oddly matter-of-fact way in which Joe had mentioned her. *If it hadn't been for Hazel* . . . As if Grant would understand the rest of it. And the flash of sudden wonder: Hazel, a girl he had known from babyhood; a girl who long ago from the height of her year or two of greater age had taken his hand sometimes on the way home from school when he was six or seven. In a city now which he had never seen, among people he did not know. People she did not know. He felt his mind astir again with the thing he had begun to see months ago. Years ago, it seemed now, on the steps at Frank Graham's. The fatality in Stella Graham's voice: *what she can do—there's nothing—*

This feeling remained in his thought. A sharp regretful consciousness of the things people had to face, other people as well as himself and the Gordons. Next morning, as he walked to church with Dan Graham and Stan Currie, joined at the cross-roads by Joe McKee, and as he listened with half his attention to the sermon, and as he stood around the church afterward, he was nagged by a troubled absent-mindedness.

It was there when he got out of bed next morning and saw with the active part of his mind that the weather had hardened. A thread of strange sadness, woven into the fabric of private pain that lay there, far back of the day's concerns. And yet, separate . . .

He went out to do the barn work and returned to the house for breakfast. Stewart, after eating, went out after his habit to scan the sky. With frost had come a break in the steely greyness of late November. The morning dusk was lightening; cold sunlight struck thinly through the kitchen's east window and glanced along the crockery on the shelves of Josie's cupboard.

Grant finished his tea and rose and went to pick his cap and jacket from their nail near the window. He shrugged into the jacket, thinking that this morning he and Stewart had better fix up the hauling-road that led across Frank Graham's land from the fire-wood they had cut in the back reaches of The Place. One or two soft spots needed poles put down. He felt the early sun on his face and glanced across the room. Josie sat by the table, her face lighted by the single window in the south wall.

He had continued now and then to light for Josie small candles of conversation which might wake an answering spark in the grimness of her mood. He was careful in this. He dropped into light conversation only when some circumstance made the fact of speech natural and easy. Pressure could raise an awareness in them both, recognition of a barrier that must remain unrecognized if he were to continue doing what he had to do. Besides this, a small inward stubbornness had begun to grow. You couldn't go on forever being sunny to a blank wall. He could feel at times an impatience with Josie, an irritation that wryly amused him.

But he spoke now without any design at all, the thought feeling its way into words from the simple image in his mind.

He said, "You know, next spring—we might put a couple of new windows in, here." He glanced speculatively at the single windows in east and south walls. "Make it brighter."

His eyes ranged, seeing in imagination new frames set close to those already there so that two narrow windows would make in effect one wide one. Experiment. People didn't put in windows like that on the Channel Shore. It would look attractive, and give Josie a wonderfully sunny kitchen. He could feel the satisfaction in working with wood, cutting through the brown old boards, fitting new frames, re-shingling around them, painting.

Josie said nothing. Presently he became aware of her silence and turned his head to look at her, and realized that he had spoken out of the thought within him, without design. Her fingers lay idle in her lap. She sat erect, head slightly lifted and slightly turned to the window, and on her face the look withdrawn, hard, unnameable.

He was suddenly at a loss, feeling his forward-looking imaginings darken and drain away. He moved toward the door and stood at the opposite end of the table from Josie, not looking directly at her, and when he spoke it was out of his long impatience, though his words were soft.

"It's—I know how you must feel about Anna." He thought, *how I feel* . . . But that was something not to be said, not when you had lost the right . . . "But—well, she'd hate to see you . . . she'd hate . . . it's . . ."

He shook his head, feeling for a moment the relief of speech but no longer able to find the words for what he was trying to say. Vaguely sorry now that he had spoken at all, that the thought had broken through.

Josie's voice startled him. She spoke shortly, with a kind of anger. The words sprang like beads of blood in the track of a knife-graze: "Anna's dead. There's no shame—" She cut the sentence off abruptly and went on, the only expression in her voice a grudging exasperation, a thin contempt; an impatient astonishment that this should need saying, that anyone lived who could not guess: "There's a girl alive . . . a child, maybe . . . Don't talk about it . . ."

Grant stood where he was for a second, his hand on the latch, and then went out quickly to join Stewart. There was nothing he could say.

Hazel McKee . . . Josie Gordon . . .

Death among earthly things was final. In time there would come a placid acceptance, about Anna. Years from now Josie would reach the sort of peace that enclosed Stewart, mercifully carried in a space of days far down the healing road of Time.

Shame was another thing. To Josie, shame was another thing. This now he understood. A time would come when the sound of Anna's name would be a small and distant bell, a sweet faint ringing in the mind. But what of Hazel McKee?

There was more in this than a revelation of Josie. He had been thinking of Richard and Hazel as people caught in the snare of a hard disgrace. The thought of them as people, known

165

and liked, was an ache in the heart. But the nature of the disgrace . . . he had seen it as something on the screen of a motion picture, in the plot of a story. Now the heart of it was clear, a thing of flesh and blood, as much a part of life as the people who faced it: *There's a girl alive . . . a girl alive . . . a child . . .*

21

AFTERWARD, when the detail of things planned and done that fall and winter was blurred by time, and other memories, and crowding labour, Grant could never recall exactly when it was that the final resolution formed itself. Nor was he conscious of a definite motive.

The earlier decision to free himself of the ties of blood and to translate this freedom into service to the father and mother of Anna Gordon had been clear and sharp. He could say where the sun stood in the sky when Bill Graham crossed the turnip rows with the word of Anna's death. He would always remember the face of the clock in Gordons' kitchen as he touched a match to fire. Clumsily, he could have put reasons for those decisions into words.

But years later when he came to talk of it all, once, to Renie Fraser, he could not say when it was that this further decision became the shape of something he must do. Or why, exactly. Many things came into it. Things seen and heard and felt over many days. The face and voice of Richard McKee when he spoke of Harvey Marshall, and of Hazel. The face and voice of Josie Gordon. The look and manner of young Joe. The memory of a hand in his on the road from school. The memory of words heard through a kitchen window. The imagined voice of the Channel Shore . . .

The thing that happened in his mind was like the discovery at last of meaning in a sequence of events imperfectly understood. And the development of understanding was such, that, looking back, he seemed always to have known.

But he did not feel the urgency until he was embarked upon it, and his motive lay submerged in feeling, deeper even than the feeling that had freed his heart from James. He was never sure even after he had talked to Renie that he had snared the truth in words.

The only certainty in his mind in the days following Josie's revelation of her heart was the need to see Richard McKee. That, and a current of inner excitement, like the thing he had felt as he faced the clock in Gordons' kitchen. But far less well defined, and purged, or almost purged, of grief and the dregs of anger.

There were things he had to know that only Richard could tell him.

He had walked up to McKees' for the mail several times since his meeting with Richard on the beach; with Dan and once or twice with Joe while Joe was working in The Place. He had sensed in Richard a private welcome. But always there had been others there. Eva, silently dispensing papers, breaking her silence now and then with a little rush of talk, remembering her pride and the front she must put up. People from up the school-house road, or Alec Neill. Or Fred or Will. Now and then Aunt Jane.

He wanted to see Richard alone, to share again in the companionship sensed on the beach. And he wanted to ask a question.

In the afternoon of the last day in November he left Stewart splitting wood in the door-yard and went up to McKees' alone.

A raw day. The road's muddy shoulders were hardened, the ruts and gutters skimmed with ice. Light snow fell thinly and he noted this with satisfaction. A decent snowfall, and he could get going, get the fire-wood to the door-yard and logs to the mill. He felt an urge to have this done, to get this place of Gordons' set for the siege of winter, and the stuff for his own house ready for the saw. The logs for the house lumber could wait, for that matter. But he had to have snow. He glanced up at the sky, muffled in a high dark sea of grey, and saw the snow was there.

There were sounds from the shop—the dull thump of a wooden mallet on iron. Richard was splitting out staves. He glanced up as Grant came into the little building and again he saw the nameless welcome. A pot-bellied iron stove stood in the middle of the shop. Richard had a fire going. He put the froe and mallet down, waved a hand in the direction of the heat, moved toward the stove and squatted on his chopping-block. Grant perched on the shaving-horse and stated his errand. He had come to borrow Richard's brace and a quarter-inch bit, he said; and felt suddenly foolish. He had thought himself fairly smart, planning ahead the exact size of the bit he would ask for.

168

Now he realized that he could have borrowed the tools nearer home, at Grahams', Curries', Neills' . . . and he hadn't even figured out a reason for needing them . . .

Richard merely nodded sideways at the array of tools hanging over the work-bench. "Anything you want." He spread his hands to the stove. "Everything all right?"

They fell to talking as men will whose days are not fixed to schedule but filled with work that has to be done, making of blended talk and silence a pleasant link between the periods of labour. Grant looked around him curiously. Richard's stave-junks were piled in a corner of the shop. His eye noted the truss-hoops on pegs, the implements of cooperage on the bench: draw-knife, crumbing-knife, compass for marking out barrel-heads.

He said, "Uncle James used to set up barrels, but he gave it up a while ago. I never could get the knack."

Richard gave a small chuckle. "Joe can't, either. But don't let on."

Grant echoed the laugh. "Joe don't have to worry. He'll get along all right. Anywhere."

Richard said, "He's all right."

Grant said, "Pity there's not more—" and hesitated, made a small movement with his hand. It was a pity there wasn't something to hold people like young Joe on the Shore. But that was the sort of thing you expected to hear, like a kind of ritual, from older men, not from Grant Marshall.

Richard said indifferently, "Yes. It's a pity . . . How're you comin' on with The Place?"

Hadn't done much lately, Grant said. He'd been working at the wood. If enough snow fell to make hauling he might get it to the house and then get out and look for a job some place else for a while. For a couple of months or so. If Stewart was all right to leave alone. Something better than chopping box-logs. He'd been thinking of making a trip to Boston, or maybe Upper Canada—Montreal or Toronto. Boston wasn't so good any more. The Americans, their immigration people, were getting fussy at the border.

Richard nodded. "You're not thinkin've pullin' out for good, though?"

No, Grant said. No. He couldn't do that, and didn't want to. Just something to put in time. A while away.

He turned to Richard with a small show of casual interest, as if thinking of that, the world outside, had brought something to his mind.

"Hazel . . . It's Toronto where she is, isn't it? She getting along all right, Mr. McKee?"

The question was a matter of form. Anyone who left the Channel Shore would be getting along all right—in the conversation of their relatives back home.

He felt cold as he asked the question, and suddenly a hypocrite. He knew Hazel's story and Richard knew he knew it. Yet—this indirection, this way of saying things, was necessary—if you had to say them at all . . .

Richard said, "Yes . . . Oh, all right, I guess." He spoke almost indifferently. Too indifferently, perhaps. Grant had a feeling that Richard recognized his distaste for hypocrisy and the impossibility of asking after Hazel in any terms but these. And yet, was not displeased that Grant *had* asked after her.

Richard went on meditatively, "Dress-makin'. She don't say much. Says she's all right. But I don't know . . ." He hesitated, frowning a little. "She wasn't—I didn't think she was any too well when she left. Still, we'd hear, I guess."

He paused, but Grant felt he had not quite finished what he had to say. After a little he went on: "She's with a cousin of Eva's. Stays with her. The one that . . . what's-her-name . . . Mason. Married a man by the name of Mason. Lives on some street"—he shook his head—"what is it, now? Peter Street, I think it is . . . Peter Street."

Grant went on to talk of other things. When he got up to go the brace and bit had slipped his mind. He caught himself in the doorway and went back for them.

22

It was not till he stood on the station platform at Truro that he was gripped by a sense of utter urgency.

He had driven to Copeland with Adam Falt and ridden the Sydney-Halifax train west to catch the Maritime Express for Montreal. All the way down the Shore with Adam and all the way up through the eastern counties with train-wheels clicking under him, his mind had turned inward and backward, still concerned, for the sake of Stewart and Josie, with the public appearance of the thing he had to do. The thing conspicuous and unexplainable and still not quite defined.

On the morning after his hour in Richard's shop he had wakened to a sense of things altered, of something new and difficult and desired and within reach. He had cast off the drag of sleep and gone to the window to peer into morning darkness, and seen that from the woods to the Channel the earth was white.

By half-past eight that morning he and Richard, with horse and sled, were on the way to their piled fire-wood in the clearings between the fields and the lake. The snow had lasted a week, firmed up by frost and an additional fall. When a wave of warmth moved northward in early December, the winter's wood was already in the yard.

Until this was done Grant had said nothing to Josie. It was going to be hard to talk to her at all. Impossible to make this journey sound reasonable to anyone. A trip to Upper Canada. It was a thin story he had told Richard. Somehow he knew that to Richard this mattered not at all. But others . . . He could not stay away, or announce an intention of staying away for a period of more than six weeks or a couple of months. More than that and it would seem . . . he would seem to be dropping the things he had set his hand to. But two months . . . the money a man could make in two months would barely keep him and pay his train fare back. That also would cause talk. On any basis, it was all a piece of craziness.

171

Personally he didn't care. The deed to the place was in his bureau drawer. Since the land had become his own, bought and paid for, he had lost his last fear of the unusual as it concerned himself. Let them think and say what they liked. But there were Josie and Stewart to think of in connection with his going, and with the curiosity it would arouse.

He had thought of taking Josie into his confidence. He could armour her privately with a frank admission. He could tell her why . . .

He had pulled up sharply at the thought. He could tell her —what? He had no certain plan. Only an urge that tingled in his blood. To bring reassurance to Richard McKee. Somehow to soften the haunted look of Josie Gordon. And beyond that an indefinable ambition, disturbing and queerly tender, in himself.

In the end he had decided not to break the surface. To let things lie. He told Josie less than he had told Richard. He was going to Upper Canada to look around. He'd be back by the first of February. He would leave things in good shape, and get the fire-wood sawed before he left.

He told Josie this one evening when Stewart, after the night barn work, had gone up to Grahams' by himself. Grant and Josie were alone in the kitchen, with a hardwood fire singing in the stove.

When he had told her, he sensed her looking at him steadily for a moment. All she said was: "Well, you better tell Stewart yourself."

You better tell Stewart yourself . . .

A moment of understanding came to him in which he could see as though he shared it the weight of pain on Josie's spirit. More clearly even than when she had spoken of Hazel, it came to him in the tone of this thought for Stewart.

Disappearance and death, and shame, pity and fear. All submerged from day to day beneath the hard calm of her resolution; hinted only in simple words, rarely, on the tongue of impulse.

The moment lightened his heart a little. There were things more important to Josie than any conjecture, any gossip, his going might cause. And she had handed over to him a responsibility. Behind her words, half-querulous, almost irritable, a grudging recognition . . . *You better tell Stewart yourself.*

He said, "Don't worry, I'll tell him."

That small scene came back to him now as he stood on the station platform, waiting for the west-bound express. The pool of lantern light swinging round his moccasined feet and Stewart's as they came in from the barn after feeding the cattle. His own words, as he glanced at the towering wood-pile in the dark: "Enough to last till March, anyway. I may have to make a trip, Mr. Gordon. But I'll be back long before that . . ."

Stewart halting in his tracks, the pool of yellow light on the mud-streaked snow of the yard: "A trip? Away?"

Again, his words of explanation: "Yes. It's a piece of personal business. Something I can't help. I wanted to tell you about it because I'm a little worried . . . Just—I wouldn't want Mrs. Josie to think—well, that anything'd be neglected. So we'll have to explain to her . . ."

And Stewart: "Sure . . . You're not—you'll be back, Grant?"

His own words, his reassuring laughter: "Oh, yes, Mr. Gordon, I'll be back. I'll be back, all right. This is where I live . . ."

He had done his best. Nothing could make it reasonable, but that he couldn't help. He stood here alone now on the station platform at Truro, in the chill of a winter evening; under the lights, under the restaurant sign projecting from the long brown-stone station building, his suitcase at his feet.

On the far track where the Sydney-Halifax train still stood there was a bumping and shunting as a car was dropped. Grant knocked one foot against the other. The snow was gone, but the air was cold, the night wind raw. His feet, used to woollen socks and work boots or moccasins, were cramped and cold in Sunday shoes.

The comings and goings of men and women continued. Walking off to buggies and automobiles, entering the station, lining up on the platform.

He walked out to the platform's edge and up and down a little. Most of the waiting passengers remained in the warmth of the waiting-room, but a few like himself had deserted the thickness of that atmosphere. His eyes ranged over them: a bulky man in a black overcoat and derby hat and spats, carrying in a grey-gloved hand a green tasselled bag, angular with books; a boy and girl self-consciously holding mittened hands; a short middle-aged male figure with dwarf-like bowed legs, in a blue yachting cap; an elderly woman in Hudson seal, a polka-dotted veil, and hatpins . . .

173

They stood in little knots along the platform, waiting for the luxury of sleepers, the green plush of first-class coaches, the leather-seated seconds.

There was not among them a single face he knew or had ever seen before.

For the first time in life, a stranger. Even in the army he had never faced the full impact of this feeling. Even in the darkest days of his indecision, even on the day of Anna's death, around his aloneness there had been known faces, voices, hands . . .

He tried to shake this away. It was ridiculous and childish . . . And in his flesh he could feel a turning tide. At one moment behind this feeling of aloneness was the old concern for appearances, fear of talk, the conjecture of the Shore. Suddenly this was gone. In his flesh and nerves there was, suddenly, the urgency . . .

The door of the waiting-room opened behind him. Men and women began to come out and move toward the platform's edge. Over a ridge of trees down the line a desolate hooting rose and died. In the well of following silence he could hear the beat of wheels.

1945

ANSE sat hunched forward with elbows on thighs, the beer glass clasped in his hands. He straightened, raised the glass and took a thoughtful swallow and half-turned toward Bill, faintly grinning. The words and voice were careless.

"The Head? How the hell would *I* know? I should be asking *you*."

Bill felt his mind go still and falter and begin to race. He said, "You never went back?"

Anse drained the glass and shook his head. A suggestion of finality edged the tone of his indifference.

"No. I never went back. Never wrote. Never heard . . ."

This chance contact was coming to an end, petering out. Whatever interest Anse Gordon might have had in Bill Graham was running down. All it had ever amounted to was a moment of surprise on the palace lawn; and now, this small moment of understated drama. This pose—or was it a pose?—of disinterest. This obscure satisfaction in an incurious reticence.

For Bill the oddity in this meeting, stranger even than the coincidence of seeing a Channel Shore face in the palace gardens, was that Anse Gordon knew even less than he.

He felt a sharp brief anger, the impulse to pierce this self-possession, to say: "For Christ's sake! Ask, then! Don't you want to know?"

As if in answer to his thought, the question came, light and sardonic:

". . . Did *you*?"

Bill checked a rising impulse. No. Leave it to Providence, whatever she might have in store.

"No," he said. "No . . ."

He got off the bench and carried his glass to the bar. Anse rose behind him.

"Well," Bill said. "If you're around London—I'm living in Eaton Mews. Number 24. It's not far from here. Or call me at C.M.H.Q. Any time."

"Sure," Anse said. He drawled absently, "Seeing you," and walked off, leisurely and arrogant, toward Sloane Square.

In the days that followed, Bill lived much with the Channel Shore. At his desk in Cockspur Street; at night, in the converted chauffeur's quarters where he slept; anywhere, doing anything, he would find the movement and the colour coming up through the sameness and the hurry of later years. At such times it was the nearer past that seemed vague and distant, while that single summer of his boyhood was lively, vibrant, increasingly distinct. There was nothing in this of the absent mind, nothing that distracted him from the routine of his work. It was simply that after years in which he had rarely thought of it, the Shore was part of him, a habit in the flesh, like breathing and sleep.

Back of it all, the recollection of discovery. One scene was particularly clear—the scene that had flashed in his mind at the sight of Anse Gordon's face. Four boys at Kilfyle's Hole, and Stan Currie talking of settlers who were dead and gone, leaving their names on the land . . . Lowries . . . Kilfyles . . . McNaughtons . . . Clearer even than Stan and Joe and Dan and the dark amber water and Anse Gordon, was the thing he had felt that day.

A curious thing had been happening to him in those first days of his summer at The Head. He could feel it happening. Andrew Graham was a professor of mathematics. He had all the austerity of the country boy who achieves academic honour through work and denial in the time of youth. He did not often talk of his boyhood. But sometimes, in the house in Toronto, he would lapse into a diffident mood of reminiscence, a speech coloured by irrelevant allusion: "Frank and I were after trout at Kilfyle's . . . Used to be good rabbit country around Lowries' . . ."

These notes on the margins of memory were brief and rare and Bill as a boy of nine, ten, eleven, had stored them up with a special regard, had fashioned round them a Channel Shore of the imagination. By that Sunday at the hole, the first strangeness of the Shore had begun to wear off, but his growing familiarity with the fields and the water was in itself strange and inwardly exciting. It was like exploring in fact a land that had existed only in story. And finding in the shape of an actual hill, the sound of a stream's voice, the lines in a face, the truth and light and colour—the confirmation of a personal hearsay.

That was the explanation of this sense he had now, a quarter-century later; this possession of a knowledge, a familiarity, more pervasive surely than anything you could trace to a single summer.

It came to him in a slow flash of recognition, definite as the inner revelation of love. He was back on the Channel Shore in the hot days of July and August. And again it was not simply the inlet at Currie Head that he saw, and the fish huts on the beach there, but these things lighted by something farther back: his father's voice when he was eight or nine or ten: "Your grandfather fished mackerel with Joe Currie. Frank and I and Hugh and Rich McKee used to pick net-rocks . . . We had a boat on the inlet, a kind of scow."

That was how he had known the Shore in his fourteenth year. The Shore was more than a summer holiday. It was a country that had been explored for years in a boy's mind, a timeless country. In this country people lived in a setting of cleared fields and wooded hills. There was the quick sound of brook water, the slow sound of sea heaved by tide and wind. In this country lived not only old Hugh Currie and old Frank Graham and old Rich McKee, but young Andrew Graham and young Hugh and Frank and Rich, a fellow named Tim Kilfyle and Bill Graham himself.

This now, after a single contact with Channel Shore flesh, was happening to Bill again.

The night of the storm . . .

The extra weeks he had asked for and got, on his promise to go to school, were almost up.

In these last days he had found himself overcoming an earlier diffidence. Asking questions that were almost absurd: "Uncle Frank, did you and Dad ever go right up the Black Brook? Clear up where it comes from? Did he ever trap mushrats? Where'd they get the name of Andy?"

His mind had seemed in a fever to cram into memory all he could pack there of present perception and incidental knowledge of the past. His uncle answered with off-hand care, amusement tempered in sympathy, as if he sensed a meaning in the curiosity he had previously laughed at. Something not quite clear, but worthy of affectionate respect.

"The brook? It comes out of Round Lake. Never been up there. No call to go . . . We let the mushrats alone, but we used to shoot pa'tridge out back . . . Your pop was named after Andrew Macnab, a Scotch schoolteacher they had here before the women took over the teaching business. Drunk himself out of the church, the ministry, before that, they found out later. But a good schoolteacher . . ."

He had been thinking of it all that night in bed, the night of the storm. The sheets had a chill to them. "Fall coming on," Dan complained. Bill was glad of Dan's closeness under the bed-clothes.

After Dan had dropped off to sleep he remained awake, listening to the straining of the wind's formless body against the creaking timbers. Once or twice a far-off change in tempo, a shudder, thudded bluntly in the long impersonal waves of sound.

Lying there against Dan, listening to the soft regularity of Dan's breathing, under the giant overtone of storm, he was part of the Channel Shore. The house in Toronto—home—the red brick school-house, even Dad . . . they seemed less real, less actual, than this old wooden farm-house under the lash of rain. Less real than Uncle Frank, laughing and hiding his twist tobacco in the shop, because Aunt Stell wouldn't stand it in the kitchen. Edith, friendly and remote in her young womanhood. Colin, in the west, whose picture stood on the parlour mantel. James Marshall, a bearded prophet from the Old Testament, sending the same little shiver up your spine. Grant, Anna, Stewart Gordon, Anse; Joe McKee, and Hazel. Stan Currie and his father, Hugh . . . Adam Falt and his horses . . . In the little world of aloneness contrived round him by the storm, Bill was not alone. There was nothing strange in Rob Currie helping Alec Neill mend nets on the west coast of Africa, which was also Currie's Beach. Nothing strange in great-aunt Fanny being Edith's age, while Aunt Stell was still Aunt Stell . . .

Not merely the simple memory of outward things, but the memory of recognition . . .

It was this that touched him now, twenty-six years later and in another country, as the Channel Shore came back.

He found himself on Hugh Currie's doorstep . . . *Handsome woman, Fanny Graham . . . it was quite a thing at the time* . . . Back in the woods at Grant's Place, with Anna teasing, and James Marshall striding down the path from the road . . . Back in Stewart Gordon's kitchen while the lines drew together in the stories of Grant Marshall and Anna Gordon, Anse Gordon and Hazel McKee.

Back in his father's study on Huron Street, far from the Channel Shore and at a later point in time; but still part of it, still part of summer and the Shore, the last thread in an all-but-forgotten story . . .

He had stayed home from school with a cold, that afternoon in late December. A ring at the door.

He listened for the house-keeper's step, and not hearing it, went to the door himself. The shabby overcoat, the cap; a tradesman.

"Hello, Bill."

"Grant!"

Already, the Shore had begun, a little, to slip away. It was still clear and coloured in the mind, but other things were beginning then to come between. But in that instant it was back. Grant!

He could not remember now, a quarter-century later, the things they said in Andrew Graham's study. He could see Grant sitting there confident and quiet in the tight blue suit. Queerly out of place, away from the woods and hayfields of the Shore. He could see the black leather of his father's chair, the golden oak desk, the paperweight in the shape of a silver stag. But except for one final sentence of explanation, he could not recall the words, or his own questions.

Only the facts as Grant had told them. He was living with the Gordons now, Grant said. The fall work was done. He had decided to make a trip, then. He had come to Toronto. He had seen Hazel McKee.

Hazel. Bill himself had thought of her, thought of trying to find her, and rejected the impulse. What could a boy say? What could you expect but embarrassment?

Grant had seen Hazel. She wasn't well. Wasn't too well. Oh, she would be all right, but . . . It was when he left, as he explained that he couldn't stay to dinner, couldn't stay to meet Andrew Graham, that Grant spoke the sentence Bill remembered word by word: "I ought to get back to her. It's this way, Bill—Hazel and me—we got married this morning . . . we're going home to-morrow."

The word in his mind was wrong. It was not a story.

That was how he had thought of it in that first hour with Anse, walking toward the Antelope, looking forward with excitement to the finish of a tale.

There, with Anse on the bench beside him, learning that Anse knew less than he, he had begun to see that nothing is ever finished.

This no longer was a tale heard. This was life, and woven into it were living threads of his own youth, alive again in this

179

older body, crossing Trafalgar Square, taking the underground at Charing Cross, climbing a narrow stairway from the litter of Eaton Mews.

On the Shore they knew. A postage stamp, words on a page, would bring him the truth, or at least the facts. But what he was thinking of were the voices, the faces, the gestures. The look on faces he had known and faces he had never seen. Through years of which he knew nothing, life on the Shore had flowered into impulse, motive, act. At this moment it was going on. In the woods and on the beaches. In fields, work-shops, kitchens, barns . . . At Felix Katen's, Grant's Place, Josie Gordon's, Frank Graham's, James Marshall's.

The liveliness and the anticipation . . . Out of the far past he was looking into a nearer past and a present. Both unknown to him. But alive on the Channel Shore.

PART TWO

Winter 1933-1934

ALAN

GRANT

RENIE

MARGARET

1

ALAN MARSHALL halted on the road's frozen shoulder and turned to glance down past Grahams' to Gordons' turn. An hour ago, just after breakfast, Grant and Dan Graham had gone that way to follow the hauling-road out back.

Alan grunted to himself. He didn't dislike school; with Renie teaching, it was all right. But school interfered with other things . . . He turned again and glanced west along the road and north along the snow-covered hills, and thought about the crew Grant had working in the woods back of Ed Kelley's, far to the northwest. With the Christmas holidays beginning Saturday . . . But the Kelley lots were old stuff. What he was hoping for was a chance to see new country, the uncut woods back of Felix Katen's.

He looked back, and grinned. Margaret's small figure came pelting through the gate, the tail of her red stocking-cap absurdly wagging against the intent face. She brushed it aside impatiently and reached for his hand.

"You go without me, Lan . . . I hommer-hommer-hommer."

"You wouldn't, would you, Mag?" Alan said. "Ol' Lan? Anyway, you're not big enough. Or too big. You're not as tough as y'were when you could *really* hommer-hommer-hommer."

He closed a fist and brought it down in a series of quick soft blows on the stocking-capped head.

Margaret let out a small roar. "I am, too!" and burst out laughing. There were times at home when they could hold a pretended quarrel all day, to the exasperation of Grant and Renie; Alan teasing Margaret with the repeated claim that the girl was getting soft since she had grown out of a furiously active babyhood. But when they were alone together they lapsed quickly into a mood in which each regarded the other seriously—the protective thirteen-year-old brother, almost fourteen now, and the going-on-nine sister who found in him an adult she could talk to without losing the fellowship of childhood.

Alan squeezed her cold hand. "Mag, you've forgot your mitts again. I ought to send you back . . . You'd lose your head if it wasn't sewed on."

"'s not cold," Margaret said "Listen! *You* can't talk. *You're* bare-handed."

"I'm older and tougher. Stuff your hands in your pockets."

He disengaged his fingers. It was time, anyway. Bert Lisle would be popping out of Hugh Currie's any minute. Alan liked the feeling of being the fellow in charge that Margaret's hand gave him when they were walking alone, the two of them, but with others around it was different.

Margaret pocketed her fists and walked slightly behind him, a little rebellious, but knowing her place.

Bert Lisle clicked Currie's gate and said, "Hi, Alan . . . Hi, Mag."

"I *am not* Mag."

Bert grinned. "You are, too, Mag. Little Mag."

"I'm—." Margaret lapsed into a furious calm. She said coldly, "Fatty. Fatty. Fatty."

Bert's plump body shook with laughter. "Mag. Mag. Mag."

Alan said, "For Pete's sake! Cut it out!" He added, off-hand, in a tone that recognized the small girl's crotchets and asked indulgence for them, "Lay off, Bert. Le's have a little peace." He didn't know why Margaret resented being called Mag by anyone but himself, nor why she called him Lan, a special name, when they were alone together. But that was the way she was, and her wishes were entitled to respect.

Bert slouched along on the opposite shoulder of the road, out of the frozen ruts grooved into the surface of packed snow.

He said, "Didn't know if you'd be coming today. Mr. Graham was over last night. Mentioned your Dad and Dan were headed out back today."

Alan said briefly, "Yes. They went early. Katen's back lot." No point in saying more than that. If Bert hadn't noticed that you were never kept out of school to help in the woods or around the place, so much the better.

His mind went back to Grant's words last night: "Dan and I'll do the cruising tomorrow, but I'll need you Saturday. And through the holidays, maybe. Likely be some roads we'll have to swamp." Grant always seemed to know what you were thinking, what you wanted; always went out of his way to make things clear, to answer the question in your mind and give you something to look forward to.

Bert said, "They're still workin' back of Kelley's though, ain't they?"

Alan laughed, keeping the pride out of his voice. "Well, you know Grant; he's just looking ahead . . . What it is, we're not chopping. He's thinking of a dicker with Felix. They went back to cruise it, see how long it'll take to clean her off when we get around to it."

"Later on, you mean. Next summer, maybe. You'll be choppin' next summer."

"Guess so," Alan said. "Same as last."

He spoke with satisfaction. It might be that you were kept in school when the winter woods work was on, and steered away from other responsibilities you would like to take a crack at, but working with the pulpwood crew in vacation time was all right. Peeling pulpwood in hot weather is nasty work. Wear all the mitts you like, the fresh balsam cakes the skin till you have to scrub with kerosene to get clean for Sunday. But it was sharing a man's work, Grant's work, a known enterprise on the Channel Shore.

They slowed, dawdling, at the top of the slight rise where Marshalls' gate opened on the drive sloping down to Uncle Fred's house. Fred's two school-age kids, Jackie who was twelve, and eight-year-old Beulah, were coming up the slope, sheepskin book-bags flapping.

Alan's eyes ranged the Channel while they waited, the cold blue stretch of it and the hazier blue of the Islands.

Bert Lisle said idly, "Not a sail . . . Mr. Currie says years ago there'd be hardly a day you wouldn't sight something . . ."

"I know." Alan had heard all that. Grandfather McKee talked that way sometimes, when he bothered to talk at all. "The bankers, into Princeport for bait; and coal schooners coming up to Morgan's Harbour."

Directly across the miles of blue-cold water he could just make out the white dots of houses, far apart, hard to see against a land veiled distantly in snow. And farther east, the clustered specks of Princeport. Once when he was ten he had gone there with Grant and Renie and Margaret on a visit to Mr. Bob Fraser—Big Bob, everybody called him—Renie's father, and her sister, Aunt Bess. They had driven to Morgan's Harbour and taken the boat down the south shore of the Channel, the Islands' shore. He had talked about that for a long time afterward, about the look of the Atlantic from the other side of Middle Island, about the fish wharves and the general store, and the invitation Big Bob had made to him to come back and stay a while. That would never happen now. Big Bob had sold out and moved to Halifax to spend his old age. But Alan still thought of that trip to Princeport as a kind of adventure, the one time he had been away from the Channel Shore.

His mind ran on, to the invitation Mr. Fraser kept pressing . . . a trip to Halifax. It would be all right, for a week or two. To see the city and the harbour and the ships and then come home to Currie Head, a traveller with things to remember . . . to brag about to Bert and Jackie Marshall and talk about to Grant.

He was not introspective beyond the normal inward-looking of boyhood, but he wondered now as he had wondered before, whether Jackie Marshall or Clyde Wilmot, for instance, ever got the same feeling in their fathers' presence that he did. It was like having a father your own age, except that you didn't want to get smart, as you would with a boy. Sometimes he thought people must notice this, this about himself and Grant. There were wisps of memory; curious looks, low-toned asides . . . He couldn't imagine how Bert Lisle felt. Bert came of people who had moved away from The Head before Alan was born. He had been sent back to work for his board at Hugh Currie's and go to school. He was fatherless.

It was all pretty good, Alan felt, except for the few things you were not allowed to do, and those didn't matter in the light of the long companionship. There was one other thing, a definite apprehension that came up to bother him sometimes. It had crossed his mind just now, called up by his thought of Big Bob Fraser and Princeport and Halifax. But it was nothing close or soon, nothing you had to deal with now.

"Come on, you bunch of slow-pokes," he said. "I got a fire to build."

They trailed him across the road and took the path up through the Marshall upper field and back pasture, a short cut used for four generations, that brought them out on the schoolhouse road just below the school.

Alan snapped open the padlock on the storm door, slipped it out of the staple, and entered the hallway, a passage narrowed by piled stove-wood. The big room beyond was cold as sin. He shovelled dead ashes into a pail, piled in kindling and paper while Bert and Jackie carried armloads of dried hardwood in from the hall. When things were ready, he struck a match.

A pleasant sense of responsibility came over him: possession of the school-house key and the duty of building fire. He touched the stove with his fingers. In the cold metal, a hint of warmth. He took his books from the bag and stowed them in the double desk he shared with Bert.

He still felt a touch of regret that he wasn't out back on Felix Katen's lot, but there was no resentment in it. A few hours of *Beginner's Algebra* and *English History* were ahead of him, and a couple more at Mrs. Josie's wood-pile. But after that, Grant and Dan would be back.

After that, sitting across the stove from Grant with the lamp lit and supper cleared off, he would hear about it. And after that there was Saturday, and Christmas, and the days ahead.

By the time Renie arrived at five minutes to nine the room was beginning to lose its chill. She noticed that all twelve of her pupils were on hand this morning, from little Syd Kinsman, the youngest, up to Clyde Wilmot, who came when he felt like it, and his sister Jennie, and Sarah Laird, who was struggling through a second year of grade ten.

She smiled a little absently as she hung her cloth coat on her special hook in the corner and glanced into the small square mirror that hung there. A fullish face, slightly freckled, smiled absently back. She met the grey eyes briefly, ran her fingers through a mass of short rust-coloured hair, streaked with grey, and turned to the desk at the head of the room. When you were a tax-payer's wife and the mother of two of the kids you taught, there was no formality. No *Good morning, teacher . . . Good morning, pupils.* Renie had never been able to go through such formalities, anyway, without the feeling she was simpering.

The smile lingered round her mouth as she ticked off the names on the register without calling the roll. Years ago it had been different. As a first-year schoolteacher, new at The Head and fresh from Normal School at Truro, she had read off the names meticulously each morning: "Frances Freeman . . . *present* . . . Dan Graham . . . *present* . . . Stan Currie . . . *present* . . . "

She had thought, in those days: *Currie Head. I'll remember Currie Head when I've gone on from here and taken a degree. When I'm Miss Irene Fraser, B.A., principal of the High School at Morgan's Harbour, or the Academy at Copeland . . .*

But looking back on it now she knew that even then she hadn't believed in that particular day-dream; day-dreaming of any kind had never meant a thing. The day itself, for Renie, had always been too immediate to permit a dream to dim its realities. Was too immediate still.

The imagined picture of herself as a spinster of thirty-four, tapping a blackboard with a pointer, was so ludicrous that Renie almost laughed out loud. There was a blackboard behind her now. The difference was that she tapped it not for a living, but as a person who lived in the place, helping out because teachers were hard to get. And she was not a spinster.

She called Margaret and Dolly Wilmot and Willie Laird up to the desk, stood them in a line, and heard grade four spelling. Once she called "Alan!" sharply, and rapped the desk with a ruler. She knew what it was. He couldn't afford to behave like a teacher's pet when his step-mother was the teacher. The flipped dart and the whisper to Bert Lisle were stage business. So were the sharp word and the rapped desk. Twenty years from now, perhaps, they could admit it.

She could see Jennie Wilmot, Clyde's twin, stealing long side-long glances at Alan. She could understand that, too. Good looks were on him: the wiry body, the dark hair falling in a lock over the left temple, the high cheek-bones, the dark mocking mouth, the frank brown eyes and the easy grin. There were times, thinking of Alan, when Renie came close to envy, regret that Hazel McKee's flesh and not her own had had the sprouting of him . . .

At ten-thirty she announced recess. At quarter to eleven she closed the copy of *Anthony Adverse* Grant had borrowed at the library in Copeland, and stepped to the door to ring a perfunctory recall with the hand-bell.

Laughter, and shouted admiring mockery . . . It was Alan again. There were times when all you could think was *that boy*! Not, as far as Renie was concerned, in exasperation, but in a kind of wonder at the impulses to original action that coursed through his mind. He had climbed the taller of two firs that stood in McKee's pasture and was perched twenty feet above ground, feet stirruped between branch and bole, gripping the slender top and rocking in the wind.

Renie's nerves jumped slightly. What she felt, as Alan dropped straight down from hand-hold to hand-hold on the branches, was not alarm but a quick sense of relief that the youngster had learned not to do that kind of thing in Grant's presence. The only sharp words she had ever heard spoken to Alan, except for her own stage business in the school-house, were curt commands that grew from

187

the fear of hurt to the boy himself: the quick order to a running eight-year-old to close an open jack-knife; the refusal of permission to go hand-lining on the Channel with Bert Lisle unless Dan or old Hugh Currie were along.

There was something vaguely disquieting in this to Renie. Once she had remarked to Grant, tentatively, "Perhaps there's such a thing as being too careful." He had replied, "Maybe. But he's my son." The slight accent had been on "son", not "my", but the implication was there, conscious or not. The drawing of a boundary, the definition of a relationship in which no one else could fully share, no matter how complete her sharing of a maturer love. And a further implication, without reproach to anyone, but clear as day to Renie. Grant might have said, ". . . my only son."

It was at moments like these that another picture was sometimes realized in Renie's mind. She had never seen him except in the images derived from hearsay, but Anse Gordon's lounging figure would sometimes cross the field of her inner vision with the furtive clarity of a character in fiction.

"My son . . ."

A paradox was stated here in terms of flesh and blood and fierce affection. A paradox that had created in Renie's mind an immeasurable respect, a response like the response to courage. And yet she knew that this was something, despite Grant's slow careful recital years ago, that she could never fully understand. Something that could be fully understood only through the intuitions of personal experience, the life Grant Marshall had begun on the day of Anna Gordon's death and shared with Hazel McKee . . . She shook her head at Alan as he came, laughing, into the school-house.

In the high woods at ground level the heavy white flooring was unbroken under the trees. Boughs supported crusty gobbets of snow, and the black water of Katen's Creek, slow and small at this distance from its outlet in the Channel, was half-hidden under broken panes of ice.

Grant Marshall and Dan Graham were wearing woollen socks and cowhide moccasins. Every once in a while Dan would glance back along their tracks for evidence that he was walking a straight line, but the growth was too dense in places to give him much of an idea. Running compass lines was new to him. At intervals he stopped, paced a circle, and put the callipers on the trunks of spruce and fir while Grant noted down the called figures. Finally a laugh slipped through.

Grant put the notebook in his pocket and pulled on a mitt.

He said, "Not bad . . . What's funny?"

Dan said, "Nothing much. I was thinkin've the way you always want to measure the woods before you knock it down. Anybody else'd go in and take a look and cut."

Grant laughed, a little self-consciously. He said, "I guess the old-timers can tell by the look of it, all right."

He had learned to map land and figure the cordage of standing trees during three seasons with a timber-cruising outfit in the west end of the county, in the early years when he was grabbing at every job that offered. He liked to apply the practical knowledge he had gained in that period, even when guess-work would do as well.

At odd moments such as this he had flashes of insight in which he caught a glimmer of how such proceedings might cause him to be regarded as a kind of special character, give him a flavour of oddity, or add to the flavour of the unusual he had earned in youth. But long ago, he told himself, he had given up thinking of such matters.

He said absently now to Dan, "A shame to cut this stuff for pulp . . . all this stuff in here." From the slope where they were standing, unbroken woods stretched north and east to the sky. "Look at it. As good a cut as you'll find any place. If the market was right, and you had a mill . . ."

Dan said, "Well, Rod Sinclair . . ."

"No," Grant said. "Rod's not interested in anything but box-shooks. And he's getting old. Anyway, in this kind of country a permanent site's no good. I wasn't thinking of water-power. What a fellow'd need would be a diesel outfit he could move around where the timber is."

Dan was non-committal. "Might be something in it."

Grant was turning it over in his mind. "Pulpwood at four or five dollars a cord . . . roughly seven hundred feet of lumber in a cord. And lumber's—what?—maybe thirty dollars a thousand." His mind went at it.

He said, "Of course, one strip wouldn't go far." He spoke thoughtfully, as if talking to himself. "Not much more than eighty thousand on Felix. You'd have to tie in six or eight lots to make it worth while. Not worth fixing the roads up for less."

"S'pose not," Dan said. "You could pick up the stumpage though. Next strip north belongs to your Uncle James, don't it?"

Grant frowned. He hadn't really meant his speculative talk to be interpreted by Dan in terms of personal intention. He said, "I wouldn't cut on Marshall land. Not till it's Fred's."

Dan said, with blunt curiosity, "Why not? You bought The Place—"

Grant noticed Dan's quick hesitation, halting the flow of speech. He regretted having spoken at all of what was in his mind, but he said evenly, "Oh, that was different. The Place belonged to me."

He didn't want to go into it, any of it—his present ambition, which had led accidentally to talk of the past, or that past itself. He could think of that time matter-of-factly, but talking about it was different. He had got along well enough without explaining anything to anybody; except Renie, long ago. It wasn't the kind of thing people questioned you about; Dan had let the question slip through and then caught himself.

Apart from the long reluctance to discuss that personal thing, any attempt at explanation would only confuse Dan. But Dan was a friend. You could skirt the surface and give him some kind of answer.

He said, off-hand, "I'd done so much work there I hated to give it up. So I just asked Uncle James if he'd sell it. He did. He's fair-minded, you know."

Dan said, "Well, why don't you go after his woods, if you want it?"

"No," Grant said. "That's something else again."

Dan let the matter drop.

As they tramped toward the single white birch Dan had picked as his next compass point, Grant's mind roved involuntarily. Dan's question had started him going back, thinking it over, the outlines of his life. The time at Gordons', the time with Hazel, and Hazel's death . . . the jobs he had worked at, anywhere and everywhere . . . Renie . . . the three-roomed house he had built first, for himself and Alan and Renie, and converted into a workshop and garage when the new one was complete.

He grinned inwardly, considering how for years now he had scarcely thought at all of what his actions looked like to others. He supposed there must have been quite a bit of talk about useless gadgets—running water, a furnace, a bathroom. In a region where there was little essential change except birth and death and moving away, perhaps it *was* odd to contrive something new . . .

He felt a ripple of well-being . . . Renie, Margaret, a kid like Alan. He called a halt. He and Dan pulled sandwiches from their pockets and stood there, knocking their moccasins occasionally against exposed roots, for warmth; lunching off cold pork between slices of home-made bread. Finally Grant threw away a last crust and said, "We've seen all we need to see on Felix. Le's just take a look in some of this stuff east of here."

They began to climb the long slope into uncut timber.

One of the informalities Renie had started when she had accepted the Currie Head school again, after years of preoccupation with her family, was an extra half hour at the noon break. Usually she walked home then to get away from the school atmosphere and eat the meal with Grant, if he happened to be at home. But as he had been working in the woods all day since early fall, she had fallen into the youngsters' practice of bringing a lunch with her.

As she put the kettle on the stove she was clearly conscious of happiness, of the goodness of her life. Right from the first, happy. She glanced at Margaret, precisely setting out sandwiches on her desk, using a page from *The Herald* for a table-cloth . . . And what she saw was another nine-year-old, in a green dress, running down the steep and crooked road to Bob Fraser's wharf, her father's wharf, in Princeport. To watch the mackerel boats come in . . . Big Bob himself, then, at a later time. Broad and tall, the red face stubbled with a week's whisker . . . *Good God, Renie! If you don't like house-keeping, come into the business. But school-teaching!*

Whenever Renie thought of Big Bob she smiled gently and a little wryly, to herself. For Bess had gone into school-teaching too; and now the business itself was gone, swallowed up in a federation of fish companies; and Big Bob, an old man, lived in Halifax and ran a corner grocery for something to do . . .

Her happiness was in the people who were hers . . . Big Bob and Grant, Margaret and Alan. In the host of others she knew, and had known, the work she did from day to day.

But halting to think of these things was unusual in Renie. Pictures of the past faded with the meal. Dishes were washed, school resumed. The afternoon began to slip by, a small uneventful passage of the uncomplicated present. At four o'clock Renie said, "School's out!" and smiled at the youngsters.

While she put on her coat and pulled the old felt over rusty hair, she could hear them horsing around, squatted on the piles of wood in the hallway, putting on rubbers and overshoes. She paid little attention to it, the kid-talk, the boy-talk, but she gathered, absently, that Clyde Wilmot was trying to persuade Alan and Bert Lisle to go home with him for a while, up the school-house road, to see the pair of young mink he was attempting to raise in a pen behind the barn.

"Can't do it today, Clyde," Bert said regretfully. "Mr. Currie'll want me. How'd it be if we come up Sunday afternoon? Christmas eve? I'd like to see them animals."

Alan said, "I can't, today, either. I got to get home to chop wood. For Mrs. Josie."

"Aw . . . You guys!"

The taunt in Clyde's voice caught Renie's ear. Impatience at the small ordinary sense of duty in Alan and Bert. Impatience at interference with a desire to feel superiority, the chance their company would give him to show off something new and strange.

"You guys! Always worryin' about the boss . . . or your old man. Or—" an odd hesitant daring ran like an undertone in Clyde's voice—"or your grandmother."

Renie's hand stayed where it was, tugging the felt hat down. Jennie Wilmot cut in on her brother roughly: "Shut up, Clyde. Who cares about your darn stinking mink? . . . Anybody'd think you had a million-dollar fox ranch."

The chatter petered out.

Renie felt herself possessed by unreality, cut off from the smooth unworried ways of life by careless words, a boy's voice . . .

"Or your grandmother" . . .

Or was this reality? This sly hint of the past and its pattern, living in Channel Shore memory, traced again in half spoken allusion; something said perhaps more by inadvertence than malice; something said in gossip or anger, in the hearing of a boy whose heart was open and ignorant and therefore vulnerable?

Or was she imagining it all?

It came home to Renie suddenly, a drifting thought, secondary to the actual import of Clyde Wilmot's slanted words, that the objective images in her mind, the things without special sharpness, were drawing in with the force of personal experience . . .

The images of Grant had always been clear in her mind, personal to her, since a day in the winter of her first year at The Head. He had driven into the school yard with a sled-load of hardwood, a young man in mackinaw and high-laced moccasins. He had grinned with impersonal friendliness when she remarked on the size of the logs. "Yes; Joe and I'll saw the stuff up and split it. It *is* kind of big. The place hasn't ever been cut over . . ."

The story had been fresh then, a new thing. The successive sensations of Grant Marshall's break from his uncle, his living with the parents of Anna Gordon, who was dead . . . his departure and return with Hazel McKee . . . A sick girl, they said of Hazel. Taken to the cottage hospital at Copeland and on her back a month before the boy was born; and dying now at Gordons' . . .

The personal pictures as they related to herself and Grant began that day in the school yard. Something had puzzled her that afternoon. She had not been able to reconcile a previous conception of Grant Marshall—acquired she supposed by hearsay—as a boy shy and almost sullen, with this self-possessed man who was caught in tragedy, but whose eyes were direct and un-shadowed and whose manner was sure.

Pictures of life thereafter crowded her memory. A spring funeral, and late snow falling on the graveyard behind the church at Leeds. A summer wedding, more than a year later, with the sun checkered on the parsonage floor at Findlay's Bridge. Uncounted pictures, until the screen, the fabric, was a tapestry; a Channel Shore tapestry in which Renie's mind enlarged and picked out with special colour the scenes of which her own flesh were part.

Hazel McKee had been merely a figure in the cloth, a figure vivid in the pattern seen by Richard McKee, by Eva, by Grant; but important to Renie only by association, through a weaving that was indirect and allusive; by the fact that Hazel had something to do with the qualities in Grant, the positive kindliness, the hard realistic independence, the calmness in the face of cir-cumstance, that were to Renie a continual quiet delight and still could take her by surprise.

But now . . . these things and people, the things and people she had seen as only indirectly related . . . these things that belonged to a time before . . . Drawn close, suddenly, in the raucous taunt of a schoolboy; made personal to her, merged with the living images of life.

Or was it all imagination?

She couldn't tell.

You couldn't tie it down. You couldn't count the sources of possible revelation. She had never thought of it in quite this way before; and she wondered now, walking down the short cut through the top of McKees' pasture and then Marshalls' whether this was something—this possibility of revelation—that all these years had lived in Grant's remembering mind, a grey fear behind the affectionate possessive sense of fatherhood.

Once, long ago, she had raised the point herself, in the one conversation in which they talked of that bitter time, of Alan and his origin.

She had said: "You've thought of the risk?"

And Grant: "Hell, Renie, we'll take each day as it comes."

She didn't know. All she was sure of was that she would have to tell him. The long easy silence would have to be broken. She would have to talk to Grant.

2

RENIE washed the supper dishes by the sink at the east window. Margaret worked beside her, twirling the dishcloth over plates and saucers competently, like a small old woman. The kitchen was singing gently with the comfort of slowly-burning hardwood, a comfort visible in the narrow red rectangle between stove-door and damper and felt in the drowsy warmth of the indoor air.

Margaret went up on tip-toes to pile dishes on the cupboard, and dropped back on her heels. She pressed a hand against the lower pane of a window to feel the cold of it in contrast to the warm and lighted room. The night had clouded up; it was already black outside. All she could see were the lights of Frank Graham's house and Mrs. Josie's, hanging like small yellow stars on the lower edge of the sky. The whole room, even its windows, turned inward now from darkness, inward to the fireside and the light. In the dark panes for a moment Margaret watched the reflection: her father sitting by the wood-box, back to the window, smoking; and beyond the stove, in the spot where he liked to sit, Alan; partly in the circle of light from the shaded reading-lamp, partly in shadow.

Renie emptied the dishwater down the drain and sighed. She said regretfully, "It's prayer-meeting night. And choir practice for the Christmas service . . . I promised Edith I'd go up with her. She's taking the sleigh . . ."

Grant said, "All right. We're old enough to look after ourselves, I guess."

Renie twitched off her apron. She said, "Bed at nine, now," to Margaret, and crossed to the downstairs bedroom, the one she shared with Grant, to dress for the evening out.

Margaret said precisely, "Yes, Mother," and opened her Fourth Grade English Reader on the red table-cloth.

Grant, sitting in shadow, studied for a moment the small serene face between the tight brown pigtails. His own in miniature. The resemblance was ludicrous.

There were times, times like these, when the simple fact of family, of possessing Alan and Margaret, thumped in his blood like the beat of a march-tune. Sometimes this feeling was accompanied by a trace of fear, as if his own boyhood stood up in memory to remind him. Remind him that of body and spirit there is no right of blood possession, only the gentler ties of affection and respect . . .

Sometimes he would send Margaret home, when she followed himself and Alan around the hayfield and into the barn. Send her home or encourage her to go over to Grahams', where Edith Kinsman had two smaller girls for her to play with and take charge of. Sometimes, working with Alan at any of the man-and-boy jobs they did together, he would withhold both the praise and impatience of parenthood, seek to work and talk as person to person rather than father and son.

He had followed this in his mind, sometimes, to the point of wondering whether this in itself, this attempt at a matter-of-fact personal as well as a family relationship might be weaving threads of feeling of another sort. But all he really knew was that no matter how much of a friend instead of a conventional father he tried to be, there were still times when he was all father, inordinately proud of Margaret's mature and knowing ways, and Alan's alert judgment in the woods and around the place. Inordinately cautious, inordinately annoyed when the boy showed a trace of forwardness, off-handedness with other people, or the girl an occasional abruptness with children of her own age. Inordinately proud, amused, impatient. Inordinately regretful, when he thought of it, that some time in the normal course of things on the Channel Shore, these two would have to choose a road and go. Inordinately swayed by tides of unreasoning protective love . . .

Renie came into the kitchen again and tucked her hair into a woollen toque as she stood by the window, listening for the sound of sleighbells.

She was not a possessive woman. She enjoyed getting out among people. But she could never close the door behind her on a common scene like this without a feeling of reluctance.

In her earlier years, when teaching school had been a job instead of an incidental filling-out of life, she had been troubled at times by the violences of normal living. Rough talk had never bothered her when it was good-natured; she had listened to a lot of it, with childish appreciation, on the wharves at Princeport. But flaring violence between children in the school yard could set her shaking; or sharp words from parent to child, heard in the houses to which she had gone as a guest to tea or Sunday dinner. It all seemed so unnecessary.

It was simply her reasonable nature, she thought, rather than any unusual sensitivity that caused this personal distaste. And gradually this reasonableness had created in her a sort of immunity to the harsh and the violent. She had come to see that in people along the Channel Shore there was much generosity and courage, and even kindness. She had ceased to dwell on the other qualities, the occasional meanness and cruelty, the gossip and intolerance and pride.

But it was still true that there were some people you liked more than others. The Grahams, and old Richard McKee, and Josie Gordon . . . The Shore had no word for such people, but it had a word for the quality they did not have. They were not *small*.

No place she could think of was as free of smallness in that sense as her own house. Renie never came back to it, to Grant's casual glance and Alan's energy and Margaret's moods of chatter and silence, without a little upward sense of release.

And so she always left it with a touch of reluctance and regret. As she left it now a curious feeling stole into her mind; there were personal radiations, changing in character and intensity as circumstances changed. Herself and Grant: alone together, going somewhere or at home, or even in a crowd—that was one thing. When all four were together, that was another; you governed what you said and did by its effect on all. When Grant and Alan worked around the barn or in the woods, the combination was changed again, the personal radiations concentrated between these two in a manner wholly masculine, a manner they themselves were not aware of. Regardless of how close and intimate four people were, intimacy changed and increased when the circle was reduced.

As she went out now into the raw night, hearing Edith Kinsman's "Renie!" from the sleigh at the gate, she knew the radiations were changing, changing pattern with her own departure, drawing in from the atmosphere of the family complete to the special atmosphere of Alan, Grant and Margaret.

A thought took hold. What if something should blunt the radiations, shake the faith that gave them their special quality, their confident warmth?

The sense of ease in this house was such that while she went about the common business of getting supper, washing dishes, changing her dress, the afternoon's apprehensions had seemed remote. Merely something she should mention to Grant without emphasis. Something he should know about.

Now, outside, it was different. Now, as she left the house and Grant and the children, her family's living flesh, the breathing evidence of tolerance and affection, fear gripped her imagination with a troubling strength.

As she walked up the frozen path to the gate her instinctive reluctance to leave the house was sharpened to urgency by the need to get back and talk it over, the need to get it off her mind.

Grant knocked the ashes from his pipe, went to the coat-closet for his notebook, and drew a chair to the end of the table farthest from the stove.

Margaret looked up from her *Reader*. Her eyes moved from Alan to Grant and back to Alan, quizzical with the small ridiculous thought that stirred behind them.

"Homework," she said, gravely.

Alan laughed. "Yeah. Even the boss has to do his homework. But he don't have to show it to Renie, I guess."

Grant said, "You mean 'doesn't'," and thought, That's what being married to a teacher does for you. His pencil ran down the figures recording the diameters of trees sampled along the cruise-lines. "I s'pose you could call it homework, but you never know the answer till you work it out with an axe . . . We ran across an otter-slide today, Alan. You could see where he slid on his belly down a snow-bank into the brook."

Alan's eyes came up in mid-sentence from *A History of Canada for High Schools . . . Though not part of the loyalist movement, the Scottish emigration to Nova Scotia belongs roughly to this period. Economic conditions in the Highlands . . .* His glance travelled across a brush-drawing of bearded kilted men, marching ashore from a beached longboat, a full-rigged ship far off against sea and sky. He shoved the history aside and sat with chin on folded arms, watching Grant's pencil, while his mind roved the eighty-acre lot his father and Dan had cruised that morning. It noted the otter-slide as an incidental fact, part of the variety and interest of the woods, but of no importance. He said, "What's out there, Dad? When d'you plan to chop it out?"

"Haven't figured that far yet," Grant said. "Have to dicker for stumpage first. Why? Getting anxious?"

Alan said, "I was just wondering."

"Well . . . there's enough stuff up back of Kelley's to keep the boys busy for the rest of the winter, I should think. Maybe we'll figure on Katen's and another couple of lots out there for the summer. Small crew, working when we get a chance.

198

Not worth while to build a bunk-house, I guess. We can walk in, mornings. A short day. Peel the stuff, maybe, and pick up a few extra dollars that way. Should be enough water in the creek by early fall to run it down to where we can pile it by the road for the trucks." He paused, and added thoughtfully, "Unless we get into something else . . ."

Alan made a pretence of going back to the settlement of Nova Scotia . . . *in the Highlands of Scotland were the principal cause. In 1773 the vanguard arrived* . . . The printed lines meant nothing to him. He was thinking of other things. The Katen lot was not to be stripped this winter. Summer work. They'd be cutting this summer. Grant and Dan and himself and two or three others, perhaps. In the slack time between spring planting and haying time.

Across the table, Margaret was studying the *Reader*. Something in her manner caught his interest. She was listening . . . intent on the skating race from *Hans Brinker* but listening to himself and Grant . . . Amusement tingled in Alan's mind. He began to remember a little scene from the summer before last. The two of them loafing under the maples by the road on a Sunday afternoon. She had said: "Lan, how can we keep so much stuff in our heads?"

He had answered her slowly, "How do you mean, Mag?", careful to get to the root of what she was driving at, warning himself not to laugh no matter what it was.

"Well," Margaret said, "Katen's car. It just went up the road. But I remember all the other times it's gone past. Remembering —Why don't it squeeze out something? That story Renie told us about how she got to know Dad—when he hauled wood to the school-house. That's kind of a long story . . . You'd think a person'd have to forget something to make room for that. Why don't we?"

He had taken his time. His first impulse was to tease, to say, "How d'you know we *don't*, Mag? If you forget it, it's gone. You wouldn't know you ever knew it, now would you?" He could have had some fun that way, could have made up a mythical tale and proved to Margaret that she had known and forgotten it, and that in the fact of learning it again she had been forced to forget something else to make room for it.

But he couldn't tease Margaret about anything she took seriously. He had an instinct about the family, especially Margaret. He thought: Maybe she's worried about it; maybe she *does* think you have to make a hole by forgetting something old before you

199

can put in something new. Furthermore, he suspected Margaret was smarter than himself. He had to do his best against the day when she would think of his answer in the light of her developing knowledge.

He had said, "What happens, you start out with a blank brain. Putting in a thing like a car going by don't take up the millionth part of a pinpoint. That story of Renie's'd be less than a smitch. You want to remember something special, you pick a speck and put your old magnifier on it." He couldn't resist a little teasing at the end. "All the stuff you got in there so far, Mag, looks like a fly-speck on a barn door. You might fill up a quarter of the waste space by the time you're a hundred and ten."

Alan thought of this now in the warm kitchen, perhaps reminded of it somehow by Margaret's alert divided attention, carefully veiled; her mind, curious and quick and taking in all kinds of things at once . . .

Margaret glanced across at Grant's bent head; conscious of Alan's amused and affectionate glance. She had sped with Gretel Brinker along the ice of a Dutch canal, heard the hoarse cheers at the end of the shining mile, but she had not missed a word of talk about the otter-slide or the plans for Katen's lot.

It gave her a small secret pleasure to realize she had shared in this, been permitted to listen briefly to words about the world of men and boys and work. There was something else. In the fact of Alan's casual and confident knowledge of that man's world, the work-world, a richness and pride were added to her own personal experience, the intimate half-teasing relationship between herself and him. Listening to this talk, Margaret now was a small mistress taking joy in her lover's devotion to battle and venture and discovery.

She raised her eyes to the alarm clock on the shelf behind the stove. Two minutes to nine. Gravely she watched the long hand move in tiny jerks to the middle of XII, and dropped her glance to regard Grant and Alan.

"It's my bedtime now," she said primly.

Grant always went upstairs to say good night to Margaret when Renie was out. He returned to the kitchen now and found Alan hunkered in Renie's rocker, his feet on the nickeled fender of the stove. As he settled in his own chair by the wood-box, Grant felt again the tingle of intimate affection that always touched him when he and the boy were alone together—something you couldn't find the words to say, even if you wanted to; and of course you didn't want to. His love for Renie was a continuing quiet passion, his love for Margaret a lyrical lightness of heart. The thing he felt for Alan was something else. Something farther back, rooted in the time of Anna Gordon and Hazel McKee. Rooted in winter, the time in which he had worked his way to calmness and deliverance, a personal integrity.

For Alan, being in the house with Grant when no one else was there, when there was nothing to do but talk and listen, or even sit in silence, was a special feeling. Different from the man-and-boy relationship in the woods or the barn or the hayfield, which was a companionship of work, more a thing of action than communication. Different even from the spirit of lazy half-hours together on the back doorstep in the evening; then, the sense of the passing moment was always there. In this kitchen-feeling there was a kind of continuing permanence. This would happen again. You were in the house, among the long-known things: the table with its dark red cloth, the conversational stove.

All the past times you had sat there melted into the present. Without the memory of separate facts or special detail, the spirit of a hundred evenings combined and flowed into one.

Here he had heard stories of Uncle James, the old man crippled with rheumatism now, in Uncle Fred's house up the road. Of Uncle Will, who had gone away and had his own lumber business in Halifax; of Uncle Joe McKee, and Dan Graham, and Dan's brother, Colin, who hadn't been home in years. And Dan's cousin Bill who had spent a summer on the Shore a long time ago. Of Currie Headers who had been born there, and grown up there, and gone away. A good deal of the Channel Shore had become part of him while he sat across the kitchen stove from Grant.

Sometimes an incidental revelation of personal feeling would enrich this mixture of usual things. The curious quiet tenderness with which Grant said "Hazel . . . your mother" on the rare occasions when her name was mentioned. The odd meditative way in which Grant had once recounted how James Marshall had travelled to the States to bring him home. Almost as if Grant knew he, Alan, couldn't really like Uncle James, and told that story in a kind of wish to be fair . . . Alan carried in his mind a picture of that small boy on the plush of a day coach seat, dim lights, and rushing darkness. He always tried to remember this in the presence of the stern cold man he was taken to see, sometimes, in Uncle Fred's house.

All, a part of the texture of these evenings . . .

The things you'd felt, that were now part of the sum of feeling, came back, though the circumstances in which you'd felt them once were lost, were not important any more.

Once in the fall of the year, more than two years ago, Grant and Alan had come back from Graham's Lake after dark, with a string of trout, and found the house deserted. Renie and Margaret had crossed the fields to Grahams'. After Grant had pulled out the damper and shaken up the fire, Alan had inched the rocker up to the warmth and leaned back, sock feet on the fender, already drowsy with comfort and alert for the male companionship, the Grant-and-Alan feeling of warmth and kitchen talk.

Suddenly Grant's voice, rough and exasperated: "Get yourself out of there!"

Alan had stiffened, pulled his feet to the floor, sat up erect and rigid.

Grant had turned, still in a half-stoop, his hand reaching down toward the seat of his chair, his face startled and incredulous, touched with alarm. "Alan—" The voice was a mixture of amazement and reassurance—"Good Lord! You didn't think I was talking to *you!*"

Alan had grinned and put his feet back on the fender. Grant smacked the cat lightly, driving her out of his chair, and laughed. "Cats are all right, but . . . you have to let them know who's boss." The laughter had in it a trace of disappointment, an edge of hurt that his son should even consider the possibility of being spoken to in a tone like that.

This touched Alan's mind lightly now, along with all the other odds and ends of personal intimacy; not the memory in detail, not even the fact of occurrence; merely the softly nagging sense of a thing half-forgotten, the rush of affectionate feeling, the strength of its essence.

Something Grant had said earlier tonight stuck in his mind, anchored by a question mark.

The answers always came. You could ask Grant anything and be sure of a reasonable answer. That was part of the person-to-person way in which he dealt with you. But Alan had been building up a private theory: it was better not to ask. It was more satisfying to hear the answers dropped casually or developed in action. Years ago on an evening like this Grant had said:

"There's a good bit of pulpwood-cutting going on. If a fellow could get a crew together and go into it in a bit bigger scale . . ." That fall and winter he had bought stumpage on a number of back lots northwest of Graham's Lake, and with Dan Graham had begun the operations that made him a contractor. It almost seemed to Alan that in some Arabian Nights fashion the whole thing had grown out of that spoken thought, absently voiced while Grant smoothed an axe handle in the kitchen lamplight with a piece of broken glass.

There were evenings when Grant would sit wordless, absorbed in his reading or merely thinking, but tonight Alan knew with the instinct he had for family atmosphere that his father wanted talk.

He said, without too much show of interest, "It's a good piece of woods, is it?"

Grant said, "Better than you'd expect. Not been cut over, much, that far to the northeast. Oh, there's places where they took out fire-wood . . . but most of it's solid spruce. Some fir. A little hardwood. Not just Katen's. Miles of it. We took a walk east. I'd been through some of it before, but just never realized how much there was."

"Hard to get out, though, I s'pose," Alan said.

Grant nodded. "Yes. . A lot of it's not close enough to any kind of a stream big enough to drive on. You'd have to cut roads and haul. And I don't know . . . The profit's not too big, even when you're close to water."

He hesitated, and went on thoughtfully. "I kind of hate to knock down stuff like that for pulp, anyway. If a fellow had a portable mill, a diesel outfit . . . He could set up in there, a place like that, and turn the stuff into lumber. Right there. Payload to the railroad or boat'd be a lot bigger."

If we don't get into something else . . . That was the thing that was anchored in Alan's mind. The scope of it seized his imagination; the images began to form. He said tentatively, "Lumber's pretty low, though."

Grant laughed. "Low enough. And hard to figure where you'd come out at. Something like the story Hugh Currie tells about old Walter Lisle, years ago. Walter couldn't read or write, but he liked to keep things moving. One summer he had nine barrels of salt mackerel. He loaded them into his boat and crossed to Princeport. Sold the fish for eight dollars a barrel, seventy-two bucks, and bought a horse. Walked the horse into his boat and traded him in Morgan's Harbour for a sow and a litter of pigs.

Took the pigs aboard and sailed down to Findlay's Bridge and traded them for a yearling steer. Came back to The Head and traded the steer to Sam Freeman's father for a wheelbarrow and a dozen Plymouth Rocks . . . All in two days. Fritz McKee pointed out he'd kind of traded himself thin. Walt said, 'Yes, sir. Maybe I did. But I was doing business' . . . Something like that, lumbering. Can't figure everything, if you're going to have the fun of doing business." He laughed again. "Not that I think a fellow has to be as anxious to turn things over as Walt Lisle was. Should be able to have some fun and still come out even."

The picture formed in Alan's mind: a low slab-sided bunk-house somewhere out back with logs yarded shoulder-high and more being snaked in. The snarl of a forty-eight-inch circular, the mutter of the diesel and the drive-rig. Ten or a dozen men busy at the gliding carriage, the skidway, the edger and trimmer. A pile of edgings always burning, and sawdust growing in great pale heaps on the moss-floored yard. Trucks coming down to tide-water or going on out to the railway sidings at Copeland or Stoneville . . . thousands of board feet of yellow deal . . .

There was in this for him more than a second-hand interest in something that was turning over in Grant's mind. It had gone past the stage of being turned over or Grant wouldn't have mentioned it. It was an enterprise in which he himself would have a share, however small. He felt that, from the way in which Grant had taken him into his confidence. He thought, maybe it'll turn out I can run the trimmer.

He could feel the excitement of it, and the fading of a remote but certain worry, the thing that had crossed his mind on the way to school that morning, the thing he had shared with no one. This dated from the previous spring, when they had chopped from the shed floor, with sharpened hoes, the winter's accumulated layer of sheep manure. He remembered Grant's exact words: "This is absolutely the worst job we've got. Worse than picking stone." He had looked up and laughed. "You'll get a great kick out of this, thinking about it—when you've got your own business. In Halifax or somewhere."

In Halifax or somewhere . . . He hadn't thought much about it at the time, but the words remained in his mind. Then, last summer holidays, he had mentioned to Grant that Rod Sinclair wanted a boy to cleat box ends for a week or two. Not asking, just mentioning. Grant had said, "You won't be making a living around circular saws when you get older, so why take a chance on losing a hand?" He hadn't pressed it. There was nothing to be gained by mentioning that cleating ends didn't take you near the saws. And Grant had taken him into the woods for the holidays, anyway.

A number of outwardly unrelated things had begun to add themselves up: the little careful restraints, the insistence on school. The meaning was there when you thought about it. He had heard Frank Graham say more than once that Currie Head, the whole Channel Shore, was a place to be born in, to grow your teeth in, and to get to hell away from. That didn't make sense, when you thought of Grant working hard and happily there, his whole life tied to the Shore. But it was something you would have to meet and deal with some time. Trips to places like Prince-port were fine. Seeing new things was fine. But the idea of going away for good . . .

Tonight, in some subtle way, had changed the picture. It might be that he would leave The Head eventually. But it might not. If Grant went into milling he would make a go of it, as he did of everything. If a man had a business like that, what should his son need or want beyond a chance to work at it?

He asked, audaciously and putting laughter into it so that Grant could laugh it off if he wanted to: "Have you ordered the rig yet, Grant?"

Grant started. Not at the use of his name instead of the usual "Dad". Now and then Alan would call him "Grant", humorously, as if mimicking someone else. Or, with dead-pan solemnity, "Mr. Marshall". Just as Margaret, in the privacy of home, often called her mother "Renie". It was a joke among themselves, without meaning except for the laughter in it. No, it was not the "Grant", though that was unusual unless Renie or Margaret were there to hear. It was something else that startled him; you kept thinking of Alan as a boy who was all action, and then he shook you with a word or look that came straight out of the odd direct insight you didn't know was there . . .

He said, "Well . . . I haven't said anything about it yet, even to your—even to Renie. I know where we can lay hands on a pretty good fifty-horse-power diesel, though."

Light footsteps sounded on the porch. Renie came in then, a dust of melting snowflakes in her hair. Her face was flushed with the raw cold of the damp snowfall, and warm with the sense of coming home.

Faint sounds came from upstairs, the sound of a door closing and a window going up. Now the relationship was down to two again, Grant and Renie. She wondered how she could lead into what she had to say. Never in more than twelve years of married life had she found Grant hard to approach about anything, but this was something that went back to a time they had talked of only on his initiative, never on hers.

It was characteristic of Grant that once having talked of it without reserve he had never returned to it directly again. There was no barrier in the mind. No open avoidance of Hazel McKee's name or Anna's, or even of Anse's if they happened to be mentioned in the reminiscent conversation of the Channel Shore. But that was of the surface. Of these people and himself, the inner thing, he had not spoken, except rarely and by indirection, since an evening in May a little more than a year after Hazel's death.

The scene was interwoven in Renie's mind with the smell of sawn lumber and the sound of running water; lumber piled behind the roadside maples at Grant's Place and the rush of Graham's Brook.

She had walked down, that evening in the spring of her second year at The Head, to have supper with the Frank Grahams. Afterward, Frank had remarked a little slyly that she and Grant Marshall always seemed to find something to talk about when they happened to fall in with each other.

That was not strictly true. They had done little talking. But she had admitted to herself, thinking about it, that she found satisfaction in being near him, a satisfaction that left her still unsatisfied and yet was heightened by recognition of something in Grant that turned toward her, and matched her feeling, and waited.

As she walked home from Grahams' in the early dusk she heard Grant piling lumber in The Place, noticed the glimmer of white planks through the trees, and turned in at the path down from the road.

He dusted off his hands and laughed.

"Well, Renie . . . come in and sit down."

They had relaxed on a pile of planks, the stuff he was planning to put into his house.

His fingers were suddenly busy with cigarette papers and a small tobacco-bag. She was pleased that his voice and smile were light with humour. That was a quality of which she had seen little . . . Not much wonder, she supposed, considering the lifetime he had lived in twenty months. But tonight he laughed, and his mood was catching.

She said impulsively, "Roll me one."

He said, "Ida Freeman'll smell your breath. She's not quite as full of conversation as Hat Wilmot, but you'll hear about it . . . or others will."

He went on then to roll her a cigarette with careful fingers. "Not much good at this. Haven't been at it long enough myself."

Renie had never smoked. The impulse was one of curiosity mixed with an obscure urge toward closer companionship. She choked on the first drawn breath. Grant took the small ragged cylinder from her fingers, pinched it out against the edge of a plank, and tucked it into the tobacco-bag.

He said, "I'll stand for a good deal, from clergymen and schoolteachers, but nobody can waste my makings." The look in his eyes was a blend of amusement and something that startled Renie's blood: frank, open affection. Still half-choking, she bent her head, coughed into the bib of his overalls, pungent with dried balsam, and clasped her hands round his neck.

A little later, as the mild spring evening darkened, he had talked of Anna and Hazel and Alan. As he told her of the conversation with Anna on the beach, of his awkward effort to explain the existence together of a sure love and an apprehensive uncertainty, she had had a curious understanding of the link between the uncertain boy of two years before and the man of that day. Something that didn't change. Once again he was trying to make things clear, to put on record for a woman loved his heart's findings. The difference was that now there was no uncertainty, no conflict of loyalties. And now he could find the words . . .

He had talked simply, without obvious feeling, almost as if he were speaking of someone other than himself. "You've heard a lot of talk. I know how people talk—they can't help it. About me, going to live with the Gordons; marrying Hazel. As a kind of—what would you say?—atonement, maybe. For Anna. But it wasn't just that way. There's not much you can do about things like that when they're over. I didn't feel entirely guilty . . . At least that wasn't the whole of it. I was mad, sore. Hardly knew what at. But free. Uncle James—anything I owed Uncle James was paid up. I did what I felt like, without a doubt in the world." He halted, and said reflectively. "It's a queer feeling, not to have doubts. It didn't come, finally, till I went to find Hazel McKee . . ."

He rolled a second cigarette and lit it. "Funny thing. You're thinking Hazel and I were—well, hardly what you'd call in love . . . But we were closer together, maybe, in that little time she had, than lovers ever get. Don't go round with any idea it was just—self-sacrifice; marrying Hazel. She was in a bad way, and nothing could make things any worse for me. When I said 'free' I didn't mean 'happy'. We'd have been all right, if she'd lived . . . All right. In the end we both learned something. Not a damn thing matters but what people can do for each other, when they're up against it."

In the pause, Renie said, "That's your religion, is it, Grant?"

He said, "Yes," and then, returning to an earlier thought, "Hazel did more for me than I was ever able to do for her. I've got Alan."

His tone startled her, and what he said next was an answer to her thought.

"I s'pose most people, if you look at the outside of things—I s'pose most people would figure I wouldn't care much for that kid. Well, I can't go round denying that without calling attention to things that ought to be left alone. You know—before he was born, and when he was born, I felt queer about it. But it came over me that of all the people I knew . . . this baby was the one that had no way at all of helping himself. I didn't have to make up my mind . . . It was made up for me by everything that happened before."

He laughed, remembering. "I started out thinking of Alan as a person. You know, a kid entitled to a square show. And the next thing I knew—I was crazy about him."

She had said, slowly: "You've thought about the risk."

He said, "If you're going to be a father, you've got to take a chance, I guess. One kind or another. Hell, Renie, we'll take each day as it comes."

He had paused then and spoken matter-of-factly. "You ought to go into McKees' some time and see him. We've got him trapped in a play-pen."

"Yes, I should," Renie said. "I will, too. But . . . I'll see him every day pretty soon, won't I? Or isn't that the idea?"

He had turned to look at her and laughed, and found her hands.

She turned now from the coat-closet, from fiddling with spring clothes, aimlessly, to walk across the kitchen to the rocker beyond the range; and halted beside Grant's chair as she caught the quizzical appraisal in his glance.

She turned to him. "What now?"

Grant laughed, "The Fraser bottom . . ."

He reached out, circled her skirted thighs with an arm, pulling her close to his chair, casually. "Bess has it too," he said. "Dan's caught in the same trap."

She dropped her face in his neck, shivering with laughter and seized by a tenderness in which there was something almost sad.

"You're an awful fool, Grant."

"I'm not so bad . . . Get over where you belong, then."

This kind of unpredictable foolishness, coming up rarely from depths of quietness, had a contagion in it. But it was going to be harder now to say what she had to say. She went round the stove, pulling the rocker in.

Grant said, "Now you can tell me what *you've* got on your mind."

She was quiet for a minute, caught by this curious matter of insight in others.

She said deliberately, almost lightly, "Well—I was worried a little. About Alan. Oh . . . it's not anything about him, *himself* . . . not anything definite. Just—Grant: did you ever think about how it would be if he *heard*? . . . If someone started talking?"

"Why?"

He asked the question quickly, with a sharp interest.

Renie said, "Don't get worked up, now. It's nothing, actually. I—something brought it to mind, and I had to mention it . . . You and I, we're odd people. We don't gossip. Maybe we forget, sometimes, that others do. But this may be—oh, it may just be imagination. It was something one of the kids said. Clyde—Clyde Wilmot. Talking to Alan. He said, 'your grandmother' and I thought he meant Josie. In a kind of a sly way. Jennie shut him up. But he could have been—"

Grant said, "Oh." He added, "Thought of it? . . . Yes, of course. At times . . . You don't entirely forget."

Hat Wilmot's youngsters . . . They would be the kind who were sure to know. Perhaps the only children on the Shore who had heard the old story. Everywhere, there were one or two who would keep a thing alive; for no reason except remembering gossip, unconscious malice; and go back to it, relishing it, carelessly, with children listening. And it wasn't the kind of thing children would keep to themselves forever. Some children. Not if they remembered; not if they could enjoy a sly renown . . .

Pictures formed in Grant's mind. Himself and Hat Wilmot in the buggy behind the black horse Polo, young Dan and Bill hanging to the back of the seat . . .

Hat Wilmot and others like her hadn't changed. All their conjectures had been confirmed. They'd been cheated out of public recognition of that fact by the marriage of Grant Marshall and Hazel McKee. They had talked it out in their warm kitchens and stiff parlours, fourteen years ago. A lot of time had gone by, but it wasn't likely they'd keep still forever . . .

And he hadn't worried, greatly. Not with his conscious mind. Too many other things . . .

He thought now of a winter night, in a hotel room on Front Street in Toronto. The last of the ten strange days of first re-acquaintance with Hazel McKee. Strange? No. The only strangeness was in the sense of—what?—the inevitable. The way they had recognized from the first that the road to peace was through each other.

Grant's eyes now were fixed without seeing it on the nickeled handle of an iron lifter, standing in a stove-lid on the back of the stove . . . His mind was back in those bitter, exalted days—his own ambition somehow to solve it all: Josie's shame and the sorrow behind the gently brooding face of Richard, and Hazel's disgrace—

And Hazel. What, really, had been the impulse of her heart? Return. Return to the Shore. Return in a kind of bitter honour to the country she had fled from, the land she had escaped . . .

How their dreams had meshed! His own necessities and Hazel's need—for the Shore, for the bitter presence of Eva and the look on Richard's face.

That hotel room on Front Street. Grant could hear again the clanking of freight cars and see the gleam of stars faintly through city murk. They lay on its fringes still, but the city had been already behind them.

Behind Hazel, the months of dreary work in a dress-making shop on Spadina Avenue, the weeks of illness and worry and resignation; the public masquerade as *Mrs. Gordon;* and, under the eyes of Bertha Mason, the private shame . . . Perhaps, the secret knowledge; for she must have sensed—she must have sensed the end of it, and known—

Behind Grant, ten winter days in a strange unfriendly city; days lighted by an exaltation, the knowledge of deliverance . . . He could feel this again now; and he could feel again the need to go on record, to say it to someone, that had sent him northward through the city to Andrew Graham's door. To tell Bill Graham, who had known Hazel and known Anna; who had been a witness to his shame and the beginning of redemption, and who had to know the end . . .

210

Behind them both, the grim ceremony in Bertha Mason's parlour . . . *I, Grant, take thee, Hazel* . . . And before them both the Shore.

They had huddled in bed there, on Front Street, in that odd intimacy, physical, emotional and affectionate. A relationship without passion, without even the memory of shared passion, but with, perhaps, passion expected on the other side of spring. In Hazel? The hope, perhaps. But expectation? He doubted it, now. She must have sensed . . .

Hazel had said, "Grant . . . There's something I'd like . . . I'm always wanting something . . ."

And he, coming up from the edge of sleep: "We're square, Hazel. What is it?"

She had taken his hand and placed it on her swollen belly. "This. If anything happens . . . I want him to be yours. Grow up as yours."

He had told her to shut up. Nothing would happen. And the boy was Grant Marshall's son. They'd make it so. *Go to sleep and forget it.*

One thing, he thought, they had been blind to. Or had kept far back in the closets of the mind. The thing that threatened now . . . And yet, for years the fiction had been preserved. Almost unthought of. Until in his own mind and heart it wore the shape of truth.

Other pictures . . . Alan, helpless in the cradle; black-haired and mischievous in the play-pen. A stumbling four-year-old with a tiny hand-made rake, following the hay-cart . . . The easy promise, made in bed to a worrying girl, had become the truth of life. And not because of a word pledged. Because of love, affection, the way things were. His mind skipped to a day when the boy was eleven. They were stowing away green oats in the barn when Adam Falt came by and halted the second-hand Chev in which he now drove the mail. Adam squinted through the barn doors at Alan in the mow. "I see you've got some home-grown help . . ." Grant had said, "Oh, sure, they grow up," matter-of-factly. He'd had to hide his amusement at the way Alan moved, with a stature heightened at the sense of identification with the place, the work, his father.

Grant got out of his chair now, back in the present, and stood for a little by the window, looking out into the blank dark. Josie Gordon's light went out as he stood there, leaving a single spark at Frank Graham's against the black.

He didn't return to his chair by the wood-box, but began slowly pacing, back and forth, between the window and the door of the bedroom. Renie hadn't seen him do that in nine years, not since the winter Alan lay in delirium with scarlet fever.

211

When he did sit down it was in one of the hard chairs by the table. He sat with elbows on the cloth and head up, a curious alert thoughtfulness replacing the calm of a thousand winter evenings.

He asked, "Anything you'd like to suggest?"

Renie shook her head. "I don't know what . . . I'm thinking of Alan." That was half the truth, anyway. "I was thinking, maybe . . . Perhaps he should be told. By someone . . . I mean, not hear it from somebody outside, and carry it around inside, stewing about it. I'd be willing . . . If you wanted . . ."

The fingers of Grant's right hand tapped the table. He clenched and unclenched the hand.

"No, I don't think so. That's not it." He looked down at the hand, curiously. "Something I should've been giving some thought to. You get kind of lulled . . ."

He stopped, leaving the thought unfinished. Later on, in the big maple bed, Renie lay and listened to his even breathing. It was not the breathing, softened with lost vigilance, of a man drifting down to sleep. Her body's impulse was to turn to him, to press against him, to let him feel the warmth of her slow affectionate passion, quiet and constant. With an intuition deeper than instinct she controlled the urge.

NORTH of the coastal slope, beyond the fringes of cultivation and the old second line of settlements, the woods swept unbroken over a second fold in the land. Here there are lonely lakes, swamps tucked between wavelike hills, aimless brooks and stillwaters in which are sourced the creeks that slip through hidden intervales and narrow valleys to emerge finally in bushy pastures and tumble to the Channel. Here there were miles of red spruce and fir, low wet land studded with black spruce, hills clothed with white maple and rock maple, stony plateaus of white and yellow birch.

This is the forest behind the Channel Shore, stretching east and west, rolling north until its brook-water begins to lie in secret ponds, to crawl and slip the other way, northward toward the railroad and the farms along the gulf.

Much of this wilderness had been granted long ago to early settlers, as back lands additional to their farms along the sea. A hundred years and more ago, in the time of early prosperity, the second and third generations of settlers bought up more, seeing, perhaps, a vision of villages and farms.

That dream was dead. Once in a while a man and his sons would cut a road and haul enough hardwood to rip up for a kitchen floor. Sometimes, in the mackerel-fishing days, a man would search these hills for pine and twitch it out to be sawn into planking for a two-master. Now and then when a wood-lot nearer home was chopped out, you had to go back for fire-wood. And lately there had been some pulpwood-cutting there. But much of it had never been touched by an axe.

On the southern fringe of this were the lots Grant had cruised with Dan Graham. This was where he went, with Alan, in the days following their talk across the stove about a saw-mill; the days following Renie's reminder of the past.

Friday morning, he had glanced at Alan across the breakfast table and spoken lightly, smiling. "Well—d'you think school can get along without you, for one day? What d'*you* think, Renie?"

Renie's answering smile, Alan thought, had been a little startled. He had been startled himself. Startled, surprised, and delighted. This was more than he had allowed himself to hope for. It was only one day . . . but for once work was being placed ahead of school. He felt a soaring sense of freedom.

That morning they had followed the road to Graham's Lake and turned east, walking along the lake beach and then up through scattered hardwood, chopped over long ago and now growing up again, to strike one of the old hauling-roads leading in from Katen's Rocks. This they tramped back to its point of disappearance in the timber.

Now, Friday and Saturday and Sunday and Christmas were over. Sunday you had to put up with. But Christmas, Alan thought, had been a long day. Oh, there was the laughing excitement of presents, in the morning, but . . . He felt a little guilty about this. Margaret took such delight in the young fir with its lights and green and red tissue bells and tinsel, filled stockings, wreaths in the windows, the blaze in the front room fireplace. He looked down at the slightly lop-sided blue mitts on his hands, the gift of her secrecy, and laughed . . . Must be getting older, when what Christmas meant to him personally was a day's delay in getting back to this . . . He comforted himself with the thought that it had been drizzly, anyway. No day for work.

Friday and Saturday they had spent, mainly, exploring; getting the lay of the land.

Now, on Tuesday forenoon, they were dropping small stuff in Katen's lot, trimming and cutting it to length for corduroy to bridge the swamp-holes in the hauling-road, and at the same time extending and widening the road.

Alan had been out back once or twice in previous winters, but never so far as in these recent days. He thought of the land as a vast hilly checkerboard, each of the squares owned by different men; and then rejected this idea. You couldn't see any lines. Only, here and there, the crooked traces of an overgrown hauling-road, and when you looked up, woods that sloped away to the sky; new snow, and the dark green of spruce and fir, with now and then a patch of birch or maple, and occasionally a grove of giant beech.

Somewhere far to the north the railway ran, paralleling the shore until the track curved south to join it far to the east at Copeland. Southward was the shore, the Channel's edge flickering to its curved beach at Currie Head, curling on the reefs at Katen's Rocks, stretching away east against the land—Mars Lake, Forester's Pond, Millersville.

214

But here, out back, there was no hint of railway or shore, only woods. A thought tickled Alan's mind with a mild sense of strangeness.

He said, "It's like water."

Grant spoke absently. "What?"

Alan laughed, a little self-conscious. "I was thinking of the woods. The cleared places out front, they're like a strip of land with water both sides of it. Only on this side the water's woods." He laughed again, apologetically.

Grant glanced at him. "Kind of, at that." After a minute he spoke again. "There's a tide to it, too. They dammed it back a little, years ago. But it's high again, now, with places like McNaughtons' and Kilfyles' under water. Under woods."

Alan felt better. He had been touched by embarrassment at having voiced his fancy, but Grant had gone along with the mood.

He asked, "How's it happen people own this woods in here, Dad? When nobody lives on it? . . . Why don't they?"

"Live on it? Well—." Grant drove his axe into the butt of a slender fir, fence-rail size, and straightened. "Times change. When the old people got here first I guess they figured the place would grow. Some of them took up this back land so they'd have places for their sons, I s'pose . . . or as a kind of speculation. Didn't turn out that way. The young ones didn't stay. Nothing to stay for. Better chance other places. Too far from markets here for farm stuff." He broke off and dropped the fir. "Couldn't push the tide back."

Alan said, "Well, it'll be a little lower by next fall." He waited, hoping Grant would pick the subject up and talk freely again about the woods and the mill and the summer, as he had last Thursday night. But Grant said nothing.

Alan was a little puzzled. He still felt the sense of freedom, but it was beginning to be clouded by an atmosphere he didn't understand: Grant's absent-mindedness, his disinclination to talk about his plans, even though you made openings. An oddness in other ways . . . His mind turned back to Sunday. Coming down the church hill from Christmas service, he had walked as usual with the boys, Bert and Clyde and the rest. Grant overtaking them in the sleigh, with Renie and Margaret; stopping to say, "Climb up behind, Alan." A queerness, and unexplained . . . He glanced up now, with the feeling his father was about to speak. But Grant was merely cutting the fir pole into lengths.

Alan picked up the butt and carried it to the side of the hauling-road. He said, "Where are we, anyway? About three miles in?"

"About that, from the shore road," Grant said.

"How much of the hauling-road's in shape for trucks, d'you think?" Alan asked.

"None of it. Oh, for a mile or so in from the main road maybe, there's nothing to do but a little fixing, rocks in the holes. From there in to where we are now, there's a lot of swamping out to do. Some stumps I'll have to blast. Build a bridge or two. We'll go out that way tonight when we go home."

This, to Alan, was part of the strangeness. Grant's words on Thursday night had been confident and definite. They had carried a promise, almost; and in them he had touched the body of a dream. Two weeks of work, between school and school. Two weeks in which they would swamp roads, make plans, clear land for a mill site. Perhaps with Dan, or Lon Katen, along. So that in the spring, when the chopping back of Kelley's was finished, they'd be set to make this further venture. Ready to go.

But now they were puttering. And there was no talk of plans. It wasn't like him. It wasn't like Grant to be casual about work in the woods.

Grant glanced up now at the sun. "Let's knock off and eat a bite."

They sat on a pile of trimmed wood in a little natural clearing, scarcely more than a wide place in the hauling-road, where the sun came through. The snow was crusty, here. Over Sunday and Christmas it had warmed up and drizzled and then hardened again. As he unbuckled his book bag and dug out thermos and sandwiches, the thought kept running through Alan's head that they wouldn't get much done, in the two weeks of holidays, at this rate.

As if he understood the unsaid things, Grant said: "No hurry about this, I guess. I've been thinking it over, and I don't know. Might cut pulp again next summer. Wait awhile on the other business. Lumber's low . . ."

Alan felt in his veins the tide of disappointment, a sorrowful anger. What had Grant talked about it at all for, if this was the way it was? And he was talking in the singular.

He looked up, sideways. Grant's expression was abstracted, his glance intent on something far from Felix Katen's woods. This that he had said, perhaps was what he had been about to say for the last four days. But that wasn't all of it.

He filled his pipe and lit it. His tone was tentative, his voice a little hoarse.

"Did you ever think what you'd like to do? After you go away to school, I mean. What you'd like to train for . . ."

He couldn't let the question lie. He had to go on, fumbling with words, trying to make too much of it before he halted for an answer.

"You could take a business course, like Will Marshall after the war. He's done all right, I guess. But if you want to go through for—oh, law; or medicine, even—or just, well, general stuff; and see what you want to do after . . ."

He let the words fade, looking down at trampled snow and skeletal brown ferns around his feet. He had done it awkwardly and bluntly; he recognized his own failure as an actor. You tried to work up to this. You tried to lead into it by talking of men who had left the Shore as boys: Will Marshall, going up through accounting to a contracting business; Dan Graham's brother Colin, an engineer with an oil company in Venezuela; Dave Neill, growing fruit in California; Dan's Uncle Andrew, a professor of mathematics in Toronto. His cousin Bill, who had come down and spent a summer on the Shore, years ago—something now in advertising. Stan Currie, whose name you saw sometimes over stories in the newspapers. But the boy hadn't been interested. You never got a chance to turn the talk easily from what Stan Currie and Col Graham were doing in the world outside to what Alan Marshall would find to do there.

He hadn't been able to put it off any longer. He'd had to get it settled. There was nothing he could do but ask a forthright question. When you dealt with things that lived in your marrow you couldn't dress them up. An old fault, a double-edged failing: the inability to rest content while a thing remained unsaid and unsettled, and the inability to say it in anything but the bluntest words.

Something flickered in his mind. The sound of leisurely swell on the beach, sunlight on grey shingles, the smell of brine and tanbark and a girl, turning to him . . . *I'd feel the way I do now; I'd feel this way.* The embrace he had turned away from. Queer how time lived. Well, when this scene, this memory of today came back to him, a dozen years from now, it would not remind him of a gutless indecision.

But the fact was bitter as gall. The fact that to keep your son, to preserve the heart of truth from creeping gossip on the stairs of time . . . you must send your son away.

Alan said, "No. Not much. Thought about it, I mean. I—"
Grant waited, and went on.

"I guess we have to. Think about it. Nobody stays here if they want—When I think of the people we know—there's more Shore people in the States, Upper Canada, out west . . . The smart ones leave. Renie and me—we've been doing some thinking about it. You're a kid yet, but in some ways you're grown up. It's better to get used to . . . better to rub up against people, before you've got

217

to, well, leave for good." He went into it abruptly. "Big Bob's been after us again. He wants you to stay with him. This winter and spring."

He paused again. Alan said nothing, and Grant went on.

"It's a good time for it, the holidays. You can start right in with the after-Christmas term at school in Halifax. The one your Aunt Bess teaches at. Learn something about Big Bob's business; help him out . . . It would be kind of a way of breaking in, getting used to being away, before you go to the Academy in the fall."

Grant stopped talking. No need to say now that it wouldn't be the Academy at Copeland. By next fall the tendrils of habit would have begun to fray. The fascination of the world be at work. His mind ran on to picture the future: the Academy at Cardinal, across the border in New Brunswick. University. Summers at paying jobs, away from the Shore, and occasional visits home. Grant Marshall's boy, back for a day or two between terms, and finally not back at all. It was a Shore tradition. There was nothing strange about it.

Alan asked, "When would I go? To Big Bob's?"

"In a week or two. When the holidays are up. We've got some things to do . . ."

You couldn't be in too much of a hurry about it. You couldn't tell him one day and send him away the next. You couldn't be conspicuous. But there was little danger in vacation-time, and until the day came, you could watch, guard, protect . . .

Throughout the afternoon Grant tried to convince himself it was all right. They talked naturally of common things as they chopped and trimmed in their stretch of timber lost between the Channel and the far-off railway. But not about Grant's mill and not about Halifax and the future. Something about it was unnatural. Something was artificial and strained.

At the end of previous days they had walked home by the lake shore, but tonight, following Grant's promise to look at the road, they took the hauling-road straight out to where it met the highway at Freeman's mill. Neither said much. They did not stop to examine the road and discuss it. Grant turned in his mind Alan's silent indifference. Under the surface of his regret, small annoyances crept along his nerves, a nagging anger. This went back through Alan's silence to the non-committal look on Renie's face when he had told her of the decision he had come to. The annoyance sharpened. Bad enough knowing this was necessary, knowing this was what you had to do. Bad enough knowing that, without the crawling sense of aloneness that grew from the boy's quietness and Renie's unspoken doubt.

Sinclair's mill was shut down, a long low building squatting across Katen's Creek with its race empty and dry. A little farther on, Katen's store was lighted. You could see figures moving across the windows, inside. A stretch of woods, then, along the road. Vangie Murphy's place. Vangie's front field, once a hayfield and later a wilderness, was all stumps now. The tangle of bush had paid off, in the end, in pulpwood—a dozen cords between the house and the road.

All the way through the woods and up the shore road Alan had been thinking about it all, beginning with the cold tingle that had coursed along his backbone at Grant's words . . . *Did you ever think what you'd like to do?* After you go away . . .

He had let Grant down. He should have shown excitement, a looking ahead to venture . . . There should have been questions and talk to express that. There had been nothing. There *was* nothing, now. Only the slow cold flush, the numbness. The long aching disappointment.

He didn't give me a chance. He never asked me if I want to go. He just said I'm going.

Vangie's place. Gordon's turn. It was early dark, the air cold and wet. They'd lighted the lamps. Clouds were piling up, black and melancholy, in the northwest, back of Mrs. Josie's.

Frank Graham's. Dan was on the way in from the barn . . . A little farther up the road a small figure slipped through the gate under the row of maples and turned down to meet them. Margaret must have caught sight of them when they rounded the turn. Home . . .

Renie cleared away the dishes quickly and washed and dried them with Margaret's help. Her mind never had to bother much with household tasks. Renie's career, though she had never formed the thought in this way, was being a person. House-keeping and teaching school were incidental. Easily accomplished and not unpleasant, but incidental.

Tonight her hands went through the motions with even less thought than usual about what she was doing. Supper had been a silent meal. She had talked a little herself, feeling that to let that kind of silence grow was to acknowledge and submit to the strangeness and the strain. When that sort of thing took hold, unresisted, it got to a point where it was pretty near unbearable.

She had asked a question or two about the woods, and Grant's answers had been easy enough. But none of these exchanges had

219

developed into casual talk or the kind of conversational silence they were used to. She sensed that was not to be expected and neither she nor Grant had pressed it. To keep up a run of talk could be as bad as a tightened silence. The best you could do was say a word that took no trouble to think of but still broke up the strain.

She stacked the last plate in the rack, moved to the table and leaned across Alan's shoulder to turn up the lamp. His eyes came back from some unfathomable distance to the black print of his *High School Reader*.

He closed the book and got to his feet. "Think I'll run over to Curries'," he said. "See Bert for a while."

Grant said, "All right."

Margaret followed Alan with her eyes, gravely, as he put on his wind-breaker and hurried through the door to the porch. Just as he stepped out he half-turned and winked at her, secretly; but he wasn't grinning. Her insides had the feeling they got when there was something going on she didn't understand. Something odd and frightening you didn't want to ask about but had to know.

Renie made herself comfortable in the rocker with her knitting. Her eyes placidly asked a question.

Grant said, "Well, we talked it over . . ."

Renie turned her head toward Margaret, an off-hand note of explanation in her voice.

"Grandfather Fraser wants Alan to stay with him in Halifax for a while. This winter, and the spring."

Margaret looked at them both. Across the table at Renie, across the room to the shadows where the smoke from Grant's pipe curled in a faintly drifting haze. Renie was conscious of a childish feeling in herself, as if she were under the scrutiny of someone old and wise. But there was nothing old in Margaret's voice. Only something young and unbelieving.

"Halifax? Does he want to go?"

Renie started, her mind caught and held as her heart turned with a sense of tender pride and something close to rueful laughter. You skated all round a thing and a child went to the heart of it.

The moment of private wonder died in the harshness of Grant's voice. The long exasperation, the anger at circumstance, came through in unconsidered words, snapped out as he straightened in his chair.

"Want to? Why *wouldn't* he want to? You'd think—"

He caught himself, stood up and reached for his wind-breaker. As he moved through the porch door he was humming softly the air of "Sleepy Time Gal".

> *You'll learn—to cook—and to sew—*
> *What's more—you'll love it—I know . . .*

The half-whispered tune was a kind of regretful apology.

Renie said to Margaret, "Things'll turn out all right, you know," and reached into her knitting basket. She could feel the thoughts that would be moving in Grant's mind while he walked, the endless reasoned argument. Why *wouldn't* Alan want to go? It was something new and even venturesome, the sort of thing he used to ask to do. In his own hurt, in a mind hardened to something hard and necessary, Grant wouldn't make distinctions. Wouldn't see, just yet, the difference between joy in brief adventure, the passing urge to new experience, and the fact of exile. Not yet. Later it would come to him.

How odd it must have seemed to Alan, to find the old cautions dropped, the sense of personal companionship gone; and no real explanation. The urgency must have been great in Grant, Renie thought, to have blunted his usual sensitiveness to such a degree that he could choose the woods out back, alive in Alan's mind with the vision of work and companionship, as the place in which to tell him he must leave the Shore.

Later on, Grant would see. But even then, unless you wanted to tell the truth, what could you do? What could you do except what Grant was doing?

While her fingers moved, her mind went back to Thursday, the feeling of her new identity with the past that had possessed her, as she walked home from school, and of the past's identity with the future; Grant's quiet attention to what she had to say, and the sound of his breathing as he dealt with it in the dark.

She had known next morning that he had reached a decision, when he had taken Alan with him to the woods; and what it was, that evening, as he sat at the desk in the room, writing to Big Bob Fraser.

He had told her, but he hadn't tried to explain or justify. He hadn't asked her opinion. She understood that. The responsibility was Grant's; it went back to a time she couldn't really share. Under his personal code no one could share the decision or the risk.

What he had in mind was clear. Protection through absence. Departure. As quickly as it could be arranged without seeming suspiciously sudden. Everything matter of course.

But Renie couldn't help wondering. She couldn't erase the pictures that kept moving in her mind: the two of them, walking up through the lower pasture, driving the old ewes to the barn in a sleet-storm . . . building haycocks against threatening rain . . . Grant coming in from a day's work in the woods, his eyes roving the yard for a sight of his son . . .

He would be on the road now, tramping it off. Dropping into Hugh Currie's for a while, later, to walk home with Alan.

You couldn't argue about it. There was no way of telling what was right or what was wrong.

She smiled across the table at Margaret. The small girl met the smile evenly, in acknowledgment. Behind the acknowledgment was a look of tolerance, an understanding of the fact that there were things neither Grant nor Renie could be expected to know.

4

WHEN Josie sat by her kitchen windows she was likely to think of the past; not dwelling on special incidents but simply noting they were there. The kitchen, the southeast corner of the house, faced both daybreak and the noon sun. The windows in its walls belonged to the strange time between the past and the present.

The summer after Alan's birth and Hazel's death Grant had set extra windows into the kitchen walls, on each side of the ones already there. Now, the wide south windows caught the afternoon light. She and Margaret sat facing each other by the long sill, the small girl's outstretched wrists moving a skein of yarn from side to side, slightly, as Josie's fingers rolled the yarn swiftly into a ball.

Her mind touched lightly on that older time: not the continuing torment, the soul's knowledge of shame and death and absence. Those were things that had lost their sharpness, until you were able almost to forget. No, not to forget, but to think of the Josie Gordon to whom they had happened, not as this present flesh sitting in clear sunlight in silent communion with a little girl, but as another person, a neighbour across the fields of time.

Whenever she looked far back, the slow recovery, the achievement of a tranquillity that was inward as well as outward, seemed interwoven with little things, with matters of no importance.

There had been one definite turning-point; a look, and words said in a hospital room in Copeland. Without that, perhaps, she would have gone forever unhealed and hopeless. But beyond that, it was the little things that came to mind. Deliverance was merged with the small routines, the incidents of living . . .

Grant, fixing the cellar steps and drawing Stewart out of his lethargy to mortise window-frames and whitewash pickets. Grant mending harness, filing and oiling tools. Grant rigging a scheme to heat Anna's old room for the girl he had brought there, the odd girl Hazel McKee. Years later, Grant smiling in cautious sympathy, almost amused, it seemed, when Stewart in absent-mindedness, the mild aberration that had affected him just before his death, would look up and call him by name . . . "Anse".

223

Josie said to Margaret now, softly teasing and in order to break a too-long silence, "Terrible quiet today, Marg'ret. Quieter even than usual."

"D'you think so, Mrs. Josie?"

"Well, maybe it's not a bad way . . . People waste a lot of time on talk, sometimes, it seems to me."

Margaret said, "I'm lonesome."

"Lonesome?"

You never knew what to expect from this child. That was one of Josie's small joys. But she was startled. She was still the austere silent woman of years ago; that was in her nature, apart from the shame and grief she had had to bear. But with Grant's children, with Alan and in some degree with Margaret, she found herself sometimes lapsing into a curious ease of manner, almost a playfulness in speech. Now she was a little startled. It was hard to imagine loneliness in Grant and Renie Marshall's house.

Margaret nodded. "Yes. When I think of it. This spring . . . and Lan away. It's awful."

She thought to herself: I used the name. But she didn't care. She had said now what she felt about the thing closest to her heart, something that was part of herself. Something she couldn't say to Dad or Renie because that would seem like exposing a weakness, like calling attention to yourself, trying to get round something by crying.

You could say it to Mrs. Josie because she was a person who seemed like one of the family, and yet—was not. You knew she wasn't, but her vague position in the flow of life didn't worry you or make you curious. And when you talked to her you preserved the secrecy of talking to yourself while you got the relief of talking to a listener. You never felt yourself made smaller by laying bare your curiosity or misery or joy.

It wasn't quite the same thing as telling things to Alan. With Alan you didn't care whether you made yourself small or not. But this was something she couldn't say to Alan, because he was feeling bad enough himself.

"Oh," Josie said, hesitantly. "Lonesome *that* way."

Renie had told her of the plan to have Alan spend the rest of the winter with Bob Fraser. Josie had thought of it simply as a chance for the boy to see something beyond the Channel Shore. Grant's willingness to let him go was strange, but it had not occurred to her that this had any particular meaning. It was, she supposed, merely his wish to see Alan started toward a life that could give him more than he would find at Currie Head.

Her own affection . . . She was interested to find as she examined it now that this affection was rooted in Alan himself and in her feeling for Grant; that the fact her own blood ran in Alan's veins had hardly occurred to her in years. Not, at least, as a thing to think about. There must be a kind of relationship, she thought, of place and touch and word as well as kinship. Her affection was deep and warm. But the prospect of his going hadn't stirred her with regret. Going away was normal. She thought: queer how you can accept something, a little thing, and not realize it may be a bit of hell to someone else. But Margaret always seemed so self-possessed, so self-sufficient . . .

She kept the pity out of her eyes and voice.

"Lonesomeness's not so bad, lots of times. It makes coming home all the better."

She knew this was poor comfort, nothing but the old trick of turning the mind to the dream world of faith and hope, beyond tomorrow. It was the best she could do.

Something stirred in Margaret's mind. Mrs. Josie. Lonesomeness. Coming home. There was some old story, overlaid by newer and fresher stories and events that in themselves were growing small and dim, fly-specks on the barn door of memory. Anse. Anse Gordon. The one who had disappeared . . . She had a sudden pang of remorse for talking about lonesomeness. She turned in sensitive embarrassment to look through the window, while her hands kept adjusting the diminishing skein to Mrs. Josie's winding. Across the Channel the Island hills were blue and grey and streaky white. She could see a few white specks lower down at the line of the water. The houses at Princeport. Her eyes came back to the Shore. Opposite the Grahams', with a lumpy bag on her back, Vangie Murphy was coming down the road.

Vangie walked the shore road, slow and almost stately, her strong body not unpleasantly tired by ten miles of plodding travel.

Her habits of thought had developed in one direction until something of the sententious and the insinuating was implicit in everything she said and did. In her pace, the form and figure of a worn-out woman, badly used by life but facing up to it, deserted by her children and without friends, making her way alone.

She had dropped in at McKees' on the pretext of seeing whether anything had come in the morning mail but really to sit and nurse the illusion of social equality, and a continuing malice because this was something she could never really win. She had walked into Eva McKee's kitchen without knocking, set down her bag of supplies, smiled at Eva and eased herself into a rocker. As Jane Marshall might have done or Hat Wilmot or Stella Graham. But it never quite worked.

She had said, "Anything for me today, E—", and lost courage and begun again: "Anything today, Mrs. McKee?"

"Nothing, Mrs. Murphy."

As she walked the road now Vangie felt again the flick of anger. Never the intimacy of first names. Only the empty title they had given her, the cold camouflage of respectability.

At McKees' she had tried again: "Well, I can wait. I have to. You work and slave . . . and they leave you and forget. They forget you."

Eva's impersonal voice had cut her short. "Oh, I don't know, Mrs. Murphy. It's hardly a week since you had your cheque from Tarsh. Last Thursday night."

This was a problem Vangie had never quite solved. How to play both parts—the deserted mother, piecing out a poor existence, and the matriarch supported in comfort by her absent family. The latter role was closest to the truth. Tarsh in Halifax and Etta in Boston sent money. The Shore knew it. But there was a wide streak of human paradox in Vangie. There were times when she felt her best chance at social acceptance was in the wearing of her newest dress, appearances at church, praise of her children's generosity. When that failed, she went back to the baggy sweaters and work-boots, and walked to The Bridge for flour and tea instead of having Adam Falt bring them down in the mail-car.

She would have admitted to herself, had the thought occurred to her, that she liked best the role of road-walking sloven. She had never taken satisfaction in keeping a neat house and sitting by the fire when the work was done. On the road there was a hint of the carelessness, the freedom, that had coloured her younger days with a harsh excitement. And you could drop in, at this house and that, on the sly look-out for the recognition that would serve as a substitute, now, for the earlier abandon.

But recognition was something you didn't get. You got a sort of withdrawn politeness from the women, and from the men a word, kindly enough, without malice, but touched with unconscious mockery.

She had smiled as she left McKees'. The anger didn't show in the smile. Vangie rarely risked the little she had by forthright protest about the things she couldn't reach. It merely added up: one more resentment in the smouldering compost that would die with her. That broke out now in sly runnels of insinuation, feeling

226

their way on doubtful ground. They smoked and crawled as she walked down the road past Marshalls', Neills', Curries', Grahams'.

Eva McKee. Knitting and not listening. And not so much to be proud about. Her own daughter, fourteen, fifteen, years ago . . . her belly filled by Anse Gordon . . A little shock of personal pleasure could still travel in Vangie's spine as she thought of Anse. But that pleasure had not been as full as her satisfaction in the knowledge that one of the good ones, one of the respectable ones, had been caught in the same net that life had set, years ago, for Vangie. Nor had the pain of Anse's going been anything to compare with the unreasoned rage she had felt at Hazel McKee's escape. Grant Marshall, stepping in to poison a pleasure that could have lived in Vangie's soul for life . . .

It was all there as she walked down the shore road. On impulse, though she was nearly home and there was no excuse for such a visit on the plea of rest, she turned in at Josie's Gordon's gate.

Margaret said, gravely wondering, "She's coming in!"

Secretly she was afraid of Vangie Murphy. Something in the smile and the husky ingratiating voice set up a current of revulsion in her flesh. She felt this whenever they met on the road or on the rare occasions when in the course of her rounds Vangie dropped in to sit in Renie's kitchen.

Surprisingly, Renie had noticed this despite Margaret's efforts to hide it behind a careful serenity. She kept Renie's words in her mind: *Don't let yourself brood on things, or people, if they make you feel bad.*

It was all right to say that; but it was not Margaret's way. The thing she had to do was go to meet a feeling, good or bad, accept it fully, puzzle out its qualities until she could see what made it so. She had never been able to fix in definite form her fear of Vangie Murphy.

Josie said matter-of-factly, "So she is . . . we won't wind any more, now." She gathered up the lapful of balled yarn, stowed it in her knitting-basket, and turned her serene face, with a murmured greeting, to Vangie Murphy coming through her door.

"Mrs. Gordon . . ." The smile was expansive, but Josie was one woman Vangie never even started to call by her first name. "And Margaret . . . I haven't seen you for a dog's age, pet . . . Just seemed I couldn't go a step more without a rest, Mrs. Gordon. I'll sit a minute, if you don't mind."

"Certainly, Vangie."

Somehow in the way Josie Gordon always said it, there was no satisfaction at all in the use of the name. It was too remote, too kindly and vaguely sorrowful.

". . . a dog's age," Vangie said turning to Margaret. "My soul, she looks like Grant, don't she, Mrs. Gordon? You're the spit of your father, pet . . . It comes out as they get older, don't it?"

She paused, and added, "Young Alan, now. He was down past my place the other day."

Vangie's tone joined "the other day" with all the days along the Channel Shore. She had come into this house on impulse but the sight of Margaret and Josie Gordon was blending with her smouldering anger at Eva McKee, her dreams of years ago. The little runnels flared in the small audacity of smooth remembering words.

"Just the other day . . . There's not much McKee in him . . . not much McKee . . ."

She was talking literally over Margaret's head, carried along by a garrulous daring.

"Took me back . . . years ago. When we were young, and your boy . . . When young Anse was a boy, going down to Katen's . . . He's the image . . . it must remind you, Mrs. Gordon . . ."

Josie said, "Vangie!"

Vangie caught her breath and grouped her features into an apologetic smile, a parody of apology.

"Oh! . . . yes . . ."

She glanced at Margaret and away again.

Josie said evenly, "Margaret, you might as well run home. That's all we'll do today, I guess. Your mother may be wanting you. I kept you longer than I should've, maybe. You run home now, and come over tomorrow if you like."

"All right, Mrs. Josie."

Margaret said the words naturally and rose to go, but she was not through here. Her mind was on the undercurrents of this conversation from which she was being banished, and on her feeling about Vangie Murphy.

While her instinct was shrinking from Vangie's "pet" she had almost run it down. Part of it at least was fear of contact, of touching . . . As she walked toward the door she stubbed her toe deliberately on the edge of the rag mat between the stove and table. Stumbling, she caught herself with a hand on Vangie Murphy's plump knee; Vangie's hand came up to catch her—"Oops, pet!"

Margaret straightened and said, "Excuse me," and opened the door to go.

Part of her was satisfied. She was not going to be afraid of Vangie Murphy any more. Only the dislike remained, and a new nagging curiosity. She closed the door behind her and hopped down the porch steps.

"Vangie," Josie said, "you ought to know enough not to talk that way. Not any time. But in front of a child . . ." Her voice was scornful and exasperated.

Vangie was soft and regretful.

"I know, Mrs. Gordon . . . It just came over me and I didn't think. I was feeling . . . You know, I often think how hard it must *be* on you, Mrs. Gordon. Not able to—and seeing him brought up a Protestant, and—"

"Vangie, hush!"

Josie could not remember when her insides had been so harshly torn by anger. But anger was something she couldn't afford. Anger was something that could serve only to harden this probing curiosity and malice . . .

It was odd how things like this could recur, in waves. She remembered the sly hints after Alan's birth, after Grant had brought Hazel and her baby to the house from Copeland hospital. That strange time, when the bitterness of inner shame had begun to fade; when, through the voice and presence of Hazel McKee, she had begun to feel the tide of life continuing. The sly hints . . . *You must be specially fond of him, Mrs. Gordon.* The glances. The silences. At that time she had only begun to see how life could grow, healthy and even pleasant, from the seeds of shame. But her instinct had been right and the tone of her reply had been right. Trite, sententious and effective: *I'm fond of all children, since I've none of my own . . .*

Not in a dozen years had she heard a suggestion . . . There must have been talk. But mostly guarded talk, without malice, between men and women careful to say nothing that would rouse curiosity . . . There was quite a bit of kindness on the Channel Shore. But now, perhaps, a wave . . . returning.

She said, "Vangie, something wrong was done, years ago. Grant Marshall made it right. If people use the sense God gave them, there'll be no one that even remembers—in time . . . Let me tell you something, Vangie. There's nothing I wouldn't do to keep things . . . If anybody's vicious enough . . . There's nothing I wouldn't do . . ."

She checked herself. You couldn't make it clear to anyone who didn't know by instinct.

All you could hope for was that such people would be dominated by the force of your person into accepting what you said. Josie was not overly optimistic. In people who gossiped there was little capacity for personal respect. For the second time that day she thought: It's the best I can do.

5

On Friday Grant and Alan set up the stationary gasoline engine in the yard and belted it to the small circular Grant used for sawing fire-wood.

They had not been out back since Tuesday. Wednesday had been a day of forced idleness, with high winds and snow and sleet. Thursday, the wind was still up; too unpleasant for the woods, Grant said. Today was fair and cold but he had said nothing about the Katen lot. They hauled the engine out of the shop and begun to cut into stove-lengths the year's supply of fire-wood.

A question asked itself in Grant's mind. He ought to be thinking, planning, arranging for stumpage. Figuring, deciding whether he'd let Dan run the pulpwood-cut back of Kelley's while he himself went on with work out back, preparing for a mill. Except for the few days' work he and Alan had put in, nothing was done. . . .

Why?

This was the question which in various forms he had asked himself for days. Asked . . . while he knew the answer; the answer —itself a question.

How could you throw yourself, whole-hearted, into anything— when the zest of life was dulled by a bitter and burning loss?

It was only in these last days that he had begun to realize how much his son had figured in his ambition to saw lumber from the woods of the Channel Shore. The thought of a mill, of logs coming into the yard, deal going out, neighbours on a pay-roll: these things were all good; but the colour went out of them unless you thought of them in relation to one dark-haired youngster—the boy who was always there. Always wanting to work at whatever you were working at; always around the yard, always there across the stove in the evenings.

There was no end to questions when you started to ask and examine; never an end . . .

He grew bitter with himself at his own inconsistency. You built up the idea of departure, planted it in the boy's mind for his future's sake. You tried to keep him from getting too closely wrapped up in home, too interested in the Shore. And then when the time came you started crabbing to yourself.

What if it *had* come a few years early? You couldn't have it both ways.

You could keep him with you a year or two longer and run the risk of losing the curious tie, the instinct of blood relationship. Or you could send him away and keep that tenuous thing for years. Perhaps for ever.

Loss? There was loss in it, either way. But the lesser loss was in departure, in the gamble to keep alive the long illusion.

Or was it? Hadn't you learned long ago—a knowledge etched in acid by slow degrees—hammers tapping on a barn wall, words across the muddy rows of a turnip field—hadn't you learned that blood ties do not matter?

The thing that matters—hadn't you learned that this is the feel of fairness, affection, kindness, good nature? Between person and person? Hadn't you tried to avoid possession, to treat your children as people, not merely kin?

That was your theory.

Well, then.

Well, then, you were learning now that hearts don't beat on theory.

Suppose you could school yourself to take the chance of revelation. Suppose you took the risk and kept him home . . . You were back then where it all started. How could you weigh the damage to a boy's heart at the stroke of that shameful knowledge?

Always at this point a shadow of doubt plagued Grant. *Is it Alan I'm thinking of, or is it me? Is it the hurt to him that scares me, or the hurt to me?*

Another thought would come, then: the realization that behind the long plan for departure, education, life in cities, there had been a hoarded hope. Always a secret hope that for Grant Marshall's son the Shore would be enough.

Sometimes as he turned these things in his mind he would find his heart clutched by an old, a forgotten, panic. Again he could feel the reasonless thing that had crossed it, years ago, when he had sensed that Hazel was marked for death. And after. The knowledge that this, an end to living, had been the portion of both: the girl he had loved and the girl with whom he shared deliverance from the past. The sense that he, and all who touched him, were fated . . .

He shook this off now as he had shaken it off then. To let the mind harbour such fancies . . . What was the word?—morbid. Morbid. Worse than that. It was close to being touched, unbalanced. The thing had never really gripped him; it was too far beyond the circle of reason. It had merely crossed his heart, the brief blinding fancy . . .

He shook it away impatiently, the heart cleared by the mind's reason. But Alan—and Alan's going—There were things about this, now, that reason would not clear.

The alternatives were too confused to be sorted out. The long argument, futile and endless, lived like a tumour in his mind. The rankling question, the hard conclusion. It was with him as he kindled the breakfast fire, as he turned the cattle out to water, as he worked in the shop, as he played checkers with Margaret in the evenings; as he lay in bed, listening to the soft lapse of Renie's breath.

It was with him now, under the irregular bark and chuff of the engine, the brief repeated whine of the saw as he and Alan loaded the tilt, heaved it against the snarling blade.

There was nothing wrong with the plan. While Alan worked with him, through the holidays, he was out of danger. Beyond that was Halifax and the long reprieve. People knew the affection old Bob Fraser had for Alan. Knew he'd been after him to visit. Nothing wrong with that . . . Already he had told people, casually, that Alan was to spend some time with Big Bob. Nothing surprising in it if the visit lasted . . . lasted in the end until it merged with the road away . . .

Nothing wrong with the plan . . .

But there were days now when he grudged every minute of Alan's absence; and yet found in his presence a continuing ache.

Today, working with him at the sawing, watchful to stay between the boy and the whirling blade, his mind was laden with these thoughts. He worked silently, more than once conscious too late that Alan had spoken some casual word and gone unanswered.

Grant shook his mind back into balance. The cold fact was that in a week now the boy would be gone, away from the danger of wagging tongues, away from . . .

He had better begin to get used to it. And there were other people to think about. Long ago he had seen the unspoken thing growing between Alan and old Richard McKee.

After dinner he said, "I've got to go down to see Rod Sinclair this afternoon. We'll leave the rest of it till later. You might

233

take a run up and see if there's anything you can do for your grandfather."

Alan said, "All right. Sure."

Margaret looked quickly at Renie.

"I guess so," Renie said. "You might as well . . . I'll give you Mr. Alec's bread to take in while you're at it. And you'd better go in and say hello to Uncle James and Aunt Jane. See how they are."

The lower pastures were deep with snow. They kept to the main road, walking on the inside of the shoulders where sled tracks made the going easy. Bert Lisle was piling wood in Hugh Currie's door-yard, with old Hugh, who had been sickly lately, wandering in the cold sunlight, muffled up in an overcoat. Alan thought briefly about Mr. Currie. A friendly absent-minded man. He had spent his early manhood away from Currie Head, Dad said, and come back and sent his son away in turn. People did come back, then, sometimes. But not often. Not for good, anyway. For a day or two, or a week every couple of years; like Stan Currie, who was never home long enough to share in anything that made up living, like haying or the herring-run.

He never asked me if I want to go; he just said I'm going . . . He didn't ask . . .

Well, then, the mind argued, tell him. Tell him what it is you want to do.

He had thought of that, thought of saying—But how could it be said? How could you break the habit of acceptance when this was rooted in you as a part of life?

He remembered how it had been long ago. Whenever he asked about a thing denied, the careful explanation had left him feeling childish, feeling he should have known without being told. And in these later years there had been something more than that. A kind of foreknowledge of what you wanted. And if there was something you couldn't do, or something you didn't want to do but had to, the explanation came without asking, in some casual aside. It was as if Grant knew by nature the need to make things clear.

All you could say was, "I don't want to go." And if you said it you were saying good-bye to the warm wordless communication of needs and desires. You were questioning the judgment you had learned to accept. Rejecting the explanation you'd been given.

Well, was that it? Or were you just afraid?

Once, this morning, he had come close to it. A wave of feeling had submerged both habit and thought. He had turned, as they walked back to the wood-pile for another stick, beginning the words. Then he had seen Grant's face, closed and hardened, his look turned inward on something personal and strange. Grant hadn't even noticed he had been about to speak.

That was failure. Thinking of it now as he walked the road with Margaret, Alan knew that this was something he couldn't stand again.

Alec Neill was working behind his wood-pile, pointing posts with an axe. He looked up and saw Margaret and Alan coming through his front gate and started for the house, limping slightly on his one bad leg which was twisted by arthritis. Alec lived alone now, since his wife's death three years before. He had been a bachelor for years, had married late and fathered sons—Dave in California and Harry in Truro—and now was a bachelor again, doing his own housework as well as tending his salmon net in July and August and farming the year round.

Alan grinned to himself. Next to Grandfather McKee's, Alec Neill's place was the one he liked to visit best. Renie baked Alec's bread for him; whenever he and Margaret took the loaves in, Mr. Neill met them at the back door with a grin in which there was a kind of shared amusement at the way he lived, but no apology.

He said now as pushed open the porch door, motioning them ahead of him, "Come on in. Sit down a spell—if you can find a place to put your sitter-down."

Then, gesturing largely, to Margaret: "I don't keep a very neat house."

Margaret said, "No, you don't, Mr. Neill," and perched herself in a rocking-chair.

Alec laughed as he took the bread from Alan and stowed it in a wooden box with a leather-hinged top on the shelf back of the stove.

Alan thought of what Mrs. Frank Graham had said: Alec had no one to make him take notice. Mrs. Hattie Wilmot was more specific. She said Alec's place smelt like a fish-hut. It did smell a little like a hut, Grandfather McKee's on the beach, or Alec's own. A good salt and tanny smell. The hundred coiled fathoms of a coarse-meshed salmon-net-leader lay in a pile in one corner; in another the back numbers of all the magazines Harry Neill subscribed to in Alec's behalf at Christmas-time. The unwashed dishes of at least three meals were piled on the table. Crumbs and crusts littered the checkered oilcloth. For dinner Alec had eaten a boiled salt herring. Its backbone still lay on the plate, beside a small heap of potato skins.

Alec reached for a lifter and shook up the fire.

"Don't put wood on for *us*, Mr. Neill," Alan said. "We've got to go on to Grandfather's."

Alec added a couple of sticks of wood to the fire and reset the stove-lid.

"I'm tired workin' anyway. Think I'll spend the afternoon in the house . . . just lazy."

He eased himself into his private chair, a low-cushioned one he had built to his own special angles, and fingered his beard. This was something he had cultivated in the last few years for the fun of it, and, as he told Alan, to give the women something to talk about. "James Marshall's got fur on his face," he had said. "I got the same rights as James." His eyes always laughed above the grey brush, the unkempt parody of James Marshall's trimmed and tended beard.

"On your way to Rich's, are you?" He laughed to himself, an absent-minded chuckle at some private joke. "You'll find him gettin' ready to cooper up some bar'ls. He's been threatenin' to. Easier to buy 'em, but that wouldn't satisfy him. 'D I ever tell you about him tryin' to teach Joe?"

Alan shook his head and glanced secretly at Margaret. "No, I don't think so."

"Rich don't say much. Never did. Curious fellah . . . There was that puncheon. Puncheon's a handy thing to have 'round, to keep a salmon net in, or salt fish, most anything. I used to speak for the empty molasses-bar'ls from Morgan's store. White oak casks. But they don't use 'em any more. Rich decided he could make a puncheon out've birch, and by God he did. Never said a word. I come down to the beach one mornin' and there she was, in the hut.

"I started to tell you about Joe. It's tricky, cooperin'. Rich had quite a time with Joe. Couldn't get the hang of it. Joe tried one on his own hook, when he was your age, one time Rich was away. Leaked· like a collander. Joe heaved it in the Channel. Come in with the tide, later on, one forenoon while we was guttin' herrin'. Rich looked it over and looked out at the water, and back at the bar'l, and then at Joe. All he said, finally, was, 'Joe, I'll tell you . . . You can't hide murder.' "

Here in Alec Neill's untidy kitchen, Alan thought of Uncle Joe McKee, growing wheat in the Peace River Block, and wondered whether he ever remembered the derelict barrel and the look on his father's face. He could see the scene as if he'd been there; from Alec Neill's words and his memory of Joe, the one time he had come home, and his knowledge of Grandfather. Under the laughter that stirred in him he was struck by the oddity of things, the thought of people all over the world who at one time or other had been boys on the Channel Shore, and had got a feeling of being grown up from doing the things their fathers did.

The thought was fugitive. Alec Neill was talking again.

"Odd people, the McKees. Mind their own business and get along with anybody, even fellahs like James Marshall." Alec caught himself and said, "Your Uncle James used to be considered a wee bit stiff."

Alan grinned, "Yes. I know."

"A bit stiff," Alec repeated. "You know, most people along the Shore are fair-to-middlin' people. But now and then . . . Well, your uncle always had a reputation. Never knew the taste of liquor or tobacco, they said. No sir, he never did. That's what they said."

He felt in his pocket and began to shave a pipeful of Master Mason into his palm.

"You wouldn't remember Fritz McKee, Richard's father. Your grandfather's father. Fritz always claimed he knew different. Said he could prove James *did* know the taste've booze."

Alec reached over to scratch a match on the stove, and began to draw on the pipe, making small smacking sounds.

"Seems, one hot day in July, twenty-five, thirty years ago, Fritz took James out off the Rocks in his dory. Fritz was runnin' trawl. Hot weather, too. He'd took along a pint flask of Felix Katen's rum in his jacket pocket. Seems he'd leant over to haul trawl when the little jug fell out. Eleven fathom, off there. Fritz watched it go, sinkin' slow, him droolin'. Couldn't say what he thought, either, on account of James . . .

"Well, minute or so, James says, 'It's too hot to live, Mr. McKee,' says he. 'I'm going to cool off.' Strips himself down to his drawers and dives in . . . Minute goes by. Two minutes. Fritz looks down over the gunnel. No sight've anything. Hitches a piece of cod-line to a net-rock, to ballast him, and goes down after James. Two fathom, four, five. No sign. He goes right to bottom. Fritz used to tell it good. 'You know what I found?' he used to say. 'There was James Marshall, in his drawers, sittin' on a killick-rock drinkin' my rum!'"

Alec leaned back in his chair. He said, seriously, "Of course, I don't believe that story. Some people do, but I don't. There's one thing wrong with it. Fritz must've made it up. James Marshall never went out in no dory. That family was all dry-footed."

It was odd, Alan thought, going up the road, how you could be sort of numb inside and still be able to laugh, still enjoy the fun in a man like Alec Neill. They were passing Uncle James's now. He deliberated over going in, and decided to postpone it until after they had been up the road to Grandfather's, until their stay at Uncle James's could be cut short by the necessity of getting home for supper. Uncle Fred was all right, and Jackie; his heart lifted at the thought of Jackie and Jackie's mischief; but Uncle Fred and Jackie had gone to Town . . .

He glanced down at Margaret, his mind still lazily concerned with the people who moved in it; Bert Lisle, Mr. Currie, Alec Neill, Uncle James's crowd; but vaguely conscious of a difference in this walk up the road from all the other walks they had taken together. He realized in a moment or two what it was. She wasn't talking. Always when they were out of earshot of others, Margaret talked. Questions, mostly. But today she was silent, walking in some sort of dream world of her own. Not even Alec Neill's fooling had shaken her out of it.

Margaret . . . He felt the shiver of emotion he had sometimes felt when she was smaller, a baby, and he had visualized the horror . . . a speeding car . . . an open well . . . a sickness . . . There had never been anything morbid in this; it was more a thankfulness that she was as she was, healthy and fine. She was growing up, tough and small and strange, and that fear was something he had hardly felt for years. Now, walking beside her he thought of the Lee Wilmots. Lee hadn't made a go of it in the States; he'd come home to his brother Clem's with an American wife and a year-old baby. A baby with something wrong, a leg and arm that wouldn't work right; would never work right. Alan felt a wave of thankfulness about Margaret. A wave of thankfulness and fear. In all these months away . . . how would he know . . . how would he know . . .

She walked beside him, the expression on her small face puzzled and withdrawn. Alan started to ask a question and broke off. She'd tell him in time.

A rhythmic splitting sound came from Grandfather McKee's workshop. As they went down the path from the road, Alan felt the eagerness that always took hold of him around the McKee place. Now, with his senses edged to special perceptiveness, he thought with a small thrill of surprise: Grandfather's something like Dad. It was odd that Grant should be like Grandfather McKee when they weren't even related. And different from Uncle James.

He said, "You go in the house, Mag. I'll come in and see Grandmother after a while."

But Eva McKee opened the porch door, watching them approach.

Eva could never be an off-hand woman. Time does not change much the outward characteristics, even though it harden softness to resolution or soften intolerance to a kind of understanding. Nothing could alter the primness, the lines of habitual slight disapproval in her face. Nothing could change the habit of her speech, seasoned with complaint. But in some manner the years had turned the tone's edge; and in some manner, though the mouth was still straight and thin-lipped, the eyes had learned to smile. At Richard and at children.

She was thinking she was going to miss Alan this winter. So was Richard. Joe'd only been home once since he'd gone west. Anyway, Joe was grown up. Richard sort of counted on Alan. Grant and Renie were good about coming round on Sundays and letting the children come up whenever they wanted. She knew Richard had planned on asking Grant to lend him Alan for a while in July. Richard wanted to set a fleet of herring nets and have a boy in the boat again. Odd how you understood these things better when you got along in years . . .

There had been a period when the sight and sound, the name and thought of Alan, had meant to her a hard and bitter time. The time of Hazel's return to the Shore with Grant Marshall, believing you could cancel shame by marriage . . . that kind of marriage . . .

The time when she, Eva, had been forced to lend herself to that fiction since there was nothing else to do. Since only in that way could you salvage the shreds of pride.

The time when pride itself had begun to lose importance . . . She was not quite sure how that had happened, but the image in her mind was that of a bare room in Copeland hospital, and Hazel there in bed, her body swollen under the bed clothes, white-skinned, but with the tell-tale spots of red already burning in her cheeks.

The thing she remembered best was the look in Hazel's eyes. For her, Eva, a kind of dumb regret. For Richard and Grant, tenderness . . .

239

It was that moment that had started the downfall of pride—Made possible humility; even in the face of the girl's wish to be close to Grant at the last. And not in Eva's house, but where Grant lived, at Gordons'. Made possible the curious truce between herself and Josie Gordon, as they joined their skills to bring health and strength to the tiny life Hazel had left behind . . .

All past and gone, grown dim with time. The one vividness, the one thing that would never lose its form and colour, was the year of Alan, the year she had nursed and kept and tended her daughter's son; and returned him, when the time was right, to Grant. Grant and Renie Fraser.

The curious thing, now, was that pride had been reborn; softened by time and children's voices. For Hazel had been right. You *could* cancel shame . . .

She said, "Your Grandfather's splitting out hoop-poles, Alan." What she thought of that occupation was in the tone, or rather, what she had thought of it years ago. "Come in, Margaret. It's a raw wind."

Richard McKee was slightly deaf with the deafness of age beginning, an access of inattention, of preoccupation with things past and present, moving in the mind while the hands work. He did not notice Alan at first.

Alan watched him for a minute as he opened the end of a hoop-pole with a deft stroke of his adz. He moved into his grandfather's line of vision.

Richard looked up with an absent-mindedness that smoothed out into a slow smile as he saw who it was.

"Well, boy . . . I'm bogged down."

He had obviously been working in the shop for days. The shop floor was carpeted with chips and shavings.

Alan grinned at him and went to a corner for the broom, worn past further kitchen use, that Richard used to keep the shop floor swept when he thought of it.

"Don't lug all the kindlin' to the house," Richard said. "We'll need some for the stove here"—he gestured at the heater, giving off a comfortable warmth—"and the cresset, when we get around to it."

This was the usual progression, from some common task to the mysteries of whatever craft he happened to be engaged in. Last fall he had shown Alan how to mend nets, with twine, mesh-board and net-needle. Before that he had taught him to row on the inlet, sitting in the stern of his old flat while Alan struggled with the oars. When he said now, "We'll need some . . . for the cresset," he was laying out a course: We'll see whether you can cooper up a barrel.

This was one of the out-of-date crafts that survived on the Shore in Richard because, now as always, there were times when he did what he liked. Each winter he cut hoop-poles and measured and sawed into stave-junks a few fir trunks. When there was nothing else to do, or even when there was, he split staves with froe and mallet, shaved and joined them and set them up in truss-hoops, scorched and steamed them to pliability with his cresset fire, drew them into barrels with his creaking windlass, finished them off with crumbing knife and croze.

The amusement that kindled in Alan's memory was shadowed by the present. Last fall, as they worked on the nets, Richard had said, "Maybe you can come out, some mornings, when the run's on."

Unless he got back in time, he was going to lose that chance, the chance to feel the swell of the Channel under him in the early-morning darkness before the wind came up; nets heavy with twitching fish, coming up out of dark water; the boat low, the landing on wet gravel; the blowing sun. Grandfather McKee, foreshadowing the building of barrels, didn't mention his going away.

There was never much talk between Richard McKee and his grandson. When you went to see Alec Neill you expected to be entertained with speech, colourful and salty and a little coarse. You expected the twinkle in the eyes and a grin behind the whiskers and you missed something when the words were sober and the face uncreased by laughter. With Grandfather McKee it was different. His presence and what he did were more important than anything he had to say.

Richard rarely smiled and didn't talk much. Even when he was showing you how to flip twine off a net-needle and knot it around a mesh-board, it was a matter of hands rather than speech. Broad hands with heavily knuckled fingers, the skin leathery, the creases marked with a fine graining of earth and net-tan, the inworn dust of barn floors and harrowed fields, hay seed and dried cow-manure, that soap and water could never quite erase. More than in his face, which wore an expression tolerant, withdrawn and non-committal, Richard's character was in his hands.

His character, his history and his skills. Once in a while, as he bent over you to re-set your grip on the scythe handle or the oar, you would feel the contact of his hands. Sometimes he would put one, absent-mindedly, on your shoulder. It wasn't a caress; it was simply a casual communication. In all Richard's attitudes, in his body moving or at rest, there was communication. When Eva swept the kitchen floor, round the door-sill, with a glance at Richard's boots, his body relaxed in the cane-bottomed chair kept saying: A bit of mud won't hurt you; it's all in a life-time.

And in the shop, or anywhere else, the touch of his hands said: This is the way you do it; try it again, now. Or, rarely, on your shoulder, one of them said something that wouldn't translate into words.

After Alan had finished sweeping, Richard nodded at the ladder leading up at the end of the shop away from the stove.

"Might go aloft and pass me down some staves."

On the loft floor where they had been piled to season, Alan gathered unshaved staves and passed them through the hatchway. When Richard gestured that he had enough to go on with, Alan turned again to the dusky space under the slant roof. He couldn't remember that he had ever been in the shop's loft before.

Bundled herring nets hung from iron spikes in rafters from which the bark had dropped, leaving a surface intricately runnelled with the track of wood-worms. The wheels of a dismantled buggy lay in a corner. One of them had been stripped of its iron tire. Alan guessed that was where Grandfather had got the iron to shoe the handsled he had made for him two winters before. In the opposite corner a spinning-wheel stood. The place was strewn with old rubber boots, old iron, the detritus of years making a rusty litter of the past along side the present materials of Richard's busy hands—his split staves, hoop-poles, nets and lumber.

Alan felt the sting of curiosity, the little thrill of interest about to be satisfied, the sense of strangeness sometimes found among things so old they are new again. Nothing in the attic at home went back much beyond his own memory. The house was new, they had moved into it when Margaret was a baby. He could remember his wonder at having your own electric light plant, and water by turning a tap, and a bathroom. But it was all new. Even what they sometimes called the old house, where the truck was kept in what had been the downstairs bedroom, and Grant's tools in the one-time kitchen, and where he himself had slept in the loft, there was nothing really old. But here at Grandfather's there were traces of years far back of that, of time continuing.

Under the spread legs of the spinning-wheel a sea-chest lay, its green paint scratched and flaked, blurred with dust and time, its corners blunted by wear and casual handling. Alan got down on his knees. The box was heavy; as he dragged it out by the rope handles let into its ends, one of the loops parted. Someone had locked the chest, but apparently for no reason except to keep its contents from spilling when it was lugged from one place to another. There was nothing secret here; the key was still in the hole. It grated around in his fingers.

The box was half-full of stuff Grandfather called odds and ends and Grandmother called junk. Alan lifted and held in his hands a round brass container streaked with verdigris; under its cracked and deckled glass the compass-card swayed and steadied. He set it down gently by the chest. He would have to go through the formality of asking, but this was his. He turned back to the rusty treasure of the chest. A length of shotgun barrel, sawed from the stock for some reason perhaps no one living could remember; a pair of work-boots with soles worn through and eyelets chopped out. He recalled that Grandfather had used boot-eyelets for halyard-blocks in the schooner-rigged play-boat he had shaped and hollowed and decked over when Alan was six. A ball of blue carpenter's chalk, scarred where the cord had rubbed, and a plumb-line. A gobbet of beeswax and a hank of cobbler's thread. Half a dozen door-hinges of brass and iron.

He picked out of the litter a flattened circlet of stiff leather, studded with a brass plate pitted like a thimble—a thing he'd never seen, but recognized, out of some untraced memory of men's talk, as a sail-maker's palm. He slipped the hardened leather on his hand, trying the feel of it, and put it down beside the compass.

His hands roved and probed as his eyes explored the chest. A jumble of worn objects, unrelated to each other, but all linked with some aspect of life on the Channel Shore. Linked, most of them, with ways of doing things that had changed and faded and been replaced by tools and methods of the present. He fingered again the brass-studded palm, and for a brief moment had a curious vision, a sense of knowing the past, when wind in the tanned sails of two-masters had been the Shore's transport, when the road was a track and buggies few and gasoline unheard of. He felt a little sad, not at any sense of old things lost and gone, but at the realization that the present things, the tools they now worked with, the lumber truck, the saw-mill they didn't yet possess, would some time go the way of these mouldy tags of living stowed in the workshop loft. But there was revelation in the feeling, and this submerged the brief sadness. When present things were gone, new ones would take their place. For the first time, he was conscious of glimpsing yesterday, today and to-morrow as part of a continuing whole. It put things in balance, and in a kind of abstract way was comforting when you thought about it.

It didn't, he found, do much to change the face of the immediate tomorrow, the personal tomorrow you didn't like to think about . . .

His attention was caught up from this uncharacteristic musing by a small noise on the ladder. Margaret scrambled into the loft.

"It's you, is it, Mag?" Now that his mind was back in the present he realized something was missing—the sound of Richard's draw-knife. "Where's Grandfather?"

"In the house," Margaret said, "looking for an oilstone."

Alan laughed to himself. It was typical of Margaret not to intrude in the man-world that fascinated her until the proper time, not to come here until he was alone.

She picked her way across the littered loft floor, grave eyes on the battered green box.

"A sea-chest," Alan said. "Grandfather's. Or *his* father's. Old Fritz's, most likely."

He clawed at the rubbish.

"Look at this, will you, Mag?"

Old, once-useful things like a ramrod or a candle-mould you might expect. But skates . . .

They were streaked with rust, screwed to girls' boots with high tops turned down and tucked in, parcelled together with a strap of stiffened leather.

Margaret said, "Your mother's."

He looked up at her, a little startled. He hadn't thought as quickly as that. He said, "I s'pose so," and then, "Hazel's." His mind went back to the photo in folded tissue in his dresser drawer, the picture he had never tried really to merge with the idea of an actual person. Now, with the skates in his hands, a queerness began to crawl through him.

He put the skates back, withdrew his hands, and half closed the chest; then tilted the lid back again and began to uncover whatever was left to see. From under the end till, weighted down by a package of boat-nails and an unopened can of enamel, he tugged a brown book, bound in boards. *Songs for the Home.* The fly-leaf bore the name and date in ink in a hand swift and angular: *Hazel Evelyn McKee, Christmas, 1918.*

Alan fanned the pages. Snapshots lay together in the middle of the book. Originally black and white, they had faded to a vague sepia. He examined the face and figure of the girl, the face with high cheek-bones, wide mouth, luxuriantly piled hair. He knew them all from the photo in his dresser. A slender, angular figure in white middy blouse and long dark skirt, against the background of a bridge railing, the bridge over Katen's Creek. He picked up the second print. The background was the same. But this was a man. A young-ish man with dark hair falling over the left temple. The Brownie hadn't missed much. The smile had something in it that was faintly superior, the outward cast of an inner knowledge, satisfying and unshared.

There was something familiar about this picture.

"I know," Margaret said. "That's Anse Gordon."

Alan glanced up at her again. "How d'you know *that*?"

"I saw a snap in an album in Mrs. Josie's parlour closet. In his uniform. About the time he came back from the war, about the time he went around with Dad's first—with Hazel. When she was a girl."

Alan almost said, "Say: you know more stuff than I ever heard tell of," but caught himself. The odd thing was, it would disappoint Mag rather than gratify her to know that he was ignorant of anything. He said, "Yes, so she did, I guess . . . Where'd you ever hear about stuff that happened *that* long ago?"

"Just people talking," Margaret said; and then, "Lan—"

He sensed in her the same hesitancy, mixed with the need to ask, that he had felt when they were coming up the road. He began to tuck things back into the chest, carefully casual. "What's on your mind now?"

Margaret said slowly, "Mrs. Josie—the Gordons. What's she got to do—Are they any relation? To us?"

Alan considered. This was something new. He said, "Don't think so, Mag. Never heard of it; the Gordons've always been Catholics. Only thing I ever heard, was, Grant kind of liked Mrs. Josie's girl. When they were kids. The one was killed." He looked at her curiously. "Where'd you get *that* idea?"

For some reason she didn't understand, Margaret was a little afraid. There were times when she wished she could get over wondering, get over the need to know, get over the feeling that scraps of guarded talk had to do with things that were important, get over the sense of something unfinished that drove her till she knew.

She felt now an apprehension that was mixed with her revulsion for Vangie Murphy.

It was the tone of Vangie's words that had given this importance in the first place. But Margaret had a feeling now, a wish that she had left it all alone.

Her speech stumbled. "Oh—nothing." Suddenly she blurted, "Vangie Murphy. She was talking to Mrs. Josie about Anse. You and Anse. She said you're the image of 'him."

Alan laughed. "Vangie's crazy . . . You can't listen to anything she says. Not to believe it."

He was speaking mechanically as he refilled the chest. The song book with its two snapshots went back under the till. He kept out the compass and the palm.

Downstairs he heard his grandfather's faint tuneless whistle and the crunch of boots in curled shavings. He said, "Come on; we'd best get down. You go in the house now. Soon be time to start for home."

Richard looked with faint absorbed interest at what Alan held in his hands. He took the palm and held it in his fingers. "Not been used for thirty years. Your great-grandfather was a good hand at cutting a suit of sails." He added in an off-hand voice that attached no importance to the matter, "Keep it if you want to."

The compass he held longer, studying the card, setting it down finally on the work-bench and watching while the starred points slowed and stopped to the pull of the pole. He was smiling slightly when he handed it back to Alan. "When you get to Halifax, you can set this up. From Big Bob's place. Let me see—The Head should be pretty close to nor'-east . . . maybe a bit more easterly . . ."

He turned back to the shaving-horse and the staves.

Margaret was chattering again. As they walked down the road Alan listened with a kind of attentive indulgence, not saying much, letting her talk slip through his mind. Mrs. McKee was hooking a rag mat—Margaret always said "Mrs. McKee" or "your grand-mother," careful not to make any personal claim on a relationship that belonged only to him. Mrs. McKee had set the frame up in the kitchen, Margaret said. The design wasn't the usual roses and scrolls. She was hooking-in a schooner, black rags for the hull, white yarn for the sails, on a green sea. It was for the parlour; you couldn't use a mat with white in it on a kitchen floor.

This was talk you could reply to with simple attention; it was all right as long as Mag knew you were listening. The fact that she was talking again showed that her mind wasn't puzzling itself to pieces over anything. Alan wondered about this. Nothing he had said in the shop loft had really been an answer to her question: *Mrs. Josie . . . the Gordons . . . Are they any relation? To us?* and yet as she walked beside him now, down the road from Grandfather McKee's to Uncle James's, there was none of the withdrawn brooding he had noticed earlier.

The explanation came to him with a shock, the small shock of realized responsibility. *She's got it off her chest now; to me.* And that would be good enough, to Margaret. Again he felt the weight of eldership in the bond between them, a bond that in itself was different from the rowdy half-antagonistic loyalty of brothers and sisters in the families they knew.

It was not the difference that occurred to him as important. That was something that had always been, as long as he could remember. It was not possible for him to bark "Shut up!" or "Get out!" to Margaret, as Jackie Marshall sometimes did at Beulah, or one of the Wilmot girls at Clyde. And Margaret's manner toward himself in the presence of others was almost ridiculously like respect. He had a sneaking suspicion that in this the two of them were regarded by their contemporaries as slightly soft. There were times when he had tried to snap at her, to put their relationship for public purposes on a basis of the usual. He could never quite do it.

No, it was not the difference that touched him. It was the renewed sense of this secret phase of it, the eldership and the responsibility.

Troubling and prideful, it merged and flowed and was part of something else. Margaret might resolve her doubts, ask her questions, and be satisfied with the words he gave her. But unless you were satisfied yourself, the need to know was merely transferred. Something in Margaret's questions, something in an old sea-chest in Richard McKee's loft, something that touched a sensitivity heightened by thoughts of departure, was stirring now in the depths of Alan's memory.

The old vague realization . . . Something odd sometimes, reflected in look or word, about himself and Grant . . . The thing he had thought was there because of the free and easy relationship between them. Less vague in his mind, now. Less vague, and linked with scraps of talk.

Scraps of talk about Anse Gordon. Pictures in the mind. The Exhibition at Copeland, years ago, when you were seven or eight. Motor-boats thuttering on the harbour under whipping flags; you could see them from Exhibition Hill, beyond the red brick clock-tower on the post office. Crowds of people on the hill, moving in and out of the Farmer's Building. More people than you'd ever seen: driving home that night, when you closed your eyes you'd been able to see them moving across your mind, like a dream; though you hadn't been asleep.

Something from that time that came back now. The smell of orange peel on grass, and bright red strawberry pop. The thud of hoofs, horses wheeling and scoring on a dirt track swept with dust. Someone looking up at the grandstand, under a peaked cap pulled back so the snap-fastener showed like an emblem. He couldn't

247

remember the face; only the cap with the fastener and the words, spoken with a kind of rakish reverence: "Renie Marshall; God, I'd like to . . ." A hand had fallen on the speaker's arm. Faceless he had glanced at Alan and glanced away. "Oh . . . the kid . . ." And, floating out of the sound of hoofs and wheels and scattered yelling, "Anse Gordon . . ."

It had meant nothing then. It meant little now. But a strange excitement moved in Alan, a curiosity as to why this meaningless incident should have come back to him, why he should be seeing this crowd, the wheeling horses, hearing that casual voice, across time. And a feeling that this was not something isolated, but was related to other incidents, other brief incidents that moved with colour and life, other scraps of talk that lay in the mind, unremembered but not forgotten. They plagued him, these unremembered incidents, with a sense of existence known but elusive and unproven. It annoyed him to have to turn in at Uncle James's and put off until later the long and troubling pursuit.

James Marshall sat by the north windows of his parlour, facing the road. Since arthritis had taken hold of his knee joints he kept to the house. There was something undignified about leaning on canes or hobbling between crutches as he had to do when the thing was at its worst, and something common about sitting around a kitchen. He had got Fred to cut a door through his bedroom wall to enable him to get directly into the front room without shuffling round the long way through kitchen and hall. There he could look out at the three ash trees in the front yard, and up the slope to the road, forty yards away, and argue with God.

He thought of it as prayer. A kind of communion. He was still the head of this house. But always now behind his consideration of when to order the ploughing and planting, when to mow the oats and let the ram loose among the ewes, a preoccupation absorbed his thought. He was speaking now silently and almost unconsciously while his hands gripped his useless knees . . .

Why, oh Lord? . . .

The pleading note in Mr. Marshall's addresses to God was habitual and reflexive, the result of years of unconsciously memorizing the public prayers of a dozen ministers on the Channel Shore circuit. He did not, particularly, think of himself as a son. The relation was more of a partnership.

For all his austere dignity, there were two qualities James had never quite known. Resignation and humility. He continued now to ask God for health. The request was phrased in established forms, as men use over and over the hackneyed forms of business correspondence. But behind the form was a demand.

A demand . . . ungranted. He stirred restlessly. He had felt lately the beginning of an obscure frightening anger, and blended with this, a reservation. Out of this anger and this reservation, with no preamble of conscious reasoning, a thought so terrible that it left him cold and shaking would sometimes flicker through his mind.

What if you're talking to the wind?

When this happened, he would pray again. For forgiveness. And the act of prayer would shut out the spectre of doubt until it returned again in another form . . .

A just God would answer. If not by granting prayer, by some recognition that prayer was heard. *By some sign* . . . He found himself asking God to prove existence, and arguing with himself that this was senseless, like the riddle of where space ended and time began. Proof was a thing of time. Belief belonged to eternity . . .

There were times when he brushed it all away, the knowledge of God's truth and the spectre of denial. Wipe it all away, everything you can depend on. Admit you don't *know*. One thing is sure. There is still your own strength, your own mind. Still James Marshall.

It was hard to find comfort in that, even though for sixty years or more you had found your mainstay in it, along with the thought of God. Hard to find comfort in it now when the mind lived in a body tottering between canes. It shocked him to learn how much of the physical was woven into the mind's strength. Always he returned in the end to prayer.

He didn't look up as Jane entered the room, talking. She had in her hands a cup and saucer.

"Soup . . . Supper'll be late tonight. They're not back from Town yet. Now, why don't you pull the curtains back . . . how you can see . . ."

She set the cup down on the wide arm of his chair and turned to fuss with stiff white lace curtains, to raise the blind a foot, and pull it down to its original level, and to stand for a moment, small and straight, gazing out at the fields and the road, singing under her breath.

Seeing her there, James was embarrassed by a memory. He found himself living a memory so clear that it had the reality of present illusion. A memory of Jane, standing by the window this way, long years ago, watching the people leave after the wedding

249

supper. She had turned to him from this same window and pressed against him, clasping her hands fiercely together against his back. Her body beginning to tremble, slim and soft, had shocked him. Such actions . . . they were not for women . . .

Jane . . . Why should he feel regret? At the thought of that other woman, the younger one, the words of this present Jane fell half-heard on his ears.

". . . youngsters. Alan and Margaret. Turning in. They're coming in. That's nice. I must ask Renie . . ."

Alan. Margaret. Renie—Grant's wife. Grant. He had hardly come back to the present before the past was ringing in his mind again. The same odd feeling of something lost, continuing from his memory of the young Jane to the thought of Grant, and through that back to Harvey. Impatiently he shook his head.

Moments passed. He could hear them talking in the kitchen, though he couldn't make out the words. Jane's interminable chatter. Alan's laugh. Margaret was the quiet one.

He would have to see them both, he supposed, and his pleasure in Margaret, in noting the fineness of line, the blue-grey eyes, the calm pride of a Marshall face, would be cancelled out—erased by an unreasoning dislike for other eyes, dark and flecked with hints of laughter; for a face that was all surface charm. A Gordon face. A face that took him back to years of health and strength and the bitterest defeat he had ever known.

Something struck him now with strange force. Something he hadn't thought of. Prayer. He hadn't prayed, that summer . . . Hadn't prayed about Grant and Anna Gordon. He had been too proud then, too sure that his own will was enough. Had it been a judgment? Was that why no one answered now?

"How are you, Uncle James?" Alan said.

"Poorly, in some ways." There were times when he lapsed into the colloquial without thinking. He did not ask them to sit, but peered at their faces with eyes speculative and probing as they stood before him.

"How are things at home?"

"Pretty good, sir." .

Never once, he thought, could he look at this boy without reliving that moment in Stewart Gordon's house. *No, Uncle James, I'm staying here* . . .

The ghost of a smile crossed his lips as he turned slightly to Margaret and looked beyond her to the old enlargement under its convex oval frame, above the mantel. Harvey . . . Grant . . . Margaret . . .

Without explanation he said to her: "You have the face; you're all Marshall," and turned back to Alan:

"I hear from Fred's boy you've been in the woods."

"Yes, sir. Dad wanted me for some work out back, for awhile."

"Oh . . . I suppose . . . He won't be keeping you out of school, though . . ."

Alan hesitated. Uncle James hadn't heard, then.

He said, "No, sir. I'm going to finish out the year in Halifax. Mr. Fraser's invited me to stay . . . to stay with him a while. Him and Aunt Bess."

For a moment something more than polite interest flickered in James's eyes. His mind turned this fact and examined it.

Grant. Was Grant tired of raising as his own the boy he'd given his name to? Grant. James had always acknowledged to himself a grudging respect for Grant. For what he had done. For the vows he had taken to save a pregnant girl from shame. But the shame remained. Sin was something you paid for. To escape payment was to cheat life. He realized without remorse, merely noting it as a fact, that what he had felt at the wild idea of Grant's disowning Alan was a hope, anticipation of a personal pleasure. Briefly, a sensation of power claimed him. He thought: I could do it myself. I could tell this boy, this Gordon boy, just how it is. I could tell him now what right he has to the name of Marshall . . .

This was new, this sense of power in this particular connection. But he knew at once, as his eyes moved again to the picture of Harvey, that there was no cutting-off in whatever Grant had in mind for Alan. And he knew at once that whatever Alan might learn of an old and miserable story, he would learn nothing from James Marshall. That was the kind of thing you left to God.

He hardly heard their good-byes. He was back in his curious introspection, glimpsing vaguely the softness, the warmth, the strength of personal relationships and shared passions; emotions he had never permitted to trespass beyond the selvage of his life. Again the slight brief touch of regret. He turned to the window. Alan and Margaret were going down the road, toward Grant Marshall's house. In the kitchen Jane was making a needless clatter around the stove as she got things fixed for supper.

Alan always felt relief at getting away from Uncle James. Until today he had accepted this fact without thinking much about it. But now, after talking with Alec Neill and spending the best part of the afternoon with Grandfather McKee, he felt his recognition of the contrast with a sense of guilt. You were supposed to like your relatives. There was something wrong if you didn't. At least, you were supposed to be what Mrs. Josie called "clannish". You had to defend your family against anything.

Once on the way up the school-house road to Sunday school as he passed the Wilmot place he had seen Clem Wilmot chasing Clyde with a length of harness-leather and had heard the smack of the strap and Clyde's howls when overtaken behind the barn. And yet, a week later when Jackie Marshall had referred to Clem as Pondwater Wilmot—a scurrilous name of which even the origin was lost in time—Clyde had smacked Jackie between the eyes without even waiting to speak.

Alan didn't think he would feel that way if he heard someone running down Uncle James. Now that he thought of it, he *had* heard things. Someone outside the church at Leeds, after evening service: ". . . best place at The Head. But they'd have to bury old James before I'd want to be in Fred's . . ."

Again—that odd pursuit of hidden memory. The plaguing things you couldn't find by conscious search. They had to come up, it seemed, when the time was right, touched to life by something else, a thing somehow related.

Another time, another voice: ". . . queer about it, the way Grant changed after Anna . . . but it must burn old James, to see . . . raising Anse's kid . . ."

Margaret took his hand as they reached the stretch of road screened by their own maples, and dropped it reluctantly as they passed through the gate.

6

AFTER Saturday night supper Alan left the table quickly. There was Mrs. Josie's barn work to do. He did not glance at Margaret. He sensed her stillness, waiting for the look of invitation, as he opened the door to go out. But tonight he had to be by himself. She would be a little hurt, but that was something he couldn't help.

The weather had hardened again but Grant had said they wouldn't go out back that morning; he had gone to see how Dan was getting on, back of Kelleys'. To Alan this was finality. The dream of a mill was dead.

Outwardly serene though unusually quiet, he spent the day splitting wood, in the morning at home and in the afternoon at Gordons'. The serenity was outward only. The pressure of a nameless fear, of things guessed at and half-remembered, pressed without ceasing in his mind. It was as though the aching certainty of departure had given the field of imagination a fertility in which surmise and conjecture were thriving with a nightmare growth.

As he walked down the short stretch of snow-packed road he wondered suddenly, why . . . Why he was going to Gordons' . . . Why Grant looked after Mrs. Josie . . . In these last few days all kinds of things at Currie Head, things you had taken for granted as part of life, were emerging by themselves, sudden and strange, out of the flowing picture of the whole. But their meaning —that was something you did not know.

In a curious way this new and nameless fear, vague and pervasive, made the fact of departure seem less important. That was something certain, known. But this . . .

Less important, unless . . . unless departure and the causes of this growing fear were linked. There was something there, a possibility, too shattering to admit to the surface of the mind, too terrible to haul out and examine . . .

He had never in his life felt anything like this pulsing pressure. There had been a time of worry a couple of years ago that no one knew about. Grant had spoken casually of an ache under his shoulder blade and mentioned the possibility of a touch of pleurisy. Renie had cautioned, "You ought to have an X-ray." Grant said perhaps so, he'd see about it next time he went to Copeland. Until he had heard Grant say, weeks later, that the plates had shown nothing, Alan had lived afraid; almost forgetting what it was he feared, but clutched again and again by moments close to panic, and always conscious of a shadow on the heart.

What he felt now was like that, but more troubling because less definite, less able to be measured and recognized.

Scraps of talk. *She said you're the image . . . Anse Gordon . . . must burn old James to see . . . Anse's kid . . . or your grandmother . . .*

Alan went into the back porch and got the milk pail and went on to the barn. Milk drummed thinly against tin. He stripped the cow, carefully coaxing the last thin streams of milk from warm and flabby teats, and wondered briefly how it was that you could do your job, well and thoroughly, when you felt like this. The smell of hay, the smell of dried manure, the warm glistening feel and smell of the cow's side, the pail's weight between his knees; they remained the same. Only his own insides were different, aching with fear and the need to know.

For a little while, after the cow was dry, after he had climbed the mow and thrown down hay, he stood in the door between the cow stable and the sheep shed, looking in at Stewart Gordon's old two-master, incongruously sheltered there, bottom up, on the shed floor.

On the way in from the barn to the house he made up his mind.

While Josie put the milk through the separator in the pantry, he waited in the kitchen, sitting quietly in Stewart's old chair. She came in, and turned up the lamp. The small yellow crown of flame diffused a widening pool of light.

He said, "Mrs. Josie . . . Something I wanted to ask you."

The tone surprised her. There was something thoughtful in it, and strained. Alan's voice usually was edged with laughter or enthusiasm or curiosity. Rarely with nervousness or contemplation.

"Ask me . . . All right, ask away."

"Mrs. Josie—what is it—about us? About me . . . Grant and me. What is it people talk about?"

Josie sat down in her rocker.

"Talk about . . . I don't know as I see what you mean . . ."

She knew as she said it that her voice was not the voice of ignorance or casual surprise.

Alan said, "You better tell me. You better tell me what it is. What it is about—Anse, when they mention Dad and me—"

The final words came in a hard halted rush. "I got to know . . . I can't stand wondering . . ."

Josie was not a psychologist. She was simply a woman past middle age—she thought of herself as an old woman now—who had come to know a good deal about what suspense and uncertainty can do to the mind. This knowledge was a part of her, as if memory had become an essence in the blood. The memory of days when she had wondered what it was that went on between Anna and Grant Marshall, what it was that absorbed Anse. Later, of how Hazel McKee . . . The memory of waiting, of doubt worse than certainty. The release of knowing, of the worst known. Something you could deal with and accept, because at last it was definite, lifted out of the shadows of hope and fear.

Regretful anger flowed through her.

Why? Why?

Years ago she had given up asking why. Beneath the hard immediate concern of the moment, it rankled now to find this old questioning of life revealing itself immortal in a sinking spirit and a hand that shook.

She reached out deliberately for calmness, for the steadying pattern of sensible and common thought.

Lies. Lies were easiest. With a little sense of escape she realized that the moment could be lied away. This boy . . . he was leaving Currie Head. Lies, to hold him while the mind's questions died . . . She looked at Alan, and what she saw was a boy away from home, a week, a month, a year . . . away from the warmth of the usual, and questions that would not die . . .

She knew about lying, the tragedy of lies exposed by time.

She said, calmly, "Did you ever ask Grant about whatever it is you've got on your mind? Grant or Renie?"

Alan shook his head. "No."

No. It was not something he could ask Grant or Renie. You can't reveal doubt when your whole feeling for people, and theirs for you, is based on things you never think to question.

For a moment her mind encompassed Alan's, and the question growing there:

Is it true? I'm not your son?

No one could ask that question. Or answer it.

That was why he had come to her; someone he could ask. Someone he could come to for the knowledge that was better than fear.

It was forming in her mind. What he had to have was more than fact. Somehow it had to be truth. Somehow it had to be the way it was . . . the way it was now . . . and that was some-

255

thing Josie wasn't sure she had the words for. Only the understanding, the insight that had come to her late in life; the knowledge that facts and the truth can be different. As different as black from white.

She glanced at Alan where he sat in the cane-bottomed chair Stewart had sat in. Behind the composure she could see the strain, and something that was almost eagerness. A lock of dark hair fell across the left temple. Josie felt the crawling pang of mingled love and anger and regret.

How could you give this boy the facts? And leave in his heart the truth? The truth as it was now? As time and love had made it?

She said, "Have you got a picture of your mother, Alan?"

"Mother?"

"Hazel."

"Yes," Alan said. "A photograph . . . And there's some snapshots at Grandfather's."

"You can tell the kind of girl she was, then," Josie said. "Good-looking . . . impulsive. I've never felt before or since the way I did when we began to know she wouldn't live . . ."

Her voice halted. She had made her statement deliberately, to contrive an effect. But it was true. Now she knew it was true.

Years. It was years since she had really thought of all this. Thought of it as a whole. Parts of it at times came up out of memory . . . Grant's letter from Toronto: he was bringing Hazel back. Bringing her home. Would it be all right if she lived with him at Gordons'? Until his house was built . . .

Grant's return, alone. Hazel . . . a haemorrhage on the train, almost within sight of Copeland.

Days of uncertainty. Her own obedience to impulse. The long cold trip down-shore with Adam Falt. The low brick hospital. The room. The girl.

The girl, and the quick understanding . . . "I know how it must've been for you, Mrs. Gordon." The understanding, and the revelation. He hadn't known; Anse hadn't known. That was the gift of Hazel. The girl, she supposed, must feel that this fact made a difference to Josie. Even though it was not a fact you could talk about, make public in extenuation . . . because you couldn't shatter the fiction Grant Marshall and Hazel McKee had brought to life around themselves. Themselves and an unborn child . . . But, actually, it was not the fact itself that made the difference to Josie. What Anse had known or had not known could make no difference now. What made the difference was Hazel; Hazel and her strange happiness—in Grant, in return to the Shore, in being able to tell this small and secret truth to Josie, and in the painful and precarious life she clung to . . .

It came back to her with startling clearness, Hazel's carefully undramatic voice in a moment when the end was close. "Try not to mind this, Mrs. Gordon. I don't, much. Except for Grant . . . And for . . . But I don't know . . ."

She *had* minded. Hazel *had* minded. Had minded dying, had sought to cling to life and Grant Marshall and her child . . .

Josie thought of Anna. There were times when Anna and Hazel McKee were almost mixed in her mind. Both dead, long ago. Both in their separate ways a part of an old story; a story that lived in memory, the separate memories of men and women on the Channel Shore, men and women who were sympathetic, indifferent, curious, careless, malicious. A story that lived too in living flesh and blood.

Anna. The sound of the name. She said to Alan, "I don't know . . . Did you ever hear your dad speak of Anna?"

"Oh, yes," Alan said. "I know he went around with her, Mrs. Josie." He was looking at her shyly. "And then she died; and he married my mother."

Josie nodded. "That's right. A kind of boy and girl thing. Grant liked Anna, and Anse . . . Anse went with Hazel. They were—they planned to marry. There was trouble about religion. D'you understand those things, Alan?"

Josie thought: Lies. I lied . . . No one had ever mentioned marriage. Except perhaps, in a moment of desperation, and too late, Eva McKee. She hardened her will, with no excuse to the saints. A lie was safe when no one could prove it false. When it helped to preserve the truth. What she was after was the core of truth, the truth as it was now.

"You've heard about Anse, I guess. The way he disappeared, I mean. I blame myself, a good deal. He told me what they wanted to do. I . . . I told him 'No'. I don't know what got into his mind—what happened. Maybe he went to find work."

Josie's mind went back to the old fictions she had tried to cheer herself with, years ago.

"Work. So he could come back and get her . . . without being . . . oh, dependent. Dependent on us here."

Alan's face was tranquil and interested. The strain had gone out of it. This was a story of the Channel Shore. He knew that into it his own life was somehow intimately woven, but the tenseness had gone out of him. This was the beginning of certainty.

257

Josie went on. "He didn't come. We got word of Anna's death. Grant was good to us. We'd always been friendly enough, religion or not. And there was that special . . . that feeling for Anna . . ."

She broke off and went back. "You know, I think he—I think Anse must've been . . . killed. By accident, maybe. Among people who didn't know, wouldn't know who to send word to—who to send for. Something like that. He and Hazel—he'd've written . . . There was a special reason. They thought of themselves like married people do. Like they used to in Scotland a long time ago . . . Married, between themselves. A queer thing, and not—recognized. Not done any more. And not understood. Some people on the Shore can be—narrow . . ."

She spoke with a note of reminiscence, almost absently. "Hazel. It all came down on her, because they—Well, because they'd lived together. Though he didn't . . . didn't know . . ."

She studied Alan's face briefly, keeping her scrutiny outwardly indifferent. His look was full of interest and sympathy and a growing understanding.

"He never came back," Alan said slowly. "Hazel—and Grant, then. She married Grant."

He seemed to be trying the words over in his mind, looking at them to see what they meant; tentatively and with a certain wonder, but without surprise. And waiting for other words to make the tale complete.

Except that it would never be complete. That was something Josie knew. Never complete. And the course of it, onward from this point in time, depended now perhaps on the skill she could summon to her tongue. Suddenly she rejected skill. Blunt words, few and forthright, would have to do it. A boy's faith in a neighbour's word and her own faith in his will to understand.

"Let me tell you something," she said quietly. "And don't you forget it. Your dad and your mother—they'd been through the mill. There's a kind of—love—comes from that, sometimes . . . stronger than any other kind. There was only one thing they thought of more than each other. That was the baby born while she was in the hospital, the winter they were married, a couple of months before she died . . . I remember Grant coming in and looking at you in the cradle, after the funeral. It was a mean day, cold and raw, and snow blowing, even that late in the spring. He wasn't sorrowful, you know. He's tender-hearted, it was all a blow—but mostly he looks ahead when looking back don't do much good. He took a squint at you. You were sleeping in the cradle he'd made for you out of pine left over from my husband's two-master. He took a squint at you and laughed and said to me, 'Josie,' he said, 'I've got a son on my hands.' Then he said to you, 'Kid we're on our own,' and went out to tend the barn."

What more could you say to plant the seed of truth, to fix belief in that kinship of the spirit? Belief in this as something warm, possessive and personal; as strong and as personal as kinship of the blood.

Alan said, feeling for words, "Then really—you *are* my grandmother."

What oddity of realization had turned his mind to that? Away from the more direct revelation, the confirmation of his physical fatherhood? Josie didn't know. The words caught her unguarded. For a moment her spine tingled with the nameless craving of earlier years, the physical desire to put her arms round his body, to press him close, once, against the beat of her heart. She fought her way back with quick fierceness to a hard reserve.

"That's the kind of thing you're not to think. It's not true. Not in any way that counts. I don't come into it. Don't come into it at all. The Gordons don't come into it. You're Grant Marshall's son, in everything but—you're Grant Marshall's son . . . I'm a neighbour, that's all. That's all I want to be . . ."

She walked to the window and looked out at the dark, and came back and put a hand on his shoulder briefly, and returned to her chair, facing him.

"You're a neighbour's boy to me . . . The reason I told you this . . . Well, you asked. And it's better to know than wonder. If things were so you wouldn't 've ever . . . That's the way it should've been, because—What I told you, it don't mean anything. Not to you, or Grant. But people . . . I'm scared, Alan. Grant would skin me, if he knew I'd . . . You're what he lives for. You're what he plans for. An education. A chance. But people . . ." Josie's voice was querulous. "I know the Shore. Some time . . . They're always talking . . . Like Vangie. You've got to know. So nobody can take you by surprise."

Alan got up out of Stewart's chair. He looked at Josie as if she had misunderstood him, and as if he couldn't quite explain.

He said, "Well, I guess I'll go home. Thanks for telling me, Mrs. Josie . . . And don't worry. I understand it." He turned in the doorway and looked directly at her. "It won't make any difference, y'know . . . And—thanks."

The air was cold, yet soft. The Channel was grumbling, a giant sighing on the winter beaches of Currie Head. A light was on in Grant's workshop and Alan could hear the sound of an axe. *Difference. It won't make any difference.*

The axe stopped going in the shop, and Grant came to the lighted door. "Hello, kid. You better report in. Renie's looking for you."

Alan said, "All right, Dad," and went into the house. He spoke almost absent-mindedly. A new feeling had taken hold and was spreading through him. He put off thinking about it while Renie told him what she wanted—a gallon of kerosene oil and a pound of tea from Katen's.

On the way to Katen's he walked slowly, letting the kerosene can bump his leg. A tightened ache throbbed at the back of his throat. But it was not himself he was thinking of. He was thinking of the girl who had lain upstairs in the stove-pipe room at Gordons', that spring fourteen years ago, and the man who had lived there, working in the woods and cleaning stables, milking cows, coming in at supper-time. Joking with Mrs. Josie, going upstairs to say a word to the girl before he sat down to eat.

And, sometimes, holding in hardened hands the small warm breathing body of a boy, lifted from a hand-made cradle.

Hazel and Grant. They were people in a story, a sad kind of story that was not all sadness. Grant . . . It was like knowing as flesh and blood the people in a book, as if you could come home and talk to someone like Starbuck, the mate of the *Pequod* in the story about the white whale . . .

A staid, steadfast man, whose life for the most part was a telling pantomime of action, and not a tame chapter of sounds . . .

Not quite Starbuck. Grant was steadfast, but not staid.

Hazel and Grant. The child. He had been thinking of the child as a nameless character in an ancient tale, a stage property. But that was not the way it was. For the story still went on, the story was life; the child was a boy, walking beside him, taking the same steps, thinking the same thoughts.

The cold thought that was not a thought, the apprehension he had never quite admitted to the lighted spaces of his mind, could be taken out and looked at now. Looked at and utterly rejected.

Grant. Grant would never send the child away because it was not the child of his body. Some stupid fool might think that. Might say that. But that was not the way it was. Not when you knew . . .

260

He felt for a moment a kind of enlarged view, as if he could see the other side of the Islands, and past the woods, north to the railroad. As if he could talk on equal terms with Alec Neill or Grandfather McKee or Uncle James. The Channel Shore—it was not a little world, now, from which people went and to which they sometimes returned, but a living part of a larger world, a part of the whole thing, like Halifax or Boston or Montreal. He saw the Shore now not as the one place loved and friendly and known, but as his own particular part of something larger, embracing all, the bright and the ugly, the familiar and the strange.

Grant . . . Closer, now, than ever. That winter, fourteen years ago, and all the seasons since: more than woods work, more than farming or snaring rabbits or going after trout together. It was something hard and bitter they had shared.

No one was in the store yet, under the gasoline lamp, but Felix Katen and one of his grandchildren, Lon's son, a ten-year-old they had christened Burford. The youngster came out from behind the counter eagerly, calling, "Hi, Al!"

Alan said, "Hello, Buff," and punched him lightly in the chest. He had helped little Buff Katen set rabbit snares in Felix's lower pasture one Saturday before Christmas; and even while his mind was fixed on other things, he felt a brief amused lightening of spirit at Buff's obvious devotion.

Felix looked up from a newspaper and peered over his glasses. While the kerosene gurgled into the can, his mind came back, to Halifax, the trip away. He waited until he had the full can in his hand, until he was on the way up the road, to think about it.

He never asked me if I want to go; he just said I'm going . . .

For days the resentment had quivered through his mind, swirling at last along the surface of a darker tide, the clouded sea of a darker apprehension. Now he could look at this boyish hurt with a curious detachment.

That afternoon in Katen's woods: *The smart ones leave. Renie and me—we've been doing some thinking about it . . .* This was still something he didn't understand. But in his new maturity it was a problem to meet with calmness, not something to be nursed and worried over.

He asked himself, once, "If that's what he wants you to do, why don't you do it . . . take it, without griping, and go?"

But that was not the answer. A series of curious pictures, all one picture really, came into his mind. Alec Neill, limping out from behind his wood-pile, alone. Limping into a cold house with a salmon net in the corner, and a pile of old magazines . . . Grandmother McKee, hurrying to unlock the mail-bag, fingering through the thin sheaf of letters for one with a Peace River postmark.

Mrs. Josie . . .

The flowing pictures moved on the surface of his feeling, his certain knowledge. The answer was there. The answer was in something that bound him to Grant in a kind of exalted sonship. Resentment and frustration and unquestioning acceptance belonged to childhood. In their place now was a strong and growing purpose. To live according to the story. To hold in the heart, secret and sharp, the knowledge of a kinship stronger than blood. And holding that, to be Grant Marshall's son.

How could you make it certain, acknowledged, visible?

All right, perhaps, for sons who were really sons to leave, to go away; the tie of blood remained.

But when you were not. When you were not. When the tie was another thing, private and tender, its source unshared by word or glance between you . . .

How could you make it true? How could you affirm it in the sight of all, by action, manner, habit? How? How—except *with* him; working, talking, belonging to his life and purpose, and on the Channel Shore?

If he had never gone questioning to Mrs. Josie Gordon . . .

That thought, now, was like considering the possibility of never having known a person loved.

He was passing Vangie Murphy's, watching for the gleam of Mrs. Josie's lights round the turn, when he began to feel a new slow excitement.

He had the courage, now. If he could find the place, the words, the moment.

It might not change the hard necessity. But he could try.

7

On the morning of New Year's Day there was no talk of going to the woods. Grant went out to the barn, absent-mindedly, without telling Alan what he wanted him to do. Renie saw the omission for what it was—an absorption so complete in a problem without solution that for once he had simply forgotten that he had to try to be natural, had to try to play a natural part.

She said to Alan, "You might clean out the shop if Grant doesn't need you for a while. Anything that'll do for kindling, put it in the porch."

He was glad to be alone this morning. He carried in and dumped in the kindling box the odds and ends of boards left over from Grant's work in the shop, and when this was done built a fire in the shop stove and patched a couple of inner tubes for the truck. After that he sat on the shaving-horse for a little, whittling and working on the purpose in his mind.

He was going to get it said. How, he didn't know. The difficulty still was how to say it. The only words he could think of were as awkward as Grant's had been in Katen's woods. All day Sunday he had tried them over in his mind, on the way to Sunday school, at dinner, and while they idled in the house in the afternoon.

I'd like to talk to you a minute . . . I don't know whether you know it or not, how I feel, but what I'd like to do . . . I don't want to go . . . I want to stay here, for a while anyway . . . Till I see what I want to do . . .

No matter how you varied them they were stilted and awkward and unconvincing.

As he sat on the shaving-horse he worked it over, testing and trying sentences, imagining situations that would make the saying easy.

Nothing could make it easy; and it had to be right. He was haunted by the spectre of thought that waited in ambush if his spoken words should fail: the sense that somehow he had missed, bungled the moment and left the telling words unsaid.

The soft compelling impulse brushed his mind again: let it slide, take it and go. Go as the rest of them go. Stan Currie, Dave and Harry Neill, Col Graham. That's what their fathers wanted for them, a chance away. That's what it means, on the Channel Shore, to be father and son.

He shook his head. That was the argument of fear and of reason. The truth he felt was deeper than reason, a knowledge in the blood and bone. He was not a boy, now, fretting at separation from known and pleasant things, but a man avowing a way of life. The chance he chose was to live and work with Grant, the chance that belonged to those who planted life in the rock and earth and woods of the Channel Shore. This, for him, was the single way of sonship. There were hard things to be done. To speak this word to Grant was first and hardest.

As noon approached, while Renie was getting dinner ready, Margaret came over to the shop. Bert Lisle was with her.

Alan felt a slight annoyance. What he wanted was a chance to go on working it over, reaching for the way to do it right. He heard Bert asking cheerfully whether he could borrow the buck-saw to use on Mr. Currie's wood-pile, and said, absent-mindedly, "Sure," nodding toward the saw hanging on the wall.

Bert lingered, leaning on the saw, blind to Alan's impatience.

"Well, I better get back to work," he said, standing in the open shop door in thin cold sunlight. And then, curiously, "When you goin', Al?"

"Going?"

"To Halifax. You're really goin', ain't you?"

"Next week, I guess. First of the week, likely." Alan spoke quickly and indifferently, unable to think of anything to pull Bert's mind away.

Bert continued with his questions. "When'll you be back, though? D'you really mean it? Bein' away all winter? How long'll you be, really, Al? . . . When'll you be back?"

Exasperation was piling up in Alan: the pressure of accumulated brooding, annoyance at the interruption in this present effort to find the words he had to say to Grant.

He barked, "Oh, for God's sake! How do I know? Never, maybe."

Bert looked at him in astonished injury. He said, finally, "All right. Keep your shirt on. You don't have to . . ." He picked up the saw and stepped out of the doorway and started for the road, wearing a kind of baffled dignity.

Angry at his own anger, Alan said: "Oh, cripes!" He drove his knife hard into the head of the shaving-horse.

Behind him then he heard the sound of crying.

Margaret sat on a pile of sash-wood, crouching forward with her elbows on her knees, hands clutching her face. Her body shook with short stifled gasps.

Alan walked across the shop floor and sat down on the pile of planed boards. He put an arm round her, his fingers hard against small hard ribs. The feel of her, while his anxious mind turned to her trouble, made him think of something almost ridiculous. Years ago one of the ewes in lambing time had refused to mother one of her twin lambs. They had had to raise it by hand, starting with warm milk in the kitchen. He remembered the way the lamb felt, the trembling ribs under skin crinkly with infant wool. He thought, just by looking you didn't realize how small she was.

He said, "Mag . . ." At the sound of his voice and the touch of his hands her will let go. She threw herself across him, burying her face in his sweater with an exclamation oddly wild with relief, crying without restraint. A minute, two minutes . . . he didn't know. She straightened and said, sniffing, "H'ndk'chief, Lan." He felt in his sweater pocket and gave it to her. She dried her eyes and wiped her face carefully, gave the handkerchief back to him, and marched out of the shop.

Alan watched her go through the porch and into the house. He could hear a metallic tapping. Grant, working on something in the stables.

He stepped down from the shop doorway and headed for the barn.

Grant was alone. There were no animal sounds, even, to give the place the feel of life. He had left the cows free, after turning them out to water earlier, to ruminate in the sunlight on the snow-covered pasture slope along the brook, and forgotten to turn them back to the stable.

Dan had both horses in the woods back of Kelley's. For something to do, Grant now patched the horse-stable floor, inserted new planking in the old partition between the stalls.

He thought idly that a barn without life in it was an empty place, almost as dismal as a house without people. The stable door was open, for light, but here on the north side the sun didn't strike. And it was cold.

He wiped his hands on an empty oats bag, standing there in the inside stall, and considered the changefulness of human feelings. One day you felt like a man on horseback; the next, you could crawl underground.

For nearly fifteen years changes in mood had not much bothered him. He had put that kind of thing away. There was always so much to do. Josie and Stewart and Hazel, first, and Alan. Renie and Margaret, and still Alan. A place to look after, a house to build, pulpwood to cut and haul and boom. Pay-rolls to meet. Not much time to be moody. Was that why it was, he wondered, that he'd always kept moving? To avoid brooding, to keep thought away? Was action the answer, the reason he had been a cheerful man?

Perhaps. He didn't know. He said, conversationally, "You don't know a damned thing about it," and made a small sound of disgust: he had known some ups and downs in his time, but this was the first time he had got to the point of talking to himself.

The barn's damned emptiness was inside him. He threw the oats bag away, walked to the open door, and glanced along the cart track to the road. Over toward his own house and Hugh Currie's, then down past Frank Graham's to Mrs. Josie's and Gordon's turn.

If he could bring it up, if they could talk about it naturally . . . things would be better. Not all right, but better. He hadn't been able to get near it. He hadn't been able to say, "How d'you like the Halifax idea, anyway? You'll have a good time at Big Bob's when you get used to it." He hadn't been able to say, "Write a fellow, will you, when you get settled." He hadn't been able to say, "We'll get down to Halifax in the spring, likely; Renie'll want to see her father."

Thinking did no good. Some kind of block in the mind made speech impossible. How could you ask him what he thought about it when it had to be done anyway? How could you discuss it easily, like something natural and agreed, like a trouting trip up the tidewater behind Findlay's Bridge, when the whole thing was forced and unnatural, an expedient you couldn't explain?

This was the first important course of action he had ever imposed on anyone without an explanation. Without a *real* explanation. The things he had said in Katen's woods were thin and artificial. The only explanation worth a damn was the true one, exposure of the thing you feared. Again Grant felt the faintly sickening sweep of doubt along his nerves. Something he had heard rang in his mind: *It's a queer feeling; not to have doubts.*

With eyes that noted the small incidents of life and movement around the place while his mind still turned inward, he saw Margaret emerge from the shop and walk to the house. Alan came and stood in the shop door, and stepped down, turning toward the barn. Even now, you couldn't fight down the feeling of lightness and warmth, the place living in the surface of your sight, the children moving through the small activities of life there. Grant turned back toward the inner stall, not to be caught standing aimless, empty-handed, glooming at the yard.

After a moment he was conscious of something odd, a feeling of being watched. Alan, standing in the stable door, hadn't said anything. Grant straightened. "Dinner-time? I'm just about through here."

Some intuition caught him. He walked across the stable floor to the door, the past and future slipping from his mind. All he saw was Alan, in this present moment, and what was in his face.

He spoke out of himself, not out of reason or prudence or fear, but out of love without caution.

"Alan, kid—what is it?"

He never asked me if I want to go; he just said I'm going . . .

Alan gulped. All he could think of was that Grant at last had asked. Not in the words he had dreamed of, but in words selfless and all-inclusive; words and a tone that were not concerned with this moment only, but probed for the source of all trouble and of every hurt to a person loved.

The sound of Grant's voice . . . the sense of something half-remembered. A dark kitchen, the smell of wet moss and the rank smell of trout; Grant grumbling at the cat, and the note in his voice: *Good Lord, kid; you didn't think I was talking to you!*

Something in the tone: *Alan, kid—what is it?*

The strength of the essence. The new sense of maturity in Alan's heart was merged with something else. With all the years of kinship.

A question had been asked.

Answer it, then.

He said, "I don't want to go to Halifax. Academy in the fall, either. I want to work here in the woods, with you; and take grade ten right here, from Renie."

He said it roughly, his voice hoarsened by the resolution that had come to him with Margaret in his arms; hoarsened by tears forced back in the throat.

Grant motioned him down to the door-sill and dropped to it himself, not touching Alan; not close enough to make it look like sympathy. He leaned back against the jamb, like a man considering something in a reasonable manner, not overly worked up about it. There was no sense wearing on your face the fact that reason had nothing to do with it.

He found, in fact, that he wasn't much worked up. What he felt was a kind of easy freedom and a gradual relaxed excitement. The odd thing was, he wasn't thinking about Alan, or anyone in particular, but about the whole of life as it included himself and his people, his place and the Channel Shore.

Somewhere he had read that dreams, even when they seemed to take all night and to cover days in time, were really over in a few seconds. The parts you remembered. Years ago at Uncle James's he had dreamed an elaborate dream in which he left home, took the boat from Morgan's Harbour to Copeland, boarded the train and went to Halifax. He could remember the coarse plush of the day coach in the dream, edited in, perhaps, from an earlier actual experience, and Uncle James standing stern and righteous on the wharf at The Harbour, to say good-bye. In Halifax he had got a job in a restaurant, dish-washing. The dream ended as he walked across the restaurant kitchen and the stacked plates he carried began slowly to topple, crashing with horrible deliberation to the floor. He wakened to the sound of the alarm clock, realizing it was his turn that morning to get up and light the kitchen fire.

He had figured later that the dream had consumed only the time it took the clock to bring him awake. He had long known that his dreams seemed to grow from some thought or consideration not followed to a conclusion, picked up later in sleep. He had been day-dreaming about leaving home; thinking, turning over in his mind with no sense of conviction the idea of how it would be if he went away and made some kind of home and sent for Anna. Some small distracting thing had called his mind away from that, but it had come back to be carried on in a dream for which the clock had been the measure and perhaps the accidental light that flashed it on the screen of sleep.

Now, the conscious considerations of his mind were like a dream in their rapidity and in the way they picked up and wove together the wisps of unfinished thought. He was feeling again his boyhood need to make a home at Currie Head, on the Channel Shore, at a time when everyone with ambition worked only to get away from it, to the opportunities of the cities and the west. Feeling again his refusal to run away. All he had ever known about that was, it was what he felt like doing.

Sometimes he had looked at this feeling in the light of reason; but he had never arrived at an explanation of it. Now, without having to figure it out, he saw it clear.

The next time Dave Neill came home from his fruit farm across the continent, and hinted that anyone with guts had left the Shore long ago, Grant knew what he would say. To himself, anyway.

Away, sure. It's easy enough to leave. Nothing new in that . . . But when you take the old stuff, the country that's under your feet and all around you . . . when you take that, and build something they said you couldn't, and grow something they said would die: that's new, boy. That's something really new.

He picked up a winter-bleached oats straw and began to chew it, squinting at the slope of the upper field across the road. He felt a good deal as he had felt one day long ago, after a spring funeral, when he had come back to a house down the road and looked into a cradle and felt the turning of his heart.

The odd thing was that this really had nothing to do, directly, with the fear that had risen in his mind as he listened to Renie across the kitchen stove . . . when was it? Less than two weeks ago. Nothing to do with it at all, when you looked at things reasonably. All the danger still remained. But reason had faded before the look in his son's face and the response in his own blood. There were times when you did what you felt.

Somehow now you knew that the thing you feared was less important, less dangerous, than the artificial thing you had thought up to defeat it . . . You knew that your way of living, the things you talked about and did and looked forward to, hardly knowing, came into this and were part of the pattern that made your feeling right.

There were times when you did what you felt.

Chances you had to take.

. . . *we'll take each day as it comes.*

He wanted to laugh. Then he remembered that he hadn't said a word to Alan. It must have been half a minute since he'd turned and seen his son's face in the door . . .

He said, "Big Bob won't like it much . . . You'll have to go stay a couple of weeks with him, anyway. That ought to be long enough . . . No idea you felt that way. That's fine. That's what we'll do, then."

1946

FORTY miles or so northwest of Copeland as you travel east and south, the land begins to flatten. This is where they built the rail line close to the shallow salt invasion of the gulf, the county's northern edge.

On the right hand are sloping farmlands, checkered with square groves of spruce and hardwood; barns and houses in fenced fields, the barns stained a dusty red against the weather, and the houses white and orderly or shabby and grey with neglect. From the train window on that side you watch the country slide, sheep and cattle standing distantly in pastures speckled with maple clumps, far away a horse-drawn cultivator moving across a side hill, here and there an aproned woman, or a child in a dooryard, lifting a hand.

But on the left, for miles, until the track swings southerly through woods and barrens to meet the southern beaches at Copeland, the traveller sees a low sweep of salt-marsh and tall grass under the wind, the gleam of occasional water.

This was where Bill began to be troubled.

It had been all right, travelling down by the day train from Toronto and boarding the Ocean Limited at Montreal. He had been touched then with the same forward-looking excitement that had come to him a year ago in London, planning what he had to do. But these marshes, this shallow cloud-reflecting water from the gulf, were the first land and water he could recognize, the first fringes of the country he was coming to. These fringes he remembered from twenty-seven years ago, and with recognition came doubt. Doubt and the lurking fear that Andrew and Helen had been right.

The two scenes were clear. They merged slowly with dark grass moving past the train window, the slow dragging creak as they pulled into station yards, the matter-of-fact mourning of the engine whistle, the dull white of banked clouds between sky and water.

270

Andrew Graham, thin-faced and white-haired, leaning back in the worn black leather chair by his study window, fingering a paperweight, a tarnished silver stag; speaking with the old precision but with more gentleness than Bill remembered: "It seems odd. An odd thing. But I think I know what takes you back. Some sort of illusion. It might be kinder to memory—" he hesitated and went on: "Suppose the illusion lives. Harder, perhaps, to—" Andrew waved a hand. Bill finished the sentence in his mind: harder, perhaps, if you see a kind of rough well-being, to reconcile yourself to the nagging regret, the ice of surface living.

Andrew Graham in his seventies was less absent-minded than he had been at forty-five. Now he noticed things, and tried to be encouraging; with a small reminiscent laugh: "Remind Frank . . . And remember me to Alec, and Rich McKee . . . I hear Hugh Currie's dead."

All his life, Bill thought now as he watched the marshes, Andrew had covered his shy gentleness with the other thing; the hard determination, the streak of granite that had carried him through the small college first, and then McGill; a master's, a doctorate. Finding all of life in books and in ambition. Bill regretted for a little that in his shyness he had never really reached the heart of Andrew Graham, had merely caught a glimpse of him in odd moments when a softness crept into his voice unrealized, in some rare allusion to his boyhood. It shocked Bill now to realize that he regretted this more than anything he could think of. More, perhaps, than even the wall of difference that stood between himself and Helen.

Helen . . .

What was it, really, when you tried to see . . . Merely that mud tracked into the front hall, in that first apartment on Castlefield, had been more important to Helen than the rush of feeling that hurried you in through the front door to reach for her. Merely that getting off a tram-car first, and raising an arm to hand her down, was more important to Helen than a word of endearment in the dark. The hand's touch that was never there, nor the look in the eyes . . . When you tried to measure it, that was all it was. That was what it amounted to. Added up for eleven years.

That was the apprehension he had been feeling, walking along the Mall, before he had seen Anse Gordon. Return, a sharp brief joy, and in the end, the wall . . .

Helen . . . commenting on his resolve to spend the summer at a place she had hardly heard of: "It'll look queer to a lot of people. How long have you been home? Seven weeks? Eight? . . . It's not only myself. Jock hardly knows you."

271

"I know."

There was nothing you could say just yet about the feeling it gave you to have an eight-year-old who called you, politely, "Sir." That was the kind of thing that took time. You couldn't hurry it.

"You won't get anywhere running away from things, Bill. You've tried that."

That surprised him a little. He hadn't thought of Europe in wartime as running away. He was ready to admit that his motives were no nobler than a wish to get into the show, and, far back, the thought of a boy growing up, coming to know, some time, where his father had spent the early and middle years of this decade. But he had not thought of it as running away.

He said. "I suppose so. I'm going down to have a look, though, Nellie." He had been pretty gay about it, with the free and easy feeling which a little stubbornness can give you; speaking lightly the old name he had used in mocking affection before the wall cut off the impulse to such fooling. He had caught the almost startled glance, and said, "I don't suppose . . ." and let it drop when the glance vanished.

The nervousness he felt now as the train emerged on the gulf shore was not directly the result of his father's doubts and Helen's. These had not really disturbed him; his consideration of them was a symptom of his own disquiet; they had expressed a possibility which was an apprehension in himself.

Once as a small boy he had found in one of the city parks, near Andrew Graham's house, an island of green moss under young hardwoods that met overhead to form a small leaf-walled house, a chapel. He thought of it as a den. He had spent most of an afternoon there, on his back, thinking of almost nothing. Next summer the place had come to his mind again, and he had found the path and gone down toward his den with expectation. Winter had made changes. One of his trees had splintered under the weight of snow; its dead top hung down, spreading brown boughs across the floor of moss.

What Bill felt now was a nervous fear, a fear of the same kind of change, intensified a thousand times by the weight of his greater expectation and of time.

Perhaps what he had felt in London was pure illusion.

Perhaps Andrew and Helen had been right. Perhaps you couldn't go back.

The occupation of thinking of them, of the doubts they had voiced, brought quietness to his mind . . .

He had been thinking of all this for the best part of an hour. What was the last station they had passed? Stoneville. You could get a bus there, the trainman said, that would take you in to the west end of the Shore at Findlay's Bridge. But he had chosen to do it the old way, the way he had come in nineteen-nineteen. Down to the other end of the Shore at Copeland and back up the road. Two more stations. Now the train ran parallel to the shore. Currie Head was over there, somewhere, twelve or fifteen miles away to the south. Unbroken woods, now. They were turning away from the northern water, beginning to cross the county's eastern end. One more station and it would be time to start getting the bags down.

He settled into a kind of fatalistic peace. The tree-house might be destroyed, the illusion gone. What of it? It would be something new, then. If the old thing wasn't there, you could take a look at whatever there was in its place. Bill grinned at the way his mind was working, and told himself he felt all right.

The train's desolate hoot faded overhead. This was the last grade down into Copeland. He caught sight of water, not the green shallows of a while back, but the distant dark blue of the Atlantic, and nearer by as they pulled into the station, the murky slop around the coal wharves. He reached up for his suitcase, adjusted the dunnage bag under his other arm, and swung down the coach steps to the plank platform.

Two coaches up, the mail-car's sliding door rumbled open. A clerk in white shirt and black satin sleeve protectors began handing down bags to a moustached man in faded blue overalls, who stowed them in the back seat of a dusty Chev. Bill stacked his two bags together by the station door and watched the mail transferred. He let himself be absorbed briefly in a small interesting thought. This was, that a man of forty-odd, seen by a boy of thirteen, never gets any older. Adam Falt was just as he had been, on this platform, twenty-seven years ago. Just as he had been a year ago, in the time-less land of memory.

PART THREE

Summer *1946*

ALAN

MARGARET

GRANT

ANSE

1

At Marshall's mill on the Mars Lake flats Dan Graham was switching the diesel over to gasoline for the evening shut-off. Alan brought the carriage up on its last run, pulled off his gloves, batted his cap to knock the sawdust out of it, and walked off the mill floor into late afternoon sunlight.

He glanced up at the spruce piled back of the skidway, the stacked lumber, the open mill-rig under its sheltering roof, and began to feel the laughter.

There were two periods in the day when the force of it was clear: just before seven in the morning, with the crew straggling into the yard; and again at shut-down time, when the flesh looked back in a kind of physical reverie, relaxed, feeling again the shuttling thrust of the carriage, the repeated droning snarl of the saw.

This was something that was always somewhere in the shadowy depths of feeling. Now and then it would break the surface briefly while he worked. In an idle moment, perhaps, when Buff Katen was slow in rolling a log down the skidway to be clamped on the carriage. Sometimes at such moments he would be consciously aware of Dan feeding planks through the edger, Sam Freeman squaring them off at the trimmer, Lee Wilmot piling them in the yard. Consciously aware of the conveyor slanting up and out beyond the broad low roof, pitching slabs down to the smouldering fire. Consciously aware of sawdust heaps behind the mill, piled logs and stacked lumber in the clearing beside it.

Sometimes it would come to him during the noon hour, a recess full of small concerns and eating and idle talk.

But moments like that were brief and occasional, dropped by chance into a busy monotony; it was in the morning and after shut-down that he could really feel the tide of well-being, always remotely washing the shore of flesh and nerves, come in to flood the inlets of his mind.

He glanced up now and laughed.

Sam Freeman tucked his pipe under his moustache and said, "See you in the mornin'," and walked off with Lee Wilmot toward the Wilmots' ancient car, parked at the side of the short stretch of hauling-road that led out past the western end of the lake to the highway. Lon Katen lounged after him and Buff followed them slowly, lingering.

Dan pulled the tarpaulin over the diesel and sat down on the edge of the mill floor. He said, "Grant's late."

Alan said, "He'll be along. You go ahead with Lee if you want to, Dan. I'll wait."

Dan got up slowly. "May as well, I guess." He called to Lee to hang on a minute and crossed the yard, moving lazily in this time of leisure after the day's work.

A car came up the hauling-road then, pulled round Wilmots' and crunched over sawdust and edgings in second gear. Grant got out and stopped to exchange a word with Lee and Sam and again for a moment to run a glance over the piled lumber. Then, erect and compact, he crossed the yard to the mill.

Watching him, Alan felt again the private pulse of liking that always quickened in him when he saw Grant after even a brief absence; whenever he saw this figure in stained khaki and creased flannels, and the grave face still boyish under greying hair. He thought, *a good-looking character.* Some time he would have to tell Grant so. Since coming back from overseas he had found himself saying what he felt like saying. But this . . . it would have to be kidding, said in fun.

He said casually, "Hello, Pop. 'd you get the cars?"

Grant said, "After a little argument."

Alan laughed. Grant usually got what he went after, even when things were scarce, like the freight cars he had gone to Copeland to arrange for today.

He saw then that Buff Katen had turned and was coming back with something on his mind.

Buff said, "You won't forget, will you? You'll be down?"

Alan said, "Sure. We'll pick you up, Buff," and turned to walk with Grant toward the car.

Grant hesitated there, his hand on the car door, frowning slightly, his glance following Buff Katen and the others until the sound of Wilmots' engine died down the hauling-road. He glanced again over the yard. "Not much left in the way of logs. We'll have to haul . . . Be haying time soon, anyway. Why don't you take a few days off? While you can?"

Alan climbed into the car, pulling Grant after him with light words. "Look, Pop. If you don't like my sawing, say so. Take her yourself or get a *real* sawyer. I'll go to work with an axe, in the woods . . . But be damned if I'll sit in the parlour . . ."

He grinned as he said it. Grant had never liked to saw; he had always said he wasn't enough of a screwball. But Alan had taken to it from the first. Even before the war, old mill hands like Sam Freeman had said his planks looked as if they'd been through a planer.

Grant said with a faint reserve, "All right . . . You ought to have some fun, though."

"I wouldn't worry about that." Alan was backing the car, turning. His voice was gentle and absent. Memory touched him briefly. Years ago he would have quit work and gone fishing, even if he didn't particularly want to, if that was what Grant wanted. But he wasn't a boy any more.

How could you make it plain? He knew what puzzled Grant. It wasn't natural for a person who had been through these last years in England, France, Belgium, Northwest Germany, to settle down as if he'd never been away. Such a fellow should be lazy for a while, should observe the forms of gaiety, get a girl perhaps; attend the receptions they were holding for the boys coming back; make appearances in the uniform with the sergeant's stripes on the sleeves.

What he could not explain was why he wanted none of that. This was all he wanted. To get up at six in the morning, eat breakfast, drive to the mill, listen to the mutter of the engine, walk up to the carriage and rip out deal. It was good enough. It was more than that. You didn't have to bother about anything. Didn't have to look ahead, even though each day, complete in itself, ran on always into a sense of the next. Even though there was a curious expectancy . . .

Work and tiredness. The look of Sam Freeman's moustache. The look of Lon Katen puddling the sawdust with brown tobacco-juice. A drive on Sunday or in the evenings. Home. Down to Katen's to hang around, kidding with Buff. Down to the mill to file and refit, with Margaret perhaps roaming the yard in the dusk. That was all.

You might say, Look: *This was what I hankered after for six years* . . . But you couldn't. That was corn. And it was not strictly true. Not when you had trained yourself to hanker after nothing.

He said absently, "I like it this way," and sheered away in thought. Grant was silent.

278

As he turned out of the yard, Alan said casually, "If you're not using the car tonight I'd like to have it for a while. Margaret and I thought we'd take a drive."

"Did you?" Grant spoke slowly. "Dan's cousin's home. Bill. I thought we might go over to Frank's. I used to—Bill was here, once, years ago."

"I know," Alan said. "Dan was telling me." He was regretful about this, knowing the pride Grant would take in being with him at Frank Graham's, seeing him introduced to the newcomer —Grant Marshall's son, home from the war. But Bill Graham would be at The Head all summer. He said, "Look—if it's all the same—Margaret and I—we thought we'd take a look at the dance. Down at The Pond."

After a short silence Grant said evenly, "That's not much of a place for Margaret. You either."

Alan worked the car round a hole in the hauling-road. Words formed in his mind . . . *When you were my age you'd been married twice. I can look after Margaret . . . The real reason the women don't like dances . . . the real reason is, the people are Catholics. Down-shore Catholics. You and Renie get the Methodists to put on a dance and we'll go to that.*

But that was arguing. Even though he had grown into a habit of speaking frankly, he disliked argument. Argument with Grant . . . He shook his head as he edged the car over the culvert where the hauling-road joined the highway, and straightened out for the run to The Head.

He merely said, "Oh, they're quiet enough these days, I guess. It's just for a look, anyway. Something new."

Grant said nothing. There was no answer he could make in words. The answer was in a habit of living. He checked himself. Through some odd association in memory he had thought of James. In what he had been thinking and saying, was there something of James? Was that it? James Marshall, dead more than four years. How much of his hardness had been belief? How much of it had been regard for appearances, the kind of thing that nagged his own mind now?

Grant didn't know. There was no logic in his feeling. For weeks he had been urging Alan, off and on, to take things easy, have some fun. And now he could feel a futile anger because the kids were going to a dance.

His mind turned for a moment on his own youth, the shyness of it . . . Here was Alan, grown up into a man whose confidence and ease he would have envied, years ago. And wasting it on people like the Katens.

He shook his head, bothered again by something from the past. He was seeing Alan in the summer of 'thirty-eight, a boy still, without this lean maturity and ease. Seeing Alan, standing by the mill—they had moved it east that spring, but it was still out back—standing by the mill, looking north: "Some time this fall, Dad, why don't we take a couple of packs; hit through the woods? See what's there. Till we strike the railroad . . ."

It had been a Plan. To take a compass and belt-axes and maybe a shotgun. Cross the narrow end of the county on foot, northward to the railroad and the gulf shore. Grant felt an unaccountable lonesomeness. They had never got round to it, and now in this summer of 'forty-six Alan hadn't mentioned it, or anything like it, again.

He grunted, irritated at the unreason of his thought.

Alan said, "You're talking in your sleep, Pop," and laughed.

"Guess I am," Grant said. His mind tightened at the half-teasing affectionate *Pop*, the word he was hearing now instead of the old *Dad*, the occasional half-daring *Grant*.

He couldn't help it. It was like a small inner hysteria, beyond the will. He felt again the shock that had barely touched him, far back of the rush of affection, when Alan had stepped down from the train at Stoneville after more than five years away. The grave boyhood lost in maturity. The dark grin, the lock of hair falling across the left temple. And the look he had seen, or thought he had seen — afterward, in the eyes of others . . .

In the big dining-room facing the road Margaret was setting the table.

Gradually the family had got into the habit of using The Room as a living-room, more formal than the kitchen, less formal than the parlour. Grant had built into it a stone fireplace, and in these later years when he could afford to care less about time and money, he and Renie had begun to think about leisurely things: comfortable furniture, hardwood for the fireplace, china and silver for the table.

In winter, the family spirit born in the kitchen continued here, and in summer, though no one was much in the house except to sleep, this was where Grant read the paper in the hour or two before bed-time, where Renie sewed and knitted, where Margaret and Alan sat for a little, relaxed and inactive, not needing any small activity to accompany passing time.

In summer, too, for coolness, they ate supper here. Ordinarily this was a casual performance except on Sunday or when there was company, but in the weeks since her return from Halifax Margaret had been giving it a touch of formality. She spread the white cloth now, got the plates and cups and saucers from the dish closet, and went through the kitchen to the refrigerator in the pantry for sliced tongue and potato salad. She was placing knives and forks when Renie came in from the garden, her hands full of narcissi, and began to arrange the flowers in a slender-stemmed vase in the centre of the table.

Renie glanced across the table and smiled. She was thinking that Margaret, beyond the white cloth, looked curiously slim and childish. Odd, too, how one could look so much like another while individual features differed. Margaret and Grant . . . She saw the brown bobbed hair, like polished walnut, the dark blue eyes, the short nose slightly broadened at the base, the face narrowing to a delicate chin not quite pointed, the mouth with its over-full upper lip and curved half-hidden lower; the body small and slender and unconsciously voluptuous. Renie thought: Some man, some time . . . and almost uttered one of the off-hand observations The Head had come to expect of her. Instead, she smiled.

It was a smile of understanding and wisdom, but of an understanding that did not dissect, a wisdom too gentle to be analytical. Not a knowing smile, in the sense of expressing knowledge of hidden motive or feeling. All Renie's smile expressed was that a woman has a right to her oddities, and that perhaps Margaret and herself possessed more oddities than most.

A flush darkened Margaret's cheek-bones. For an instant she felt a small sharp sensation, as though she had been discovered in some thought or feeling almost unknown to herself. This passed at once into a suspended moment in which she saw Renie as a woman. She was not conscious of the fact that for twenty years she had taken Renie for granted. The past didn't come into it in deliberate memory. What she saw for an instant was a woman in a green dress, a roundish face unlined except for laugh-wrinkles; short hair that was nearly all grey; strong shoulders, large hands. A woman who had given her a look of understanding untouched by criticism.

Once, in Halifax, Will Marshall had taken Margaret to dinner at the Young Avenue home of the man who headed the construction company Will worked for; a man who had occasionally bought lumber from Grant. One of the guests was the character woman of an English stock company then playing the Capitol. Margaret had been ill at ease, not at any lack of poise in herself, but at the effort her host and hostess felt they had to make to reassure her by their manner that it was all right, Channel Shore people were all right; in time she'd get used to this sort of thing.

She had glanced across the table and caught a glint in the Englishwoman's eye, a slight twitch to the thin-lipped mouth; a look as personal as a guarded wink. She had felt an odd sense of intimacy, an intimacy based on recognition . . .

Something of this was what she felt briefly now about Renie, who could recognize in a smile their own differing peculiarities, without curiosity or criticism.

Her blush faded. She giggled as Renie's smile broke up in a husky laugh. The moment dissolved in a sense of warm silliness, leaving no sense of violated confidence. Margaret turned to the east window, reached up to part the curtains, and rested her hands on the sill, looking out.

Renie pulled a cushioned wicker chair round to face the north windows and the roadside maples. She leaned back and crossed her ankles. The window was open, propped on a framed screen, and an air of wind touched her face lightly as half-thoughts touched her mind. The ability to enjoy doing nothing, between the activities of the house and the farm, was a quality she had always had. Since she had given up school-teaching there was more time to indulge it. She thought: minutes of rest; they're my vice. Her mind ran idle, thinking of brief restful moments between cooking and gardening, sitting alone or with Janet Currie on Stan's porch, or lying in the curious half-sleep before sleep, unwilling to let yourself drop away . . .

This was a quality she was thankful for and she knew its rarity. Margaret, now — Margaret didn't have it. Though all her attitudes might indicate ease and a quiet mind, it wasn't there. Margaret and Grant were alike; they had a deliberate quietness, a detachment lightened by humour. It made you think of them as easy-going. They *were* easy-going. But it was a *schooled* ease. When you knew them, you knew their minds were never still. You knew that while Grant smoked in the kitchen or lounged on the back steps, his face untouched by anything but the moment, his mind was ranging in time and distance. Ahead to next winter's cut, to next year and the next, back to . . . back to boyhood, perhaps. Ranging and planning. Never quite able to let things lie.

How hard he had tried to achieve that sense of acceptance. How well, in regard to his fears for Alan, he *had* achieved it. How well he had preserved that calm, touched with laughter and shared, continuing love.

But that questioning of time and space and circumstance was always there, far back. Ignored, brushed out of the mind by a kind of reckless resolution. And yet existing; brought to the surface once in years, perhaps, by some word half-caught, a glance, the look on a face. Renie was faintly worried. There was something — the way Grant seemed bothered now —

But her worry was slight. She smiled, shaking it off. Renie understood Alan, she thought. He had grown up. Alan was a good deal like herself. More like herself than Margaret was, the child of her body.

Her eyes came back from their surface brooding on the road and the maples to take in again, in concert with her mind, the figure of her daughter standing by the east window, watching the fields and the eastward curl of the road.

Margaret ... her daughter ...

Drawn toward the girl in that slight warm moment of wordless communication, Renie's mind continued casually reflective.

Margaret ...

In years of living with Grant she had come to know when matters other than the concerns of day-to-day living were moving in his mind. To guess a little even of what they were. But about what Margaret thought and felt, despite that recognition, the understanding that a woman's moods were there, she realized she had no hint at all.

Outside a car slowed and stopped under the maples.

Renie said, "It's Beulah."

Margaret turned from the window. The screen door clicked. Beulah Marshall came through the front hall and hesitated in the dining-room door, a little flustered at seeing the table set for supper.

She said, "Oh, Aunt Renie ... Margaret."

"Come in, Beulah," Renie said. "Sit down."

Margaret said indifferently, "Hello, Beu."

Renie felt a quirk of irritation. It wasn't that Margaret ever said anything objectionable. But this polite stand-offishness . . . When you lived in a place you had to go out of your way to be friendly.

She said to Beulah, "Stay around a bit; we'll be having supper soon. The men are late tonight . . . Why don't you eat with us?"

Beulah shook her head. "Oh, no, Aunt Renie . . . We've had supper. I just drove down to . . ."

Margaret said, with no special emphasis, "He'll be here any minute."

The irritation in Renie sharpened. If Margaret wanted to tease she would have to put some laughter into it. She felt a shock of surprise. Half a dozen girls at The Head followed Alan with their eyes. Was there some kind of resentment in Margaret? She had a sense of let-down. There had been a little while ago that moment of understanding expressed in warm and foolish laughter. Now, this reasonless antagonism.

Beulah flushed. For anyone else she would have had a bantering retort, but the acid in Margaret's voice had sealed off banter with dislike.

"Oh, I . . ." Beulah said. "Look, Papa's driving up the Head of the Tide this evening to Aunt Isabel's. I thought—we thought— some of you might like to come for the drive, and—"

Renie said, "That'd be nice, Beulah. I don't think we—Grant and I—perhaps Margaret and Alan would like it. Bel Falt's fond of Alan and she hasn't seen him . . . Don't you think so, Margaret?"

She could see the girl's contrition, the self-distaste after rudeness and betrayal of personal feeling.

"I'm sorry, Beulah," Margaret said. "But I don't see how we can. Alan — we've got something on, tonight. We're going down to Forester's Pond. It's dance night."

Renie saw the eagerness drain out of Beulah's face, and the tide of astonishment.

Her instinct of family defence began to form. She said, "I guess they're not as rough as they used to be. When I first came here no one would . . . They were all right for the people who believed in that kind of thing, of course."

Beulah said, "I s'pose so." She had risen quickly and moved now to the hall door. "Well, I'm sorry you can't — Well, good-bye."

Renie waited until she heard the sound of the motor. She said mildly, "D'you think it's wise, Margaret? People around here . . . I don't see anything much wrong with it myself, but . . . It's what those dances used to be . . ."

Margaret had returned to the window. She said, "Oh, it's not . . . It's just something new, Renie. We're going down to look."

Renie said, "Well, if I were one of the Pond people I don't know as I'd feel too good about a bunch from The Head coming down as if they were going to a circus."

Margaret said impatiently, "It's not that. You're twisting . . . Things are always the same here. It's just, oh, something new. Different."

Renie nodded. "Yes, I know. Well, there's not much that's new in a place like this. But . . . Well, if it's more life you're looking for, you know we wouldn't put any obstacles in your way. There's always Halifax."

Margaret felt the tingling flush of fear. Halifax. There was nothing now in Halifax. All she wanted now was here, on the Channel Shore. Clear and definite and denied to her.

A car swung into sight round Gordon's Turn. She said to Renie, "They're coming now." For the moment that would have to do. The daily departures, the casual arrivals. There was always time . . .

2

ALAN shook his head at the mirror as he knotted his tie, impatient at a slight uneasiness, a shadow drifting in the quiet lake of thought.

He was, he told himself, making too much of it. Grant's slightest wish . . . through boyhood it had been his law, a law observed in an eager and careful ardour, a law without words. But now . . . He was twenty-six years old. Now there was an obligation to himself and to Grant to be himself, his own man. To be anything else was forced and artificial, and noticeable—the mark of a dependence that belonged to boyhood.

He grunted, feeling the ridiculousness of even arguing about this in his own mind. All Grant had said was a quiet word about a dance, a small thing on which their judgments differed. He hadn't even mentioned it after supper when he'd tossed over the car key.

Making too much of it. But the irritation nagged. He was half sorry now they had thought of going to the damn dance. He had no particular interest in it, except to talk to a few downshore people he had got to know before the war, when they had been lumbering there. People he liked. But there was Margaret; she wanted to go. And Buff. Buff wanted the pride of having them with him. Alan grinned, thinking of Buff.

He went downstairs, still conscious of the drifting shadow, and found Margaret on the veranda steps, arms about her knees. Renie sat in a wicker chair on the grass out front, placidly knitting. She gestured with the needles as Alan and Margaret went up the path to the road.

"Have a good time, now. And don't be too late."

He said, "We won't, Renie," and glanced down at Margaret as she scrambled into the car. "Nice dress, Maggie."

She said, "Thanks, Alan," and leaned back, stretching tanned stockingless legs straight in front of her.

Alan laughed. For more than five years Margaret had lived in his mind as a girl of fifteen, shorter and scrawnier than average, trying to carry angularity with dignity. Then, when the *Aquitania* docked in Halifax two months ago, he had been embraced by a woman of twenty, no longer angular.

Margaret said, "What's funny?"

"You are," Alan said as he put the car in motion. "What do they call that thing you've got on?"

"Oh, natural linen," Margaret said. "Off white."

"Hard to make you match up with the girl you — with nineteen-forty. You're more like the one that wore a red stocking-cap and mitts on a string round her neck."

Margaret made a small meditative sound and was silent. What he said was true, in more ways perhaps than one. In the years just before the war there had been an outward slackening in their curious intimacy. Her own awkward age and the period of Alan's passionate preoccupation with Grant, and the mill, and growing up. No change in feeling. It was just that the expression of feeling had been more remote. A quick occasional smile instead of the long sessions of question and answer on the way to school. Now, in another sense, the first relationship was back. Back without the small-girl-and-big-boy chatter. Back in a sense that was clear to Margaret, but which, she thought, Alan had never stopped to consider or define . . .

If it's more life you're looking for . . . There's always Halifax.
Her mind went back to Renie's words and the dread there was in them. Halifax was all right. It had served its purpose. She remembered the sense of freedom that had come to her when Grant agreed to let her study stenography and get a war-time job. Escape from the Shore and from the emptiness of everything. In Halifax you could be alone with the aloneness. You didn't have to act, to pretend interest in Red Cross meetings, the Young People's League, the endless little running talk at the post office and Katen's. There were times on the Shore with Alan gone when even Grant and Renie had seemed to her intolerable.

Halifax was pot-hooks at the business school, streets crowded with uniforms, convoys gathering in Bedford Basin, ships moving in single file past George's Island. Halifax was a job, hard work, and doing what you could, and freedom to be alone. Freedom to admit what you felt, uncomplicated by the implications of the old and the familiar.

Sitting silent in the car, Margaret felt the moving images come up, the moving moments, flowing to the balanced, the precarious present . . .

Lights. Lights, long ago, hanging at the lower edge of the sky, and a red table-cloth . . . A small cold hand in a warm one . . . words . . . *You'd forget your head if it wasn't sewed on . . . It must remind you, Mrs. Gordon* . . . Richard McKee's shop loft, and an apprehensive curiosity . . . *Where'd you get that idea? . . . Vangie's crazy . . . you can't listen . . . not to believe it . . .*

School. Sunday school. Words, voices, in the dark. Walking home from church . . . *No. Not even his half-sister. Didn't y'know?* Whispers. *If her father hadn't . . . he'd a been a bastard . . .*

That was how you knew. Anger, first. Anger and hurt. And then the shock. To find that the realization, when fully understood, didn't strike you with a sense of loss or loneliness at all. Filled you instead with a throbbing excitement.

The loneliness—that came later, when the excitement was a thing you hid, while the old relationship of sister and brother subtly changed. Changed for you alone, in the nerves and blood and mind; while on the surface, for Grant, for Renie, for Alan, for the Channel Shore, it must appear unaltered . . .

A subtle singing joy . . . until the war had taken him. Then, Halifax; escape from the reminders of his presence and of the accepted thing, the sense of family.

But there was nothing now in Halifax. Everything was here. It was something, at least, to *be* here. Not enough, but something. She would have to be careful not to upset the balance; she would have to be friendly and interested; she would have to check the impulse that stirred behind the reserve and the control.

Alan laughed to himself. Mag was having one of her quiet spells, but there didn't seem to be any unasked questions in it, and a mile or two of silence in a car didn't amount to much. Something about her had reminded him of that long strange time of war, the something you couldn't explain. Her letters. In spite of all that you could do, there had been islanded hours in that careful separate existence when in spite of any precaution you found yourself across the border into the old-time world, felt the pull of loved people, saw the Channel marching under spring wind, heard the road's gravel spurt under turning wheels, smelled the wet smell of sawdust. Something familiar in the slant of a field in Normandy could do it, or the sight of a farm-house with late sun on the windows. And the way you felt when mail overtook you, up the line. The feel of the thin blue crumpled airmail forms, the look of known handwriting.

Grant's, brief and matter-of-fact; little of the communication in his voice came through when Grant wrote a letter. Renie's, easy and unlaboured, more like bits of spoken conversation. Margaret's . . . Margaret's were hardest to shut out when you were done with them, hardest not to take out and read again. More herself than the self you remembered. In her written words the old faint reserve was luminous, transparent. A veil that emphasized, that did not hide . . .

He slid the car to a stop beside Katen's gas pump. There were few loiterers this evening. Only Dan Graham, with a stranger, sitting on the store's low doorstep, and Stan Currie's two boys, Hugh and Duncan, hunkered on the grass beside them, sucking cokes through straws. It was still light with the clear luminous light of late June, but as they got out of the car the store windows and its open door bloomed white. Old Felix had turned on the electricity.

Dan and the stranger got up as Alan and Margaret walked toward them across gravel. Dan said, "I'd like y't'meet Bill. Cousin of mine. This is Grant's boy and girl, Bill."

Alan took Bill Graham's hand. He said, "Pop's talked about you," and glanced up as a screen door slammed in the Katen house on the knoll. He waited attentively, the shadow of a grin on his face, while Lon Katen's son came round the corner of the building.

"Buff! Well, I'm damned. What is it? A secret weapon?"

In Buff the sardonic Katen face was softened by an habitual cast of friendly curiosity and faint puzzled surprise. His carrot-red hair would not lie down under brushing. He had treated it with oil. He was wearing blue serge with a green shirt, a figured red-and-yellow tie, and ox-blood shoes.

Dan said, "Y'can't blame Buff. There was a war on."

Margaret said, "Leave Buff alone. He's teaching me to square-dance."

Alan laughed. "*Blame* him? I'm not blaming him. I wish I had the nerve . . ."

Buff said. "This is my goin'-t'-Mass suit. Shut up!"

A wave of good humour broke down whatever slight edge of constraint the presence of a stranger might have caused. Alan turned the car, stopped as if reminded of something, and turned back to Dan.

"Listen . . . Why don't you come on down? The dance, I mean. You and Mr. . . . You and Bill."

289

He waited expectantly, looking from one to the other.

Dan shook his head, looked at Bill in a kind of hesitant questioning. "I never learnt . . . We're not dressed for it." He glanced down at his unpressed pants. Neither he nor Bill had bothered to shave or put on a tie.

Buff Katen looked up. As a regular attendant at down-shore dances, this was his business. He came out of his silence. "That don't matter. Any kind of rig's good enough."

Alan said, "Oh, come on, Dan. Do Bess good to miss you. We'll be back early. If we can drag Buff away. He's got work to do tomorrow, same as you and me."

Abruptly, Dan turned to young Hugh Currie. "Step in on the way home, will you, Hugh? Tell them we're down-shore for a while, with Alan."

Alan laughed, thinking of Dan. From 'forty-one on Dan had never got home. Georgetown . . . Dakar . . . Capetown . . . the Red Sea . . . Bristol Channel . . . and never a long enough turn-around at Halifax to get to The Head. Now he wouldn't go down-shore without letting them know where he was.

They climbed into the car, Alan and Bill in front.

"How long's it been?" Alan asked.

"Twenty-seven years," Bill said.

Alan shook his head. "That's quite a stretch."

Something in Bill Graham's presence set him considering the small continual migrations, the people who left the Shore and those who came back. Rarely to stay, merely to be lazy for a month or so every second summer or fifth or tenth, or once in a quarter-century. Andrew Graham had been born here and was old Frank's brother, and so this one, this Bill, was a Currie Header — one who had stayed away longer than most.

They should have Stan Currie along, he thought, to give a kind of tourist lecture. Stan didn't talk much, but sometimes the words came in a tide, and Stan was a kind of expert on the Shore. As far as you could be an expert, with mostly guesswork and hearsay to go by. A queer one, Stan. He claimed that along the Shore you found all the differences that make up nationality: different ways of doing things; differences of up-bringing and religion; differences between Findlay's Bridge with its touch of village superiority, and Currie Head; differences between Currie Head, full of Protestant Scots and English, and the Irish Catholics of Katen's Rocks and Mars Lake. Differences between all these and Forester's Pond, which kept that name though the last Forester was gone, and where, although the Catholic Church was there, you began to get a sprinkling again of the up-shore kind of people. The Channel Shore — a little nation.

All getting along in a kind of working tolerance but divided by difference . . . Differences that came down to people in the end. Differences between people. Grant didn't like the Katens. He let them work for him, he'd work with them, but there was something about them he didn't like.

The road passed the outlet of the hauling-road in to the mill, curved around a hardwood hill, crossed a wooden bridge, straightened out until they could see the Channel curling to flat sand a quarter-mile away, beyond low pasture; and on the left a blue-flag swamp and scrub spruce with the glint of fresh water behind it.

Alan nodded sideways to Bill.

"Mars Lake. The Pond's next."

"Yes," Bill said. "I remember."

3

THE heart of Forester's Pond is almost a village. You come out of a gulch in the land to higher ground and find buildings clustered round the approaches of an iron bridge. Under the bridge a creek slips down to lose itself in the brackish water of the pond, a narrow salt lagoon lying inside the Channel beach. The tides find their way in and out at the pond's eastern end and at high water reach up the creek bed to low meadows beyond the road.

Just west of the bridge John M. Clancy has his grocery and feed store, south of the road. Across the bridge the land rises abruptly. The Catholic church stands at the top of this short hill, on the pond side, with the square mansard-roofed glebe house behind it. Across the road is the parish hall, a hip-roofed building with dormer windows.

A pick-up truck and two or three automobiles were already parked haphazard by this building when Alan pulled up there. Inside an orchestra was playing. A printed bill tacked to the grey shingles by the door identified it as the Copeland Rhythm Boys. Piano, drums, banjo and sax. The Rhythm Boys were playing "Blue Skies". Through the open door and lighted windows Alan saw several couples, dancing earnestly.

Dan said, "No fiddles? I thought they had fiddles."

There would be fiddles all right, Buff said. Not much square-dancing any more; but they always had a few sets, in between the other stuff. John M. and John B. would be there with the fiddles. That was the best of it. That was dancing.

Three or four young men were hanging round the hall door, waiting for full darkness and a bigger crowd before going in.

To the middle-aged woman at a small table inside the door Alan paid two dollars and fifty cents. He said, "Dough, Mrs. Clancy." She looked up and smiled. Another car pulled up. Three men and a couple of girls got out, laughed, and took their time coming to the door. "Lot of visitors tonight," Mrs. Clancy said.

"Copeland people, these are . . . Nice to see you, Alan." And to Dan, "Good evening, Mr. Graham."

Alan nodded, feeling a rush of friendliness for John B.'s wife. She was being matter-of-fact, not making any particular point of the oddity of Currie Head people at a Forester's Pond dance. He drew Margaret and Bill forward and introduced them and edged Margaret out on the floor, grinning at Buff Katen.

"You can have her in a minute, Buff. This is all I'm good for. You're the square-dance man."

They were playing a moderately slow tune he didn't recognize. He slipped easily into the rhythm. He wasn't much of a dancer, he thought. He got around on a sense of timing, but had to keep his mind on it. He noted with surprise that Margaret was highly competent, and grinned down at her, a little mocking. She was lost in some rapt imagining; her eyes came back to regard him with gravity. She wrinkled her nose in a small swift wordless answer.

Benches at the edge of the dance floor were well filled by the time the number ended. The two Clancys, old John M. and his son John B. tuned up their fiddles. Old Jay Katen stood up to call off the figures for the first square-dance. After the couples had swung into the stamping rhythm, Alan saw that Buff had persuaded Margaret into it . . .

Buff, he guessed, was a little gone on Margaret. But it was under control. It would do Buff good to see a lot of someone like Margaret, and do Margaret good to learn that the qualities Buff had, the loyalty and soundness, could develop in someone who had grown up in rough surroundings, a rough home. Buff had lied about his age to enlist with Alan. He would hear no word of criticism about Buff Katen.

He heard Margaret's laugh. The girl continually surprised him. Along with her reserve, her quiet, she had a streak of casual hilarity, rarely roused. For a moment he stood bemused. Something in this scene, this atmosphere, had brought to his mind the image of another girl, an image made of pure fancy, a name scrawled in a song book, a fading snapshot, an old photograph, words heard by chance . . .

Why should he think now of Hazel McKee?

Alan glanced at his watch and saw that it was nearly midnight. There hadn't been much sense of time passing; only of laughter, and a hall full of people, the shuffle of fox-trot and waltz, an occasional change in tempo as the floor was cleared for a square-dance.

Amused, he had seen Margaret dancing with Bill Graham, even inveigling Dan into a few simple steps on one occasion. He had left her pretty much to the others while he danced with the daughters of down-shore people he had known before the war or run into since Grant had moved the mill to Mars Lake. He had one more duty dance to go, with John B.'s daughter Sadie, a plump dark girl just home from the States.

It was while he danced with Sadie Clancy, while they were caught momentarily between couples near the side-lines, that he heard a snatch of conversation. Someone asking about himself or about Margaret.

". . . girl . . . with Alan Marshall?"

". . . sister . . ."

There were words lost under music and the slow shuffle of the dance, and a word faintly echoed.

". . . sister . . ."

Something in the way the word was said, a questioning. Was it merely a passing interest, or a mocking remembering knowledge? A recollection across the years of a story deep in time?

He shook the thought off, told himself he was developing a crazy imagination, and led Sadie Clancy back to the benches as the music died in a spatter of clapped hands.

A square-dance, next. He sat it out and as Buff and Margaret came back toward the side-lines, got up to meet them. He said, "Well, one or two more—and I guess we ought to go."

Buff nodded. "All right." The orchestra was getting into the slow beat of one Alan liked, an old one, one Grant used to hum . . . "Sleepy-time Gal."

He turned toward Margaret just as a young man in checked green tweed—Alan recognized him as having come in one of the Copeland cars—put out a hand to claim her for the dance. This was a little unusual; there had been no introduction that Alan had seen, nor any informal contact that might have brought Margaret and the Copeland man together. And there was a kind of rough conventionality about this dance. Not that Margaret would mind . . .

But Margaret shook the hand off, lightly, without looking. An unconscious, meaningless act; she was listening intently to "Sleepy-time Gal", looking at something far away, her hand in Alan's arm. They slipped into the step together.

Over her shoulder he saw the other's face turn dark. Someone near him laughed. "You nearly had her that time, Del."

When the dance ended Alan led Margaret back to where Buff waited near the door with Dan and Bill Graham.

Behind them someone said conversationally, "Y'know, it's too God damn bad we're not good enough for these up-shore people."

Alan turned slowly, puzzled.

Someone said, "Shut up, Del."

The voice went on, pointed and provocative. The man in green tweed was looking straight in front of him, talking to no one, or to a figure set up in imagination, so that all could hear.

"Too bad their — women can't get loose from their own damned pretty-boys . . ."

He used a word to qualify "women"— a word as common in the army as a drawn breath but completely shocking on the Channel Shore.

Alan felt the shock of it and the curious rancour in the voice. Someone said quickly, "Rum . . . rum talkin'. Pay no attention to . . ."

Black anger shook him. He turned.

He had time for nothing. Buff had moved in front of him. He sensed rather than saw the blow. The man in green tweed folded, crashed backward through the doorway, fell on back and elbow across the porch railing and sprawled on the gravel beyond.

Buff Katen, his face white and contorted, walked out to stand on the porch, looking down at him.

As he drove home, past black stretches of woods and fields vague in after-midnight dark, Alan was concerned with one thing. Quickly, in the morning, he would have to tell Grant. Before someone else did.

He had been careful to play it down for Buff's benefit, touching Buff's shoulder lightly with a hand. In the midst of the little crowd that formed round the hall's entrance while the Copeland man named Del was being helped to a car, he had given Buff a tempered grin with a touch of admiration in it. But it wasn't anything you could dismiss with a grin. This was the sort of thing the women of The Head had meant, years ago, when they said with loathing in their voices, "a down-shore dance."

This was an incident blatant and public. Even in the old days when there had been nothing unusual in fights at dance halls, they had occurred among the hangers-on, the youths with caps slanted over one ear, who came to a dance to watch, brag and drink. They had taken place in a moment's passion, sometimes simulated, half-theatrical, behind a building or on the road. To-night Forester's Pond had seen a piece of old-fashioned rowdyism on the dance floor, and brought about by others than its own. Buff in a sense belonged. Perhaps the green tweed man did also. Alan and Margaret Marshall did not.

This was what Grant had meant when he said it wasn't much of a place for Margaret, and added, "You either."

Alan heard Dan Graham in the back seat say a reassuring word to Buff. Buff had come out of a glum silence to mumble a word of self-blame and regret. "Oh, hell," Dan said. "What else could y' do? . . . Talk? Sure, they'll talk about anything. But what else could y' do?"

What else could you do? Behind the disturbance in Alan's mind was a realization and a small regret that had nothing to do with his distaste at the prospect of telling Grant. He had never been able to fathom the drives that set the thud of fist against face between neighbours. The necessary team-anger of men fighting for life against a common enemy he could understand; that was some-thing he had shared. But hatred of an individual . . . Now, he realized with surprise, he understood it. He had been slow. What Buff had done was his own impulse, in action. He had been slow . . .

What else could you do? Well, Grant would say—no, he might not say it, except with silence. You could stay out of false positions, situations in which you either had to be less than a man or act with scandalous violence. Except . . . you couldn't stay out, always, and be yourself.

He stopped the car at Katen's. Buff got out and stood hesitantly, his hand on the door. Margaret said evenly, friendly and casual, "Good night, Buff. Stop worrying."

It came to Alan that in his own personal worry, he hadn't given much thought to Margaret.

She was curiously tranquil. There had been a brief moment at the door of the hall when she felt her body trembling and afraid, and had found herself, surprisingly, clutching Bill Graham's hand. She had a confused memory of voices, placating and under-standing; of other voices, competent and profane, in the back-ground.

Now the trembling and the fear were gone. She began to feel small responsibilities. In some way she would have to make clear to Buff that he was not to blame. She would do that, later; Buff was the kind of boy who would need assurances. Margaret knew Buff Katen. Knew that what he felt for her was merely a focusing of what he felt for all her family. For Alan, particularly. People who were different from his own. This was not disloyalty in Buff. It was a recognition of different qualities in others and a willingness, almost an anxiety, to know about these; to be familiar with different people and other ways of behaviour. A kind of receptive admiring curiosity. The best thing she could do for Buff was simply continue being natural.

She wondered, worrying a little, what Alan was thinking, how she could ease the anxiety she knew must plague his mind. At that moment he withdrew his right hand from the wheel and let it rest on her forearm. She slipped her hand back until his fingers rested on the back of it, turned it and held him by the hand. Not with the grasp of one either seeking or giving comfort, but with a light almost indifferent pressure, a contact conveying no special understanding, a reminder that between them the obvious symbols of understanding were unnecessary.

The wide garage doors Grant had cut in the side of the old house were propped back. Alan ran the car in and braked and let his dimmed lights flood the wall for a moment. The family had moved into the new house in the fall of 'twenty-seven, when he was seven years old and Margaret was a baby. In that time of young boyhood it had seemed odd, for a while, to find the old house being used as a workshop and storage-place, but after a little the strangeness went out of it. Like everything else, it was something you got used to. Now without warning his heart was brushed by a tenuous recognition; not the boyhood excitement of moving across the yard into a new house with electric lights and running water, a house fresh with paintwork and the smell of lumber, but something farther back. With his hand on the light-push he waited, letting it come.

The pattern of the wall-paper: this had been Grant's and Renie's room. Once when he had wakened screaming in a night-mare of whirling wheels, of a car that travelled like lightning yet did not move, Grant had taken him into the big bed between himself and Renie. Across the lapse of more than twenty years he remembered it: the sweat-dampened flannel sleeping-suit, the hard comfort of Grant's arms around his shoulders and under his thighs; the soft warmth of Renie: the drowsiness, and after the relief of oblivion, sunlight streaking the pattern on the wall.

When Grant got his first truck, Alan himself had bracketed up the shelf that ran across the wall to hold oil-cans and car tools. He had patched inner tubes here, changed spark-plugs, filled the

297

cups with grease. He had used this room a thousands times; but not till now had he noticed the smeared remains of wall-paper with anything but the most careless corner of his mind.

An endless formal pattern of white-sailed ships on dark-blue waves, against a lighter sky. The car's head-lamps in some manner created an illusion of freshness, restored in the reality of memory the repeated pattern, and with it the feel of the mattress, the half-fearful relief of nightmare gone, and the morning sun.

A moment of truth that flowed imperceptibly into other moments: Richard McKee's attic and the sense of old things useless and rusted, yet having in them the colour of vanished life; the road to Katen's, and the vision of a girl in the Stove-pipe Room at Gordons'; a door-step, just beyond this dark partition with the papered wall, and Bert Lisle's question on a cold day white with snow, and the feel of Margaret's smallness in his arms.

Alan switched out the light and got out of the car and followed Margaret to the garage door. The night was dark; a young moon had long since set. Halting in the door, Alan laughed, a low laugh with something like a question in it, a wondering, almost a deprecation of this mood that unwilled had possessed him briefly with insight and sadness and a sense of flowing time.

He felt Margaret turn toward him, questioning his laugh, and said affectionately and faintly self-mocking: "Wall-paper."

It was this about Alan that you didn't understand. With Grant you expected the laughing shrewdness and the casual word that revealed the subtle understanding. With Grant you had to be careful, you had to watch yourself; underneath, the two of you were too much alike.

But with Alan . . . It had always been the open frankness she loved, the unsubtle companionship, the hard masculine strength. And yet, at long intervals, he would let fall a word, his face would reflect a glance, that showed you the existence in this active flesh of something you hadn't known was there. It was when this happened that the tranquillity of love was displaced by a wild wanting excitement; and the control, the recognition of the need to wait, by passion and the need to know.

Alan said, "Wall-paper," and laughed again; and in her answering laugh he heard a note that was strange to him, a recklessness, a casting-away of reticence, a careless delight.

She turned to stand against him and her hands went up to close behind his neck. He drew her close, hard, for a moment beyond thought or reason, the flesh informed only with instinct and feeling and emotion; tenderness and a kind of wondering passion, an emotion he could not name.

4

GRANT shook his head when Renie glanced at him at church time. After she and Alan and Margaret had driven off he took the county map from the wall-closet and spread it on the dining-room table. The action was almost aimless, like that of a man opening a book read long ago and known by heart.

The map's crossed lines, its small figures indicating elevation, its streams and roads and headlands, were merely reminders. On linen-backed paper the county did not change. But in his mind the county lived as earth and rock, still lake and running water, barrens and clearings and standing timber, never quite the same from year to year. Behind the fringe of front lots the best of the woods had been stripped for miles. Hardly any place within easy hauling distance where you could set up a mill and feed the saw with wood from all around it. The best you could do was find a convenient spot like the one at Mars Lake and haul from far away and from scattered patches nearer by.

Something out of time past came to him: the tide of timber. Lowries and McNaughtons and the Frenchmans now were like isolated pools in hollows of the sand when the tide drew back. Why had he thought of that? And of the picture that went with it: himself and Alan, working on the hauling-road in Katen's woods, the winter he'd got out of pulpwood and into lumber? He felt the brief ache of passing pain, brushed the picture from his mind as one turns quickly a page black with hurtful words, avoiding the detail of memory.

Frowning, he rolled the map and tucked it back in the closet, and walked out through kitchen and porch to the yard. Warm, sunny and windless. His eyes travelled down the slope of the lower field, the slanted pasture with the beech trees in the middle of it, the spruce along the spine of land that bordered the beach. The Channel was like glass this morning.

Restless, he wondered whether the whole Graham crowd had gone to church. Probably not. Frank liked to loaf on Sunday mornings.

And if Bill were home . . . He hadn't yet seen Bill. With Alan gone down-shore, he hadn't gone across to Grahams' Friday night, and last night, troubled by other things, he had lacked the heart for it.

He climbed the bars in the line fence and crossed Frank's pasture now.

Bill came down off the front steps to meet him, sticking out a hand and mixing a grin with a cautioning nod toward Frank, stretched on the veranda lounge.

With Stell out of the way at church, unable to nag him about making himself conspicuous in full view of the road, Frank had made himself comfortable. His eyes were closed. Something between a sigh and a snore escaped him. His thin frame was clothed in baggy blue serge pants, an unbuttoned vest and a clean white tieless shirt. The serge had faded until it was more brown than blue. Frank's shoes lay by the end of the lounge. One hand hung over the side, thin and brown, big-knuckled and mapped with blue veins. The throat was sinewy and hollowed; the bristling grey moustache had a mock ferocity, and about the nose there was something almost hawk-like. The silky grey disordered hair on Frank's head reminded Grant of the first soft hair on a blond infant. Seventy-six years old. Colin in the west, Edith married and away, Stell and Dan and Bess and little Frank at church. Frank Graham's body, slouched on the lounge, stirring within itself in the slight rhythm of breathing, expressed an ultimate placidity.

Grant and Bill stood for a moment, their eyes on Frank in a communion of amusement, and walked quietly round the house to the back steps, looking east and south to the Channel.

There wasn't much to say, Grant found. It was pleasant to see Bill Graham again, to ask him what he'd been doing for twenty-seven years, to consider that here was flesh and blood, grown to man size that had known the Shore briefly as a boy. There was none of the constraint he sometimes felt still at making a new acquaintance, the search for something of common interest to talk about. The Shore and their common knowledge of its people were enough to make reunion easy for two who had known liking long ago.

There was not, of course, any resumption of that peculiar intimacy. It was too soon for this, and they were not now a man and boy. Time had levelled up the years and made improbable that kind of sensitive confidence. But the knowledge that it had existed was there, leaving no sense of embarrassment. Lightening, rather, the mere conversational attitudes of re-acquaintance without breaking down the reticence men owe each other.

In the midst of talk, casual talk about surface things, Grant's mind ran idly on how, years ago, he had talked to Bill about The Place. He had no wish to recall those days, nor did Bill mention them. And that, perhaps, was a little odd. Bill knew the story, or part of it. It was woven into the intimacy of their first acquaintance. Was it delicacy that kept this conversation in the nearer past and the present?

Grant watched the smoke haze behind the Islands. There were forest fires there, on the Atlantic side. He flexed his hands. Two things . . . He had an impulse to cut through the avoidance of a subject, to talk to Bill about Alan. Not of the heart of the story, but of the surface, of Alan Marshall, his son. He had an eagerness to talk to Bill Graham, who remembered, casually as one might talk to a friend who did not know . . . The other thing was a commoner craving. He wanted to know whatever there was to know about the fight at Forester's Pond.

He admitted this, the core of his disquiet, to the front of his mind. It was accompanied by a wave of anger. This was partly directed at himself—in his morbid curiosity he was like a lover jealous of a woman's past.

He said, "I hear you were down to The Pond with the kids."

Bill said, "Yes, I was there." He laughed.

Grant said, "Alan was kind of close-mouthed when he told me about it. What . . . What *did* happen, anyway?"

Bill grunted. "Oh, a fellow started swearing. He'd wanted a dance with Margaret and she hadn't noticed him. Simply didn't notice . . . Buff slugged him. He cracked a rib or two on the porch when he fell, I guess. That was all."

Grant said meditatively, "It's about enough. I don't like that kind of thing. I don't like the Katens. They're violent people . . . But you can't give orders."

He thought: you can't give orders. If your son's ways are reckless and loose and on the edge of violence, a laughing arrogance . . . Of what use are orders when . . . He let the bitter thought take form: of what use are orders when the qualities that make behaviour are born into you, brewed in the blood?

Bill said doubtfully, "I don't know exactly why, but I kind of like Buff Katen. When you come down to it, the way he . . . Well, how else could you handle a thing like that? I thought what Buff did was, oh, a kind of natural courtesy."

Grant was lost in thought, a bitter private abstraction. He said nothing. Frank Graham came round the house then, in his sock feet, walking gingerly, yawning and running fingers through his

301

hair. He said, "Hello, Grant. *Thought* I heard somebody talking. You skipped church with the rest of the heathen.'

Grant straightened and rose, all the meditation in his manner gone. He said, "If *you* can risk purgatory I guess *I* can . . . I'm taking Bill home to dinner with me, Frank."

He did not want to let go of this companionship. The thought of his own house filled him with a kind of loneliness.

It was a relief to Renie, home from church, to find Bill Graham on the veranda with Grant.

Throughout the drive to church and back Margaret had been silent and Alan carefully talkative. Renie felt like telling him to hush, he was betraying the uneasiness he tried to hide.

Something was wrong. The scattered wisps of feeling she had sensed these last few days were being spun into tightening threads. She did not know what it was. Something you couldn't say was due entirely to Friday night's brawl at Forester's Pond. Though that, perhaps, was a surface symbol . . .

Something off-key in the radiations. The personal radiations. Wrong, whatever the combination—herself, Grant, Alan, Margaret.

It was a relief to shake hands with Bill Graham, to sit on the veranda a few minutes while Margaret laid the table in the dining-room, to find the combinations altered by another person, a new face and voice breaking up the habitual patterns. And it excited her interest to meet again, as a man, someone she had forgotten, and identify him with a youngster who now came back into conscious memory, a kid who had studied under her in grade eight for a single month in that far time before she had known Grant.

Once, after they had gone inside to eat roast lamb in the breeze-cooled dining-room, she looked up and noticed that when Bill turned to speak to her the look he gave her was a studying look. She did not mind. There was something easeful in his presence.

The men were talking with casual interest about the back lots. In his boyhood summer at The Head, Bill said, he had got back no farther than Graham's Lake and the Black Brook. In those days there hadn't been a clearing that you could see, in the hills beyond that.

Grant said no, that was before the pulpwood-cutting, even. But now there was hardly any timber worth going after; not within easy hauling distance.

Some of the cut-over land, though, Alan said, would soon be up to pulpwood size again. Spruce would grow anywhere in this country; faster here than anywhere else in the world . . .

302

Only Margaret was silent. Only to Margaret was the presence of an outsider an annoyance. She knew that having Bill at table was making Grant pleasanter and more talkative than he had been for days. It seemed also to have taken the tightness out of Alan's manner. But as far as she herself was concerned, the presence of a visitor did nothing but force her own presence at dinner. If only the family had been home she could have pleaded a headache, a sick stomach, anything, and shut herself in her room.

Through the shield of her private knowledge she heard the meaningless words go on. Then suddenly they were close and clear. Alan was talking to Bill, off-hand, without emphasis.

"Oh, there's still a lot of timber in the province. I'd like to see what it looks like over west. Like to have a look at the way they do things over there . . . Maybe I'll take a shot at it, some time soon."

He meant it, then. She had not doubted that. But it created in her an aching hopelessness to hear him preparing the way.

It went against the grain to be less than forthright, Alan found. He had been forthright with Margaret this morning while they sauntered around the yard before church, talking casually, as far as anyone who watched could tell. He had been forthright while they stood by the barn with their eyes on the swallows, home from Peru, house-keeping in the shadow of the eaves. He had tried to get across to Margaret the sense of impasse that was woven into the exultance of discovered love. The thing he had felt, seen, heard in his blood as he lay in bed in the room next to hers, thinking of her and of himself and of Grant.

Lying in bed there he had tried to face it. There were moments in those first hours of revelation when all he could feel was the wonder and the exultance; the memory of Margaret's small body in his arms. The memory that went back to that other day, when he had held her briefly, crying, in the shop and had gone out to the barn to say what was in his heart to Grant.

Grant and Margaret. Always, for him, it had been Grant and Margaret.

The thing he felt for Grant was clear, defined long ago in flesh and nerves and brain, rarely thought of, like a religious faith, a part of him.

And now, Margaret.

Last night, yesterday, the night before . . . As the moving scenes came up he had found that in all of them was Margaret's image, a small repeated figure in the pattern of time.

It was Grant, years ago, his realization of what Grant was, that had fixed his purpose to stay on the Channel Shore. And it was Margaret, the protective tenderness he felt for Margaret, that had broken his final fear, sent him to the barn that winter day to assault with feeling the barriers of reason.

Margaret and Grant.

But this, now, was something he couldn't take to Grant.

He had moments of recurring panic, hearing in his mind the story they would tell on the Channel Shore. Of Grant Marshall's boy who was not his son but Anse Gordon's bastard. Hazel McKee . . . He had a wry twinge of regret that he had never known her. Mrs. Josie long ago had softened that story. He knew enough now, he had heard enough allusions to Anse Gordon, enough reminiscent words of Hazel, to guess how it had been. Hazel . . . a wilful girl who had grasped at what she wanted. He felt he would have liked her. Her problem, in another version, survived in himself.

The story of Margaret Marshall's brother who was not her brother.

This was something that must come before they could talk or think of love.

For the second time in his life he faced a thing he was afraid to do. And afraid not to do.

There was no such simple answer as to blurt from the heart to Grant his own desire. He had tried to make this clear to her. All he could do was go away. Take refuge in time. He had told her this. She had said nothing.

He had been forthright with Margaret. But he could not see himself going to Grant, without preamble or explanation, and saying: "Pop, I'm going away."

Now at the dinner table he had voiced his intention casually, as a possibility, an inclination. Voiced it· to an outsider while Grant was there.

". . . the way they do things over there. Maybe I'll take a shot at it, some time soon . . .

Grant hardly seemed to notice.

He mentioned his own years in the Queens County woods, and along the Mersey and St. Mary's rivers as a timber cruiser, and went on to question Bill Graham about the advertising business.

On the veranda when the meal was over, he filled his pipe. He found himself biting the stem of it, holding hard against a rising impatience. When Bill Graham got up to leave he schooled himself to walk slowly across the yard with Bill to the bars in Frank Graham's fence, and slowly back. He dropped to the steps, waiting a moment. Through the open window he could hear the homely clatter of the table being cleared. He spoke with a casual abruptness over his shoulder.

"You really want to try it . . . somewhere else, away from here?"

Alan said, "Well, I've been thinking about it, Pop. Just for a while, y'know. I've been thinking it over . . ."

He did not add to that. He could have said lightly, "I think you were right; I ought to take some time off . . ." But it was not time for play he needed, or planned to take. And he could not carry his acting quite so far as to pretend that it was.

Grant nodded. "All right."

In each of them was an emptiness like long hunger.

THE mill was idle. They had sawed the last of the logs in the yard on Monday and Grant had turned to trucking from a lot back of Millersville they had logged the previous winter. Alan spent the early forenoon of Tuesday hauling slabwood to Josie Gordon's back yard and began cutting it up, in the hour before dinner-time, with a buck-saw. Today he preferred to work by hand, putting his back and shoulders into it.

The chore was his by choice. The Katens and the Wilmots, with some local help loading, were enough to handle the trucks and his instinct told him he was better off alone. He had always liked working at Mrs. Josie's anyway. On coming back from overseas he had picked up again where he had left off years before, relieving Grant of the small necessary jobs around her place.

Shortly after noon Josie opened her back door, stood looking out for a moment, and walked across the yard to him. To Grant, to anyone else, she would have called out dinner in the normal way from the door. What she felt for Alan, the private half-realized relationship, was singular and different. There existed between herself and Grant a strong adult respect and a silent understanding rooted in the sharing of a bitter time. What she felt for Alan was blended of tenderness and a kind of continuing excitement. So now, she walked across the matted chips and grass toward him.

She said, "Come on in, Alan. It's ready."

He leaned the buck-saw against the saw-horse and straightened. "All right, Mrs. Josie. So am I."

He laughed, teasing, and slipped an arm lightly around her as they walked to the house.

"What've we got? Herring? I smell 'em frying."

To Josie the small easy ways of obvious affection were always a sense of wonder. They were something she could not herself achieve. In some people she saw them with an inward doubt. But in Alan . . . In Alan they were right; she could feel the light warmth of them, and in her heart, in little things like the easing of her tongue's restraint, she could respond.

He had come down the road alone, the afternoon of his return from overseas, taken her in his arms with a quiet laugh and kissed her between the eyes. In the months since then she had watched with interest the new and casual manner, the way in which he found laughter in the smallest things, even small annoyances; his off-hand attitude with people of any age, even in Grant's presence.

It was not new, really. As she watched him slosh water over hands and face at the kitchen sink, running wet fingers through the dark straight hair, Josie's mind repeated the realization that this was Alan's natural person, the kind of person that had been hinted in his early boyhood. Through the later years of a secret knowledge, of the caution bred from it, of thinking toward a single purpose with a boy's devotion, the lightness and charm had been covered up, held back, the voice and gesture harnessed in a boy's deference to the presence of his father.

Now it was free. Freed by war and the sense of full manhood and the fact, perhaps, that whatever of sonship and fatherhood had to be proved was proved.

Josie dished up the fried herring and boiled potatoes. Alan pulled his chair in to the oilcloth-covered table.

"Grandfather?"

Josie nodded. "Richard sent them down by Adam this morning. Makes it handy, mail making both trips the same day now, what with cars and the road fixed."

Alan put his fork into the crisped herring skin and uncovered the white flesh beneath.

"Good eating. If they weren't so darned bony . . . Every time I eat 'em, though . . ."

He hesitated and let it go. Every time he ate fried herring he thought of a day during the summer when he was fourteen. A day when he'd been out to the nets with Richard. A cold wet morning, for July. Rain sloshed down in torrents on the hut's roof after the catch was cleaned. Rather than go out into it and home to dinner Richard had made up a fire in the round iron stove, a relic of a time when men at The Head would spend all day at the beach and sometimes sleep there. They fried herring in an ancient pan from which Richard scoured the rust with sand and an old newspaper, using butter from their morning snack for frying-grease. That was the one July he had fished with Richard. The next summer he had spent in the woods and the bunk-house back of Katen's.

In the thought now of that day under the drumming roof, a thousand thoughts were drawn up and mingled. He could feel again the wonder of that summer, the exultation, the purpose, the pride and the fear.

Exultation at remaining on the Shore; the purpose—to be as Grant wanted him; the pride in a story learned from Josie Gordon's lips; the fear that in some way—his own resentment at a veiled sneer, thoughtless words, betraying knowledge—the fear that he, or anyone, should break the long illusion.

Josie's dry voice cracked the crust of his abstraction.

"Must be something kind of weighty."

He said, grinning, "Well, now, maybe it is. Would you like to take a guess?"

Josie said, "Oh, a girl, most likely . . . It's natural. They all come to it."

Alan pushed back his plate, laughed, and went to the stove for the teapot. It was curious, the effect Mrs. Josie had on him. Here in her house, with her, he was careful to keep up an easiness, an exchange of banter, as though the ache in his heart did not exist. The curious thing was that this was no effort to him; he enjoyed it. At home was Margaret, and in the woods back of Millersville, Grant. The problem of his love for both was all his life. And yet here, with this drying apple of a woman, he could be himself. Something in the sense of time. Josie, flesh and blood, seventy-five years old; the mind alert, the heart courageous and, for all its reticence, affectionate.

He poured tea into Josie's cup and said, while he filled his own, "They grow them pretty down the Shore, Mrs. Josie."

She buttered bread and raised the cup to her lips.

"Heard you were down. News travels, around here."

Alan said, "Always did . . . Did you go to dances, Mrs. Josie?"

"Yes . . . oh, yes." She considered. "They were big affairs in my time."

Her mind drifted . . . Images of Stewart Gordon, stiff in broadcloth . . . buggies tied at the hitching-rail back of the hall . . . satin puffed out at the shoulders . . . Lord Macdonald's Reel and The Irish Washerwoman . . .

She said, meditatively, "Grant wouldn't like that kind of thing much," and had a moment of misgiving. Never except on that one evening years ago had she talked to Alan about anything but surface matters. The self-revelation they had shared that day was woven into the background on which the pattern of their everyday relationship was traced, giving it strength and substance, but it was not a part of that pattern. Now, she thought, she had gone a little deeper. She had intruded into the wordless world of feeling.

308

Alan seemed not to notice. He tipped back his chair and fished out a cigarette. He said with a short rueful chuckle, "He didn't," and continued: "Well, I guess it won't happen again. Not this summer, anyway. I'm thinking of going down around the Mersey . . ."

"Are you?" Josie seemed mildly surprised. "You know, I've never in my life been farther away than Sydney. I s'pose the more you see the more you want to. I'd 'a thought . . . Wasn't France, those countries . . .?"

". . . enough, like?" Alan finished the sentence for her. "Too much, sometimes." He let the chair's front legs drop to the floor, got up, and began to clear off the table. "Let's get these dishes washed."

At the sink by the east window he stood at Josie's left, wiping while she washed, stacking dishes on the sink-board and looking out over the summer fields and woods.

There it was again, the thing you couldn't quite explain. The separate existence. He didn't know how it had been with the rest of the Canadian army; except for the members of his own family he had never tried to look into the minds of others. But for himself . . .

Suddenly he laughed, and in answer to the question he could feel in Josie, said: "You know, over there, this was one place I tried not to think about. The Shore. I didn't know about the rest of them. You heard it said, about guys living on—oh—hope. The thought of home and so on. That was never any good to me. Had to put it out of my mind. Think of what I was doing. What I had to do next. That way, you got through today and first thing you knew it was tomorrow . . ."

That was it. From the day he had put on khaki he had belonged to a world different from the world of home. Whether by home you meant the Channel Shore or Copeland county or Nova Scotia or the whole idea of the future. He had kept no more than an open mind about the chance of getting home. If you didn't count on anything except what you felt and smelt and tasted, if you didn't look past tomorrow, you could stand the army and the war. Not otherwise. Let the long future take care of itself.

Looking back on it with a kind of curiosity he saw that in a way he had written the future off. Once you did that you could go ahead with what you were doing. Your mind would be keyed up, alert, but still in working order. But it was not the kind of standpoint from which you could afford to look forward or back. That was why, morning and evening at the mill, he had wanted to laugh. He had come back, unbelievably, to a reality that was both old and new. The world he had left in nineteen-forty. But now every word and act and gesture that went into it, every log and piece of machinery, every man and woman and farm animal, every moment, had a sharper outline than before.

"First thing . . . it's tomorrow," Josie said. "Killing time. I know what you mean."

Alan felt a quirk of amusement at the old-fashioned saying which expressed so tersely the truth. There was something else in her voice. For a moment he felt sharply what the old ones must have felt, and the young, the ones who were left behind: Grant, Renie, Margaret, Josie. What they had felt, onward from the dawn of a June day over the French coast . . .

And Josie—did she mean too that other waiting, years ago, the waiting that never ended, that was edged with shame, and that now must certainly be finished? His mind played with a strange thought: had Josie dreamed, ever, in these last years, of Anse Gordon alive? Returning, perhaps, to stand in her kitchen door? And in that dream, what feeling would be uppermost? Love? Hope? Fear?

He shook the fancy away and his own moment of insight with it, and gestured at the window. He said, lightly, dismissing it: "All gravy. You couldn't count on it, so you tried not to think about it. It was all gravy, when you got back."

It came to him as he lit another cigarette, sitting by the window with the dishes done, that instead of making up a story for Josie to explain his going away, he had been talking as he had talked to no one before, not even Margaret, about his war-time battle with dreams of home. Talk like that added up to a question: *Why don't you stay here, then?* But if Josie noticed the inconsistency she said nothing. She had got out her knitting and relaxed in the rocker by the south windows, across the room from him.

He felt lazy and could see no reason why he shouldn't indulge the feeling. The day was reasonably cool and an air of wind through the screen flowed over his face. He sat, feeling little, letting his body relax and his mind note that when he wanted to he could go out and get to work with the buck-saw and then go home.

After a little he heard the throb of a motor below the turn and saw Grant drive by, headed homeward, and noted that he must have left the crew in charge of Dan.

From where he sat he could see the eastern reaches of the Channel. Beyond it a long low white cloud bank shawled the Islands. He could make out a tiny whitish glint, perhaps a sail, at the entrance to the hidden dog-leg between Middle Island and the one they called The Barrens. Time passed over him; he was not conscious of Adam Falt's mail-car as it rounded the turn and slowed at Josie's gate.

A man got out of it and came through the gate. A tall man, oddly graceful despite the slouch in all his movements. Through the screen of his puzzlement Alan saw that he was decently dressed, as if for Sunday, white shirt and blue tie, carrying the jacket of his grey flannel suit over one arm, swinging a canvas sea-bag with the other.

Turning, oddly, to approach the back door . . . Alan heard a small sound, a gasp or a cry, a whimpered exclamation or a prayer. He turned to Josie. She had risen from the rocker and was supporting herself with both hands clenched on the table's edge, her face turned toward him. As he stepped quickly across the floor to put an arm around her, he realized the truth.

The door opened. The stranger who stood there was dark-haired, though grey was showing in the lock that fell across the left temple. The sardonic lines from the flare of the nose to the mouth corners were deep, the skin weathered. But he was one of those thin ageless men who do not thicken. A man whom time had dealt with lightly.

He said, "Well, anybody glad to see me?"

Josie said, "Anse—"

Alan drove the pick-up out of the yard by the barn gate, turned west on the road and stopped. He took his time, walking slowly back to close the gate. He climbed into the cab again with deliberation. As he let in the clutch and the truck began to move, he questioned life with a wry annoyance and a dull resentment. Once was enough. Once, for days . . . months . . . years . . . he had lived an acted part until the acting had become life itself. Until, across time, he was barely conscious of the caution, the study and the restraint he had put into it. He had gloried in it, once. Gloried in establishing for all time a kind of exalted sonship. And *had* established it. Established it in the sight of the Shore, until it was not second nature but nature itself—a thing you didn't have to think of, the very soil of yourself in which you could grow to your own bent, the seed unquestioned . . . almost unquestioned . . .

The audience of the Shore had been lulled, convinced . . . But now, a newcomer in that audience—the one, the only one, whose presence there could prove the long performance false. And now again the old cautions, the care, the foresight, the study and the restraint . . . He must put them on again. Wear them with a deft-

311

ness, a subtlety he had never reached before. A newcomer, and—
the audience would know it—a malevolent partner in the play.

Now, again . . .

Almost at this minute it must begin. Had already begun, back
there in Josie's kitchen.

This was the beginning. Why must it fall to *him* to be the bearer
of this news?

He had stayed in Josie's house long enough to steady himself
and to see that whatever emotion swept her, Josie was in command
of it; and to show, himself, the shy excited curiosity that would
be expected in anyone who had ever heard the name of Anse
Gordon. The images of that half-hour were clear, but with the clearness of a remembered dream, the sense of experience evoked by a
story heard or read. The look on Mrs. Josie's face: what had it
mirrored, of the three emotions he had imagined there? Love?
Hope? Fear? The slouching arrogance of Anse, with the touch of
mock humility as he and Josie clutched forearms in a barren reticent
embrace . . . The familiarity of face and figure, and Josie, flustered
but working her way to calmness. Josie saying, hurriedly. "You remember . . . No, what am I thinking . . . Alan Marshall, Grant's
boy . . . Grant's . . ."

Now the images began to lose their unreality, to become life,
the beginning of a whole new story— a story that must fit itself by
word and recollection, by glance and touch, into the pattern of the
Channel Shore. What ravelling-out, what industrious re-weaving
. . . Even now, in the house behind him, Josie perhaps would be
telling Anse.

With a tingle of shock he realized what it was that had given
him that sense of the familiar. An inch or two in height, and thirty
pounds in weight, and twenty years and he himself . . .

His mind went back and found a boy who had walked this road
preoccupied on a winter evening a dozen years ago and come into the
yard to the sound of Grant's axe in the shop. He could hear the
words, the off-hand tone he had found in which to say them . . .

Grant, now, was washing the car in front of the house. Alan
slid the pick-up into the garage and walked over to join him. Grant
paused, rubbing the hood, and glanced up quizzically as if sensing
something unusual. Now, Alan thought, now . . .

He said quickly, brisk with news, "This is a hot one, Pop . . .
Mrs. Josie's got a visitor. The son. The prodigal son. He's home."

Grant frowned, puzzled. His face cleared, stilled, grew lively with
interest and unbelief.

"What d'you mean? Not—it can't be *Anse?*"

Alan nodded. "Yes, sir. Anse. It's him, all right."

Grant said, "What . . . Where's he been, then? What's he been doing? Where'd he come from?"

"Don't know," Alan said. "I didn't hang around long. Didn't like to. Josie's—well, she's kind of upset. Oh, she's all right, but . . ."

Grant began meditatively to rub a mudguard. "I can imagine . . . Well, I'm damned."

No false notes, Alan thought. Whatever had gone on in Grant's mind his manner had been merely that of a man hearing unbelievable news. And knowing . . . Alan thought, he knows I know; he *must* . . . But he couldn't be sure. Never once by word or glance or silence had either of them come close to breaching the long illusion. He went into the house, looking for Renie and Margaret. Whatever else, he must tell the tale, wherever it was told, as news and nothing more. In his own house he must rehearse the words and moods and manner, of a life that once again demanded the playing of a part.

A part in which with every telling word and act he sealed a wall between himself and Margaret.

Renie was opening the refrigerator door, bending to get at the vegetables for supper. He could hear Margaret's light step on the stairs, coming down. She came into the kitchen through the dining-room, and for a wild moment his heart went out before him, oblivious of the story and the Shore . . .

The moment passed.

He said, "Well, I've got some news."

As he told them, he realized that already he had accepted the renewed responsibility.

He had seen this without thinking of it. He could not go away. No one should say that Alan Marshall had gone from the Channel Shore because Anse Gordon had returned to it. He could not go away.

Anse sat on the open front porch in a red plush rocker he had hauled out from the unused parlour. He lay back, in shirt-sleeves, feet braced against the rail, and waited. He was oddly amused, excitement as close to him as it ever came. Amused at being back, at sitting here watching the Islands, the Channel and the road. Amused at the conflict in Josie, the swift flicker of doubtful love and wild hope that crossed at times the unreadable resolution in her face. Excited, for all his native indifference, at the position he was in. They wouldn't talk about much these next few days at The Head and The Rocks, except Anse Gordon. Up the road at Leeds and Findlay's Bridge, down the road at Forester's Pond and Millersville, people would be stopping Adam Falt . . .

Idly Anse considered this. Considered Adam, and those others with business up and down the Shore. The news. Anse Gordon? The middle-aged and the old would stare, remembering. The young would ask and learn.

Anse grinned. There was another excitement. A thing that had briefly astonished him. His mind turned with satisfaction on the brief exchange of words with Josie after Alan Marshall had left the kitchen three or four hours before.

"Anse," Josie said, as if trying the word over. And then, directly, "Anse. What brings you home?"

He had walked across the kitchen, settled in Stewart's chair, and waited until she returned to her rocker before he answered.

"Well, Old Lady—," the voice was light, amused, affectionate. "I had a mind to look things over. See how you were getting on. And all my old friends." There was mockery in that. A chiding note in what he said next. "You get to the questions fast. A fellow'd think you might be glad to see him, *without* too much asking. For a while, anyway."

Her still, alert look had puzzled him a little.

"Glad? . . . Yes, I s'pose so. There's something I've got to say. It's a little late for coming home. The mortal sin . . . It's been righted. Long ago. By others. Now . . . It's a little late."

There seemed to be nothing in her voice but meditation and the need to say something she had to say. He said, "What d'you mean by that?"

She told him then.

"The spring after you left, Hazel McKee died. Sick, and she never got over the birth. The child. The boy you just saw. She was Grant Marshall's wife."

Anse said nothing, letting his mind absorb it, and quelled the impulse that rose in him. The impulse to demand, "Child? *What* child?"

No use protesting that. In that moment he had a prevision of the summer days to come, and the prospect was pleasant. Let them think he'd known. He didn't give a damn for them. Let them think the final villainy, the villainy of accident and impulse, had been the villainy of a calculated will.

Now, thinking about it on the porch, he gave a hard throaty chuckle. It made no difference. He'd have gone anyway, if he had known. Faster, likely.

This was what he was thinking now, after an hour's sleep sprawled on the parlour lounge, and a silent supper. Let them think what they liked and like it. In a little while they'd be dropping in. Tonight. Tomorrow. Making errands past Gordon's place, so they could call and have a look at him.

All of them. If he had come back a year or two or three after his departure his name would have been an obscenity then to the prim stiff-mannered women of The Head. But twenty-seven years . . . Time had woven its mellow intervention . . . There wasn't one of them, not one, who wouldn't stop when they met him on the road, recognizing, for all their holiness, the flare of something special. And all of them a little envious.

Envious, and cautious. He laughed inside, thinking of Adam Falt. Adam, after his first shock of surprise, had said, "You'll find things changed." Anse had answered, "Yes. They do change." He had asked no questions, and Adam had gone silent on him, volunteering nothing. He had learned from Josie of Stewart's death and Anna's, still without asking. But what she had told him first was the thing about Hazel McKee . . .

Josie came through the front door onto the porch, dragging a kitchen chair. Anse did not stir from his position. From up the road now, echoing against the hills, the rattle of an ancient car . . . It grew louder; the car passed the screen of poplars Grant had planted twenty years ago, pulled over and stopped opposite the gate.

Josie said, "The Wilmots. Word must've got around."

Talk at the supper table was concerned with Anse Gordon, where he could have spent the years, why he had come back, whether he would stay, what he would do . . .

Outwardly Grant could recognize only a normal interest in himself or Renie or Alan or Margaret. Even while he made the effort of restraint, smoothly casual, his mind was touched by a wisp of thought: how odd it was that people could hold a surface naturalness, masking with unconcern the conflict of nerves and heart. The children, of course, would be oblivious. Or would they? At the edge of Grant's mind a speculative cloud gathered and hung. Did they know? Did Alan know? He turned away from it, swept it from his thinking, as he had done a thousand times in years past. He had settled that, pushed it away from him, on a winter day twelve years ago . . .

Oblivious. But Renie knew. And Renie's face was serene. Behind her effortless manner worry must now be nursing at the

315

breast of memory. Worry for him, about him. But nothing showed in the smooth tanned planes of her face. And farther back, behind the worry, that essential light-heartedness. A gift. A thing she had given him, a thing he had shared but never, really, achieved in his own being.

After supper he stood for a minute or two by the veranda steps while the others relaxed.

He said, "I think I'll go down and see. I don't know . . . Wonder whether she'll want us to—whether we ought to bother about the work . . . Anse was never much of a hand . . . Probably leave her to do her own milking. But it'll look odd to keep tending to her."

Alan said, "It *is* kind of awkward. I like hanging around Josie's —"

Grant said, "We'll see," and added evenly, "But you won't be around long anyway."

Going down the road, he reflected that it was just as well Alan had made up his mind to go.. Something about that planned departure still puzzled and disappointed him; it was all a part of the oddity of this grown-up Alan. A doubt touched him . . . Perhaps now if the boy knew, he'd be held at The Head by curiosity, by something stronger than whatever whim had turned his mind to the thought of departure . . . Suddenly, Grant wanted him out of it, away.

He had hoped that his first meeting with Anse could be un-observed by others, except perhaps by Josie. Clem Wilmot's battered car, standing on the shoulder of the road, halted him. He had an impulse to go into Frank Graham's and postpone the moment. But there were people on Gordons' porch; they had already seen him. Better, anyway, to get it over with. He went on and turned in at Josie's gate.

Hat Wilmot, Clem, Lee, and Lee's crippled youngster Skimp were sitting with Josie and Anse on the porch. He felt talk stop as he turned in, and walked up the path in a waiting silence.

Anse got up from his chair grinning, saying nothing. As Grant took the outstretched hand he realized that Anse was entirely self-possessed, as if he were back from an honourable absence at honourable labour, in the States or the West.

He said, "Well, Anse; nice to see you back," and sat down casually on the top step. With his shoulders against a porch post, he greeted the Wilmots and Josie with an inclusive glance.

This was the pattern. This had to be the pattern. A natural friendliness, casual, tempered perhaps with a little reserve. The reserve anyone would feel and perhaps show, for someone returning to the Shore—someone whose behaviour had been questionable, long ago. So long ago that you treated it indulgently, since there was nothing in it that touched yourself.

He was glad now that there *had* been people here to see. Hat Wilmot would spread the story of this meeting. He thought with a faintly bitter amusement that Hat must be disappointed. Seeing him walk up the path, she must have hoped for drama. She would spread the story, and the tone and burden of it would be the flatness, the ordinary quality of his meeting with Anse.

He glanced across the porch at Hat, remembering the night he had gone to Katen's and found her there. He could recall the mischief in Anna's eyes, and his own self-examination later as he drove Hat home in Uncle James's buggy, with Dan and Bill Graham standing in the fly . . . And another time when he had thought of that drive, a night in the kitchen, and Renie . . . memories of memories . . .

Hat and Clem were making conversation with Anse, and Grant put in an occasional comment. It appeared that Anse had spent most of the years at sea, but he was not communicative. Unwilling, apparently, to dispel a veil of mystery that must add to his stature in the Shore's eyes. He mentioned tersely, off-hand, a torpedoing in the North Sea, rescue by an E-boat, years in a prison camp.

Grant thought: He hasn't changed. Until this moment he hadn't considered the possibility of Anse changing. Hadn't considered the possibility that Anse might have come back—well, "repentant" was as close as Grant could come to it. Anxious to avoid hurting others, ready to live and be liked. Well, on the evidence of manner and attitude, it was clear that no one need waste any thought on that.

Grant joined in the conversation now and then, but he found himself almost absent-minded. Something to do with the Wilmots was there to be tracked down in his thinking, and finally he knew what it was. He had been looking at Skimp, sitting with Lee on the porch swing. Skimp had been born crooked, with one leg slightly shorter and one shoulder higher than the other. The child was withdrawn and sensitive.

The thing about the Wilmots was that they were Currie Head people, Channel Shore people. Hat might talk, and there might be danger in her talk, in the fact that it would sharpen an old story in the minds of people who preferred to forget. But the story was going to be sharpened anyway by Anse Gordon's presence. And no one on the Shore would blurt out a statement or a question that would pull it into the open, imperil publicly Grant

Marshall's relationship with his son. The pattern was being formed here, now, on Josie Gordon's porch.

Anse was speaking to him.

"Would you have any pine around the mill, Grant?"

Grant said, "Might be a stick or two. Why?"

Anse said, "Thought maybe I'd drag the old man's boat out of the barn and fix her up. She'll need some patching."

Clem Wilmot asked bluntly, "What for?"

Anse didn't answer him at once, letting the moment draw out until it amounted almost to a calculated insult. He said finally, meditatively, "What for? Oh, fun."

After a little while the Wilmots left, piled into the wreck of a car and went on down the road to Katen's. Hat would have some purchase to make to explain the journey, Grant thought. But the real purpose of coming down the road had been to call at Gordons'.

Josie had risen. Anse said, lazily, "Going in, are you, Old Lady?" She did not answer him. There was something in the manner of her going that suggested to Grant she was leaving it to him. Leaving it to him to say what must be in his heart to say to Anse, or to say nothing.

He said, merely, "We've been doing a few odd chores for your mother. Milking and so on. I s'pose . . ."

Anse said, drawling, "That'll be all right. I'll look after it . . ."

In a little while Grant said, "Well . . ." and got up to go.

6

In the early dusk of Saturday evening Alan came downstairs and walked out on the veranda, irritated by a general restlessness, a wish to be doing something; a feeling heightened by the fact that it would not harden into a desire for any certain action. No one had suggested any of the activities that usually marked the week-end, a drive to The Harbour for the movie, or anywhere along the country roads, simply for the drive . . .

The morning after Anse Gordon's return Alan had taken over the truck Lon Katen was driving on the haul from Millersville. There was no advantage any longer in being alone. The feeling between himself and Margaret was a remote crying ache at the back of his heart, displaced by a danger more immediate. The immediate thing was Anse; and to meet this he must be close to people. Must hear their spoken curiosity and share their speculation and live the part of Grant Marshall's son as he had always lived it.

This now he had done for four days. They had cleaned out the Millersville yard, but would not go back to sawing for a while. It was getting close to haying time.

Margaret, in white blouse and dark slacks, was curled up in the swing, reading in the fading light. She looked up to exchange glances, her own non-committal and almost impersonal.

He said, "Mag, what d'you say we go up and see if there's any mail?"

Indifferently, Margaret swung her feet to the floor. "All right; d'you want to walk it?"

He said, "Sure. Let's walk it."

They walked in silence. Past Stan Currie's and Alec Neill's and up the slight rise toward Fred Marshall's. Thought moved in Alan's mind. In that house, behind those windows reflecting dying daylight, Uncle James had lain for years helpless. Alan had seen the old man seldom in the years just before the war. He remembered the painful immobility of the figure in bed, the eyes

319

in the caved-in bearded face, oddly alive for Margaret but with only a hint of impersonal recognition for himself.

The thought of it clutched his heart for a moment with a strange sadness. James Marshall, forty, thirty, twenty years ago a power on the Shore . . . dwindling to the shape of an old man in bed, dwindling to a memory. And a memory of what? Even to him, Alan, Uncle James as a personality was no longer clear, except for the remembered hardness. He had passed from the Channel Shore story, except as the things he had felt, said, done, remained in the flesh of others.

The figure who was clear to Alan was Jackie, small and full of hell. Nesting apples on the way to school, and in a grass-lined recess under the roots of a maple in Clem Wilmot's pasture. Jackie, sweating green lumber out to the piles in the mill yard at Katen's lot. Jackie, in 'forty-one, coming down to Surrey on leave with the crown and stripes of a flight sergeant on his sleeve. Jackie, who had died in fire over Duisberg.

Yet, behind that sharp sorrowful anger when he thought of Jackie, there was now this vague touch of sadness about old James. Or rather, about all those men and women whose power on the Shore had faded with age, dwindling into death. He found himself remembering a boy in Richard McKee's shop loft, and useless things in a sea-chest that had for a moment, then, caught his heart with an aching pain.

He shook his head and said to Margaret, "It's queer when you think of it, isn't it? Frank Graham still says 'James Marshall's place'. Even Dad says 'Uncle James's.' But we say 'Fred's' . . ."

Margaret said, "Yes. I know."

Alan thought: she does know. For a moment he felt a strange relationship. Something he had caught a glimpse of years ago and saw now for a moment clear and sharp. Something of which the old big-boy-and-small-girl thing had been a surface manifestation. Something far back in the mind and memory, the instinct and the spirit. Farther back, he thought with a start, than this emotional and bodily magnetism that had found them out. Even if by some miracle this present craving should die, even though minds and hearts should come to the clash of anger, this inner thing was there: not a bond—it was more like a shared freedom.

In this small moment of recognition he was lifted briefly into a climate of emotional peace. The recognition, or the memory of it, would remain. He was realist enough to know that the peace itself would come rarely.

Behind the personal tenderness and the realized love, something almost impersonal, almost remote . . . As he came to know this, and was left with the sense of always having known it, the immediate and the physical for the moment were almost unimportant.

And yet, there was a strange new splendour in the tenderness and the love.

Margaret, surely, had known it long ago.

Anse Gordon tipped his chair against the wall of Richard McKee's kitchen. Annoyance was beginning to edge his inner amusement. It had been exciting to walk into McKees' for the mail and to sense the hard hostility in Eva, the cold "Well," with which she had greeted him after twenty-seven years. She had not offered him her hand.

First meetings with people whose lives had been changed by his departure were a series of small excitements. It was highly amusing to consider that not one of them dared to translate hostility into words or actions. In the interest of their own peace, and for Grant Marshall's sake, they had to preserve the fiction. Hide their hate under friendliness, and stand it.

He was beginning to be annoyed. Eva, simply by silence, was coming close to getting round that necessity. There had been an awkward moment, after she had handed him Josie's copy of the Halifax paper and turned back to her chair by the table, leaving him standing. Richard's indifferent, "Sit down, Anse," had ended that. But he was getting nowhere with Eva. He had said, "You've been well, have you, Mrs. McKee?" and she had answered, "Well enough." He had said, "Everybody looks pretty good," and been answered by silence.

He should have been foresighted enough, Anse thought, to visit the McKees when others were there. With no one else in the room, only Richard lounging in a rocker in the shadows, she could get away with it.

He was about ready to let his chair fall forward and rise and leave when he noticed Eva's hands halt in their aimless sorting of letters. Her eyes were on the window. A moment later Margaret Marshall came through the back door into the kitchen, followed by Alan.

There was a moment of suspended time. Eva's hands were motionless on the table top. Richard's face, turned toward the door, was still.

Alan said, "Hello. Hello, Mr. Gordon," and to Richard and Eva, softly, "Hi. No mail, I s'pose?"

Eva said, "Yes. A letter or two, I think, here somewhere. And the paper . . . I'll light a light."

Alan said, "Oh, don't bother doing that, not for us," and found a chair. He stuffed the letters she handed him in a shirt pocket and glanced around. "Oh—Mr. Gordon, Margaret. My sister."

Margaret crossed the room to sit by Richard. She said, "We've met. I saw Mr. Gordon the other day at Mrs. Josie's."

Anse grinned. For a moment the strain had been too sharp for comfort, but the kids had eased it. Covertly he examined Alan, lounging there with ankle over knee, searching his pockets for cigarettes. Anse got up and handed his package over.

Something about the boy made people easy. Something of his own nonchalance, but with a difference. Easiness, Anse knew, was not the feeling his own presence usually called forth.

He glanced at Margaret with appreciation. Momentarily, when he had first seen her at Josie's, he had felt a slight regret that women no longer lighted in his blood the slow fires of earlier years. The cunning with which he had pursued the satisfaction of those early fires was still there. He had considered for a moment the havoc he could raise if by some wild achievement of personality he could fox Margaret Marshall into an infatuation with himself. In Anse's mind this was not beyond the possible. He could see in her a quality . . . and he doubted the likelihood of its response to the young men he had seen and heard of at Currie Head. A wanderer, with a touch of the world about him, and a reputation . . . It might be done . . . it might be done. But with physical desire no longer a driving force in him, the victory though spectacular would be chiefly of the mind. And it would be brief. Anse had no illusions that he, in this generation, could carry on an affair with anyone on the Channel Shore in secret. Or that the forced friendliness that fed his private amusement would continue in the face of that.

For reasons which he did not directly examine he wanted to avoid a break, to go on enjoying his power over Currie Head, the Marshalls, the McKees, the Grahams, all these people who were . . . respectable. A drawn-out, continuing victory, climaxed perhaps—

He glanced again at Alan, and was struck by a curious feeling. Alan Marshall was someone over whom he felt no urge for power. In whom he wished to see, toward himself—what? Certainly not dislike. Certainly not the revulsion the pursuit of Margaret would arouse. What, then? He felt a curiosity, personal and strong: did the boy know?

That question Anse put away in the back of his mind, with the unformed dreams gestating there.

Alan said, "How're you getting on with the boat, Mr. Gordon?"

The boat, already, was beginning to excite interest at The Head. Lon Katen had attached himself to Anse. The two of them had hauled the hull out of the barn and propped her up in the yard. They would sit for hours on Josie's steps, doing nothing, as if they took some peculiar secret satisfaction in conspicuous laziness while the industry of the Shore went on around them.

Anse said, "All right. She's sound. We've not done much to her, though. Not yet. Have to get her down to the water to soak before I start patching her up. Reminds me—you got a rig could handle that?"

Alan considered. "We've got a cat would get down Currie's road as far as the inlet, I guess. It's grown up, across the neck. We could rig some kind of trailer, maybe. Need a couple of men to steady her. Shouldn't be much trouble."

Anse said, "Well, I can get Lon and Buff. What d'you say? Tomorrow night?"

Alan shook his head. "Better make it Monday. After supper."

Anse chuckled. "That's right. Tomorrow's Sunday . . . I forgot." He said, "Richard, *you've* cut sails?"

Richard stirred. He could feel no active hatred for Anse Gordon. Only a kind of indifferent distaste. He said, "I cut the odd suit of sails years ago. Cut the sails your father had on her, matter-of-fact."

Anse said, "I thought you did. I've got to get a new mains'l, anyway. Rain got in on the old one. I'm sending to Halifax for the cloth."

He let the moment lie, briefly, and then got up to go. "Good night, Richard . . . kids. Good night, Mrs. McKee."

Eva had risen to get down the lamp and light it. He gave her a slight friendly smile, only faintly touched with mockery, as he turned to go.

Alan and Margaret stayed until it was fully dark outside. They talked a little, of small things, but not much. To them Richard's house, even though there might be periods of a week or a fortnight when they never went there, was like home. A place where a person could be silent if he wanted to, where it wasn't necessary to make conversation.

323

Richard hadn't put in electricity when the hydro line went through. Except for new oilcloth on the table, a change in the calendars on the walls and in the patterns of hooked mats, this kitchen was as it had been for forty years. Sitting in the dimmed edge of the lamp's light, Alan felt something of this continuity. He was content to sit, almost empty of thought and almost happy.

It was only after he and Margaret were back on the gravel of the road in overcast darkness that his mind began to turn again on the hard facts of the present, and people, and circumstance. The way in which he found himself acting naturally in Anse's company was curious to him. He was keyed up to it, he supposed. At any rate, it was only in his imagination of situations, not the situations themselves, that he faltered. And it was only when he had time to think, time to consider, that despair and anger clutched him.

Walking beside him, in the shallow opposite rut beaten by the wheels of trucks, Margaret stumbled slightly. He started to put out a hand and let it drop back. The shock of this instinctive caution struck him like a blow. He was suddenly angry, angry at no one. A fact that had faintly surprised him at Richard's came to the surface of his mind.

He said, "I didn't know you'd run into Anse. Before tonight, I mean."

Margaret said, "Oh, yes. I kind of like him."

He said, non-committally, "You do, eh?"

It came to him that he resented this off-hand reference of Margaret's to Anse. And yet—he had no cause for resentment. The reticence between them that made of Anse in Margaret's speech a person of merely ordinary importance, a person you could like or dislike casually, was of his own making. No reason why she should have gone out of her way to mention meeting Anse Gordon . . . In every act and attitude he himself had made it clear that this was the way it must be.

He told himself again that this was true. He could talk with Margaret—particularly when they were alone together—only within the circle of surface things. Any delving into the things that mattered, with its risk of an affectionate word, a touch of the hand, was what they had to avoid.

In the dark Margaret half-prayed for accidental contact. She made a bargain with herself: *If he veers from the rut, I'll veer to meet him; if his arm brushes me, I'll take his hand . . .*

324

But in a moment she shook her head, discarding stratagems and bargains, biting hard on the bullet of pride.

She now looked straightly at the fact that to her Anse Gordon's return meant not tragedy but something like hope, a strange half-sorrowful but exciting hope.

Anse. Anse could break the shell of the past and re-set the pattern of the present. And yet—there was something dark, some shadow of meanness in the thought of it. She felt the slow anger of frustration surging through her flesh in waves.

They found Renie sitting by the radio in The Room, listening to slow string music, turned low. Grant lay on the chesterfield, asleep. Alan grinned at Renie and stretched himself quietly in a chair. Margaret climbed the stairway to her room without a word.

7

BLACK spruce and juniper grew on the neck of low land connecting Currie's lower pasture with the Head. The neck was patched here and there with swamp, but midway along the eastern edge of the inlet, between the old road and the water, the turf was firm in a flat half-acre, faintly ridged and treeless.

In the early sixties Rob Currie had built the *Star of Egypt* here, a thirty-ton coaster, the only decked vessel ever launched at Currie Head. After that, during the years of the mackerel, men from The Head and The Rocks had brought their pine planks and steam-boxes, their juniper timbers and black spruce knees, their saws and planes and adzes to Rob's Yard. Nine or ten sloops and two-masters had been built there, but nothing now in nearly thirty years. Nothing since Stewart Gordon and Frank Graham had wasted a spring in building the boat and that now lay moored at the edge of the tide-channel in the inlet.

Anse in hip-length rubber boots sat for a little on the centre-board casing, watching salt water bead and seep along the joins and trickle down the inner surface of the old pine planking. He was humming to himself . . . "The Irish Washerwoman". At length he eased overside and splashed ashore.

He said, "Well, we'll let her soak. Won't hurt if she settles in the eel-grass. We'll haul her out after a while, see where she needs patches. Cau'rk and paint. She's stood up all right."

Grant asked, curiously, "What're you going to do with her, Anse?"

It was still an effort to be civil to Anse Gordon. But civility was necessary. He had welcomed this chance, in fact, to help haul the boat to Rob's Yard and to stand around with Anse and Lon Katen and Alan for a moment or two after they had got her into the water.

Anse felt for tobacco and began to roll a cigarette.

"Use her for? Don't know as I'll use her for much of anything."

He eyed the boat and said, lazily, "Lot of work on her yet. I think the spars are all right. We'll have to bring 'em down in a day or two, Lon. Shrouds are okay, too. Likely need some new rope." He added, confidently, "We'll have her under sail in a couple of weeks . . . She'll be in shape for the Holiday."

Time and purpose were of no importance. It was enough for now to serve notice that this was so, to let Grant Marshall and Currie Head know, casually and without making a point of it, that no limit was set in days or weeks to his sojourn on the Channel Shore. Let them speculate and wonder.

He let his glance drift deliberately over Grant Marshall, and on to the clam-beds, the spine of Curries' beach, the sky and the Islands. Grant Marshall. He had never been able to see, long ago, what Anna found attractive . . . And now . . . his eyes came back, to Alan.

Alan was looping up the lengths of chain with which they had stayed the hull to the trailer-rig for the trip down Currie's road. He was whistling, unaware that the tune he had picked up was "The Irish Washerwoman" and apparently oblivious of any undercurrent. He glanced up, broke off, and said lightly, "Well, Pop, we may as well get going."

Pop. Grant felt along his nerves the flush of an inexpressible annoyance. *Pop.* A word to go with the mock affection of Anse Gordon's drawled *Old Lady.* Sometimes, a thing as small as that would break the lashings of a man's control . . .

He walked over to the cat and shook his head. "I'll take her up. You go over to Frank's. Find out when they want to start the hay."

He climbed aboard the cat, swung the rig round the yard and drove it lurching up the rutted road. A picture was in his mind: two faces, one middle-aged, the other young. One carved in downward lines of selfish and self-sufficient arrogance. The other mobile and laughing, but moulded in curves and lines you couldn't mistake . . .

He wanted to be alone, to deal alone with the wave of anger and fear that washed through him, seeing for the first time together Anse Gordon and his son.

The cat lurched and crawled up Curries' road. There were times when Grant enjoyed every minute of a common task. Like this one, or driving one of the trucks, or tramping the woods with an eye on the timber. Sensing a known hill, coming into view round a turn; sensing the look and feel of this country with which his life was linked, and which without thinking of it in just that way, he loved.

Tonight, hunched morosely on the metal seat, he sensed nothing. A possibility came to him, sudden and shocking. Would Anse

327

talk to Alan? Tell him . . . ? If he didn't already know! He didn't think so. Anse was too shrewd for that. For the present, anyway. It would be someone else. Again, that searing *if*: unless he knows already.

Why hadn't Alan left? Gone as he'd planned to go? Was it curiosity? Or something deeper, more secret, a fascination, rooted in the truth known?

Why was the boy still here?

All Grant knew was that he would not ask.

Alan walked up through the pastures with Anse and Lon toward Frank Graham's house. He had not missed the narrowed glance, the carefully veiled calculation, with which Anse had looked just once at Grant. The thought came to him that this had been the one unacted thing, the one flash of life uncoloured by an instinctive pretence, in this private drama they were playing.

Private? Well, hardly. Not with Anse Gordon's face in the same county with his own . . . For a moment he had a sense of the hidden thought and guarded conversation of the Shore. The concern for Grant Marshall and the members of his family. The curiosity, the interest. Perhaps, even, in one or two, the malicious hope . . .

None of it open. None of it said in the hearing of Grant or Renie or Margaret or himself, or Josie Gordon. Or Anse, except perhaps for hints that would be broadly voiced by Lon Katen and his kind.

And yet now that he was into it, it was not as hard as he had thought. The curious thing was that he could feel nothing for Anse Gordon except a rather definite interest, the interest you'd feel for anyone . . . The ancient villainy was there, and yet for him it was not personal. Not yet. It was almost as if this middle-aged Anse Gordon were another person, separate from that younger one. And this one he knew: the son of a neighbour woman, home after years away. It made the acting easier.

They had been walking silently. As they approached the path up to Grahams', Anse said, "Ever do much sailing, Alan?"

Alan said, "Only in Grandfather's flat. He put a centre-board in, one summer. We had a sprits'l and jib. On the inlet mostly. Sometimes outside." He paused and went on. "I'd like to take a crack at it when you get her rigged."

Anse drawled, "Oh, you bet . . ." and walked on with Lon as Alan turned to climb the lower fields to Frank Graham's.

8

AFTER the first day of mowing at Graham's, Alan climbed the upper field in the early evening, turned east along the Black Brook and stripped naked on the patch of sand where the brook enters Graham's Lake. He carried clean shorts and a pullover with him and came back down the slope from the woods with his blood singing.

Curious how the mind could adjust itself: once you faced a thing and acknowledged that you had to deal with it, it became part of a new personal pattern. The mind's mechanism shifted to take care of it, leaving, still, margins for the range of feelings: pleasure, indifference, incidental annoyance. He recalled having heard somewhere the story of a prisoner who had taken delight in the companionship of a bug in his cell.

Well, he was not *quite* a prisoner. He went into the house, slipped into a linen jacket and headed down the road. Katen's was one of his hang-outs. He was sticking to the pattern of the usual.

He felt that he was, almost, over the hump. He had met Anse Gordon in Josie's kitchen and betrayed no trace of feeling. He had talked to Anse Gordon in the presence of Richard and Eva McKee. He had watched Anse Gordon and Grant Marshall together and been casual with them as they were casual. He had listened to the talk among the hauling crew, guarded and elaborately impersonal, and had joined, himself, in the speculation about Anse Gordon's return.

He had seen and heard nothing that was outwardly disturbing. Nothing beyond the sense of something unspoken, something in the silences. Nothing but the slanted grin on Lon Katen's face and the calculation in Anse's single glance at Grant.

It was working out. The other things of course would have to wait. A tide of quiet desperation filled his mind at the thought of Margaret. One thing at a time. But soon, perhaps, he could start on that. Could safely go away, away from the emotional

329

climate . . . Away among strangers where time perhaps could tell him what the answer was.

There were times when he wished he was the kind of man who could find relief in a woman, any woman. But he knew from experience without considering it as any personal mark of merit, that he was not. There had been girls in England . . . Always afterward he had been bothered by a feeling that there should be a fondness, a closeness, but that this was something they did not value or really understand, and for that reason, something of which they were unworthy. A circle of dissatisfaction . . . He envied, almost, those to whom this did not matter. But if there had been little for him in women then, what hope of finding an answer in them now? Perhaps, among strangers, there was something else.

In the meantime he must simply be himself.

Tonight he wanted to see Buff Katen, feel the friendliness of Buff. The thought came to him as he walked past the Gordon place that he had no idea whether Lon's son knew the truth. And that, personally, when it came to people like Buff he did not care who knew and who did not . . .

From Josie's kitchen windows Anse watched Alan pass. He waited a little, drumming his fingers on the sill, then rose and sauntered out through the back door.

Whenever he saw Alan Marshall or thought of him—and the thought of him now was seldom far from Anse's mind—he could feel a renewal of the tingling thing that had begun that evening— five nights ago—at Richard McKee's. And a renewal of the question: does he know?

He halted now on the back steps, caught by an impulse to go back, to face Josie withdrawn in the dusk, and demand an answer. He rejected this inclination. To ask would be to show interest, to hint at a purpose not yet clearly defined in his own mind. It would be, also, a confession of ignorance. He had thought of asking Lon, but an inner distaste had kept him from doing so. An unwillingness to admit there was information he did not have. A distaste for the slanted grin, the grin saying (if the tongue did not): *He don't know if his own son knows him!*

Lon Katen was a good-enough hanger-on, a henchman whose lack of scruples matched his own. But . . . he thought, as he walked to the gate and turned down the road, he did not want Lon, or anyone, assuming equality or edging into the confidence of his secret mind.

So far, except for Eva McKee's curtness and Lon's occasional insinuation to himself alone (and there had been a certain pleasure in these), he had seen no hint of any break in the interested but matter-of-fact manner in which he was accepted at The Head. The sense of personal power in this remained, the feeling that at any time he could break the shell of protection these people had closed around Grant Marshall and his family.

But the continuing calm was getting a little irksome. He found himself having to hold back the sneer and control the tongue . . . It wasn't time yet.

His fantastic ambition was becoming clearer.

He had thought at first in terms only of the spectacular. The broken shell. The truth made public. The secret ended.

Now he was thinking beyond that.

He was thinking of possession.

Fatherhood . . .

A wild moment at Lowries or on the Head or in the woods at Katen's Creek . . . He was thinking of how you could claim the child of such a moment, after half a lifetime, and make the claim stand up.

He was not sure how he could do it, nor was his mind clear on why he wanted to—if in fact he *did* want to. Simply to show a power more persuasive than any these people here had guessed? Or—was it really this flush along the blood when he saw the boy?

As he passed Vangie's, stimulating memories of old associations passed through his mind. Vangie was living now with Etta, somewhere in the States. She must be—what?—sixty-five or so. Grant Marshall, Lon said, had bought the place for the timber on it. Grant . . . quite a fellow he had got to be, on the Channel Shore. The thought annoyed Anse. Anything about Grant Marshall afflicted him with the bile of an old contempt. And now . . .

His musing was interrupted by a car coming up behind him—Wilmots' rattle-trap. Lee Wilmot had Sam Freeman in front with him. They pulled up. Lee made a questioning gesture, "Just going to Katen's . . ."

Anse nodded. "All right for me." He climbed into the back with the twisted boy Skimp.

Old Felix was fiddling with a battery radio he had set up on the counter and muttering to himself. Nothing was coming through but static, blurring out the faint voice of an announcer in Sydney or Charlottetown. At the east end of the store Buff and Alan were playing two-handed forty-fives on an up-ended cereal crate.

Alan turned as the newcomers entered. He grinned at them inclusively with a special welcome for the boy. "Hi, Skimp. We been looking for company. Come over here and take a hand."

The youngster flushed with embarrassment, mixed with gratitude at being noticed. He said shyly, "Hi, Alan," and looked up at his father and added, "Well, I don't know how . . ."

Cards would be banned under the code in force at Wilmots', where Hat was boss, Alan remembered. He said, "Well, that's all right," adding mischievously, "You can have a drink with us, anyhow."

He went through the hatch in the counter, rummaged in Felix's ice-box, uncapped three cokes and came back to draw Skimp along with him to the stools around the cereal crate.

Felix gave up on the radio, turned it off, and looked up without interest. People with nothing better to do had been coming here in the evening for close to forty years. All he was likely to sell was a plug of smoking to Sam Freeman. If that.

Anse sprawled on a case of canned goods, holding one knee in his hands. Sam Freeman stuck the stem of a pipe under his tobacco-yellow grey moustache, hooked a buttock over an unopened keg of nails, and got out the heel of a plug, chipping a pipeful leisurely into the palm of his hand. Lee Wilmot lounged over to the counter, dug out a crumpled one-dollar bill, and bought cigarettes. He lit one, holding it between thumb and forefinger almost reverently, in the manner of a man to whom a smoke is something real, an occasional luxury to break the monotony of labour, and let himself down to a backless chair, elbows on knees, watching Alan and Buff and Skimp.

Alan was dealing showdown, three hands a deal, with no money up; but paying Skimp a nickel when the hand he dealt the boy was high. "It's not playing cards, y'see," he said. "It's a prize you win . . . That's all right, eh, Lee?"

Lee Wilmot grinned tiredly.

Anse said, "Better than some deals Lee's had, I guess."

There was a slight cast of insinuation in it. A sardonic irony. Lee Wilmot was the the bright one of that family. Now he lived off Hat and Clem, making a day's pay when he could.

No one made any comment.

Sam Freeman said finally, "How's that boat coming, Anse?"

Anse said, shortly, "All right. There's nothing wrong with her."

Sam said, "What you plan to do, Anse, run a freight line?" and laughed heavily.

Anse drawled, "Well . . . Not up the brook to Bogtown, anyway."

332

He went on rapidly, his voice turning friendly. "It's something to do. Richard's going to cut me a mains'l. We'll have the cloth from Halifax any day now . . ."

The slightly hardened expression on Sam's face relaxed at the softened tone. Anse felt a sense of relief. He was going to have to watch his tongue; he couldn't afford yet to speak his mind with the old terse sarcasm, to stab and probe. He couldn't afford to antagonize. Not yet. If it could be managed . . . If he could swing it . . . the first public hint should come from others, not himself. And in something like friendliness, not anger.

Anger was the danger. He felt instinctively that to sneer and to antagonize would get him nowhere, would widen the breach of time and habit between himself and Alan Marshall and make impossible the incredible triumph that tantalized his mind.

Unless, of course, a bond could be woven first—a personal bond that linked him to the boy with ties of interest and liking. Anse hated the soft word affection, but there it was. A bond so strong that he could chance anger, chance anything . . .

He said, meditatively. "A great fellow, Richard is."

Sam said, "Nobody'll give you an argument there."

Anse went on, talking almost to himself, "You get a kick out of it, seeing a man smart at the things that've gone out've style . . . People had to be smart with their hands, years ago. And their heads. Richard's an able man . . ."

Felix had returned to the radio and at last had got it going. The ten o'clock news was coming in. Something about a conference of foreign ministers in Paris . . . Britain and the United States had served notice on France and Russia they were ready to organize their own zones in Germany as an economic unit . . . Three German ships were expected to be part of Canada's share of reparations, it was learned in Brussels . . . Felix grunted, "Foreign stuff," and snapped the receiver off.

Sam Freeman said, "Well," and yawned and looked at Lee Wilmot. Alan said, "See you later, Skimp," as the boy trailed his father toward the door.

Lee looked a question at them. Anse shook his head. "I'll walk up."

After the car had spluttered into life and faded up the road, Alan rose and stretched. "Time I was getting some sleep. See you, Buff. Good night, Mr. Katen."

Anse went with him. It was fully dark outside by now. The fringe of spruce along the road made an irregular saw-toothed edge against the lighter sky.

Going up the road, Anse talked about the boat, mainly. She was sound, all right. Soaked up just enough water, but there wasn't a rotten patch in her planking at all. His father had certainly known how to plank a boat. He spoke of Stewart with a kind of wistfulness, the same tone he had used of Richard McKee.

Alan was puzzled. This suggestion of softness . . . And the tone Anse used to him was one of easy equality, subtly different from that in which he spoke to Sam Freeman and Lee Wilmot.

At Gordon's gate Anse said, "We'll have sail on her next week, likely. Don't forget."

"No," Alan said. "I'm looking forward to it."

9

Renie was lonely. There were times when it seemed to her that she was an outsider in the house, as though Grant and Alan and Margaret lived in an intimate circle of their own, from which she was excluded. She knew that what these three had in common was not intimacy, but the restraint of separate private preoccupations. Alike, perhaps, and perhaps related, but certainly not consciously shared. She knew also that the care with which they excluded her was not the formal reserve of intimates toward a stranger but an effort instinctive and affectionate to keep her untouched by troubling things.

Within that circle of constraint an instinctive considerateness for others within the circle existed also, like the thoughtfulness that kept her out. Though private troubles were not shared, the recognition of them *was*, perhaps unconsciously. There was a studied naturalness, an artificial ease. Alan was best at this. Both Grant and Margaret fell into moody silences more often than before. The Room sometimes felt to Renie like a pressure chamber.

It was understandable that Anse Gordon, coming out of the shadowy past like an embodied judgement, should tear at Alan's heart and Grant's. But Renie could not see it all. She could not tell, for instance, what Margaret's part in it was. She wanted to talk, to bring the thing out of the shadows in shared words. But, remembering, she could not do so. There were elements in close relationships that tied the tongue.

No one to whom she could talk freely. Renie was not the kind of woman who could discuss the inwardness of self and family with neighbours she must live beside. She would not give hostages of confidence. Except perhaps for Mrs. Josie . . . But she could not burden Mrs. Josie with worries that were rooted in the heart and soul and flesh of Anse Gordon.

On the third Tuesday in July Renie took a dipper and went down through the lower field to the pasture. Near Frank

Graham's line fence the last of the wild strawberries had ripened. These days you could buy as many cultivated berries as you wanted, but Renie liked to search out the sweet wild ones in the pastures. She walked slowly, hearing the sound of mowing machine and raker at Graham's. Grant and Alan were busy there with old Frank and Dan. Years ago, when things were done by hand, haying time had been a season of its own, a month-long business of waiting for the sun, mowing with hand-scythes, shaking-out, turning, cocking-up against the rain, shaking-out again, bundling-up, hauling to the barn, stowing away. Now it was all machinery. They would make Frank's place in a week or less and then turn to Grant's.

Renie felt a small resentment at being out of it. As a girl on Prince's Island she had handled a fork, stowing away, and a rake behind the rack, raking after. But now Grant wouldn't let either her or Margaret take a hand.

She came to a place where long grass grew between cradle-hills, where wild strawberries grew long-stemmed and slow to ripen. She squatted there and began to pick.

The first indication that she was not alone was a knocking on a fence rail. Bill Graham said across the fence: "Can I come in?"

She looked up, startled, and laughed.

"Hello, Bill. Come on over."

She liked Bill Graham. A quick wordless friendship had grown between them in the short time he had been at Frank's. It was as if they felt some sort of rueful half-humorous alliance, the alliance of aliens in a land friendly and familiar but to which they had not been born.

Bill climbed the fence, carrying a partly-filled preserving jar in a careful hand. "They won't let me make hay. So I left them to stew in their own sweat."

He sat on a cradle-hill, holding the jar between his knees. Renie brushed red-stained fingers through her rusty grey hair and gave him a look. She said, "They won't let me make hay either. We're outsiders, Bill."

He laughed. "Maybe so. You know, Renie, seeing you here after strawberries . . . It reminded me of something."

She gave her little laugh. "Nice, I hope."

"Well, odd, anyway . . . You remember . . ."

She said, "When you 'went to school to me'?"

"Yes. Well, not that, exactly. You were in Gordons' kitchen, remember, the night after Anna was killed."

336

Renie said, "So I was." There was a little note of wonder in her voice as she went back to that time before she had known Grant, except by sight, or foreseen anything at all of the life she was to grow into in the time between.

Bill said, "It wasn't that, though . . . Something else. Not directly. A Sunday afternoon and Dan and Stan Currie and Joe McKee and I, loafing in the woods along the Black Brook. Anse Gordon stopped for a while. And after that we wandered up to Lowries and he and Hazel were just leaving there. They'd been picking strawberries."

"That was a long time ago," Renie said. "And an odd thing to remember." She spoke slowly. "You know it seems, well—a little queer. I've lived at The Head a long time—and yet—you were here first—"

Bill said thoughtfully, "Odd how things stay in your mind when you don't even know it, isn't it? I'd forgotten the Shore. Not forgotten, exactly, but it was something I didn't think about. And then when I saw Anse Gordon in London—it began to come back. I could really *feel* it. It'd been, oh, a part of me, I suppose, all the time. Then the colours started coming up . . ."

Renie said, "You saw Anse in London . . . When?"

"A year or so ago."

"And you didn't write to anyone? Didn't mention it?"

Bill shook his head. "No. I didn't write. I didn't mention it. He said he hadn't been back, you see . . . And I didn't know . . . I didn't tell him anything. Not even that Anna was dead . . ."

Renie said, thoughtfully. "You know the whole story, *don't* you, Bill? I *thought* you did."

He shook his head. "Oh, no, Renie. How can anybody know the whole story? Of anything. You'd have to put together everything a lot of individual people know, and don't talk about. Each one of them knows something no one else does . . . But I know enough. I was here, you know . . . and Grant came to see me, in Toronto . . ."

Renie said, "So you know why . . . You know what Anse means to us. Coming back, I mean."

Bill said, "I've got a pretty good idea, yes." He went on, "Grant looks the way he did when he was worrying about the old man, old James, and Anna." He hesitated. "Have you tried to talk to him about it?"

She shook her head. "Anything that goes back to that—he looks at it as a problem of his own." She said, meditatively, "I meddled once. Years ago." She had the gift of terse narrative. As she went back over that winter of twelve years ago she could feel again the tension in the house and the relief when it vanished. "And I never knew why. There was only—the sun out, and the cold. And Margaret glummer than usual. And then Grant and Alan coming in from the barn to dinner, and you could tell it was all right. I never knew why . . . But I said to myself then, I'd never meddle again . . ."

She paused, thoughtfully. Far off across the bushy slope a figure climbed the fence into Stan Currie's pasture—Margaret, going toward the beach.

Renie went on, slowly, "You're right. You can't ever know the whole story of anything. I know, for instance, that Alan's known for years . . . Mrs. Josie told me that. She never told me how he knew, only that he *did* know, and that it was all right . . . It was something she had on her mind. She figured I ought to know, but not Grant . . . Margaret must've picked it up too, long ago; I don't know. And I don't know whether Grant's ever found out that Alan . . . Oh, hell, Bill. It's too involved—and yet, in terms of feeling . . . I s'pose it's simple. That strange thing, kind of beautiful, it's been as much a part of Grant's life and Alan's as breathing . . ."

She hesitated. Bill was silent, and she went on.

"Odd, you know. Once his mind was made up to let Alan stay I s'pose Grant just stopped, well, trying to figure . . . The worry would be there, but he'd try to ignore it. What happened, it seems—as I look back—was that he lost a lot of his impulsiveness, got careful, not so free and easy. Instinct, I guess. Alan was the same. Each one kind of watchful for the other, till it got to be . . . But Alan's grown up now, and he's a little different. A man. That would have been all right, too. But Anse came back . . ."

She paused. "It's nothing I can talk to Grant about. Neither can Alan. Can't reassure him, I mean. The minute he does, it's over."

Bill said, thoughtfully, "Yes, I s'pose so. About all a person can do is stand by."

That was it. Nothing had been solved by talking, but Renie's heart was lighter for having talked with Bill. She felt none of the reaction, the sense of having exposed a personal weakness, that can depress a strong-minded person after speaking freely of inner things. There was no morbid inquisitiveness about Bill Graham. They had let each other know that they shared a recognition, a concern for certain people. That was all.

338

Renie stood up and brushed the seat of her slacks. She said, "Let's get some berries picked. Come over to supper tonight, will you, Bill? I'm going to make a shortcake. Last one of the year."

Margaret angled her way across Curries' lower pasture toward the beach. In the years when Hugh's place had lain unlived on, young spruce had over-run the whole slope, but Stan had cleared it again. To her right as she walked between small yellowing stumps toward the old road to the Head, his new-field potatoes were coming into blossom.

Margaret had found that in the last few weeks, the Currie place, the thought and sight of it, gave her a little lifting of the heart, a warmth. Something to do with the fact of Stan Currie's return with his wife and children to the land he had been raised on. Stan had come back in 'forty-one, put a new cellar under the house and installed running water, and left, the following winter, to follow Dan Graham into the Merchant Marine. This had made no notable impression on Margaret at the time, nor could she recall feeling anything in particular about the Currie house during its years of emptiness, an abandoned place. It was only now when Currie Head, home, had become vivid to her through Alan, that her heart stirred to events like Stan Currie's return. This had little to do with Currie Head. She knew that. If Mexico or New South Wales had been Alan's choice it would have been hers also. But his place was The Head. As Margaret turned south to cross the neck, the sight of Janet Currie's washing on the line, the sound of Stan's mowing-machine, helped to lighten a mood already excited with the purpose in her mind.

Her purpose was to find and talk to Richard McKee.

As she approached the swampy section of the road, an intermittent hollow tapping came to her through the fringe of black spruce to the right. Anse was working on the boat. Involuntarily she hurried a little, skirting to the left, anxious to avoid contact; she felt a flicker of surprise at her own reaction.

Anse could be the key to her problem. In Anse there was the possibility of release, the wakening of memory along the Channel Shore, open knowledge and acceptance at last of an old and hidden story . . . It was clear to her that only open recognition and acceptance could make fulfilment possible.

But for Anse himself, she realized, she felt none of the warmth that could make a chance meeting and conversation a pleasant thing in itself. There had been truth in her statement to Alan that she rather liked Anse; but the fact was that most people were unimportant to her now, a waste of time . . . Anse Gordon could be an instrument, but he would be an instrument she couldn't control, and one which in any event she couldn't bring herself to use.

As she turned west to go up the inlet shore toward the huts on Curries' beach she threw a swift sidelong glance over her shoulder. She could see the hull, propped up in the yard, and standing motionless by the stern, Anse. He was looking at her. Standing and looking.

Her glance had been a quick thing, a movement of the eyes, the head hardly turning. If Anse caught it, he did not wave. As Margaret turned to go up over the hump of the beach to Richard's hut she had a moment of prescience in which it seemed to her that all those nearest to her, the members of her family, watched each other now through a screen of work and leisure, daylight and sleep. And were in turn watched.

On the narrow flat top of the beach she came out into the push of the southwesterly. It was low tide. On the inlet side the tiny tide-channel, dark with eel-grass, wound around clam-beds covered with less than a foot of water. The fawn shallows were minutely ruffled, now and then, as gusts of the long wind brushed and passed. On the seaward side of the beach the Channel marched to the packed sand and coarse gravel in a constant leisured lop, shore and sea merging in a continual splash and grumble of slow sound.

The day was bright but now and then the banked clouds, massive with summer, would move heavy-bosomed across the sun, trailing along the beach for long moments a windy shadowy chill.

Margaret approached Richard's hut in a sunlit moment and saw that he was there.

Richard had hauled out for cleaning the single fleet of herring nets he still tended each July. The spread mesh lay cleaned of slime, drying on the slope of the beach. He was engaged today in mending a section of salmon net for Alec Neill; whiling away time by the sunny side of his hut.

The sight of Margaret coming up the beach gave him a sensation of pleasure he did not at first form in thought. It was merely a sense-perception of her small figure, buffeted slightly by the wind, merged with the knowledge that she was coming to see him.

Somewhere during the years just before the war, Alan had grown out of the boyhood habit of closeness with his grandfather. The affection was still there, evident in a glance or the turn of a word, but for a long time he hadn't seen a great deal of Alan. Richard understood that. In those years when he was growing up, the boy had grown away from an interest in old men and their archaic crafts; he had had no time for anything much but Grant; Grant and a lively activity. And then the war. For years now Richard had lacked the touch of youth around him. It was only lately that in an odd way he had felt it again, that protective sense of closeness, in his rare meetings with Margaret. Lately for some reason she had been calling him Uncle Rich.

He got up from the upended trawl tub on which he was sitting and looked around to find a seat for her.

"Never mind, Uncle Rich," Margaret said. "This'll do." She tucked an ancient float-keg under her buttocks.

Richard resumed his seat, picked up the net-needle and grinned slightly at the mesh of Alec's net.

"How are things up in civilization?"

Margaret laughed. Suddenly she knew, with relief, that she was not going to have to be gradual, groping for words, with Richard McKee. There was something in his voice, in the almost careless manner of his speech, that told her Richard was touched by little of the emotional prejudice she feared in others. She had a speculative thought that from the beginning of this story, nearly thirty years ago, he never had been.

She said, "Too civilized, sometimes."

She slipped her feet out of her shoes, tugged off ankle-length socks, and curled her toes around smooth sun-warmed stone. Chin in hand and elbows on knees she watched while Richard's knobbed and calloused hands moved with deliberate deft precision, drawing twine around the mesh-board, knotting his knot. For a moment it seemed to her that she could go on watching this indefinitely, as if there were no need to speak at all.

Richard talked intermittently, low-toned, neither to Margaret nor entirely to himself. Alec Neill wasn't too well, he said. The old leg trouble was bothering Alec, enough to keep him in the house for a spell. Richard had hauled his salmon net for him. A few snags to mend. That was all.

His voice was an accompaniment of what he was doing, of his moving hands. The thought crossed Margaret's mind that although Uncle Rich was well along in his seventies, there was no essential change. A little stooped and withered, but still the man who had been splitting hoop-holes, a dozen years ago, the day she and Alan pawed through the contents of a sea-chest in the

341

shop loft. More than half her own lifetime ago . . . But only a little time, perhaps, to Richard.

After an interval she said, "Uncle Rich. You're the only person I could talk to. It's Alan and me. We're . . ."

Her voice trailed off. Richard felt behind him on the trawl tub for his knife and snipped the twine off at a completed knot.

He said, "Is that a thing you just found out?"

She shook her head. "Something Alan just found out, I guess. I've felt that way for years."

Richard nodded, put the knife away, and sat with his hands between his knees.

He said, "You both know the whole thing, then . . . The whole story. Otherwise . . . But I s'pose Grant wouldn't think of that."

Margaret said: "He doesn't know—anything. That we know . . . Or the way we feel . . . And Alan won't . . ."

Richard said, "No, I s'pose not. And *you* can't, very well."

She shook her head without speaking. She could not go to Grant. Not without betraying Alan, living with the knowledge of betrayal in her heart.

"Well," Richard said. "It's natural. Complicated, though." After an interval, "Got any plans?"

Again she shook her head. "No. You know how he—how he and Grant feel. He was going away for a while. But then, he didn't . . . I don't—we don't know what to do."

"Some things, you got to wait out," Richard said.

"I know. But . . . Oh, we'd wait for years. But how's that going to make it any better? To be any good for us, the whole thing's got to come out, some time. How can it make any difference, waiting, I mean, when what's got to happen is that Grant stops— stops being Alan's father? No matter how long we wait"—Margaret moved her head abruptly, snaring in the gesture everything she could foresee of sensation, gossip, wonder—"no matter how long we wait, the shock'll always be the same."

Richard was dropping pebbles from one cupped palm to the other. He let them trickle through to the ground. His voice was matter-of-fact, neither sympathetic nor indifferent.

"I wouldn't say *that*, Marg'ret. You'd be surprised . . . You'd be surprised what time does in the way of getting people used to an idea. Once it begins to sprout. You'll have to do some waiting. It'll likely work out."

She said, impulsively, "Uncle Rich, I wonder . . . You don't think—Do you think we ought to—" she made a short gesture— "try to forget it, smother it, stop thinking we can . . .?"

342

She was at once ashamed. Nothing could make her forget or change her purpose. She had come to the beach for the comfort of talk, of human contact and understanding. What she was doing now was appealing for justification.

Richard smiled slightly. He shook his head, not in negation but in rejection of the question. "People got to make their own minds up. You've done that already. Helps to talk about it, maybe. But you can't go asking people whether it's right or wrong." His voice took on a note of remote amusement that included all humanity. "How can anybody know that, anyway?"

For the first time in months, perhaps for the first time since she had realized years ago the meaning of what she felt for Alan, Margaret had a sense of openness, of relief from secrecy. Even in the brief wild moment in the shadow of the house, there had been no relief from that. This, now, was a beginning.

A beginning. She said, "Suppose—"

Richard had resumed his work on the net. He looked up without breaking the rhythm of his hands, and down again, waiting.

"Suppose it comes out again. The old story. Uncle Rich, look. Even then. How could you prove it—that we're no relation . . .?"

Richard sighed, faintly amused at Margaret's switch to the practical. He finished the hole on which he was working. He snapped the twine, tucked the net-needle into an overall pocket, and turned to squint out over the Channel, forearms on knees. He felt, oddly, the thrust of irritation.

He said slowly, almost roughly, "Hell, girl—Grant wasn't even in the country . . . Anybody can prove that."

For a quarter-century he had kept his mind from brooding on Hazel . . . Hazel and Anse Gordon . . . Sometimes it hadn't been possible to do that. The brain would return at intervals to pain. What he remembered now was a bitter walk down the frozen road, the pallor of Hazel's face on the pillow, his own wonder at the thing in her mind that called him there . . . His mind turned again. There were other memories, other images from before the time of pain began. Himself, half-asleep in the room off the kitchen, and Hazel going after strawberries . . . the sound of voices, hers and Eva's, remotely bickering . . . But always, the bleak appeal in her eyes when she had told him in the hut here . . . in the hut here . . . And the wordless thing he had felt, later, when Grant Marshall had brought her home . . .

Grant. And now again, Grant was going to be hurt.

Richard found with something like surprise that there was little pain in reverie on these matters. They had mellowed and blended.

343

Old pain was distilled into present interest and sympathy. For Grant, who had taken the brunt of it years ago. For Margaret and Alan . . .

But still, there was that little flush of irritation. Margaret. Not satisfied with the comfort of talk, impatient for . . . impatient . . . His mind returned to that bleak day, the stairs to the room in Stewart Gordon's house . . . That was something he would not talk about, to Margaret, now.

He said, brusquely, "You don't need to worry . . . You wait till the time comes. Anybody can prove that."

The meal was a quiet one. No one seemed anxious to talk and Grant was glad of that. Even then, Bill Graham's presence disturbed him a little, at first. Bill by this time was simply one of the Grahams, a person you didn't have to entertain with words; but even with people you knew well, it was hard to be at ease without making an effort and it seemed to Grant that the effort must be obvious.

Tonight, however, no one laboured to make conversation and Grant let his mind drift in what had now become an endless preoccupation. He would glance up, now and then, and see his son's face, cast in the mould of Anse Gordon's.

He looked inward with a kind of wonder, telling himself how small had been the causes of his worry, his irritation, a month ago and less: the nonchalance, the casual independence in Alan. How small compared to this present apprehension. And yet the difference was in degree, not in kind. For he admitted to himself, and must always have admitted it, consciously or not, that the root of his fear was Anse Gordon—his survival in the Shore's memory, the conjecture of his survival in his son's blood.

The only change was that the fear was sharper, was definite, was made hard and immediate by Anse's emergence out of memory to become a presence on the Shore.

All this had come home to Grant particularly since seeing Anse and Alan together on the evening they had hauled the boat to Rob's Yard. The question that had plagued him then was never absent from his mind. Why was Alan still at The Head? Was it the fascination of Anse? And if that were true, was it merely the fascination of something new, a stranger from the past? Was it that, or a groping instinct? Or did Alan know? Was it the fascination a son must feel for a lost and fabulous father, appearing by miracle out of vanished time?

344

And now also, whatever the truth, the apprehension was two-fold. First, the fear of something that in a sense must be a personal and private failure, the failure of fatherhood, the failure to overcome by habit and manner and example his son's inheritance. Now to this was added by Anse's presence the old fear of exposure, multiplied and made definite. The fear of an end to the long kindly conspiracy of illusion along the Channel Shore. An end to fatherhood itself.

As he went out to the veranda with Bill Graham, Grant was aware of a feeling that had touched him vaguely earlier, in the days before Anse Gordon's return had sharpened his doubts and fears into definite outline: a sense that there was something missing in his thinking, some truth he had missed. Oddly when this sense touched him he had felt the shadows lighten. But since Anse's return he had not felt it until now.

The moment of unreasoned lightness passed. He lit his pipe while Bill got out a cigarette, and they fell into a wordless quiet.

Someone was coming up the road, round Gordons' turn. Grant said, "Buff Katen," meditatively, in a tone of slight curiosity edged with something faintly contemptuous.

Buff turned in at the gate. He called "Hello, Mr. Marshall; hi, Mr. Graham," and crossed the yard to the shop. They could hear him talking there to Alan, the sound of casual laughter.

A little later Alan and Buff and Margaret came through the house from the back.

Alan said, "We're driving to The Harbour, Pop. The movies." Grant said, "All right."

It irked him that Alan made the flat statement without asking whether anyone else planned to use the car; and he knew his annoyance was unreasonable.

He stirred restlessly after they had driven off.

"I don't like . . ."

Bill said, "What don't you like, Grant?"

Grant was silent for a minute. He said slowly, as if thinking in speech, "Damn it, I don't like the Katens. I can work with them, in the mill, because they belong to the place. But damned if I can like them."

Bill said, "Well, if you don't like someone you don't like him, that's all . . . But you sound kind of like someone talking about Jews, lumping a race or a family all together. You can't like or dislike on the basis of a whole race. Or a family. It's the person. I don't like Lon much myself. But I think quite a lot of Buff.

Don't you think — well, nobody's a copy of his father, good or bad. All kinds of things get scribbled in, from other people, other generations. Or edited out. You can't figure inheritance on a slide rule . . ."

Absently, Grant said, "M-m-m, yes. I guess you're right." He was only half-listening, his mind busy with tags of thought, images from the known past and the conjectured future.

10

BEHIND Alan the house was quiet. Grant had stretched himself on the chesterfield when supper was over. By now he would be asleep. In a little while Renie and Margaret would clear the table with a subdued clink of dishes. But at the moment the only sound was the slight intermittent knocking, faintly echoing from the inlet shore, where Anse was working on the boat.

Working . . . Alan grinned, a little wryly. Working or making a pass at it. Anse and Lon had spent two weeks puttering over two or three days' work. They had soaked the hull, hauled it out and patched, caulked and painted inside and out, taking their time. The old boat-yard now was a place for the young ones of Currie Head, and occasionally some of the elders, to lounge in the evenings. He had gone there several times himself, to avoid the appearance of staying away and because the whole thing was fascinating. A sailboat at The Head in his time was something new.

He glanced down over the slope of Marshall and Currie land and walked leisurely past the barn to the path across the pasture.

Three weeks since Anse's return. Looking back, he could see hardly any outward indication that Currie Head had been reminded of the story of his birth or was aware of its renewal. He knew that the awareness was there, sharp and alive. But there was nothing you could call an outward sign. Nothing more noticeable than a gleam in Lon Katen's eyes, as he glanced from Anse to Alan. A slight awkward hush, once or twice, among people waiting for Eva McKee to sort the mail, when Anse walked in. The hurry of Eva's fingers . . .

And through it all an acceptance of Anse Gordon that was just a shade too careful. Alan felt his heart gripped, as he walked down Curries' road, by a hard admiration. For Frank and Stella Graham, Buff Katen, the Freemans, the Wilmots. For people up and down the Shore, not relations or even close friends. People who took care to be casual with Anse Gordon, who met him with friendliness,

347

careful that no word of theirs should rouse the sleeping anger and open the gates of grief for Grant Marshall and Josie Gordon and Richard and Eva McKee.

A care almost like his own care . . .

The curious thing about himself was that he still felt almost nothing about Anse Gordon, as a person. This was so, partly, perhaps, because the heart of his concern was not with Anse himself but with a situation—with possibilities resurrected and made urgent by Anse's return, and the care he must take, the part he must play within that situation. And yet, it was not entirely that. There were times when, alone, he let the essential fact strike him. He could find in it no true sense of reality. No sense of kinship. Nor any sense of hate. He could condemn this man, this Anse, for wrongs done long ago to Josie Gordon and Hazel McKee, but the feeling had in it none of the peculiar hatred of blood for kindred blood. The feeling was impersonal.

As for what Anse might be feeling . . . Well, as far as he could see, Anse had never once implied by word or look a knowledge of the tie between them. There was only that sense of the confidential in the rare moments when they were alone together. Wordless, more like an assumption, an understanding that intimacy existed, than intimacy itself. And when with others, that wordless manner of equality, an equality Anse would grant to no one else.

Nothing, really, you could put a finger on . . . He was beginning to feel a tentative lifting of the heart, the thing he had felt the first day of haying . . . Perhaps before long he could do what he had planned to do. With the Shore's help the fabric was holding. Perhaps he could go away, away for a while from the sight and sound of Margaret.

There were no loungers in the yard tonight except Anse and Lon themselves, through for the day. The boat lay moored in the tide-channel with masts stepped and standing rigging up. They sprawled, the two of them, on the moss-grown lip of bank above the narrow beach, smoking, lazing there until the impulse should strike them to get up and head for home.

Anse looked up and grinned slightly as Alan's feet crunched the chips and shavings of the yard. He said, "Well, Alan . . . What d'you think of her now?"

Alan stood on the bank, running his eye over the boat. In the days when he had rowed to the nets with Richard and sailed the flat in the inlet he had learned something about handling small boats. But this was different. This boat belonged to a more spacious tradition, deep water and straining sailcloth. He could not have explained the fascination she had for him: the curve of pine planking round her timbers, sweeping back from the rise of the knockabout to the grace of her narrow overhang. But the fascination was there.

He said, "Fine. She looks fine. You're about through, are you?"

Anse said, "About. We'll bend on the sails tomorrow. Have her out there in a day or two. Plenty of time for the Holiday."

Alan nodded, glancing absently over what he could see of Anse's workmanship. The planking was patched here and there, inside, between the timbers. The whole painted over, a medium green. The hull, outside, was a glistening white with a black ribbon and green washboards.

The Holiday . . . Except for the war years he had attended every picnic held during his time at Currie Head, and found them dull, most of them, except for the fact that he liked people, anyhow and anywhere. Excuses mostly for the school-house road families and others back of the first line of settlement to have a day on the beach, the youngsters paddling around the inlet in Alec Neill's and Richard McKee's row-boats, wading on the clam-beds at low tide. This one, perhaps, would be different; this one would have the atmosphere of years ago, when the two-masters raced to a flag moored off the Upper Islands, out and back. He had heard Frank Graham talk about it.

Anse got up and brushed his pants. He said, off-hand, "You might as well come down when we tow her out. Lend us a hand."

Alan said, "Sure. If it's in the evening."

Anse laughed. He turned to Lon, "Lon, you got the jug? We'd best be getting home."

Lon rose and spat tobacco juice. He walked to the tool-chest, reached in, and brought out a flat twenty-six-ounce flask.

This surprised Alan. Lon was a drinker, but Anse, according to the legend about him, never hit the bottle much. Even among men who *did* drink, you didn't often see liquor produced except to mark occasions—a dance, a wedding, an election.

Anse looked at him speculatively, hesitated, and said, "Like a short one?"

He shook his head and grinned, "I guess not, thanks."

Lon drew a sleeve across his tobacco-smeared stubble and held out the flask. "Come on. After *you*."

Almost automatically, Alan reached for the bottle, grinned fool-ishly and gulped a quick drink. He had done a little drinking in English pubs and had shared an occasional bottle of Calvados

349

in Normandy, but since then had never thought of it, simply because The Head was not a drinking place.

The alcohol meant nothing to him. He was not afraid of it. But as the bottle passed between Anse and Lon and as the three of them turned to walk up Curries' road, he was irritated and uneasy. Not at the fact of taking a drink but at the fact that in some way not quite clear to him he had entered into a relationship with Anse and Lon that was closer than he liked. He had a sense of annoyance and cautioned himself not to show it.

Anse was still talking about the boat, the fun he was going to get out of her. It seemed to Alan that in his voice and manner he was including him, with Lon Katen, in something like a conspiracy.

Lon came out of one of his customary baleful silences, surprisingly, to prod Anse. He said, "Hell! The way you talk you'd think the damn boat was a woman."

Anse laughed. "Get your mind off that, Lon. You're too old . . . A boat's better than any woman. Easier to get along with. You don't have to talk slush to get round her. And you know where you stand." He added, reflectively. "Damned if I know why they name boats after women."

A thought seemed to come to him out of that observation. "They never bothered putting names to boats around here. Maybe we ought to do something *about* that. Just for a change." His voice took on slyness. "What d'you think we ought to call her, Lon?" He paused. "The *Vangie?*"

Lon Katen grunted and spat a short word with his cud of twist. Anse chuckled, glanced sidelong at Alan, and fell to humming to himself.

Alan made a small indistinguishable sound of amusement: even while a puzzled anger grew in him, he must continue to act, careful not to repel this assumption of intimacy. First, he had been drawn into the circle of Anse and Lon. Then into a smaller circle by the jibe at Lon, the old story of Etta Murphy's disputed paternity . . . A jibe in which he was expected to share.

Almost without thinking, he *had* shared it.

He examined his feeling as the three of them crossed over to the lower pasture of The Place. The time was past, suddenly, in which he had felt nothing about Anse Gordon. What he felt now was anger. Anger and a curious shame. Odd . . . That it should come to him this way, at last, the sense of kinship: in shame that a man should talk coarsely, joke coarsely at the expense of another, in the presence of his son.

Margaret walked down the road toward the Gordons'. Since her hour on the beach with Richard a week ago, a kind of active tranquillity had taken hold of her. Not resignation, or even patience; it was more like the discovery that she could put time behind her methodically by a continued busyness. In the times between dish-washing, cooking and bed-making, she looked for things to do.

Tonight she was going to see Mrs. Josie; and as she walked the short familiar stretch of road she found herself touched curiously by the warmth of anticipation she had known years ago, as a little girl, looking forward to an hour with this quiet woman who was like a member of the family and yet wasn't. A person you almost took for granted but never quite.

A stray thought lingered in her mind as she turned in at the gate, a momentary preoccupation with the old people whose lives seemed always to have been woven into hers and Alan's. Aunt Jane, the fussy woman who was all that remained of Uncle James . . . They had hardly noticed her at all, except sometimes with amusement; and now Margaret realized with a flicker of surprise that she liked her, the thought of her was gentle . . . Uncle James, whose fierce wordless affection she had sensed and with whom she felt a vague affinity, a recognition. Eva McKee—she had never been able to feel much except a formal surface acquaintance with Mrs. McKee. Richard. Richard and Josie. It was curious that when you thought of abstract things like human understanding and friendliness the concrete images that came to mind were those of Richard and Josie—quiet people who rarely smiled and hardly talked at all.

Josie as usual was sitting by the south windows of her kitchen, the windows Grant had cut years ago, the windows through which she had seen the life of the Shore pass and re-pass for a generation . . .

Outside it was only early dusk, but the kitchen was dim. Josie turned slightly in her chair and spoke to Margaret. "Well, Marg'ret. I saw you coming, but I'm too lazy to light a lamp."

With Margaret as with Alan, although the two were little alike, she sometimes felt the restraints go down, found herself talking, as if Margaret were a little girl again, come down the road to help her wind the yarn.

Margaret said, "I'll get one down," and turned to the shelf over the sink in the kitchen's southeast corner. She reached down a lamp, set it on the table, removed the chimney and touched a match to the wick. The yellow flame cast a dim unsteady light on checkered oilcloth, steadied and flowed out to the corners of the room as she slipped the chimney back into the prongs of the burner.

Josie said, "Kerosene. Grant wanted me to put in hydro, but it's too bright for me. I don't read much. Specially at night. I could get along with a slut."

Margaret said, "What?"

Josie gave her short dry chuckle. "A slut. Saucer of fish-oil and a lit rag."

Margaret said, "Oh."

Josie said, "I don't s'pose anybody's used a slut for fifty years. More, maybe."

Margaret said, "I don't think I ever heard of that." She turned to the stove in which Josie had allowed the supper fire to die, and dipped a finger in the kettle of water sitting there. It was still warm. She had noticed that the dishes were still unwashed, piled on the sink-board. She took the dishpan from its hook, sloshed in water from the kettle, and carried the pan back to the sink. Josie watched her idly and said, "You don't need to do that; I'll get around to it," but it was not a protest, merely an acceptance of the helpfulness.

Over her shoulder Margaret said, "They had pretty—expressive names for things, didn't they?"

Josie again gave her faint derisive chuckle. "Expressive? Yes. Rough. Life was a little rough." She sighed. "Y'know, when I was a girl—I used to help father with the fish. Cleaning. On the beach, in bare feet. When I was fifteen, sixteen." She paused, said irrelevantly, "People thought it was a wonderful thing, I s'pose, when kerosene lamps began to get common." She paused again. "Oh, it *was*, too, I guess. But people were independent, years ago. Not much money, but they didn't need it. Caught fish and farmed. Always a market for fish, and all they'd need to live on was the oats and potatoes and pigs and cows you could grow yourself . . ."

Margaret washed and wiped, listening to Josie's voice, the words between pauses. She thought idly that Josie, the silent one, was more than usually talkative tonight. The words hardly penetrated. What they were doing was calling up in Margaret's mind scraps of conversation heard in childhood, bits of talk heard from the few people who talked about the past in rare moments of expansiveness, of relapse from the present. Not Frank Graham or Sam Freeman. Alec Neill, perhaps. Hugh Currie. Once or twice, Richard McKee.

Words remembered, and the memory lost of who had said them . . . *Years ago things changed in this part of the country.*

352

We got into hard times. It's like a tide, only it's years between the high and low. The tide went out because the nature of things changed . . . Fish got to be business, and the mack'rel scarce . . . More money for day labour and less for what you could catch and grow. Cheaper to buy than to make . . . When a man made wages and spent them there was more to show in the house. Boughten carpets, parlour organs . . . but after a while there wasn't enough work for wages to go 'round. You can't turn the tide, so people had to leave to find what they wanted . . .

Margaret had a picture of young men cutting white pine for two-masters, gathering chips for their cresset fires, shaving staves, bending hoops, shingling roofs, replacing sills, fashioning window-frames, cutting sails, caulking seams, cleaning and salting fish, knitting and mending nets . . . they had known it all, all the skills. They were dead, and the skills gone on a turning tide.

And yet, people remembered. And people still lived on the Channel Shore, people with other skills, newer crafts, that somehow were related to and grew from the old. The story of the Shore was the story of a strange fertility. A fertility of flesh and blood that sent its seed blowing across continents of space on the winds of time, and yet was rooted here in home soil, renewed and re-renewed.

The thought turned. All these people had faced circumstance, had known love, anger, compassion. Some of them had faced frustration as hard to bear as that which faced herself and Alan. The sense of time and home and people could do nothing to ease the sharpness of that private hunger. But there was something, a feeling strange to Margaret, a feeling almost of companionship . . .

For the first time since she had come to young womanhood she felt an identification with Currie Head and the Channel Shore that could be traced to something wider than the blood call of three people—Grant, Renie, Alan. The sense of home. And with it the sense of time. Time took care of everything, one way or another. But the manner in which it took care of things depended on people . . . time in itself was not enough. Life was shaped, slowly, by the character of people, but it took time. That was what Richard must have meant, time and people. You had to put some faith in both. Margaret shook her head in her old habit of trying to find words in which to pin a thought. If people were all right, time would work it out . . .

Josie was saying, "You can't stop change, though, and maybe things are better as they are . . ." She lapsed into silence, and Margaret thought a little guiltily that she hadn't really been listening to what the old woman said. And yet she had no sense of anything missed. She had been listening to many voices. Josie's was one of them.

Footsteps sounded on the back steps and Anse Gordon came into the lamplight.

The inner anger had hardened in Alan as he turned up toward the house, leaving Anse and Lon to cut across the lower field to the road. The sudden disgust was under control, becoming now not a surface thing that set the nerves shaking, but something he would live with, a part of him.

Woven into it was a kind of resolution.

Whatever the future as it concerned Grant and Renie and Margaret, his own people, and Anse Gordon, he, Alan, was part of it. To leave the Shore was impossible. There was nothing in going except escape for himself. Well, personal escape was not enough.

Something like the resolution that had come to him twelve years ago . . . But no clear-cut course of action was possible. It was not as simple as that. You simply had to stand by. You simply had to *be* there when you should be there, when you were needed.

Renie was reading in The Room. He asked her, carelessly, "Where's Margaret?"

She looked up. "I don't know. She said something about going over to Mrs. Josie's."

He turned and went back through the kitchen, unreasonably let down. He recognized the unreasonableness. For weeks he had been careful to be together with Margaret as little as possible—no more than was necessary in order not to seem to be avoiding her, not to seem unnatural. Now he wanted to see her. Not to talk about anything, merely to feel again in her presence the closeness, the alliance; and the understanding that went beyond that, the recognition sensed on the road to Richard McKee's. In the face of what he felt now he did not fear the hurt or the temptation. The need of Margaret as a person was stronger in this moment than the fear of love. He wanted her with him, and he felt an unreasonable anger because she was not here.

He stood irresolute for a little and then crossed the yard and climbed the fence into Grahams' pasture. He crossed Frank's land well south of the house, through the bush. On the still air he could hear the chattering of Dan's kids, and Bessie calling them inside. Graham's Brook was low from the dry weather. Little more than a series of still pools linked by a trickle. He crossed this and went on across Gordons' land and into what had been Vangie

354

Murphy's. Between the remains of Vangie's house and the Channel a good deal of young softwood was getting up to pulpwood size again. In a few years it would be worth looking at.

He crossed Katen's below the house and store and came to the creek. Despite the dry spell, considerable water flowed over its rocky bed. Sinclair's mill hadn't been running for years. The dam was gone. He found a spot on the bank and sat there, lulled by the creek's guttural song.

Margaret was finishing the dishes when Anse entered. He said in pleased surprise, "Why—hello."

Margaret murmured an offhand greeting, slipped the last plate into the rack, and dried her hands on the roller towel. Both Grant and Alan, she supposed, must be uncomfortable in Anse's presence, but there was nothing in it to disturb herself, at least when others were around. What she felt mainly was curiosity, and something like bravado.

She took a chair by the table and said, "I s'pose everything's getting familiar to you again, Mr. Gordon."

Anse laughed. He said, "Oh, yes," in a tone implying that a good deal of it was too familiar, too well-remembered, too dull. There was something about this girl, in a way the same sort of difference there was about Alan, that set her apart from the rest of Currie Head. The contempt he felt for the place, always showing slightly in speech or manner, though carefully veiled, was not for them. Not for Margaret Marshall, or for Alan, his son. He was eager to talk to Margaret, as though by talking he included her and himself in an area of experience and knowledgeability apart from the Channel Shore.

From the starting-point of Margaret's work in Halifax he went on to the Merchant Navy, recalling the times he had been in port there while convoys were making up. Prewar voyages came to life in his talk, and the ports he had seen—Batavia, Curacao, Georgetown, Aden . . .

Margaret listened, and when he fell silent, questioned. She listened for an hour or more before the irony of it came to her. Across the table Josie sat by the open window, silently knitting, and hearing—related casually, in a whim of friendliness, for the ear of a girl—the story of those years which for her had been years of doubt, of not knowing, and of a fading pain that now pulsed again, a bitter burning.

Margaret looked up at the alarm clock and was suddenly anxious to get away. She said, "It's getting late; I'll have to be going."

Anse went with her to the door and stepped out, closing it behind them. The soft night was almost as light as dusk, the Channel luminous.

Standing by the door, Anse laughed and said, "You'll be safe, will you?" in faint intimate mockery.

She laughed. "Oh, I think so," and started toward the gate.

A light shone in Katens' house, but none in the store, and there was no sign of Lon or Buff, or old Felix. Alan walked up the road. He had walked the woods aimlessly without admitting any purpose to his own mind; but when the lighted windows of Josie Gordon's house came in sight round the turn, it was like the reaching of a goal. He slowed, wondering on what pretext he could go in, and then heard the closing of the back door, and laughter.

Indistinguishable words, and Margaret's voice: "Oh, I think so . . ." He saw Anse turn and re-enter the house, the tall figure outlined in lamplight.

Margaret was moving across the front of the house, toward the path. He went up the path to meet her.

She halted, startled. "Oh — it's you."

He faced her silently, his nerves tight with a black unreasoning anger, the check-rein of caution ravelled at last. Margaret half turned toward him, silently questioning. He did not try to speak. His right hand closed hard round her bared left arm between elbow and shoulder.

For a moment, quietly, he shook her, moving the fist that gripped her arm in short savage thrusts like those of a fighter panting against the body of his foe. She made at first no movement of defence at all, letting her body jolt to the thrust of his arm. Then her free hand came up and closed over the hard sinews of his wrist. Her small figure steadied. She looked him in the face.

The look and the touch . . . He found himself looking into a face in which there was neither fear nor anger. What he saw there incredibly was understanding. Understanding of the fact that the heart and nerves can stand so much, and then . . . That torment can thrive beneath a surface calm with the normal glance of eyes, the usual voice, the small familiar habits. That, sometimes, it is the small thing, irrelevant almost, that will touch to violence the aching deeps of feeling.

The look and the touch . . .

Alan was suddenly conscious of where he was, standing with Margaret in the luminous late dusk of a summer evening on Josie Gordon's path. Conscious of the still shadow of Josie's body between lamp and window, not thirty feet away, before she moved and was gone. Conscious of the soft interminable low-toned sound of the Channel, rising and falling but always low, weaving its faint background to night sounds of farms, and far away, a dog's bark.

He saw the hand on his wrist, the child's hand with short nails and dimpled knuckles. He picked it up, rubbed the knuckles across his mouth, balled it into a fist and tapped it once against his jaw.

On the short walk home neither spoke. Once, their hands touched and Margaret's slipped into his for a moment. There was no shared pressure. It was merely a confirmation.

11

GRANT came through the open shop door and stood for a moment in the yard, brushing his hands. He had just dismantled the raker; haying was finished for another year. He glanced out over the shaven fields, across Frank Graham's to Gordons' where a shadowy sea of browntop and timothy moved in the wind, and had the thought that perhaps he'd started putting the machinery away too early. He would have to talk to Josie and see what she wanted done.

He and Alan or he and the Grahams had always made Josie's hay. Now Anse was supposed to be looking after the place but he hadn't started haymaking or even mentioned it. A small thing, perhaps; there was plenty of time, but Grant felt the need of getting it settled. If he were going to have to work in the hayfield with Anse he wanted it done with. Small things, like unmade hay, were what people noticed and talked about.

As if in answer to his thought, Anse crossed the road as he watched, went through Grahams' yard, climbed the fence and headed across the slope of Grant's lower pasture toward Curries' road. Heading for the inlet and the boat. Watching him, Grant felt again all the dark dislike, a numbness, that stretched his nerves whenever he saw Anse Gordon near or far.

Well, this was a chance to see Josie. He closed the shop door and headed for the road.

Josie was sitting on her back steps, shelling peas. Grant dropped to the step beside her, picked a handful of pods from the basket and began absently to split them, forcing the green pellets out with his thumb. She looked up at him sharply once and returned placidly to her shelling.

He gestured at the fields. "How about it, Mrs. Josie? The hay?"

She said, "Anse claims he and the Katens are making it, together."

Grant said, "That's all right, then. I didn't know."

He sensed a little awkwardness in the silence that followed; he was thinking of what to say, how to spin the visit out a little,

358

how to get up and leave without being abrupt. Josie settled it for him.

She said, "It's a worrying time for you, Grant. I'm sorry."

He continued to shell peas, feeling out the meaning of her words. They were out of character. Years ago he and she had lived in this house and talked in the most commonplace terms of the events and circumstances and people who were woven into the core of their lives. Commonplace was the word for it — for the outward seeming of their behaviour toward each other and the words they had used. Never that he could remember, except for that moment long ago . . . *There's a girl alive . . . a child, maybe* . . . Never that he could remember, except then, had Josie laid bare to him her heart in speech. Nor he to her. All they had understood, the respect they had for the patient endurance and hard courage they recognized in each other, was overlaid with the common and the casual. Now for some reason of her own Josie was reaching out to him in words.

It was odd that these words should be so ordinary, spoken in so even a tone, placidly flowing out from the commonplace into the realm of feeling. Perhaps because this was so he did not find them shocking. Perhaps it was because of this, and because she was Josie Gordon, that he felt none of the hard refusal with which, years ago, he had met and turned away any attempt, by anyone, to probe this region of his heart.

He said, "Yes, it is, Josie," and then, disarmed a little by her casualness, "Nothing's ever settled, is it?"

She said, "I don't know . . . Settled for a while, maybe. Then some time — you find that what was right a while ago won't stay right. Isn't right now. Has to be fixed some other way."

He turned to look at her, frowning, and tossed the last podful of peas into the pan. An incredible idea came to him. He said harshly, "You're not —"

"No," Josie said. "I'm not thinking Anse Gordon has any claim on . . . Any claim on anyone."

She paused, considering. "In case you thought I might know — I've got no idea. What he plans to do, I mean. What he wants. What he's got in his mind. He might leave this house tomorrow, tonight. Without saying good-bye. And still I wouldn't know."

Despite the quiet voice, Grant caught something of what it cost to say this. Not even an old desertion and the memory of shame could still entirely the call of blood.

Josie went on.

"No. What I'm thinking about . . . It's got nothing to do with Anse. Nothing directly . . . It's something different. Something I think you might give some thought to." She paused for a little. "Does it ever cross your mind that Alan and Margaret are no relation? No relation to each other at all?"

Grant said, "What d'you mean by that?"

Josie set the pan of peas aside. "What I say. No relation. I mean — how would you look at it? What could you do if they started thinking about each other — as a man — and a woman —"

Grant looked at her curiously. He said, slowly and low-voiced, "Josie, you must be crazy."

She was silent, and after a moment Grant said, wonderingly but carefully, as if dealing with the notion of a child, "What in — what in the name of God made you *think* of it? They're brother and sister in their *minds*. Brought up together. How could anything like that? — When they don't even *know*?"

Josie sighed. "Grant, you've been around the Shore a long time, but not as long as I've been. I'll tell you something straight. Alan knows. He's known for years. They both know."

Grant sat without speaking for a minute. It didn't occur to him to doubt Josie. He had never known her to state a conjecture as a fact. For the moment his mind passed by the question with which she had begun the revelation. The fact of Alan's knowledge was all it could hold. Not, oddly, the fact of that knowledge as it related to the present. That, now, seemed curiously beside the point.

What seared his heart were images out of time past.

The shock to a boy, learning, years ago . . . Learning, how? From one of the Wilmots? From Lon Katen, incautious with rum, probing with words shaped in leering curiosity?

He saw that Josie's hands were shaking slightly. He said, "God damn them all. They couldn't keep . . ."

She interrupted, shaking her head. "No. You can't blame — I'm through blaming, Grant. Long ago. Except for . . . Long as people have tongues in their heads they'll talk. Even decent people. They can't help it."

She hesitated. It had taken will-power to go as far as she had gone. More will-power even than she had been forced to call on, that winter evening years ago when young Alan had come in from the barn with the question in his face. The scene came back to her as vividly as present experience. The question, the careful answer and the careful acceptance.

She said, "He'd heard enough to worry him. Make him wonder. He asked — And it wasn't fair. He had to be told."

Grant's voice was hard.

"Who by?"

Josie waited. A kind of anger was rising in her. She had gone as far as she could go.

"Who by?"

She said, stubbornly, "Not by anybody in your family. Not by Renie."

Grant said, meditatively, as if to himself, "Well, I asked for it. When I let him stay." And then to Josie, "When *was* this?"

She said, a little querulously, "Oh, years ago. When was it he went to Fraser's?"

Grant said, "In 'thirty-three. No, just after New Year's. In 'thirty-four."

"Just before that, then," Josie said.

'Thirty-three. That bitter week came back to him. Katen's lot, and evening talk by the fire, and Renie's warmth as he pulled her close for an instant as she crossed the kitchen; her restlessness and her question.

Did you ever think about how it would be if he heard? . . . If someone started talking?

Days and nights of controlled anger. At life, at the Shore, at circumstance. And then decision. Decision, and a house with the life gone out of it. And then . . . a boy in the stable door with resolution in his face.

Just before that, then . . .

He saw the significance of that but his mind passed quickly from it, teeming with confused memory. He could not quite grasp as a whole, continuing and certain, the fact of Alan's private knowledge. He could not alter in a moment the long convention of unknowing sonship that was a part of his belief. Perhaps, he thought, he would never be able to alter it, really. Would never be able to think of Alan in that time, when he thought of it whole, except as a boy, a son, innocent and ignorant of the story of his birth.

But now specific images began to come. Himself and Alan, stripping and plunging into Graham's Lake, on the way home from the first mill yard out back, on a hot evening in 'thirty-five . . .

Himself and Alan, squatting by the pool they had dammed up in the lower pasture, watching for fingerlings . . .

Himself and Alan.

Behind the laughing yell of shock at the lake's chill, behind the intent face peering down into the pool, there had been that knowledge. A shiver coursed Grant's backbone, and turned the import of his thought.

He had a moment of intense fear. That never in his life would a scene come up clear and sharp out of that vanished time without the shock of strange, fearful embarrassment.

Alan . . . growing out of enthusiastic boyhood into young manhood, controlled and careful, knowing. Grant accepted it with a wondering humility. He said, "I should have been thinking . . . earlier . . ."

Josie had never been clear about that long-ago visit to Halifax, supposed to last a winter and a spring, which had been cut at last to a fortnight. Now she caught a glimpse of the private conflict, a glimpse of something once seen and hardly noticed; understood or partly understood only when remembered now.

I asked for it when I let him stay . . . I should have been thinking, earlier . . .

She caught a hint of the irony. Of Alan learning from hints, gossip, remembered scenes, and from her own lips, finally, the thing he had to know. Learning, almost on the eve of going. And somehow imposing on Grant his will to stay . . .

It was not clear to her. She merely felt the truth. No good telling Grant that whatever it was these two had shared, it was finer than any tie of blood. No good telling him that this, also, was something Alan knew. No good trying to convince Grant that doubts were useless. There were things you couldn't be told, that you had to see for yourself.

She said only, "You did right to let him stay."

Grant said absently, "Perhaps." He added, like an afterthought: "The other thing . . . Margaret . . . What made you think of it? I don't—I can't believe that, Josie."

She shook her head. She knew, but she had done all she could. He would see it, some time.

She said, "P'raps I'm wrong. It was something that seemed likely."

After a little Grant got to his feet. He said, "Thanks, Josie," and walked out through the gate and up the road.

On the road as he walked slowly home his mind went back to deal with the full meaning of Josie's words. He had known. Alan had known, that New Year's Day of 'thirty-four. He had realized this as Josie talked, but his mind had been too concerned with the remembered tensions of that time and with the remorseful embarrassment of images from the years that followed, to consider fully what it meant.

He had known, and he had asked to stay. He had been a son, and more.

I want to work here in the woods, with you; and take grade ten right here, from Renie . . .

That's fine . . . That's what we'll do, then.

Queer how the emphasis could shift from the present . . . Now it was Alan, knowing, in those years before the war. Alan — content, cheerful, enthusiastic, sometimes almost exultant in their shared play and labour. Quiet, controlling his exuberance with a kind of deferential dignity, when they worked with others.

Being a son.

That was of larger importance than anything that faced them now. And he had taken it all for granted, taken for granted the lightness and the warmth, taken it for granted that he alone carried the shadow of that knowledge in his heart.

It was still not clear to him. The thing he had seen as change, the nonchalance, the ease he had thought of as arrogance . . . Since the war, a difference . . . A difference was there. There was still his anger with the present. The questions he had asked his mind about this present Alan, and Anse Gordon, were still unanswered. And this new thing of Margaret, to him incredible. They pressed his mind, still, with a long insistence.

But — there was that time of comradeship and fatherhood, illumined now as something more than it had seemed. More than the thing he had sought to hold. Nothing could take it away.

The past had subtly changed the present. The weight was lifted, the pressure lessened, as if others now walked beside him to share a burden he had considered his alone. He was almost calm.

He turned in at the house. He had a sense of looking at life from the outside, from above, watching the people who were closest to him, and himself among them, going about their work in space and time. For a moment he caught a vision of it. No one person, watching life from his own point of view and his own level, could see the play of act, motive, accident; or hear the multitude of voices. Even when for a moment you were lifted up, became an observer unswayed by personal feeling, all you could see were the act and the sum of the acts. The motives were still obscure. You could only guess.

12

THEY towed the boat out through the inlet entrance on the second evening in August. Anse had painted and patched an old flat of Katens' to serve as a tender, and that afternoon he and Lon had rowed off to drop the anchor and buoy the cable. Now he looped a length of tow rope round the sailboat's pawl-post, put Lon at the oars in the small boat and took the tiller himself. Alan stood amidships, sweep in hand, in case they veered close to the steep rock beaches of the tide-channel.

They took her out at slack tide, avoiding the millstream race of ebb or flow. She moved slowly, Lon holding close to the right bank where the mouth had its fullest depth.

The entrance to Currie Head inlet changes and shifts with the years. In Rob Currie's day they warped the *Star of Egypt* out at high tide in more than two fathoms. Now there is less than five feet of depth, and barely room for row-boats to meet and pass. Gales and tides have worked there. Twenty fathoms off the mouth a sand-bar has built up at a diagonal, so that a boat leaving the sheltered water for the Channel must veer to port, easterly. Lon lengthened his stroke as the tow slipped into this final reach. Just as they passed the end of the sand-spit, lipped by a lazy swell, Alan felt the slight roll of the Channel gently heaving the slowly gliding hull.

The feel of it stirred him with memory and with something new, a sheer physical pleasure, a kind of power. He had been on rolling water often, in small boats owned by Richard McKee. And again in troop-ships. Never in a craft of this size: small, a plaything compared with the smallest steamer you could think of, but belonging to a grander company than dory or flat. Built to move on marching water, under sail, beyond the range of oars . . .

He pulled his sweep inboard and steadied himself with a hand on the main shrouds, glancing up at the bare masts, swaying gently with the sway of the Channel, as Lon rowed to the anchorage.

Anse said "All right, Lon," went forward and hauled the buoy in. There was almost no wind; the boat swung gently, head to the onshore swell, barely tightening the slack of the buoyed cable. Lon climbed over the washboards and made the flat's painter fast to a thwart.

Anse had not planned to give the boat a try-out until the following forenoon when they could expect the usual summer southwesterly. But as they sat there in a moment of silence before making a move to go ashore, the Channel began to stir and patch and darken under a land-breeze from the north. Anse grinned and began to take the lashings off the mainsail. He said, "Hell, let's see . . . We can row her back if it dies . . ."

He watched while Lon and Alan ran up the old tanned jib and the bright new mainsail. Lon transferred the hitch of the mooring to the flat, and hoisted the foresail as Anse put the boat on a reach out toward the inner edge of the Rocks, more than two miles southeast.

Anse laughed. The wind was the barest breeze, and fitful. He said, a little contemptuously, "Weather for yachts." But excitement stirred in him. The excitement of having done it, of having resurrected this derelict hull and patched and rigged and painted it into a thing that sailed, as he had said he would. And there were other excitements . . .

East of Frank Graham's beach he gybed round, beckoned Alan aft, gave him the tiller, and sat beside him on the coping of the stern cuddy. The breeze had freshened slightly. It would die with darkness, but there was enough of it now to keep the boat footing steadily, even as she was headed, partly into the wind. Anse said, "Keep her off a little; we'll take her up the Channel a bit." He eased the sheets.

But he said little. His instructions to Alan were in the hunch of a shoulder, the gesture of a hand. One of the elements in his excitement was that this was all Alan needed. This, and experience. The boy had the feel of it.

There was something in this hour on the Channel that heightened momentarily in Anse his sense of power. This was a feeling he needed now. It was four weeks since his return. The sensation of that was dying out, was almost dead. If he stayed the fall, stayed the winter, Anse Gordon would be taken for granted, merely another person who lived on the Shore, like Dave Stiles, Alec Neill, Frank Graham, Lon Katen . . . absorbed by the Shore itself.

He grunted. He had been plagued lately, thinking of that . . . the dull . . . the commonplace . . . He had been plagued by impulse. To say his say, or have it said; to break the shell round the Marshalls, round the McKees, and look at the wreckage, and go . . .

That was the temptation. But there was that other thing, that further ambition . . . Alan was still casual, still friendly, a neighbour's son. Interested in what you were doing, for the sake of the friendliness and the fun he could have, sometimes, in doing it with you. But never the dropped word to tell you he would welcome, if not the public knowledge, the personal understanding . . .

Anse was cunning. Given that understanding, the rest would come. But he could not bring himself to take the risk of a personal approach. Not yet.

The nearest he had come to it, to the necessary resolution, was after a drink or two in Katens' kitchen. Lately he had been going to the bottle oftener than usual. But in the end he had always counselled himself to patience, the need to wait.

Now, tonight, for reasons no more definite than the slight lurch of a boat on gently swaying water, a hand on a tiller, an eye on the luff of a mainsail . . . Well, if the time were to come at all . . . he could feel the time approach . . .

Alan rowed the flat the hundred fathoms in from the anchorage with Anse and Lon squatted aft. They hauled the small boat up on the Channel side of the beach and turned to walk home by way of the neck and the pastures.

He considered lightly a curious thing. Everything he had learned on the water with Richard, years ago, was still there. It wasn't much, perhaps . . . And he knew that an hour or two in a light breeze in the company of knowledgeable men had little relation to the reflexive readiness you would have to develop, a second nature, if you wanted to handle yourself in different kinds of weather, in all kind of boats. But, despite the tiredness of his mind, despite his growing dislike for Anse, he felt something for the boat and the water; a liking, a kind of aptitude, akin to what he had felt the first time Grant had let him run the carriage up to the whirling saw.

His thought drifted. Anse was talking. "Y'know, they still make a go of it, over on the Island side and through the channels, on the Atlantic shore. With a boat this size, put an engine in her — oh, eight, ten horse-power—a man could try the Channel again. Or go through and live in a hut, summers, on the Atlantic side . . ."

Anse was talking gently, not directly to either, but the words wakened in Alan's mind the old nagging sense of something at the back of memory, waiting for recall. It came to him, finally, with a sense of tingling shock: Grant's words, in the kitchen on a winter evening years ago . . . *If a fellow had a portable mill, a diesel outfit, he could set up in there, a place like that . . .*

As he turned to go up through The Place, Anse halted.

"Not coming down?"

"Later, maybe," Alan said. "I've got to call in home first."

As usual he had been going down to Katen's a couple of nights a week, to keep up the pattern of the usual and to keep his contact with Buff. Buff's nightly exposure to the atmosphere of Anse Gordon and Lon Katen together was something he did not like. Buff and he could create a climate of their own.

But tonight he was not going to Felix Katen's in company with Anse Gordon. There was something he wanted first. The sight of Renie, Grant, Margaret. The smell of the kitchen. The sound of the clock ticking in The Room. The feel of home.

13

HIGH summer lay along the Channel Shore. Still early August, but a ripeness coloured the daylight, a thin invisible smoke; and at night the shadows of hills came earlier down, flowing into evening and warm darkness, touched by the faint chill of the sea.

Dust rose in the wake of cars and hung in wavering veils and settled, a fine tan film, dimming the yellow blaze of ragweed in the gutters and in pastures by the road.

Haying was nearly done. The fields were a shaven yellowish grey, green-speckled, patched variously by the darker shades of oats and root crops. Back of the shore, in the cuttings, the brush and tops of last year's cut were brownish red, and through the skeleton branches of earlier chopping, young raspberry canes wove their lush low canopy of leaves.

Grant walked slowly out of the mill yard and down the hauling-road to the highway. Adam Falt should be along soon; he would get a ride home with Adam.

He had gone to the yard simply to look around, checking on things, as he usually did two or three times a week when the mill was idle—to keep an eye on the place. He was walking today because Renie had taken the car to Morgan's Harbour; he refused to put a truck on the road to save a three-and-a-half-mile walk.

No hurry, anyway. He hunched on the bank of the road and rolled a smoke. It was curious, but in these last few days, since his talk with Josie Gordon, his mind had drifted in a kind of sorrowful serenity. This in itself was a puzzling thing. It would have been understandable, he thought, if Josie's words had multiplied the torment. This was not so. Except for isolated moments when fear or anger caught him, or that strange tingling remorse, he had been more at ease in these last few days than at any time in months.

Far more at ease than during those years between Dieppe and Hitler's fall . . . A thought came to him unbidden as his mind moved to that time of waiting, when every phone call and every telegram had chilled his flesh with fear. If Alan had not come back . . . There would be no doubts now, no fear, no searching of the future. He shook the grim thought away with black contempt. No doubts and no fears, only an aching emptiness, a sharing of death.

Adam Falt slowed and stopped. As Grant settled in the seat beside him, Adam said, "Hot . . . You're not back t'work yet, eh?"

Grant shook his head. "No; Sam and Wilmots've still got some hay to make. And Lon Katen, at Gordons' . . . Not much use starting before the Holiday. We'll get going next week, I guess."

Adam nodded. He said thoughtfully, "Gordons'," and then, curiously, "What d'you think that fellow's got in his mind? Stay here? . . . I s'pose nobody knows."

Grant laughed, faint derision in his voice. "Did anybody, ever? Even Anse?"

Adam said, "No, I guess not. All you could count on was some kind of devilment. Well . . ."

He dropped it, his voice on the "Well . . ." drifting into a kind of resigned finality, recognition that there were things and people nothing could be done about.

Adam had spoken naturally, Grant thought. Once he himself had mentioned the Gordons, it would have been obvious, an avoidance, if Adam hadn't come up with a question, a speculation about Anse. And Adam's way of dealing with that small situation was the way of the Shore. Concerned with his own apprehensions, Grant hadn't thought much about that, the rough tact, the common consideration . . . The thought of this now blended with the humility he felt.

The car rounded Gordons' turn. Hay lay bundled in the house field, but the rack stood by the barn, its shafts down. Gone to the beach again, Grant supposed — Anse and Lon Katen and Alan.

Thinking this, he felt again the flush of involuntary anger. Natural enough for Alan to help out with Josie's hay. Grant had suggested it himself, on the pretext that it would hurry the job, get Lon and Buff free earlier and perhaps make it possible to get back to sawing a day or two sooner than otherwise. But why he should follow them round to the beach, the boat . . .

Adam stopped by Grant's gate. He said, "Thanks, Adam; so long, now," and turned in as the car pulled away.

Margaret lay on the veranda swing, reading. She rose and went into the house as Grant came up the steps. She said indifferently, "Renie's not back yet; I'll start getting supper." Their glances crossed for a fraction of a second and slipped away in a curious conscious avoidance.

Some part of every day, it seemed, Anse must spend aboard the boat. Always there was a piece of gear to be replaced or some small repair job that served to justify a journey to the beach. He had shaped new rowlocks and nailed them to the washboards, shaved new thole-pins, fitted loops under the washboards to secure the old sweeps which would never be used except to work the boat through the inlet mouth.

This afternoon he and Lon were replacing with metal pulleys the wooden blocks Stewart Gordon had once used to take his running rigging. Alan was working aft, fitting into the cuddy a sliding panel of thin pine. Something close to childishness in some of the things they were doing, he thought. There had been a fascination in watching Anse take this abandoned hull and convert it into a thing of grace and life. Despite what the Shore might think and say of waste time and useless effort, that had been worth while, a novel, original thing. But now Anse was going a bit beyond that. Puttering. There was something — "forced" was the word Alan thought of — something forced in the trivial excuses Anse found to take him to the boat.

He had been drawn into this, himself, with increasing reluctance. But he was handy with his hands, a craftsman. If Anse asked you to do something, as any neighbour might, how could you refuse? How could you avoid it without making a point of avoidance?

He slid the panel back and forth, clicked into its staple the small brass hook that secured it, and turned on the thwart to glance ashore. No wind stirred; the floats of Alec Neill's salmon net scarcely moved; the Channel was dark fluent glass, barely breathing in a slight long-drawn suggestion of a swell, moving in, unrippled, to lip the beach without breaking and almost without sound.

He saw that Alec was limping down the hump of the beach with Richard McKee. Richard had hauled his herring nets but had been lending Alec a hand with the salmon. He reflected that it must be past supper-time. Alec was about to make his evening trip to the net. Time, he thought with impatience, to be getting ashore. Anse was speaking.

". . . don't trim quite right. Need more rocks into her, for'ard. . . . Come on, Lon . . ."

Anse slid overboard into the flat. "Just hoist the mainsail, see how things run, Alan, will you? Be back in a minute or two."

Part of the peculiar picture, Alan thought. Ballast-rocks for ballast, when the boat, on the Holiday, would be ballasted with people . . . and that off-hand assumption, like giving orders.

He pulled the sail up, heaving on the halyards with arms and body, made sure that everything ran freely through the blocks, and let the canvas down and brailed it and repeated this for foresail and jib. He could hear the sound of oars in the flat's rowlocks, and then voices from the shore and the faint sound of stones being piled in the bottom of the flat. After a little he turned and saw that Anse was rowing back alone. Lon had squatted on his heels, talking to Richard and Alec.

Anse came alongside and tossed the smooth stones aboard. He climbed into the boat and stood on the ballast, an arm hooked round the foremast. For a moment, frowning, he watched the Islands. Idle on the main thwart, Alan was transfixed with a sharp discomfort, a sense of time in precarious balance. He had a feeling . . . Anse was on the point of speech, on the verge of words for which there could be no reply . . . At length Anse made an indistinguishable sound as though touched by some obscure anger. He turned abruptly, and edged overside into the stern of the flat. He said shortly, "All right. We'll go ashore. You row her in."

As they slid in toward the beach on the almost imperceptible swell, Alan was touched by memory. A distant summer, and the row in from the nets with Richard. Richard had always let him do the rowing; he remembered now the feel of booted heels, slipping through slithering fish to find a brace against the timbers. And how when the southwesterly was up Richard would lean forward from his seat on the after thwart as they neared the beach, and put his hands on the oars and help him square away for a landing.

He had a feeling in which anger and fear and a sorrowful desperation met and blended, and which he told himself was simply a sick imagining. This was, that Anse Gordon was staging now, for Richard and Alec, a scene of casual relationship.

14

By two o'clock in the afternoon of the second Saturday in August the Holiday had begun. Most people from up and down the Shore left their cars and trucks at Grant Marshall's or down Curries' road at Rob's Yard, and walked across the neck to the grounds. Others drove down Alec Neill's road to the shore, following the practice of long ago when half a dozen boats had been berthed at landings in the inlet. For families from the schoolhouse road and places other than The Head, the row across was part of the day, but now only Alec and Richard kept boats there. Bill Graham and Dan were rowing these back and forth, ferrying newcomers round the tide-covered clam-beds to the beach.

As Grant crossed his pasture with Renie they could hear shouts of laughter and see the colour of Sunday dresses through the fringe of spruce around the picnic grounds. One of the row-boats moved out from the near shore, loaded with Wilmots. Dan was at the oars.

Renie said, "It's nice, you know. Isn't it?"

She was walking slightly ahead. Her voice called Grant's mind back from aimless speculation. There she was, moving ahead of him, in white shirt and black slacks, sure-footed on the path. He had a moment of insight: these last weeks of preoccupation and silence had been an injustice to Renie. His mind flashed to another time when he had barred her away from the things that filled his thought. That time had ended. Excitement stirred . . .

Excitement . . . the word was too strong. It was more a sense of expectancy, tingling and provocative. Accept it and wait. In the meantime there was Renie. He stepped up beside her, closing his fingers briefly round her upper arm.

"Yes, it *is* nice," he said reflectively. "This picnic's been going on for eighty years or more."

"What?"

Grant's brief laugh acknowledged the surprise in Renie's voice. Surprise, not at the continuity of a common festival, but at Grant's knowledge of this and interest in it.

"So Bill Graham says. He dug it out of Frank. Somebody—a man named Macnab—started holding a picnic here every year when school closed for the summer. A teacher, Macnab was. Frank would've gone to school to him, I s'pose. It started that way, then sort of grew to take in anybody that wanted to come, and finally got shoved over into August . . . Bill gets a kick out of things like that. When he was here years ago, a kid, he used to talk about this place, ours. It was in the Graham family once, you know. Fanny's Farm. That kind of thing . . ."

Renie said, "Because his father moved away. That's all. You don't think of roots when they're under your feet."

"That's right, I s'pose." Renie's easy-going mind was sharp. He had always known this, but it never ceased to please him. He walked on beside her, letting the casual intimacy have its way. His mind moved lightly on Bill Graham and Bill's occasional interest in the past.

The past, beyond his own memory, was something he did not much consider. There had been a time when early memory . . . a voice, another voice, and green plush in gaslight . . . had woven round him a consciousness, tantalizing and contradictory; a web of possession, from which he had escaped, and a veil of doubt, of unsatisfied wonder . . . The web he had smashed himself. The wonder had been satisfied, in a curious hour on the beach, by Richard McKee . . . alders back of the school-house, herring in William Freeman's mushrat traps . . . and young Harve . . .

In continuity, when it didn't trap you, there was something, a warmth, that people like Bill Graham searched the past for, taking an obscure and private pride in their knowledge of it. Something akin to the thing Richard had given him, talking, years ago, beside a load of eel-grass . . .

Thinking of Bill, his mind played with that evening when he had sat by Hugh Currie's back steps, listening to old Hugh talk of Rob Currie and Fanny Graham . . . He and young Bill, going on into the clearing, the beginnings of The Place, and Anna coming down to talk . . . and Uncle James . . . Far away in time, but clear now in memory when you thought of it. Action . . . action had kept these images far from the surface of his mind, except as something to be acknowledged and stored in a shadowy attic rarely entered. And yet now he could see the flushed pleasure in Anna's face, feel again, though almost impersonally, as if for a moment he looked back through the mind of someone else, the thrill of her observed movement, the full-breasted supple body on the balsam stump . . . the rising fear at the sound of James Marshall's footsteps on the twigs of the path.

It seemed to Grant, and the realization puzzled him, that somewhere in these images there was a message for him, a clarification. Woven into the sorrowful serenity . . . His mind found an ancient cliché: It'll all be the same in a hundred years. But there was something more than that, something that eluded him.

Expectancy . . . This was in some way concerned with the way in which his mind had turned—consciously in these last few days, but how long had it been turning thus in the shadowy reaches of the unrealized?—to the long, the unknown past; and reawakened as something you could observe and feel, a part of the living scene rather than something dim and done with, personally hoarded and hidden, the nearer past of his own youth, the awakening and the pain.

There was something too that Bill Graham had said, recently, that nagged at his mind. Something he had only half listened to, his thoughts concerned with other things. This too was part of the expectancy. In time it would come to him.

He circled Renie's arm with his fingers again, briefly, as they climbed the incline of the inner beach to the picnic grounds. The Head's younger married women were already laying white oilcloth on plank tables. He heard Lola Marshall's casual voice, "Let's get it done; there's a sail coming; we won't get a chance when they start to eat." The older women, Stella Graham, Christine Currie, Eva McKee, Jane Marshall, were relieved of work today. They rustled about, a matriarchal reception committee, to welcome people from up and down the Shore, uttering small cries as they embraced or shook hands with visitors home from the States, smiling down at children whose first names were confused in their minds.

Along the beach, squatting with their backs to the grounds, middle-aged and older men rested in the sun, a little uncomfortable in Sunday suits on a Saturday. Unmarried men, and boys and girls, had gathered in two groups, constantly changing, one at the eastern edge of the grounds where the boys were rigging a swing, the other up the beach a little, toward Hugh Currie's disused fish hut. Bill Graham and Buff Katen had built a stone hearth there. Buff had hung his jacket on a small spruce. He was bending now to strap the tops of hip-length rubber boots round his thighs.

Grant stopped to speak to Frank Graham and Renie went on toward the tables. Bill came toward her from the direction of the swing, dusting off his hands.

More than eighty years, Grant had said. She was caught up for a moment by a sense of life and movement all around her, blending with things that happened long ago.

374

There had been a near-drowning once, in the time of the sailboat races. Renie remembered hearing about that even across the Channel at Princeport. The Currie Head Holiday was something known . . . For a moment she was lifted out of the present, seeing this day in the time of the Shore's prosperity . . . A hundred and fifty, two hundred people, gathered by boat and buggy, on horseback and on foot . . . The boats of the mackerel fleet, kept in gear after the spring run was over, for just this day . . . Joe Currie's green whale-boat, Fritz McKee's white craft with the knockabout bow, Anselm Gordon's ancient sloop . . . The flagged keg five miles southwest, on a bearing opposite the Upper Islands . . . the beat out to the mark and the run home off the wind . . . The boats loaded with children, youngsters filled with a kind of dour pride in the leathery men who squatted aft, tiller under elbow . . . Other youngsters, from the back roads, shivering a little in the bluster of wind, ducking in fright under a gybing boom, feeling the living lift and surge of an element strange to their habit and their blood. Ashore, women with aprons over satin dresses . . . Bread and butter, leopard cake, chocolate cake, sponge cake, frosted cake studded with red, yellow and green sugar-pellets, Washington pie dusted with pulverized sugar, with a filling of strawberry preserves, fresh blueberries picked from the barrens north of Findlay's Bridge . . . Boys on the clam-beds, their pant legs rolled to the crotch, plying manure-forks . . .

If a person could be given the eye to see . . . One day out of each year would be enough, back to the beginning . . . The Holiday or a Sunday service or a church supper around Christmas time. Given that sort of clairvoyance you could see the story of the Shore. And yet, what differed, across a hundred and fifty years? Horses and saddles, once; buggies later; and now flivvers, jalopies. Hand-made leather boots and homespun, then. Tweed now, from the mail-order houses. And always faces. Faces that didn't change, really, though worn by different people in different generations . . .

Renie started, then realized that the whole of her small dream had taken no time at all. Bill hadn't even noticed her preoccupation. He was looking over his shoulder at Grant, moving back to follow him. She heard Frank Graham's voice expressing good-naturedly his opinion of picnics.

"Not an honest mouthful in the lot. It's enough to turn you inside out. Cake and clams . . ."

Bill turned to grin back at her.

Frank was standing on turf matted with brown spruce needles under the fringe of trees that edged the grounds, looking across the slope of the Channel beach.

"He's got her laying where the whale-boats used to anchor . . . in the open, but good ground. Bottom's soft around east of the Head. Never gets rough from the sou'-west, though, and the Rocks breaks the easterlies. Stewart and me fished together, the two years he sailed that boat. Everybody else had the sense to quit. The last good run was in nineteen-eight. We kept after them, Alec and Richard, Hugh, some of the rest, till, oh, 'sixteen, 'seventeen. You'd get enough to salt down maybe a half-barrel. Couple've dozen a day, no more. Stewart wouldn't believe they was through. Built her in the spring of 'sixteen. Well, I couldn't see him go it alone. We never landed a damn fish in two years. Not one. It finished even Stewart. He hauled her up to the barn . . ."

The wind by this time had settled into the steady pulsing blow of summer afternoons, a sailing breeze. The Channel marched deliberately against the beach, wave following wave in deceptively gentle rhythm, curling and crumbling on loose smooth stone and flat sand. There was a continual splash, a liquid ringing in the sound as it came to the ears of Grant and Frank and Bill, standing on the level selvage of the Head, under old and twisted spruce.

Grant noticed, as a flat pulled away from the anchored sailboat, that there was a good deal of authority in this marching water. It was taking oarsmanship to straighten the swaying flat away for the beach. He saw that the one at the oars was Alan.

This was no surprise. None the less it startled Grant to see him rowing ashore from Anse Gordon's boat, with Anse squatted in the stern and Lon Katen hunched in the bow. For a moment the familiar controlled anger flushed through him, the alienation, the black tormenting doubt . . .

Lon Katen splashed into the wash at the shore's edge as the flat touched. They came up the slope of the beach, heavy-footed in rubber boots over smooth stone.

Lon grunted "Frank, Grant," as they went on into the grounds. Anse had a wordless half-sneer for them all. Alan said, "Hi, Bill," and turned his head as he passed to grin at Grant and Frank. Grant's moment of anger faded. He was feeling the quiet expectancy again, ruling his nerves. He thought, or fancied, he could see something secret in Alan's look, something regretful, tense and private and almost amused.

In the grounds a dozen youngsters gathered round Anse and Lon and Alan, waiting, their chatter stilled.

Frank said, "Used to be quite a thing. The back road kids . . . half scared to put a foot in a sailboat, but crazy to try it. I remember . . ."

Grant noted idly the youngsters waiting for the word of invitation or selection—Lol Kinsman's boy and girl, Beryl and Jack; one of the Lisles from up Leeds way; Harry Neill's young Alec, home visiting his grandfather; Hester Falt, Adam's grand-daughter, from The Bridge; Stan Currie's young Duncan . . . As usual, holding himself aloof and alone, Skimp Wilmot.

Anse was talking, his manner and voice combining in a controlled careless swagger. "We'll make a couple of trips, out to somewhere near where the old mark was, and back. Women and kids first trip . . ." He began naming them over. "It'll take three trips in the flat, anyway, to get you all aboard. Alan, you start with the young ones, and I'll go out with you and come back for the women. I don't trust Lon with no one."

Anse grinned, and Grant marvelled at the ease with which that face, lined with half a century of self-will, could smooth itself into a laughing mask of innocence.

The boys and girls were gathering round Alan, all but Skimp Wilmot. Even in that moment, before Alan spoke, Grant began to feel the small heart's-thunder of revelation. The swing . . . the trailing rope . . . the laughter in Anna's face . . . the half-impatient lilt of her voice . . .

Hey, Tarsh! Make yourself useful, kid. Give us a hand!

Alan shooed the youngsters toward the landing with a gesture. He turned casually. He called, "Hurry up, Skimp. What you waiting for?" and batted Skimp Wilmot lightly on the back of the head as the kid limped past him toward the flat.

Margaret had persuaded Renie out of the house with Grant and remained behind to pack a basket of pies and follow. She waited, sitting quietly in the kitchen, the packed basket on the table, until they had time to cross the pastures and turn down Currie's road. She picked up the pies then and closed the kitchen door behind her.

With the action of walking, thought began to flow. She was looking forward to this afternoon almost with dread. The laughter, the conviviality, the necessity of joining in, of thinking up banter, of sitting in an inverted oxbow, face to face with Syd Kinsman or Bun Laird . . . Letting yourself be swung between two swaying trees, with boys at the ropes putting in a jerk, now and then, and expected to squeal when they did it . . . Walking arm in arm on the beach with Beulah or Grace Freeman or some cousin or other from Leeds or The Bridge . . . Trying to find words, words that sounded natural . . . While all the while, all you wanted to do was work and wait.

There was no real sense of uncertainty in Margaret's mind. Ever since she had talked with Richard she had been able to imagine as something real and possible the shape of the future she lived for. But now and then, in spite of the patience she had begun to learn, in spite of the curious sense of peace she had experienced listening to Josie Gordon, in spite of the exultant reassurance she had felt in Alan's violence on Gordon's path . . . Now and then in spite of this it angered her that what she wanted must be brought about by the slow steps of time, of life unfolding in an unhurried slowly-changing pattern of days and nights and common acts and ordinary words. What she hoped for, perversely, then, was the swift stroke of drama—to tear away this web of wrongs half-forgotten and sacrifice cherished in illusion. What ought to be—she started at recognition of the wish that was in her: the thought that freedom would be whole, complete and fully satisfying, only if it came through one person, through Alan, through Alan's act, voluntary, complete and final.

She felt at this a flush of shame, remembering the truth that she herself had recognized. There was no reasoned course that he or she could take to sudden freedom without accepting the responsibility of betrayal.

Well . . . When would the waiting end? Margaret damned herself for the coloured detail of imagination and desire her mind achieved.

She walked on, across the bridge over the little branch of Graham's Brook that Grant had dammed, and on across the neck and up the inlet beach, to turn in at the grounds.

Lola Marshall, distributing knives and forks along white oilcloth, said cheerfully, "Hello, Marg'ret; time you got here." Margaret smiled shyly. Her glance ran over the older women who, after the early fluster of welcome and reunion, had settled down to talk on benches in the shade, and the six or seven others who were setting tables or waiting to be taken out to the boat.

The girls of her own age were grouped round the swing, waiting their turn, and laughing at the ones already aloft, or had paired off to sit in the sun or roam the beach.

From the corner of her eye she saw Buff plod up from the inlet shore, his rubber boots glistening, a pail of clams in one hand. She heard the small rumble of clams as he dumped them into

378

the pot over the fire. Already a group of loungers from down-shore, Mars Lake and The Pond, people she recognized only by sight, were hanging around the fire waiting to scoop opened clams from the steaming brew. If she strolled up that way Buff would detach himself; they would wander up the beach, away from this clamour of people who laughed at nothing, who had nothing on their minds but cake and clams and talk; who could enjoy these things, take pleasure in the feel of wind and sun, the sound of the sea.

The idea of such an escape was pleasant. Escape from the necessity of attention, politeness, banter, when your mind needed freedom to deal with its own concerns. She was suddenly conscious that someone had been speaking to her. She looked up, flustered. "What?" Sam Freeman's wife laughed. "Hand me the bread knife behind you, will you, Marg'ret? . . . If it's a nice dream, tell *me*." Margaret flushed, angry with herself. She forced the lightness of a laugh, a shaken head: "Just half-asleep, for some reason."

Mrs. Freeman said, casually provocative: "He's not worth losing your night's sleep over, whoever he is."

Margaret thought, *"God*—I ought to get out of this." But told herself at once she was being morbidly irritable. She continued, mechanically, slicing pie. Momentary escape, wandering the beach, was not enough.

Through the fringe of spruce she could see a flat-load of kids, with Alan rowing, tossing rhythmically as it neared the sailboat. Snatches of talk were blown back across the water, and the faint small rattle of shipped oars . . .

Despite the uneasiness he could not help, now, at the look and voice of Anse Gordon, Alan felt a swift excitement, the lift of a new thing, as the boat sliced to windward. Anse had picked a bearing, the far white speck of the Fisherman's Church on Little Upper, and beckoned him aft to the tiller. There was in this, perhaps, something of the thing he feared and for which he had no defence. Identification. A subtle, public establishment of something that linked him through the boat to Anse. But this for the moment was almost lost in the feel of the thing itself, the lift and scend of the hull, the freshness of wet wind, the fluent curve of sailcloth, the march of rolling water. All alive, all becoming part of him in the pull of the tiller along his forearm, alive in his fingers . . .

It was impossible not to feel this. Impossible not to find a sparkling pleasure in the wonderment of children, the foolish engaging chatter of women . . . of all these who lived within sight of salt water but knew nothing of its ways. He caught a glimpse of Hat Wilmot's puzzled face. Most of the older women had declined the offer of a sail, but Hat wouldn't consider herself in the elderly class, he supposed. She was studying the boat's rigging, the drawing sails. Through the screen of sound, the liquid thump and splash of water, the chatter of children, Hat's questioning voice, to Anse: "You mean, that's all there is *to* it? The wind *pushes* it along?" Alan grinned. It was a story he would never tell. No one would believe.

Pleasant, in moments caught from studying the mark, studying the draw of jib and foresail and mainsail, to watch the faces of boys and girls. Boys and girls who had perhaps rowed around the inlet in Alec Neill's flat, but who were feeling now for the first time the lift and sway of the Channel, hearing the faint creak of wood and wind-strained stays, sensing under sail the buoyancy of moving water that stretched under cloud and sun to the coast of Spain.

They were growing up, these, in a generation in which swift travel was the usual thing. Travel by truck and car, up and down the road, to Copeland or The Harbour—journeys that thirty years ago, before the Model-T had altered living, would have been unusual—such travel was no longer novel now. What *was* new and strange was this return for a day to a vanished common-place. Alan could see it in the faces of even the most insensitive, as white specks on the blue shapes of the Islands grew into small white blocks of houses, set in green and brown squares between the low white line of surf and the high shawl of woods. He could hear it in the excitement of voices, see it in the abrupt movement of young bodies, turning to watch the home shore recede . . .

He had been holding the boat on her course, a close reach to mid-Channel, for the best part of an hour when Anse began to edge his way along the ballast. He would put her over for a hitch up the Channel and square away for the run home, Alan supposed. Alan gave up the tiller and crouched with a hand in readiness on the main-sheet.

He was not sure of the intention until the thing was done. Anse let the boat fall off until her roll increased, then brought her sharply up. Spray drenched Hat Wilmot and Lola Marshall and Sarah Laird. Once more Anse smacked her into it before he put her over; once more spray fell in a splashing torrent on squealing women . . .

Even if they had known it was deliberate, the women would

have considered it nothing more than a rough joke, Alan supposed. But he had seen the look in Anse's eyes, the faint sneering grin; and knew that behind the eyes was not simple laughter but a queer contemptuous malice, impulsive and yet deliberate.

He knew, too, that Anse was aware of his observation. His own lips curved as though he shared a private dark amusement.

Some of the hungrier picnickers had begun to settle at the tables. The boat, Margaret saw, was shaking out the wind as she came up to her mooring, completing the first trip.

On the hump of the beach she noticed Richard McKee, in overalls and rubber boots. He turned from watching the boat, or the weather, or whatever it was Richard watched, and found himself a squatting-place on the stones. Margaret felt a flicker of warm amusement. It was like Richard to get here late, and not to bother with Sunday clothes, and to be alone. In a minute or two she would stroll out and sit on her feet for a while beside him. Of all this crowd here, he was the only one who knew; and her need today, she realized now, was simply that: companionship with someone you didn't have to play a part for, someone who knew and who did not condemn.

Grant had let the picnic go on around him, paying no heed at all, holding his mind free and still to accept the tide of light.

Anna . . . Anna's careless confidence, Anna's casual good nature and light-heartedness . . . alive again in Alan.

He remembered now what it was . . . the words Bill Graham had said, the words that lurked in memory: *Nobody's a copy of his father . . . All kinds of things get scribbled in, or edited out . . . You can't figure inheritance on a slide rule . . .*

Absently, he saw Lon Katen row ashore with one load of passengers and go back with another. He straightened, realizing that to anyone who might have glanced his way in the last hour he must have seemed a curious figure, lounging alone and silent against a spruce or wandering on the beach. He noticed Richard then, sitting alone on the stones, and walked across to sprawl beside him.

Richard said, "Well, Grant; nice day." The old man had taken a jack-knife from his pocket and was whittling thin shavings from a piece of broken lath he had found among the stones.

Grant watched the flat, doing its slow step-dance on rolling water, again inward-bound from the boat. Anse was at the oars.

Incredible that only an hour or two ago he should have watched the moving flat in anger . . .

An image of Alan, born of the memory of Anna, lighted by words unheeded and now remembered . . . This was reality. Strange that a memory so old and small, that words so common . . . Or was it merely that these were the mind's clues, the opening out of an inner atmosphere of light, the light he had glimpsed, listening to Josie Gordon—the light that must have risen eventually, under any circumstances, to end the darkness of his fear?

There was something else . . .

Alan and Margaret.

It was something he had to think about.

He leaned on an elbow, shielding a match from the wind, and glanced toward the grounds, his eyes seeking Margaret.

Margaret turned to see what further chore she could do at the tables. Someone had persuaded Renie and Edith Kinsman to make a pair on the swing while they waited for Anse. The boys on the ropes were driving the oxbow a little higher than usual. She could hear Edith's laugh as it rose, and the faint creak of chain, and see the slow short arc of the spruce tops swaying to the weight of the swing.

There was no hurry now. At any moment she could go to Richard. She looked back, then, and felt her heart thump with surprise. Grant was sprawled in the spot she had promised herself. He was half turned toward the grounds, talking to Richard and lighting his pipe while he leaned on an elbow. As she looked, he lifted his head and his glance caught hers.

For a moment their glances brushed, the embarrassed self-conscious stares of strangers when eyes lock by chance. The look they had been avoiding for days and weeks . . .

As Grant felt the beginning of that half-antagonistic, half-polite withdrawal, he knew what he would do. Before his mind had dealt with the matter he had sprawled beside Richard to think about, it had reached an answer. Communication. He would ask Margaret for the truth. Not now, but when chance offered. In token of faith, of unconscious promise, he smiled. He saw withdrawal crumble, in the slight forward thrust of her body, the parting of her lips.

It was a strange thing, but now that knowledge filled his mind, now that doubt of Alan was like the memory of delirium, the other thing was almost academic. He did not yet believe Josie

Gordon's surmise. But if it were true . . . if it were true . . . He could look at this possibility with no trace of the dread the mere thought of it had wakened in him. If it were true then Alan could be his son no longer. The thing was ended, the long relationship cut—as surely as if the boy had turned in fealty to Anse Gordon.

The long relationship and the long threat. This was something he had lived with throughout Alan's lifetime and more than half his own—the most-vital thing he had ever known. And yet now, considering this, he had a feeling of irrelevancy. In the face of his faith in Alan's stature as a man, he could find in nothing else, not even fatherhood itself, a sense of urgency.

On his way down to the landing, Anse halted and spoke to Richard and Grant.

"Well, this trip we're taking men."

Richard, meditatively chewing a shaving, said idly, "Think I'll stay ashore, Anse."

Anse looked down at Grant, sardonic and questioning. Grant met the look. Now for the first time he could consider Anse Gordon with no thought of caution, no thought for the necessity of maintaining a careful friendliness. His stare was brief and cold and indifferent. He turned away and reached for one of Richard's shavings.

Anse wheeled and went down to the landing.

Richard watched the loaded flat lurch out to the sailboat and realized that his only interest in all this was curiosity on a point of craftsmanship. He said, half to himself, ". . . stay ashore. But I want to see how those sails set."

That was all. He could remember the days when he and Frank Graham and Hugh Currie had haunted this beach as children, while their fathers—Fritz, Old Frank, Joe Currie—loaded their whale-boats and sailed off on the spring trip to L'Ardoise. And later days when he and Fritz had fished the Channel here, and after that, he and Hugh.

Picnics . . . There was one day, the day old Fritz had said he was through running an excursion boat for the back road crowd. Richard had taken the whale-boat out, with Hugh . . . That was the day his eyes had first fallen on Eva Laidlaw. Eva, down from Morgan's Harbour in tight-waisted black satin with close-set cloth-covered buttons down the front of her, serene and assured on the thwart, braced against the foremast, swaying slightly against him in the lurch of sea . . . The images were clear and clean; old, and as new as present experience. He had no wish, Richard found, to add to those images of days long gone an hour or two in Anse Gordon's sailboat.

As the boat headed up he could not tell whether what he heard was the actual snap of canvas, audible over the slow wash of sea at the shore's edge, or sound remembered . . . Richard sighed. Until he had put shears into Anse Gordon's sailcloth he hadn't even seen the cutting of a suit of sails in nearly thirty years. He watched now as Anse held his boat on the wind, feeling for some mark on the Islands. Everything seemed to draw.

Grant had risen and walked off toward the fire. Richard rose and sauntered after him.

The gaiety had gone out of it, Alan thought, as Anse brought the boat around for the run home to the anchorage. Anse had handled her himself on this second trip, squatted aft on the coping of the cuddy, saying nothing.

Something, in fact, had seemed to hold them all silent—Frank and Dan and Bill, Lol Kinsman and Stan Currie, Buff Katen and Sam Freeman, and Clem Wilmot and Dave Stiles; and Renie and Edith Kinsman, the only women. He had watched for Margaret to come aboard, feeling the anticipation, the thing he always felt at sight of her, and then been glad she hadn't.

Constraint . . . Even Frank Graham said little, half-crouched on the main thwart, drumming his fingers on the washboards.

Anse, Alan thought. The presence of Anse. Perhaps men like Frank and Sam and Lol resented the fact they were here on Anse Gordon's sufferance and invitation. Perhaps now they sensed that while a careful tolerance was proper and necessary in their normal commerce with Anse, there was something undignified and subservient in being aboard his boat. As if they found themselves by some misjudgment publicly recognizing and abetting personal qualities they privately condemned.

He had a sense of relief when Anse once more brought the boat up to her mooring. He leaned overside, holding the flat while Lon transferred the hawser's loop to the pawl-post.

With late afternoon the wind had dropped. Now it was six, or past it, and a hint of evening coloured everything. The Channel's blue-green had darkened, its roll was longer and more leisurely, the sound of sea on gravel deliberate and long-drawn.

A relief to have it over with. As Lon Katen headed for the beach with the loaded flat the thought came to Alan that he was not going to be able to do this sort of thing much longer. The sound of Anse's voice, in the old jibe about Vangie Murphy . . . talking of his plans, outside the Islands . . . the look in his eyes . . . the words that did not come . . .

The rebellion in himself was something he couldn't quite control.

So far, forethought and patience . . . But those were reasonable virtues. What he was beginning to feel now was the surge of something that would not wait for thought.

This was what he was thinking while Lon rowed the flat ashore and he and Anse brailed up the canvas.

When Lon returned with the empty flat after rowing two loads ashore, Anse herded Frank and Sam and Dave Stiles into it. He said over his shoulder, "We better wait, Alan, you and me; and let Lon come back for us."

Alan said, "All right." It was a small thing, but there was nothing further to do aboard the boat. The flat was loaded, but since the wind had moderated they could have gone ashore as well as not.

Anse sat by the tiller, felt in his pockets for cigarettes and handed the packet to Alan, relaxed on the ballast. For a moment they watched Lon taking the flat in over the last slow swell to the beach, and Frank and Sam and Dave climbing the slope of stones to the grounds.

Toward the bulge of the Head, on the strip of sand between the water and the stones, a group of children walked slowly, apparently looking for shells. Colour moved behind the distant spruces surrounding the grounds: women's dresses, men in their shirt sleeves. Here in the boat now, barely swinging to the lift and fall of the Channel, there was a sense of isolation, as if the life and movement observed on the beach and in the grounds, the vaguely echoing sound, and shifting of toy-sized men and women, were the life and movement of strangers on a foreign shore.

Anse turned to look across the Channel, toward the Islands. He said, "The fall mackerel'll be along soon. May be summer mackerel there now. It'd be a chance, a gamble. Something new . . . A lot of work, but fun . . ."

Alan pulled himself up and sat on the fore-thwart and glanced toward the beach. Lon had the flat launched and was hauling round to row back to the sailboat.

". . . A lot of fun. Couple of men and a boat with an engine in her. Fellow could go on from that, too. Maybe get hold of one of those little draggers that scrape up everything. The flat-fish we never used to look at; they're all worth money these days . . ."

Alan hunched on the thwart, looking down, gripped by a strange embarrassment, tense and almost frightening. Expectancy.

Of what? He didn't know. Lon was half-way back; all he knew was that he had to be casual, normal, until the flat arrived.

He moved his head in a nod of interest. He said, "I guess they are, at that," and stood up and flipped his cigarette butt far overside. He said reflectively, "I'm so hungry I could eat the drumstick off a skunk. Must be the Channel air . . ."

The silence held. He reached down to grab the flat's gunnel as Lon came alongside.

The children had long since finished their suppers and scattered again to the swing, to wander up and down the beach or row on the inlet, to lurk on the fringe of the group of men lounging around Buff Katen's fire. Some of the older people were still at the tables, with younger women serving them. Matted grass was strewn with paper wrappings and pop-bottle tops. Small mountains of unwashed dishes rose from pails.

Stella Graham, seated at the table with Frank, looked up and around as Anse Gordon and Lon and Alan passed. She said, "Better not wait too long, boys. Sit in while there's something left."

Anse nodded, "Before long, Mrs. G."

He felt the need of a pull at the bottle. He glanced over the group sitting behind the fire, on the inlet side. Someone had dragged a bench out of the grounds and the men and women who were through with supper had left the tables to sit there, watching while the kettle boiled for the day's last batch of tea. Anse jerked his head at Lon Katen and walked on toward the Currie hut.

A peculiar anger burned in him. He had gone as far as he could go, in the boat out there. Gone as far as he could go, and waited for the word. The word from Alan: "Well, why don't you try it? If you want a hand, I'll try it with you . . ."

He re-lived now that moment of waiting for the word that did not come. Powerless. He had been powerless to go further, to make the invitation and risk the shaken head, the casual regretful *No*. In that moment and his memory of it there was a sense of the dreadfully familiar. An afternoon long ago at Rob's House, on the Head . . . And a night, a Sunday night outside the church at Leeds, and Hazel McKee walking past him with Edith Graham . . . And Anse Gordon, powerless . . .

He unhooked the door of the hut, following Lon into the gloom where late sunlight leaked through weather-cracked walls, and stretched to bring down the bottle he had hidden in a corner of the loft. Holding it a moment in his hand he said, "God, I'd like to put a hot poker up that crowd of . . ." He broke off. In all his life he had never bared in words, to anyone, the impulses that shaped his acts, the emotional mechanics behind the sneering smile. He drank deep, shuddered, and held the bottle waist-high in his hand. Lon took it, held it up to the light, grunted, and swallowed.

He was reaching up to return it to the loft when Anse said, "Not so fast," and took it in his hand and gulped again.

Alan sat hunched in front of the fire, backward on his heels, feeding the red coals with split sticks of driftwood. He did not look up as Anse and Lon returned.

Half the crowd had drifted away from the grounds to lounge around the fire. The last of the tea was made, but Buff had propped on the hot stones a final pot of clams. Dan and Bill Graham with Stan Currie and Richard McKee sat on a log on the beach side of the fire. Frank Graham stood opposite them, fresh from the supper table, a cup of tea in his hand, with Sam Freeman beside him. Margaret was among those on the bench behind them, and Grant sat beside her, elbows on knees, his down-turned face absent and thoughtful.

Sam Freeman puffed tobacco smoke. He said, cheerfully, "You better eat, Anse."

Anse said, "I'll eat when I get ready . . . How'd you like the feel of her, Frank?"

Frank Graham looked puzzled. "Oh . . . the boat, you mean. Good enough. Seems to handle all right. Sailed in her myself, years ago, y'know."

No one was paying any particular attention. Small odds and ends of talk went on. Bill Graham and Stan Currie were planning a walk up Graham's Brook tomorrow, to try for trout. Bill was saying he wanted one more try before he had to leave for Toronto. One of the Stiles kids from down-shore and Dan's boy, young Frank, were tugging at opposite ends of a string of amber kelp.

Alan rose and stood looking down at the fire. He prodded it once with the toe of his boot. He had an impulse to get out of here, away from Anse Gordon, away from all these people whose lives had shaped his own. He was conscious of a curious studied moderation in Anse's voice as he talked to Frank and Sam. There was almost a note of sorrow in it. Anse was saying the Shore should have stuck to fish.

"Should've built and gone outside, or east, the way they did years ago." His voice was reasonable, calm, as if he had at last condescended to companionship with all these people whose lives were rooted in commonplace work and everyday good will. He talked as old men sometimes talked, grumbling at their own generation. "Outside the Islands. That's what they could 'a' done. But they hadn't the guts, they had to quit. And what've you got? A bunch of farmers. Sheep manure and sawdust . . ."

Frank Graham said nothing. His face reflected the fact that he was very carefully saying nothing.

Anse repeated, "Sheep manure and sawdust . . ."

He said it with the broad suggestion of a lisp, and waited.

But Sam Freeman stood red-faced and quiet. It was his wife's voice, Ida's, that broke the silence, strident and sharp and full of an outrage at last set free:

"Sawdust . . . guts . . . Talk comes easy to them that can't . . . That won't work . . . that skips the country . . ."

She choked on her own words.

Anse said softly, "You're right, Mrs. Freeman." He raised his voice slightly, putting into it a hint of reckless contempt — contempt and an odd possessive mockery, a mocking affection. "You're right. And I'll tell you this. If I'd known I'd planted a crop here, I'd have stayed to watch it grow."

Someone made a short, indrawn, hissing sound. The reaction to unexpected pain, or the sight of hurt to another.

Alan's action was unwilled, in the sense that reason had nothing to do with it. Only the years of living that had shaped his impulses to what they were, tuned his nerves to pride in people loved, to action at the touch of insult.

He had just been looking across the fire at Grant's averted face. He had slipped away from the present for a moment, thinking of Hazel McKee, and the days when she and Anna Gordon had come to picnics here. And young Grant. And Anse.

He heard the words and behind them the studied mock-sorrowful provocation. And the possession — or the mock-possession.

He turned and swung his opened right hand, backward, against Anse's face.

Someone — Grant thought it was Eva McKee — said, "Oh, dear God!"

Alan swung the open hand again, sharp and hard. There was no other sound except the long sighing grumble of the Channel.

A white triangle from nose to mouth-corners grew in Anse's face. He stepped forward and dropped his hands at his sides. The voice came clear and toneless in its venom.

"Well — I can't cut down my own flesh and blood."

Alan's voice was hard with a fierce exultance.

"No. But *I* can."

He stepped in and threw his left fist at Anse's mouth. Head lowered, Anse came at him, clawing. Alan struck through the flailing arms, stepped in to strike again. Anse fell, stumbling sideways, and dropped on elbow and hip. He lay there looking upward for a moment before the obscenity began to flow.

15

Richard and Eva were late going to bed. Fred Marshall drove them home from Alec Neill's landing and Jane came into the house with Eva. Just to *be* there with an old friend, Richard thought. There wasn't much anyone could say. But it was good for Eva to have Jane sitting there to talk to if she felt like it, while she began to get used to the feeling . . . The Shore knowing, openly at last . . .

Richard was glad Jane was there. He went to the pasture bars to milk and as he returned to the house and put the pails down in the pantry, Jane rose to go. She turned a deliberate glance toward him in the dusky kitchen. It was placid and almost expressionless, a glance of reassurance.

He knew what this meant, when Eva got up from her chair by the west window to light the lamp, without haste or nervousness. Eva was all right.

For some reason they sat late, talking hardly at all. When Eva did speak, he was startled by the thing that came into her head. She said, "I wonder if Alan — D'you s'pose he's blaming himself? D'you think we ought to go down there, Richard?"

No reason to worry about Eva, Richard thought, if her grandson's peace of mind was the thing that bothered her. The living. A wonderful thing, that was — the instinct to put the living first, ahead of pride, beyond a shame that was long ago outlived.

He shook his head. There was no reason to take reassurance to Grant's place. He had seen Grant's face.

In the end it had been Lon Katen and Buff who hauled Anse to his feet and got him out of the grounds. Richard lived again that moment of violence. The shock of it would stay with him, the hushed embarrassment of men and women and the still, lively curiosity of boys and girls. Seeing and hearing the truth at last in the thud of fist against flesh and the torrent of raging words. But it was not this, really, that engaged his mind. In the instant of its happening he had turned away from it; away from

Anse Gordon sprawled on the ground with blood trickling from a mouth corner. He had turned to look at Grant.

Grant's face was tense, controlled, expressionless. But Richard had seen the stillness change, the subtle flow of expression. What was it? Still controlled, still hard, but at ease. Lively with something like elation.

Eva got down a book she had been re-reading lately, something by a fellow called Sheldon, and read for a while. But Richard, sitting in the shadow of his corner, noticed that for long minutes her face would be raised from the page, her expression absent-minded. What her face held was a kind of relief. A relaxation.

They sat long, without speaking. Later, Richard went outside. The air was cool, a slight wind was blowing out of the southeast. He could sense high clouds, high and dark, travelling inland over the Channel, over the Head, inland from the Atlantic. The lights were out next door at Fred Marshall's, but far to the east he could see a faint spark at Grahams'.

The final satisfaction in Richard's mind was that in the end Anse Gordon had destroyed himself. In the end the word and the act that pronounced his claim and established it had destroyed whatever threat there was in it. Established the emptiness of fact in the face of warm and living truth. Established the link between Grant and Alan, and perhaps Hazel, as a thing deeper and more telling than the accident of blood.

There were questions in Richard's mind. Alan had struck after that leering hint by Anse Gordon, when nothing could have kept the story dark . . .

Would he have struck if by striking, the story could have been forestalled?

Would he have struck if the insult had been some other? If the blow itself had been the spark to end the long illusion?

Richard smiled in the dark. He didn't know.

Just then his ear caught the faint thump of oars in rowlocks, carried on the inshore wind. He waited, listening. It was too dark to see, but he thought he could hear the creak of gear, the slight whicker of canvas, from the anchorage where Anse Gordon's boat was moored. It would be like Anse, to take this way of going . . .

He went back inside the house. Eva had turned the lamp low and gone to bed. In recent winters she had slept with him in the downstairs bedroom for warmth, and for the past year or two had continued to sleep there the year round. Richard blew out the lamp, undressed and lay down beside her.

He did not sleep at once, thinking of what he must do in the morning. No one knew about the paper but himself. Not even Josie Gordon. Not even Grant. He had never looked at it since that winter day when Hazel had sent for him. Sent for him and written, while he sat by her bed, the story of her revolt with Anse Gordon and her fear and her child and her rescue.

Why?

An apprehension? A fear that the child of her body, in the years none could see, should prove unworthy of Grant Marshall? Or simply a nagging need to leave the record straight?

This again Richard didn't know. All he knew was that in the morning he would get the paper from the locked rosewood box in his bureau and take it down the road. To Grant and Alan and Margaret.

It had no legal bearing, he supposed. That part of it would be up to the lawyers; even after the lapse of years, an easy thing to prove. But it had a certain value, none the less. Insurance in the face of talk, far in the future. A value in the records of the Shore.

He dropped asleep, half-dreaming of Hazel on a Sunday afternoon, telling him softly she was going berry-picking, back to Lowries.

1946 . . .

On the Friday after Anse Gordon's second disappearance, Bill left the Channel Shore.

Stan Currie drove him to the station at Stoneville to take the train away.

As the car topped the steep hill at Leeds, Bill leaned back to glance past Stan's shoulder. The road swings inland there. From this height the fields and pastures, rimmed and crowned with spruce wood-lots and hardwood clumps, slope away south to the Channel and southeast to Currie Head. He could see Lairds', Kinsmans', McKees' upper field, and south and east of that, drawing in with distance, the tiny bluff, the Head . . .

They rolled out on level road at the top of the hill. Stan glanced south and turned again to the road.

He said, meditating, "God, I used to hate this country."

Bill jerked his glance back from the fields.

"What!"

Stan laughed. "Startles you, does it?" He broke off on a note of light dismissal, "Oh, not any more . . ."

His tone changed. "You've seen Grant and Alan and the rest of them, have you?"

"Yes," Bill said.

Tuesday morning, and Alan working with Buff Katen in Josie Gordon's hayfield, and Margaret raking behind the rack.

Dan had gone over to give them a hand, but not Bill. That afternoon he had taken the path through the pasture to Grant's.

He found them lazing on the veranda. The mill would be starting up any day now, and Grant cared nothing about the appearance of idleness if that was the way he felt. Renie greeted Bill and turned to go into the house. Grant said, "No, sit still." She smiled, shook her head, and went inside.

He said to Bill, "You know about those kids? What's happened to them?"

It was like him, Bill thought, to speak in this fashion, without leading up to it. But what startled him was the tone. Interested, touched with a curious light astonishment.

"Well . . . I was wondering about it."

"Hard to realize, yet." Grant was silent for a little, and when he spoke he had gone to the heart of it again. "He'll be living there, at Gordons'. Best way to . . . Don't you think?"

Bill nodded. "Yes." Best way to begin the new design, woven of the old. Best way to begin the change in the pattern — in the memory and imagination and knowledge of the Shore.

"Well, that's the start of it."

The start of it. That was how Grant saw it, then, not as an end but a beginning. And yet, how often, in time to come, would his mind again go back . . . ? How often while Grant Marshall and Alan Gordon worked together at the mill, the old relationship surrendered, how often would the questioning mind go back? Go back, and wonder . . . *if somehow he had never known?*

How often, no matter how the new parts were played, how often must the old peculiar warmth, a curious possession, take hold of both in the run of common tasks . . . the memory of snow-bound woods and fields and kitchen fires?

A start, Grant said. A beginning, not an end. But it was neither. It was past and present and future, eddying here in the flow of time.

Bill realized that he had answered Stan with a single word, and that this was all Stan expected. For the time being it had all been talked out — dealt with. Stan's attitude was a foreshadowing of what must happen in the lengthening run of time.

Talk? Certainly. Time would deal with it. In thirty years there would be those along the Channel Shore who would never know that Alan Gordon had once been Alan Marshall. Or would hear of it perhaps through chance words, spoken in thoughtlessness or malice or admiration. In a hundred years the tale would be part of that long hearsay, a thread in dim forgotten fabric, one with the story of Rob Currie and Fanny Graham, linked through tenuous blood-lines to the moving Now.

Stan slowed, lit a cigarette, and turned north on the paved highway that runs through The Bridge from Morgan's Harbour to Stoneville.

He said, "Not hate, maybe, even then. Heading away, and wanting to go. A lot of things come into it when a kid leaves

394

home. His father's ambition for him. His own—well—sense of venture . . .

"This place, the Shore . . . 'd you ever wonder why they came here, first? Some of them didn't like George Third. Got put into the army and sent out so they couldn't raise hell . . . Ended up here. Some got pitched off the land when the lairds began to see more money in sheep than people. I'll bet you most of them ended up here because they couldn't stand being pushed around. Highlanders, lowlanders, Irishmen, Catholics, Protestants, loyalists, all kinds . . . Only one thing they all had. They *will not* take a pushing 'round. Not for ever. They'll stand most anything from land and sea. That's all right. Nobody else is telling them . . ."

Bill had been watching the country as he listened. Bush country this, with a few poorish farms scattered along the road, and stretches of barrens. Frontier country, fencing the Channel Shore off on the north and west as on the east and south it was fenced by the Islands and the sea.

Stan was still talking. "What they did, getting out, was pull off a kind of rebellion. The only kind they could. Personal independence . . . For a while it opened out on this Shore . . . Then steam came, and other things, and it wouldn't work any more. A lot went to the States, and west, and some did all right. Then at last there was nowhere to go but cities. When you go to a city, Bill, unless you're good, in a profession or the arts, you put yourself under a boss. You're back where you were a hundred and fifty years ago. The sad thing is, you got there by following the same urge they followed when they rebelled against it . . .

"That's why I'm back, if you want to know . . . What could a man do, that had venture in it, and independence? I looked at what I'd got by leaving. Running water and central heat and something—oh, *cultivation* . . . Well, they seemed to me to be cancelled out by the pulling and hauling, the pressure to say 'Yes' when you wanted to say 'No' . . . *There was venture in coming back* . . ."

He broke off and glanced at Bill, his faced amused.

"What brought *you* back, Bill?"

Bill shook his head. "I don't know. I'm just a visitor, anyway . . . I wanted to come. I like the place. It's hard to say . . ."

Stan put back his head and laughed.

"You just said it. That's all I was trying to tell you. I like the place."

He went on. "It's the fashion now to rule out . . . to forget the past. The *living* past, I mean. A virtue not to know who your grandfather was or where he came from or what he was like. Not to care. That comes, I guess, from living in rented places. No one gets identified with a stretch of land, a park, even a street-corner . . . Nothing but themselves. They don't know they're a part of the last generation or that their kids are a piece of *them*. No sense blaming people . . . not their fault. But I'm sorry *about* it, Bill. Look, I can go down on the Head and see the ridges in the ground where Ed Currie made bricks about eighteen-ten. I can show you where Sandy Currie found a spring and walled it with rocks. Maybe I got the same kind of kick out of putting in running water and a new foundation that Ed did when he dug his first well. Or Sandy, finding a spring to save lugging water to the beach . . . I can go and take a look at Rob's cellar if I want to bother. In the parlour closet there's a tin-type of Hugh in a coat buttoned up to his chin. Taken when he went away to Boston. Every bit of it, adventure. On the Shore they don't think about those things. But it's *in* them. If they go away they know where they came from. They come back to have a look, or they look back. They look back, sometimes . . . Some of them stick to the hard living, because, whatever else, there's still the independence . . . Some of them leave, try to get comfort, ease . . . Or just for the sake of going. The best of them, now and then, take a look back . . ."

Stan's voice changed. "That's what it is with you, Bill. You got a touch of it through your dad and Frank and a little, maybe, from old Hugh and me. It hit you young and it hit you again. So you like the place."

Stan laughed. They pulled up beside the dusty red station at Stoneville, with the train hooting down the line behind them.

Bill watched the marshes come to him out of low cloud and slide by, their tall grass moving wavelike under wind from the gulf. His mind turned to the Marshalls and the Gordons and back to Stan, caught by his rambling talk. There was something satisfying in it. Stan had found words that came close to what the Shore meant . . . to Stan. Bill had a sense of regret that all he had ever been was a visitor. But this was fleeting. He had the feel of something done and yet continuing. He had also the knowledge that in blood and spirit this was the country he belonged to. He would never live on the Channel Shore. But it was home.

Already a forward-looking excitement was beginning to stir the depths of his content. He was thinking of Jock and of other summers. Fall, the time of mellowing apples. October. They said it was always fine in October along the Channel Shore. But first a summer. July and August for the beach, and Rich and Alec drying nets there. Or others, if they were gone. Summer was the time for Jock to see it first, as he himself had seen it.

The train jarred to a halt at a little red-walled station and again began to move. Bill sought with his eyes the line of the gulf, beyond that waving grass. A newer memory touched him and he tasted for a moment the curious enjoyment of remembering a baseless fear. That hour of doubt when he had last watched these marshes, travelling east . . . Andrew . . . Helen . . .

How would it be, for Andrew? A week, a month, a summer, after more than forty years? The thought filled him with a tender warmth. But with the thought, odd and startling, a flash of questioning insight.

How could he know it would be right, for Andrew? How could he know that what was right for Andrew was not whatever living dream the mind held now? A sense of conscious scholarship, of austere achievement; only, perhaps, a dimmed incurious memory of the Shore . . .

You couldn't tell. You could look a little into the minds of others, but outward with no eyes but your own. This came to him as something like discovery. He found himself thinking of Helen, without resentment or apprehension now, and wondered, again with that little start of insight, if that were true of Helen's thoughts of him.

People differed, and there was little you could do but accept the fact the difference was there. You could perhaps achieve a private integrity, an inner stature, and be alert to recognize these qualities in their differing guise in others. Preserve an evenness of mind . . .

He shook his head. He had let himself run on, building, dreaming . . . a planned future. And the essence of the Shore was that you couldn't foresee anything. All you could see were the following waves of time.

Nothing is ever finished.

He let it go. He watched the gulf shore slide by, then woods and hilly pastures as the train swung inland. But even though he had turned his thought from plans and problems and speculations, back into dreamlike communion with the living Shore, he could not keep his mind away from people.

For he was one of them. One of thousands who had taken this road away. To Boston, to Montreal, to the western prairies. To Denver and Winnipeg. To Dawson City and San Francisco. To Vimy and Dieppe and Caen.

Idly he thought of them. Of their minds turning, sometimes, to the Shore in waking dreams. Wondering, perhaps, as he would wonder, how long a time must pass before they saw this land again, and heard its voices.

A long time . . .

Already it was passing.

Toronto, Ont.—Port Shoreham, N.S.
1946-1953.

SELECTED NEW CANADIAN LIBRARY TITLES

Asterisks (*) denote titles of New Canadian Library Classics

McCLELLAND AND STEWART
publishers of The New Canadian Library
would like to keep you informed about
new additions to this unique series.

For a complete listing of titles and
current prices – or if you wish to be added
to our mailing list to receive future catalogues
and other new book information – write:

BOOKNEWS
McClelland and Stewart
481 University Avenue
Toronto, Canada M5G 2E9

McClelland and Stewart books are
available at all good bookstores.

Booksellers should be happy to order from our catalogues
any titles which they do not regularly stock.